MAROC~~~~

A Click Your Poi

BY
JAMES SCHANNEP

The eAversion Version
First Print Edition

This book is a work of fiction. Names, characters, businesses, organizations, places, events, and incidents are either the product of the author's imagination or are used fictitiously. Any resemblance to actual persons, living or dead, events, or locales is entirely coincidental. Historical elements were used to give a sense of time and place.

Copyright © 2018 by James Schannep

For the sake of irony, the author would like to ask you specifically not to pirate this book. Please do not pirate other books either, without a sense of irony.

All rights reserved.
Print Edition

www.jamesschannep.com

Library of Congress Cataloging-in-Publication Data
Schannep, James, 1984—
MAROONED: a Click Your Poison book / James Schannep
1. Sea Stories—Fiction. 2. Thrillers—Historical—Fiction.
3. Historical—General—Fiction. I. Title

COVER ART BY JAMES SCHANNEP (based on *MAROONED* by HOWARD PYLE, public domain)

This book has been modified from its original version.
It has been formatted to fit this page.

ISBN-13: 978-1724761002
ISBN-10: 1724761005

To my mother, for showing me the many worlds that await inside a good book.

Acknowledgments

Special thanks to my wife, Michaela, who it seems will never stop believing in me. Thank you for being my compass on this adventure.

A big thanks to my beta readers: Mike Beeson, Fred Buckley, Tyson Bertmaring, Sarah-Jayne, Don Ricardo Joven, Arkady Bogdanov, Martin Barnabus Noutch, Alex Rezdan, Kari L. Cowell, Scott & Jessica Santos, and Evonna Hartshorn and for the test play through by Mike "#midtableglory" Harlock, Jarred "Jet-lagged" Luko, Grant "Grunt" Smith, and James "5-color Green" Quinn.

To my copyeditor Linda Jay, and to Paul Salvette and the team at BB eBooks. Thank you all for your generosity and professionalism.

And to my friends and family, for your unyielding encouragement, enthusiasm and support.

Author's notes:
1) The Age of Sail ran from roughly 1500-1850, and the Golden Age of Pirates is generally considered to be 1650-1725. While I deliberately did not set a specific date, some of the details point to a more specific span of years inside this window. Wherever possible, the particulars of this story are true and factually correct. I admit to taking liberties in order to make a more engaging story, but if you think you've found an error, please let me know. I believe fiction has great power to educate, and I do my best to pass on my research to the reader in a fun and palatable way. While there are real-life survival scenarios, this book is not intended to be used as a survival guide.

2) As in others, the main character in this *Click Your Poison* book is supposed to be "you." That is to say, it was my intent that you should fit into this story regardless of your age, gender, race, or orientation. There were indeed female sailors, albeit usually in a clandestine role, as well as seamen of color. I did my best to keep things neutral and, for your own suspension of disbelief, I did not use the more typical address aboard ships, "Mister." Let your imagination and preferences flesh out the main character.

Here's how it works: You, Dear Reader, are the main character of this story, a youth born to prosperity in the English countryside. Now it's up to you to sail atop the vast oceans or be swallowed into their murky depths; the choice is yours. Are YOU ready for Survival and Treachery on the High Seas?

Go to the next page to begin. Good luck.

Click Your Poison Books

***INFECTED**—Will YOU Survive the Zombie Apocalypse?*
***MURDERED**—Can YOU Solve the Mystery?*
***SUPERPOWERED**—Will YOU Be a Hero or a Villain?*
***PATHOGENS**—More Zombocalypse Survival Stories!*
***MAROONED**—Can YOU Endure Treachery and Survival on the High Seas?*
***SPIED (coming in 2019)**—Can YOU Save the World as a Secret Agent?*

* More titles coming soon! *
Sign up for the new release mailing list: http://eepurl.com/bdWUBb
Or visit the author's blog at www.jamesschannep.com

MAROONED

It takes a concerted effort to keep the bile below the threshold of your throat; and though the carriage on the way to London has soured your stomach, it has not spoiled your mood. Your cousin should soon arrive in port—this very evening—after two years at sea aboard a merchant vessel.

And you? Why, you get to be the first to greet him. To hear his stories of grand adventure! Perhaps he has survived being shipwrecked, fought bravely against a raiding party of Spanish war dogs, even defended his crew against mutineers... or pirates? Could any man's life be more thrilling?

The carriage rocks again, sending your thoughts reeling back to your queasy stomach. Trying to master your constitution once more, you focus on this morning's lessons: Translating Homer's *Odyssey* from the original Greek, a task you were fully invested in before the summons came.

Another lurch of the carriage almost reminds you of this morning's breakfast too, but this time you've drawn to a stop. The partition is flung open, and the compartment fills with late afternoon sunlight.

"End-o'-the road, Guv," the driver says, holding the door open for you.

As you step out onto the muddy banks, you're greeted with the full impact of the River Thames—here waits the biggest port in the seafaring world, the Port of London: ships and commerce far as the eye can see. Hundreds of wooden vessels, of unknown make and model to your inexperienced eye, with white sails tucked safely while at anchor.

Thousands of men and women, from all nations, in all manner of dress, speaking all manner of tongues, crowd the riverbanks.

Although each one is a distinct figure on a separate mission, somehow they form a cohesive whole. Salesmen shout of exotic fruits and fishes, spices and spirits, trophies and trinkets from the barbarous parts of the world. Though you've read many volumes about bustling London, life in the countryside of Buckinghamshire could never have prepared you for the grandeur of such a sight in person.

End of the road, indeed. End of the map, too. This is no longer London, nor England; this truly is a portal to another world.

"I do believe the man's waiting t'be paid," a gruff and masculine voice says.

Your eyes go to the driver, his hand extended expectantly. In response, you place the requisite money in his open palm, then turn to face the speaker. The man's hardened, suntanned skin is peppered with sores and scabs. A rugged jawline of ruddy whiskers frames his gaunt face, made tighter still by hair tucked and tied beneath a bolt of deep blue cloth. His shirt, probably once bright-white, hangs loose, revealing his taut, muscled frame.

"Cousin... James...?" you stammer, still not convinced that the man who stands before you is the same youth of sixteen who left England only two years ago. His eyes twinkle with the same mischievous quality as the river to his back, until a smile finally breaks across his face. With the dreamlike quality of the encounter, your mind reverts once again to Homer. These words pour from your lips almost unconsciously:

"Sing to me of the man, Muse, the man of many ways, of twists and turns; that man skilled in ways of contending, the wanderer, driven time and again off-course...."

The smile disappears, and in its place there is now a grave countenance. It's a sudden change in demeanor; you fear you may have said something to insult him. But just as soon as it departed, that mischievous grin returns.

"Christ Almighty, I need a bloody drink!" James says, laughing. "I should've known mother'd send an escort t'see me home. Still, does me well t'see a familiar face. You've grown taller, coz."

"The driver," you say, not quite able to regain your senses just yet, "will take us—"

"The driver's paid and gone."

Somewhat panicked, you turn to see the carriage disappear past the muddy banks of the Thames and down the cobbled London streets.

"Same condition could be said-o'-me as well, now I'm free-o'-that bloody ship," James adds, walking towards the shantytown of shops lining the port. "Come, cousin. 'Tis awfully cold and lonely at sea, and I aim t'grant a good portion-o-me wages to the first woman who'll make me feel warm and welcome. I imagine 'tis well past time you tasted the kiss of gin, too. As luck would have it, there's a tavern right here in port where we can pay to wet whichever end we please. Don't look so troubled, now—I'm buying!"

The driver has left, and now your cousin aims to go on a bender as his first act in port. This is not going according to plan! Thinking quickly, you decide:

➢ Maybe a drink will do him good? Even the most spirited man becomes more amiable once he's supplemented with a few more spirits. Part ways to find another driver while James ties one on. Go to page 265

➢ James has clearly spent too much time in the sun. Your aunt has entrusted you to bring your cousin back home safely, and you intend to honor that commitment. Don't let him go! Go to page 142

➢ Though you know it's taboo, you've always wondered what the inside of a brothel looks like. James is celebrating; what could a peek hurt? No one back home has to know.... Go to page 100

The Accused

A collective gasp pulls in a wave of murmurs like a ghostly tide rising to meet the shoreline. Even the new pirates have heard of Captain Bullock's fate, it would seem. Rediker, for his part, stoically considers your words while the others whisper their speculations. They look at one another with renewed skepticism, wondering who you might indicate as the killer.

"Bluffing," Marlowe mutters in a huff.

"And I can prove it," you add.

"But how?" Chips asks. "We left ya here 'cause it couldn't be proved."

"I've had nothing but time and memories. The clues were all there, laid out, waiting to be ordered and solved. I've been here in exile for a crime I didn't commit—but maybe there was a reason for it all? So I'd have time to discover the truth. Pirates or no, I don't believe you'll leave me here once I clear my name. Now, once and for all, you can prove if there truly is no honor amongst thieves."

"Let's hear what ya have t'say, Saltboots," Rediker says.

Not standing on ceremony, you report:

➢ It was Billy Greaves, Bullock's mate. Go to page 19

➢ It was your mate, Barlow. Go to page 14

➢ It was you, Rediker. Go to page 244

➢ It was the surgeon, Butch. Go to page 245

➢ It was the carpenter, Chips. Go to page 36

➢ It was your quartermaster, Marlowe. Go to page 184

➢ It was the bosun, Joe. Go to page 161

➢ It was the cook, Dudderidge. Go to page 71

➢ It was the gunner, Robin. Go to page 254

Acting Commander

⚓

Captain Longwick leaves the *Hornblower* in Dalton's hands, taking a few able seamen with him into a longboat and embarking towards the flagship. Once these men have rowed the Master and Commander out of sight, Lieutenant Dalton turns back and appraises the ship with new eyes.

"Midshipman Ward, what say we leave the ship in better hands than we found her?"

"Aye, sir," you reply.

"Excellent. There's much to be done. Not the least of which is tending to the scrapes and bruises sustained by both the *Hornblower* and her crew. And if we manage to see to those before the Captain's return, well, there's always plenty in need of scrubbing."

"Aye, sir! I'll personally see to…

- …the wounded. The men who sacrificed their bodies for our victory deserve our best thanks." Go to page 143

- …the repairs. The *Hornblower* is our England; let's get her back shipshape and Bristol fashion." Go to page 156

Action Stations!

⚓

As soon as the order is given, the whole ship comes to life with the excitement of impending battle. The prospect of fighting a pirate ship is especially enticing, and not just because of any romantic notions of heroes versus villains, but because the crew is likely to be given a share of any booty returned to the crown.

What's more, many of the Royal Navy sailors have been pressed into service, while the pirates are called "freebooters" because they live the life they please. Let's be honest—there's a subconscious jealousy that might also compel the fervor. *If I can't, nobody can!* has been reason enough to kill throughout most of human history.

The drummers beat out the cadence of war and the HMS *Hornblower* sails into action. Mustering with your gun crew on the starboard lower gun deck, you peer through the gun ports, eager for a look at your foe. Though you're not privy to Captain Longwick's plans, it's clear the Master and Commander has something in mind as the ship heads into coastal waters. The smaller pirate ship has the advantage in the shallows, so he must have a good reason for the maneuver.

"Fire starboard guns!" the order comes from above.

"Stations, damn you all," Lieutenant Saffron relays. "FIRE!!!"

You dart back from the gun port just in time, shoving your fingers into your ears before the deafening explosion.

"Swab the guns! Load cartridge! Shot! Now run out the guns!" Saffron orders, and you do your part, swabbing the bore clean of sparks and heat.

In only a few moments, the team has the gun ready to fire again. But it was to be a warning shot, it seems, for no further order to fire is given. As soon as there's a lull in the action, the crew (yourself included) rushes forward to peer through the gun ports once more.

"Bloody rubber-necking bastards," the lieutenant says, shaking his head.

The *Hornblower* follows the pirate ship along the convex bend of the coast, until another ship is revealed from around the curve. A Spanish Man-o'-War, not too different from the last you've seen. She's moored in this hidden inlet, and the pirate ship dares not sail into her. This is an unexpected tactical wildcard—neither ship is allied with the Dons.

Will Captain Longwick continue the approach with the Spanish ship just beyond? It appears so, despite this new player being a much more dangerous foe. The man's of a singular mind and intensity, it would seem.

The *Cooper's Pride* turns, facing perpendicular to your approach. Then the pirates let loose a broadside of their own. The hit comes from only half a dozen guns and doesn't even slow the *Hornblower* as she shifts to return fire.

Sensing the move, Lieutenant Saffron yells, "Ready, gun crew!" and you return to your stations.

The order to fire comes from above, again relayed with precision. The cannons rip into the pirate ship, turning their gun decks to Swiss cheese. But again, one shot only. Now you wait as the boarding crews launch themselves across the open sea and onto the pirate vessel. Small-arms fire and war cries fill the air; then the clatter of edged weapons and melee combat.

Part of you wishes you could be with them, taking down the rogues, but that sentiment ends rather abruptly when there's an enormous explosion from the pirate vessel. A fireball mushrooms into the air, sending flaming debris and viscera around like hellfire and brimstone.

"The knaves have blown themselves apart?!" Saffron asks to himself.

Dozens and dozens of sailors from the Hornblower, dead in an instant—along with most of the pirate crew. Looks like they didn't want to be taken alive….

"Sink what's left of them!" the order comes from above.

"FIRE!!!" the lieutenant roars. "Swab the guns! Load cartridge! Shot! Now run out the guns! *FIRE!!!"*

The orders come again and again, until the cannons are in danger of cracking from the heat of overuse. Finally, a ceasefire arrives, leaving nothing but a ringing in your ears and air thick with haze. Once the gunpowder smoke clears, you see the pirate ship is nothing more than a heap of splinters dipping beneath the waves for good.

You've sunk the *Cooper's Pride*. Then there's another volley of cannon fire, this time from the Spanish ship. The men rush back to their stations, ready to return.

"Steady," Lieutenant Saffron says. "They're saluting us. There's only one thing the Dons hate more than the English Navy, and that's an English Pirate."

Orders are relayed for a cease of hostilities, and normal watches are resumed. It's in a somber mood, feeling a victory that came at a heavy price, that the HMS Hornblower turns and sails away from this fateful coast.

<u>Go to page 276</u>

Admiral of the Coast

Having taken Captain Longwick of the HMS *Hornblower* captive, his ship is yours. The rest of the Royal Navy crew is rounded up, and you're shocked to learn that Cousin James is among them! He was pressed into military service the same day you boarded the *Cooper's Pride,* and several of his old shipmates recognize him as Jimmy Saltboots. It doesn't take much to convince your cousin to join you, especially when the alternative is being marooned with the rest of the Royal Navy crew on the shores of the island where you careened your ship.

You tell Rediker to keep the clothing and continue the position of Captain Bloodbeard aboard the *Deleon's Revenge.* This *Hornblower* will serve as your new flagship, with your cousin as your quartermaster. Together, you're the Saltboot Buccaneers, and the man-o'-war is rechristened as the *Best Ending.*

With the enormous man-o'-war, no merchantman stands a chance. You're soon leader of all pirates, as more and more crews join to serve under your protection. As the de facto *Admiral of the Brethren of the Coast,* the seas are yours to command.

"The way I see it, we've got seven choices here," cousin James says, as the quartermaster of the *Best Ending.* "So, Coz. Which of the seven seas shall we terrorize first?"

That's it! You've survived and thrived as a pirate. But there's plenty more to explore. *MAROONED* has three unique storylines (look for anchors, skull and crossbones, and the palm tree symbols) and over fifty possible endings. And there's much more loot to be found! Easter eggs to include several references to each CYP book released thus far. Can you find the treasure buried within these pages?

Or, if you're finished, please consider leaving a review to help others find this book. It's an incredibly helpful and easy way to support the author (who thanks you in advance, and in third-person, no less!).

When you're done, don't forget to check out the other exciting titles in the Click Your Poison multiverse! You can also sign up for the new release mailing list, or check out James Schannep's blog for updates.

http://eepurl.com/bdWUBb
http://jamesschannep.com

All the Moneys!

"Damn your blood," Monks cries. He takes the dice for his own, and gives them a roll as if he suspects they're weighted. Cursed, more like. The dice were here long before you were, after all.

"That's quite a pile of sterling," Argyle notes, adding it up. You half-expect him to produce an abacus here on the spot.

"Fortunes change," Wycombe says. "Do what you will to sew a man up, come morning he could still be dead. Yet another who would bear his injuries to spite your advice will live to fight another day."

He takes another long drag on the opium pipe.

"Don't have enough coin to face this devil again," Monks says, miserably.

"It would be close," Argyle agrees, consulting his ledger.

"I can front a round or two, so long as Argyle marks it to be paid against grog rations on board," Wycombe offers.

That settled, they place their bets and turn to you for another round. True gamblers, these.

If you want to say no, enough excitement for one night:

➤ Collect your winnings and return to the bar to wait for Cousin James.
Go to page 233

Or let it ride! The winning choice has been randomized, and the outcome of these choices may or not be the same. Play the dice/coin game again, or simply pick your luck of the draw:

➤ Heads on the coin toss, or a one, two, or three shown on the die. Go to page 66

➤ Tails on the coin toss or a four, five, or six shown on the die. Go to page 308

Ancient Wisdom

Taking a pebble from the tide pool, you rest it upon your tongue and suck. The cold stone does indeed get your salivary glands working, which at the very least helps combat the feeling of cotton-mouth. It's not like you're actually going to force any fresh water from the pebble, but there's something to be said about thinking with a clear head, which is the best effect this technique can hope to offer.

The birds on this island may have taken the fish from the tidepools before you arrived this morning, but if you pay attention, they can lead you to water. Mouth closed, eyes up.

What you see, when you stop to observe, are a group of birds circling inland and other large groups leaving the circle in a more-or-less direct path to some unseen destination. What does this tell you?

- Go to where the birds are circling. That's most likely where a reserve of fresh water will be found. Go to page 157
- The circling birds are probably just looking for dead/helpless animals. Head to their destination instead. Go to page 206

Appeal to Authority

Creeping back out as stealthily as possible, you make your escape. The same logic that brought them down amongst the livery (i.e., background noise from the livestock to cover mutinous talk) now helps drown out the creaking of the planks during this retreat.

Finding Billy, you do your best to explain the situation between gasps for breath.

"Go tell the Cap'n, now! I'll get Robin and some others so we can arrest these men."

Nodding your understanding, you rush towards the captain's cabin, trepidation and exhilaration swirling in your breast. Knocking on the door, you hear a muffled reply and a clattering from within. You knock again, and the door creaks open. Must not have been latched....

The door swings wide with a lurch of the ship, and Captain Bullock falls forward into your arms. He makes a hideous gurgling noise, crimson bubbles frothing from his lips. His body falls prone and the unexpected weight of the man brings you both down outside the cabin.

You roll the captain onto his back to find the source of the suffocation, only to see his throat's been cut! Completely severed, ear to ear. There's a bloody knife inside the cabin, lying only a few feet away. Captain Bullock continues gagging for breath, blood pulsing from his wound, then—with one more sickening gasp—the man expires.

A cacophony of boots clatter on deck as the crew rushes towards the commotion. The first to arrive is Chips, who looks aghast with horror. Here you are, kneeling over the body of Captain Bullock, the man's blood on your hands. Joe arrives only a few moments later; more and more of the crew appear by the second.

"What's happened here?" Joe asks.

"Saltboots... killed the cap'n," Chips says, ashen-faced with shock.

> What? These men must be in on it, too... and now they're pinning this on you! Run now, find Billy! Go to page 291

> Stay calm as much as you can. Point out the knife, and say Billy knows there's a mutiny afoot! Go to page 58

Appressed

⚓

You stick closely, doing your best to stay just outside of the lamplight. They do indeed check the barometric pressure, and use some jargon you're unfamiliar with while doing so. You're able to gather that there's a storm system inbound, and moving fast. Even without the instruments, the violent lurching of the ship would tell the same story. It's all you can do to keep your stomach from rebelling.

"Cap'n gotcha molly-coddlin' his new Ward?" Magnus asks the lieutenant.

All thoughts of your stomach disappear and you listen closely.

"Sadly, yes," Dalton replies. "A bit of cheeky bugger too."

"The Master-of-Arms seems t'think with a storm like this'n, maybe that Ward'll have a spill, right into the drink! Find new habitation amongst the haddock, if ye get me meaning."

Dalton looks about uncomfortably, then hisses, "I trust you not to jest about such things in front of a superior! Every knot on this ship has an ear."

Magnus stiffens and says, "Aye, sir. Apologies."

"I can appreciate why you might resent this new recruit jumping forward in the line of promotion. However, if the position were to prove... *too much*... the Ward would certainly be reduced back down to Landsman," Lieutenant Dalton offers.

"Heh, aye-aye, sir. Too many duties and not enough sleep can overcome anyone."

You swallow hard. Et tu, Dalton?

What now?

➢ Tell the Captain. Go to page 285

➢ Say nothing, but keep on your guard. Go to page 222

➢ Confront the pair of them now. Go to page 46

Ashamed

"Couldn't live with the shame. Proud men, these Portos," Joe says.

Robin nods. "You all right, Cap'n?"

"I'm fine. Bosun, please alert our quartermaster to the situation, but do so quietly. Robin, fetch the surgeon to help clean this mess up, but make sure no one else comes in here."

Both men nod at your orders, then step to. You stay inside the cabin, mind running wildly. *If Bullock was poisoned....*

At length, Rediker reports in. "Christ Almighty. It's true. Look at that poor sod. Killed himself, eh? Just as well. Crew says he were a cruel master, serves him right, I say. Must've known we'd find out."

"And the prize?" you say.

"Massive haul, Cap'n. Sugar, indigo, cacao, tobacco, leather, silks, silver, gold, and jewels. Once we divide the shares, hell, I'd say each man just earned himself three years' pay! Not bad for a first-timer."

"Refit the ship first. Take their carriage guns, plus any weapons. Once the *Deleon's Revenge* is made stronger, the rest is profit."

"Aye, Cap'n. It'll take a few hours t'move all the cargo, but we should be full up. Afterwards, shall we plot a course for New Providence to unload our ill-gotten gains?"

"Do it!" you say.

➢ "I'm going to go through the Porto captain's cabin to see what I can find. He was right, I need a manner of dress befitting the name of Captain Bloodbeard."
Go to page 70

➢ "'Twas a grand first catch, Rediker. Once we make sail, open the rum stores for the men. I'd like to make another toast… to the first of many! And the start of a prosperous partnership." Go to page 137

Axes & Allies

"**K**new we had a clever Cap'n!" Rediker says with a grin. "Boarding parties, arm up. Remain below decks 'til I give the signal. Don't wanna tip 'em off early!"

Portugal and England are technically allies against Spain at present, so when you hail the other ship for assistance, they're obligated to stop for you. Most merchantmen are friendly to their kind at sea, for it's a sort of superstition, like villagers who are obliged by culture to take in and feed a stranger. They too, after all, may one day be a stranger in want or need.

"Ship ahoy!" you hail, as you've seen done before.

"Hulloa!" They recognize your flag and reply in your native tongue.

"What ship is that, pray?"

"The ship *Dos Santos*, from Rio de Janeiro, bound to Lisbon. Where are you from?"

"The *Deleon's Revenge* né *Cooper's Pride*," you say, for the old name is still painted on your stern. "From Boston, returning to London. Only we weren't able to resupply for the journey."

"No resupply, you say? Pray, what happened?"

Now you signal to Barlow. As he raises the black flag, you say, "We were taken by pirates!"

Barlow unfurls the flag; a sea of black upon which rests the iconic skull and crossbones—but with one change: There is a beard of blood sewn onto the death's head, formed by a dozen or more crimson droplets, which, when combined, give the appearance of a beard. *A Bloodbeard.*

At this, the rest of the crew rises up from below decks, wielding boarding axes, wooden and iron beams; whatever makeshift weapons they could find. Weapons aren't generally found aboard merchant vessels, so you'll want to upgrade your armaments as soon as possible. For now, it looks as though the crew has raided the carpenter's toolset.

The men aboard the Portuguese vessel look from man-to-man, unsure how to deal with this new threat. Quickly, before they have time to form a plan, say:

- "We're coming aboard to help ourselves to your supplies. Make no attempt to resist, lest you'll learn why they call me Bloodbeard!" Go to page 21

- "Send your captain over now, so we can make terms of your surrender. You have my word, no harm will come to you. We want booty, not blood." Go to page 210

Barlow

"Me—me?" Barlow stammers, eyes blinking. It's as if the poor sod is trying to figure out just how it is that he is indeed the killer.

"He was with me in the hold, planning a mutiny, when the deed were done," Rediker says.

"Ah-ha! I've just got you to admit to mutiny!" you say, pointing a finger back at him.

"I think too many meals-o'-boiled crab have gone and made ya soft in the shell, Saltboots," Rediker says, tapping his own head for emphasis. "Of course I admit the mutiny! I'm captain-o'-a pirate crew!"

Then they all laugh.

And laugh, and laugh, and laugh.

And then they kill you.

THE END

BBQ

Good choice. In all likelihood, this little piggie was left to the island so sailors like you could later come pick up her brood and roast them over a spit. Fresh meat is hard to come by on a sea voyage, so when you cook the pig's flesh over an open flame, it's the most succulent thing you've been offered in months. No matter the lack of spices, this is living!

The pig will last you a few days, though you're not the only interested party. Drawn to your kill is another hunter on the island. The nightly visitor to your camp is here again, just out of the illumination of your firelight. Though you cannot see the intruder, you can almost *feel* the presence of something or someone out there. There's a crackling sound, like twigs snapping beneath footfall, but that could again just be wood popping in the fire. Your imagination runs wild.

Though, it's not much longer until you learn your stalker's identity. The next day, you're off from camp, hiking down to the pond for fresh water, when you come face to face with a jaguar.

Its golden fur glows tawny in the early light; black splotches break up the outline of the animal, even as it stares at you out in the open. Is this who's been following you these last few days? Likely so. What was once curiosity to size you up now very well may put you on the menu. What do you do?

- Confidently walk towards the jaguar. Lock eyes to show dominance. Say, "This is my island now!" Go to page 287
- Scream loudly to frighten the animal and climb up into the nearest tree for safety. Go to page 69
- Shout, "Look, over there!" and then run in the opposite direction as fast as you can. Go to page 226
- Almost as if in slow motion, remove your pistol and shoot the beast. Can't get revenge if you're dead. Go to page 326
- Stand tall, but slowly back away. Speak calmly. Say, "It's okay, I don't mean you any harm." Go to page 306

Below the Surface

This group of three are a jolly, rough-hewn bunch who look like they were forged upon a smithy's anvil as seafaring men, rather than ever having been born as boys. The sailors introduce themselves, and you do the same, but it's lip-service only. Your eyes are locked on Barlow, trying to gauge the man.

"So ye've been crimped, eh? Gamblin' debts?" one of the seamen asks.

A grin spreads Barlow's mustache across his face, revealing a missing front tooth. "Spent most me money on women and booze—and the rest I just wasted!"

The men erupt in good-natured laughter and let the issue drop. You can see how the jibe would appeal to sailors, but there could be more to it. They wanted to know the nature of his debts, and he just rolled right over the question. Clever, that.

The senior-most seaman then says that you're all on the second larboard watch, meaning you're currently on rest and will resume duties in four hours. That time should be spent how you please and in the future will be used on sleep, sewing and repairing your garments, or simply playing cards or writing letters (depending on a seaman's state of literacy).

Heading back down towards your hammocks, you stick close to Barlow.

"So, you're Rediker's man, right?"

Barlow sizes you up for the first time. "Aye, shipmates."

"Looks like a man with a past, to me."

"Ya got a keen eye. Saltboots, was it? Well, ye might learn soon enough. E'ery ship has rats, no matter how pretty on the outside." He gives you a wink, then pulls himself into his swaying hammock. "Now if ya excuse me, didn't sleep so well last night."

➤ Truth be told, neither did you. Get some shut-eye while it's offered.
   Go to page 215

➤ Rest in the hammock, but keep one eye open—and trained on Barlow.
   Go to page 237

A Bigger Fish

The *Deleon's Revenge* cuts through the turquoise seas of the Caribbean, darting to and from the various inlets and islands, hoping to find a merchantman out in the open. It's only a matter of time before a cry of "Sails!" brings half the crew up to the deck in eager anticipation.

Bringing the spyglass up, you see the *O Rei do Açúcar* on the horizon. Another Portuguese merchantman; but from her course, this one should be at the end of a long journey from Europe. With any luck, that means she'll be laden with weapons and manufactured goods ready to be exchanged for new-world resources.

"Fly the black," you command. "Prepare the vanguard for boarding."

Then a funny thing happens. When Barlow raises Bloodbeard's flag, the merchant ship doesn't make to run. Instead, it furls sails and lets out its sea anchors; effectively stopping in her tracks to wait for your approach.

"Could be a trap," Rediker murmurs.

"Gun crews at the ready," you reply.

When you pull up alongside her, the *O Rei do Açúcar* hoists a white flag of surrender. From the looks of it, none of the crew is armed whatsoever. Instead, the captain stands at the ready to receive the boarding party.

"Captain Bloodbeard!" the man shouts. "We have heard the fate of the *Dos Santos* when she resisted. We offer full surrender and beg mercy!"

"Your reputation precedes you, Cap'n," Joe says.

"Let's cement it then. Rediker, strict orders—no harm will come to the crew or captain. We want to encourage this sort of behavior."

"Aye, Cap'n," Rediker says.

Grappling hooks are thrown to secure the two ships to one another and walkways erected as a way to ferry goods from one to the other. There's a wary standoff, but it seems the Portuguese captain is true to his intentions.

"Sails!" the cry comes.

"What is this?" you say.

"I swear, I do not know," the Portuguese captain replies.

"Spanish!" the watchman adds.

A tide of uncertainty washes across both crews. This is especially disturbing news, as Spain is at war with both England and Portugal, but furthermore, pirate ships are perhaps the most hated enemy of the Spanish Empire.

Taking the spyglass once more, you see an enormous Spanish warship, marked as the *Elige tu Veneno* headed your way. Without a doubt, the warship has 2-3 times your numbers in crew, and likely 4-5 times your firepower. This is not a fight you can win.

As captain, yours is the sole voice of authority during action. What are your commands?

➢ Hold the Portuguese ship hostage! Spain may be both our enemies, but this is a civilian ship. Go to page 63

➢ Abandon the merchantman and make to escape in the shallows! A warship of that size is not to be underestimated. Go to page 147

The Big Guns

Robin considers your arrival, then replies, "Carriage guns in need-o'-cleanin'."

They don't really, at least not by your inexperienced eye, but it seems more likely he's using it as an opportunity to familiarize you with the big gun's components. He shows you how to swab the bore, and discusses cartridges of shot, which are stored down below to help weatherproof the gunpowder. He shows you the "brass monkey" ring where the cannonballs are stored next to the guns—doesn't matter if they get wet. He shows the cordage keeping the cannons in place for firing, and how to "run them out" to return their position after recoil. Looks like quite a bit of work and heavy lifting, which may help explain his gargantuan stature.

"What do you think of the captain?" you ask, but either Robin doesn't hear you or chooses not to respond, opting simply to continue with the duties.

"Have you sailed with Captain Bullock and Billy long?" you try.

"Cap'n knows the ship. Billy knows the men. I know the guns. That be enough for me."

That's all Robin has to say about that. He continues on, trying to help you know your place aboard the *Cooper's Pride*, and you don't test his patience further. An undeniable queasiness permeates through you, worse than yesterday's carriage ride. What a difference a day makes….

Eight bells sound, signaling that your watch is over. Robin says, "Headed right into a storm, I'd wager. Eight more bells t'get some rest—long night ahead."

The afternoon was more draining than you expected—both mentally and physically—so time in the hammock could be exactly what you need.

"Up! All hands! Up, or we perish!" the cry comes, shaking you from your slumber.

How long were you asleep? It's impossible to tell, and in the commotion, it doesn't much matter. Now that you're on your feet, you feel the violent rocking of the ship that the hammock had countered. You rush up with the crew, ready to lend a hand to prevent the threat of death.

Thoughts of seasickness are replaced by sheer terror when you reach the open air. Lightning arcs across the sky with the dreadful crack of thunder only an instant behind. The sea rollicks like an open flame and foams upon the deck—beating her with great waves, threatening to pull all asunder.

One such wave nearly knocks the ship on her side, and a man who was up in the rigging of the mainsail is thrown into the sea. You recognize him as the third crimped sailor, the one in a white-and-blue striped shirt.

"Man overboard! Jack's gone in!" the sailor Marlowe cries.

Billy throws a rope, but when it hits the water, it disappears into the inky sea, and now he watches with a sort of helpless indifference as the sailor struggles for his life. It's clear the man has no idea how to swim and will soon drown.

➢ Say a prayer for the poor seaman; nothing else you can do. Go to page 196

➢ Tie a length of rope around your waist and leap in! Go to page 164

➢ No time! Dive in and help crimped Jack back to the ship. Go to page 101

Billy

Interesting choice, Dear Reader. Not sure if you just weren't paying attention during all those campfire ruminations, or if you're trying some sort of bluff, but here's how it plays out:

"The killer was none other than… Billy Greaves," you say.

There's a moment of shocked confusion, then a smile breaks over Rediker's face.

"Seeing as how the man's final words, just 'fore I strung him up on the yard-arm, were, 'Damn ye all, bloody murderous pirates, you'll pay for your crimes, Rediker. I will have justice; Captain Bullock will have justice!'—I think I can safely say there's about as much veracity in your statement as a working girl in port claiming t'be a maiden. Are ye thinkin' us for fools, Saltboots? We shall see who has the last laugh. Boys, do what ye will with the castaway here. Just make sure there ain't no breath left when you're done."

We shall see who has the last laugh, indeed.

THE END

Blowhard

"It's that Billy Greaves, damn his blood!" Butch says, too loud.

"I'd mind my tongue, were I you. Robin and Billy seem close," you warn.

"Bet ya would! But I been a butcher too long t'fear a slab-o'-beef like Robin. All men are meat, as ya seen when that crimped man went and got himself crushed. Now watch's a man short, so Billy says. Says, I couldn't save the man's foot, least I can do is take his bloody place! The nerve!"

"What does the captain think?"

Butch rubs a thick hand over his ruddy face in frustration. "How the devil should I know? The whole point of a mate, mind ya, is so folk like us don't go askin' the cap'n what he thinks for every little dispute. No, I'm just made t'suffer, is all. Lost me shop, lost me wife, now ole Butch lost the privilege-o'-bein' a surgeon. Made a mockery by bein' *Doc* in name only. Christ Almighty, what else could ye throw at me? I'd wager Job himself ain't suffered more."

On and on the man goes. It's all you can do to focus on the horizon—which seems to be rising and sinking with a greater disparity than ever before. Didn't Robin say something about rough seas ahead? They seem to have arrived. Your stomach protests against this new state worse than Butch does against his own.

Time passes slowly in this manner, winds rising and sea rollicking, but the time does pass. Eight bells sound, signaling that your watch is over. Robin says, "Headed right into a storm, I'd wager. Eight more bells t'get some rest—long night ahead."

The afternoon was more draining than you expected—both mentally and physically—so time in the hammock could be exactly what you need.

"Up! All hands! Up, or we perish!" the cry comes, shaking you from your slumber.

How long were you asleep? It's impossible to tell, and in the commotion, it doesn't much matter. Now that you're on your feet, you feel the violent rocking of the ship that the hammock had countered. You rush up with the crew, ready to lend a hand to prevent the threat of death.

Thoughts of seasickness are replaced by sheer terror when you reach the open air. Lightning arcs across the sky with the dreadful crack of thunder only an instant behind. The sea rollicks like an open flame and foams upon the deck—beating her with great waves, threatening to pull all asunder.

One such wave nearly knocks the ship on her side, and a man who was up in the rigging of the mainsail is thrown into the sea. You recognize him as the third crimped sailor, the one in a white-and-blue striped shirt.

"Man overboard! Jack's gone in!" the sailor Marlowe cries.

Billy throws a rope, but when it hits the water, it disappears into the inky sea, and now he watches with a sort of helpless indifference as the sailor struggles for his life. It's clear the man has no idea how to swim and will soon drown.

➤ No time! Dive in and help crimped Jack back to the ship. Go to page 101

➤ Say a prayer for the poor seaman; nothing else you can do. Go to page 196

➤ Tie a length of rope around your waist, then leap in! Go to page 164

Boarding Party

They consider the offer, and your crew. After sizing you up, the Portuguese captain finally replies. "Fear not, men! Look at these ragged sailors in their torn breeches. These are desperate *desperados*, not the pirates you fear them to be!"

"Looks like it's going to be the hard way," Rediker says.

"Hard way it is, then," you say. "Show them who you are!"

Here, the boarding party throws grappling hooks, drawing the prey in ever closer until they can leap aboard. The Portuguese crew does their best to cut the ropes binding the two ships together, but they only slow the progress, not stop it. Once your first men leap onto the prize ship, the enemy crew scatters, heading below decks.

Despite their leader's blustering, it appears the crew of the *Dos Santos* fears this battle after all.

"What d'we do now, Cap'n?" Barlow asks.

"Could smoke 'em out?" Marlowe suggests.

"No. We don't want t'start a fire on a wooden ship," Chips says.

"How about we rig up some *grenadoes*? Can ye do it, Robin?" Rediker asks.

The hulking gunner nods. "Might blow a hole in the ship, though, if the magazine's open."

"I say we hack our way in. Break down the door and make 'em pay for resistin'!" Butch offers.

As captain, the say is yours.

➢ Break down the door! A few axe strokes and you'll be inside. Go to page 135

➢ Have Robin rig up some *grenadoes* and blow your way in. Go to page 96

Brawl!

Your hands ball up into fists, and you send a right hook into the man with the puckered lips, aimed right at that same bull's-eye. An unpracticed boxer, you're signaling your attack and could probably be easily dodged, but the drunken man's reflexes are too slow and you ring his bell with more strength than you knew you had in you.

A terrible *crack* sounds out and you're not sure if it was your knuckles or his cartilage. Either way, a new fountain flows from his face and he curses you as he backs away.

Stunned that you even knew how to throw a punch, you look to James is if he knows what should happen next. As it turns out, he does. James whales on the other sailor with fast and angry fists. The whole tavern erupts into fighting; a powder keg that you just lit the fuse to. Glass shatters over heads, chairs crack against backs and shoulders, and fists generally let fly.

The man you punched comes back to his senses and dives at your legs for a tackle. You fall with him atop you, then beat your fists against his back while he holds tight. You're not sure what he's playing at, until he fishes a dagger from his belt.

"Fight fair, ya lily liver!" James cries, kicking the man's hand and sending the dagger flying.

The other assailant wraps James up from behind, and another seaman suckerpunches your cousin in the gut, just because he can. You go back to wrestling the phantom kisser, groaning, "Who's the buggerer now?" which only makes him clench tighter.

"Town rats!" someone yells.

"Press gang!" cries another.

"Run for it!" sounds the general refrain.

The commotion intensifies, and someone gets thrown through the front window. Several others are stabbed, beaten senseless, or bludgeoned to death around you. It's total chaos, but you can't get up, pinned beneath this sodden attacker. Wrapping your arms around the man's head, you squeeze, hoping to incapacitate him.

At length, he finally goes limp, and you make it to your feet. Another pair of arms goes to grapple and you deliver a fearsome punch—right into the face of one of the town guards. Shocked, you simply stare at the man, mouth agape, until his comrades take you in irons.

Not much choice here:

Go directly to jail, do not pass go, do not assault officers of the peace and make matters worse.
<u>Go to page 188</u>

Bread and Toasts

⚓

Captain Longwick does indeed remove his previously imposed limits on drink and the men hurrah and imbibe with great abandon. But rather than hitting the rum and grog yourself, you're surprised to learn the Master and Commander wants a dinner with his officers—yourself included. The invitation comes from the steward, Akuchi, who also brings an offer to help you prepare your uniform for the occasion. Grateful, you accept.

The ship's stores, now resupplied by the fleet's larders, proves equally up to the task of preparing for a fine feast. You're greeted with a full spread, and it takes a moment to think back to your proper upbringing and table etiquette after weeks at sea spent shoveling slop in the mess.

"Remember, we still have our watches to perform," Lieutenant Dalton whispers as wine is poured for the table.

Wine, beef, and freshly baked bread! What a feast indeed. Once you've eaten to satisfaction, Captain Longwick calls for toasts.

"To His Majesty the King!" Lieutenant Dalton starts off, and you all raise your glasses.

"And to His Royal Britannic Navy!" One of the other Lieutenants, named Saffron, adds.

"To our fallen comrades," the surgeon continues.

"To the *Hornblower*!" you say.

Round the table it goes, until Captain Longwick finishes with, "May we be true to our uniform, and uniformly true."

"Hear-hear!" all say.

The next few days are a flurry of activity. The morning starts off with funeral rights for the fallen in battle, then goes straight into resupply. Once the ship gets fresh water, provisions, and timbers, the *Hornblower* heads out towards Caribbean seas and an urgent mission to the West Indies.

Weeks go by in this way, the ocean gradually changing from indigo to turquoise as shallower seas, reefs, and sandbars threaten the ship's path. The sun hangs longer in the sky, giving warmer, near-equatorial heat, and rain becomes a welcome relief for an English sailor.

It's a particularly hot day when you're to make for port. You're sailing along a series of islands, and the men are practically frothing at the bit for some shore leave. A change of pace would certainly be welcomed.

"Sails, ho!" Lieutenant Dalton shouts.

"What colors? Spanish? English?" you ask.

"No... she's flying the black," Dalton answers.

Could it really be? A pirate vessel?! Best quickly alert the Master and Commander of the ship.

Reporting in as you've been trained, you relay the sighting of the black flag with only minimal excited stammering. Captain Longwick gives the briefest hint of a nod, then rushes out to the quarterdeck. Examining the situation through a looking glass, the captain practically growls, "The *Cooper's Pride*."

Something in your memory clicks. You've heard that name before….

"A merchant ship, under the command of Arthur Bullock, or at least she was last. A draconian captain by all accounts, but still an Englishman." Then, lowering the spyglass, adds, "Well, then, if the *Pride* has been taken by pirates, I suppose it's only proper we take her back."

"Sir, my cousin last served on that ship," you say. "I'd like to lead the attack on the pirates, with my cousin in the boarding party."

Captain Longwick shakes his head. "Too personal. Your cousin's the gunner's mate, is he not? Find out what you can from him, but he stays here. You will lead the attack, sure enough, Ward. Pray to the Almighty your cousin can tell you something useful."

He's waiting for you to acknowledge the order. Say:

➢ "Sir, all due respect, the first task you assigned me was to question the veracity of your orders. Cousin James will serve better by my side on the front lines of battle than he would in the back of my mind." Go to page 295

➢ "Understood, sir. His emotional connection might cloud his judgment. I shall learn what I can from Cousin James and use it against these pirates. Would you prefer their leader be taken dead or alive?" Go to page 192

Breaking the Seal

The tide pool provides! After a meal of mollusks, you dip down and cup your hands to drink from the shoreline oasis. Though the water is salty in the extreme (it is seawater that was caught in low tide, after all), it's at least wet, so that goes a ways towards quenching your thirst.

Now then, where to?

Wait, not yet. Seems you have the urge to relieve yourself, so first it's time to make to the nearest patch of vegetation to *micturate*. Ahh, that's better. After you finish urinating, you look about for where to head next, but the tidepool catches your attention once more.

Oddly, you're even thirstier than you were before! Well, what could another drink hurt? As it turns out, it could hurt quite a bit. This is where the phrase "water, water everywhere, but not a drop to drink" comes from. Saltwater can be deadly to humans.

Here's why. Your kidneys need to flush your system of toxins (in this case, excess salt), but even at its saltiest, human urine contains less saline than seawater. So, in order to compensate, you've got to drink more water. If you had a source of fresh water, your body could dilute that extra salt into extra urine, but when you replenish your thirst with the ocean, you're engaging in a vicious cycle.

Too much salt in, not enough salt out, which means you get thirstier. By drinking that seawater, you add too much salt in, not enough salt out, which means you get thirstier. And on and on it goes, until….

THE END

Brethren of the Coast

You step forward. "Chips, think of the flogged young sailmaker. Was that justice? The rest of you, think of the rations and pay you've been denied. Was Captain Bullock kindhearted towards any of us? Now think of the opportunity we have here."

"What're ya sayin', Saltboots?" Billy asks.

"We sail to Boston, as planned. We sell the cargo, as planned. We return home, as planned. We tell the truth of it—that Captain Bullock died at sea because the man had a bad heart—for none here can deny that. Then we all go our separate ways. But for now, I think we can agree, we're in this together."

"Aye, but only as a fraternity!" Rediker adds.

"Call me not brother, Rediker! But Saltboots has the right of it. For now, we need all hands t'sail for Boston. Once there, help ye I cannot. No matter how cruel-hearted the master, what's done here, well, 'tis mutiny and piracy in the eyes-o'-the admiralty."

Rediker steps forward, saying, "True enough. But pirate ships don't have first or second mates, so there ain't much need for the likes-o'-you, Billy. I say we string this man up 'fore he sees it done t'the rest-o'-us. Cap'n Saltboots, make me your quartermaster, and let's rid ourselves-o'-the last tyrant aboard this ship!"

"Ya lubbers won't make landfall without good 'ole Billy! I know this ship like the back-o'-me hand! Make me your quartermaster, Cap'n, and whip this dog 'fore he bites another master's hand!"

The ship starts to list, such as it is that no one is steering her. With the crew simply idling, there's real danger that the *Cooper's Pride* could turn against the wind, hit a bad patch of seas, and capsize. This isn't going as easily as you'd hoped, but at least both men have recognized you as captain, so that's a start!

Quickly, Captain Saltboots, what're your first orders?

➢ Billy's my number two. Get all hands to their stations, then get the cat to silence Rediker's dissent. Go to page 198

➢ I need both these men under me. They'll just have to learn to work together! Otherwise, all is lost. Go to page 123

➢ Rediker's my number two. We must hang Billy now, lest we all hang when we get to Boston. Go to page 328

A Bright Future

Once the English flag replaces the black, the Spanish warship fires her guns in salute. If there's an enemy more hated than the English navy, it's an English pirate.

The rest of the pirate crew is disarmed; you order a group of men to head below decks and diffuse whatever explosives were primed by that fuse. Once the pirates are all rounded up, shackled into irons, and weapons cleared, Captain Longwick boards the *Cooper's Pride*.

"Well done, Ward! Well done. Ah, this must be the piratical captain. Is this knave the one the rogue's gallery rallies behind?"

"Aye, sir. Man calls himself Rediker," you reply.

"And what of Captain Bullock?"

"Dead. Killed himself, left the crew without a Cap'n," Rediker says, defiant.

"He tells it true, sir!" the mustachioed pirate adds.

"Yes, I'm sure he does," Longwick says. "But were I you, I shouldn't stick my neck out so close to the gallows. Save your stories for the Admiralty High Court."

"Here is the pirate captain's sword," you offer.

"Keep it. Sail back to London and deliver these prisoners for trial, then tell the admiralty that Charles Longwick insists his ward take the next examination for Lieutenant. The *Cooper's Pride* is now under your command."

Head swimming, you look about, seeing cousin James grinning at your side.

"Well? What say you?" Captain Longwick prods.

"Aye, sir. Thank you, sir! But I shall need a gunner to serve on the ship."

At this, Captain Longwick's normally stalwart face exhibits the slightest smile. "You have your choice to crew your return voyage. Godspeed, Captain Ward!"

That's it! You've survived and thrived in the world of a midshipman. But there's plenty more to explore. *MAROONED* has three unique storylines (look for anchors, skull and crossbones, and the palm tree symbols) and over fifty possible endings. Maybe things would have worked out differently if you had been a crew member of the *Cooper's Pride*? Or, what if you were a pirate yourself?

Or, if you're finished, please consider leaving a review to help others find this book. It's an incredibly helpful and easy way to support the author (who thanks you in advance, and in third-person, no less!).

When you're done, don't forget to check out the other exciting titles in the Click Your Poison multiverse! You can also sign up for the new release mailing list, or check out James Schannep's blog for updates.

http://eepurl.com/bdWUBb
http://jamesschannep.com

The Butcher

Aside from your having caught the captain in his death throes, who was the last person to see Captain Bullock alive? As the ship's surgeon, Butch was summoned to the captain's cabin after tending to the young sailor whipped by the cat-o'-nine-tails, after which Bullock had shut himself away until his ultimate demise.

Butch was the only non-crimped man among the other "new recruits" on the *Cooper's Pride*, a fact that you had not given much significance until now. As a volunteer, it could be assumed that whatever grudges he might've held would be minor.

Yet a stint on a merchantman would last a year, at least. Which could be a long time to serve under a captain you'd grown to begrudge. But was this true for Butch? Did he dislike the captain?

Butch had already visited Captain Bullock's cabin before you started your watch, so you didn't actually see him come or leave, but you did hear Marlowe share his misgivings while the old man was on the same watch as yourself.

"Cap'n be medicatin' himself now, I'd wager," Marlowe had said. "Saw Butch bringing a vial-o'-something-o'-other with him to Bullock's cabin. Needs a nip t'help him sleep after having beaten a lad. Butch left with that vial empty, saw him toss the bottle overboard! He didn't think I were watching, but I saw him plain as day. And the piece-o'-parchment he carried at his departure? An order for more pharmaceuticals, no doubt. Butch were white as a sheet, leaving the cabin. Moved like a man ashamed, afraid-o'-being caught, and who wouldn't be, if ordered t'steal medicines for the ship's master?"

That had been Marlowe's take, and at the time, you had accepted the theory at face value. At the most, you'd figured that Butch had been chastised for some perceived slight. Who hadn't been jawed-down from the captain at one time or another?

But now? Something feels out of place. If you could only think back on the clues left in Bullock's cabin, maybe you could make sense of it all? Or perhaps you should just think back on the others?

> Think back to your time with Billy Greaves, the Mate and right-hand man of Captain Bullock. Go to page 140
> Rack your brain over what odd occurrences happened near Dudderidge, the sea cook. Go to page 227
> Simply stare up at the stars—the same your shipmates presently sail beneath—until you fall asleep. Go to page 252

By the Don's Early Light

⚓

After a fitful night's sleep, you head up to the quarterdeck to see how the situation has progressed. Or, more accurately, to *not see*—for the early morning brings with it a dense fog. It's a haze that glows with the promise of dawn, but the only indications that you're still on the same ocean as the night before are the lamplights from the *Don Pedro Sangre*, which illuminate your tail like fireflies in the distance.

"Lieutenant Dalton—" you start.

"Ward, *shh!*" he hisses, a finger up to his lips. He marches over and whispers, "Captain Longwick has ordered complete silence, in hopes the Spanish lose us in the night."

That would explain the lack of lamplight here on the *Hornblower*, though the plan does not appear to have worked. The *Don Pedro Sangre* still haunts your shadow. Murmurs from the crewmen, suddenly unable to help themselves from breaking the order of silence, draw your eye to the larboard side. And with good reason—the fog here glows with the lamplight of a distant ship.

"They've passed us?" Dalton says, incredulous.

But the lights to the rear haven't disappeared. Stranger still, there seem to be voices coming from every direction. More lights appear on the starboard side, in front, aft—everywhere!

"By Jove, they're speaking the King's English!" Dalton cries, his excitement getting the better of him.

Then, as if crossing some unseen barrier, you pass through the fog completely. So too, dissipates the fog of your misunderstanding. For it isn't the Spanish around you at all: you've met with the rest of the Royal Navy! Lieutenant Dalton rushes to orders, desperate to signal the fleet before the *Don Pedro Sangre* realizes the trap they're sailing into. He does so at the exact right moment, for the enemy follows into clear skies, but not before several British warships arrive to claim her as a prize.

Breaking the order of silence with the rest of the seamen, you hurrah at the sight of your countrymen, knowing that victory has saved the day.

"Well, then," Captain Longwick says, appearing on deck and looking most pleased. "I suppose I should go meet with the Admiral in accepting the Dons' surrender. Lieutenant Dalton, you're in command until I return."

➢ Stay silent, and keep close to Dalton. You'd do well to see how a junior officer assumes command. Go to page 4

➢ Say, "Sir! Might I accompany you? This would be a great event for a new Midshipman to witness." Go to page 272

Calloused

"Saw another hand flogged today, which I'm sure will be the first of many, as tensions mount and the increased workload continues to wear at the crew. With a raw backside, this sailor is now unable to perform many duties, and so leaves yet more work for the rest of us...."

You take a break from journaling to massage a cramp in your hand, surprised at how rough they feel. Funny, you'd hardly ever tired in your penmanship at home, but now it seems you've become accustomed to a different sort of work with these hands.

Eight bells rings, signaling a change of the watch. You blow on the ink to ensure it's dried, then head up to perform your duties.

Even though the storms have subsided, the sky remains covered by a thick blanket of clouds. Once the sun has set, as now, that makes it increasingly difficult to navigate. The compass will generally keep the course, but there are strict orders for any seaman who makes a sighting of the stars to take note and report in to the captain, so he can compare with his charts and make a more accurate heading towards Boston. A discrepancy of even a degree could put you hundreds of miles off-course and mean a delay of several days or even weeks into port.

You're scanning the horizon for any astronomical signs when your eye catches several figures in the moonlight. It's a trio of men gathered near the bow, unusual in a severely undermanned watch. The three of them then head down into the hold, one by one, which is stranger still, as they now leave the bow unmanned.

> Best to trust a gut instinct, and this just feels plain wrong. Follow the conspirators down into the hold. Go to page 325

> Surely they have good reason. Keep your watch. No good can come from abandoning yet another post. Go to page 205

Calm before the Storm

Barlow keeps a firm grip on your arm, leading you down into the hold, but he doesn't seem too concerned that you might fight back. Perhaps it's because he's so long underestimated you, or perhaps it's simply because he views you as nothing more than another piece of cargo; a duty to be performed.

When you suddenly lash out, he's completely unprepared.

You slam his face against one of the wooden walls, snapping his nose with a *crack* and a fountain of blood. His curses surge forth to match the flow, but he's a fighter. Barlow goes for his pistol, and you take hold of his wrist, bashing the arm against the wall to get him to drop the weapon.

Bang! It discharges into the ceiling, the shot likely stuck in the boards. Barlow drops the pistol and goes for the cutlass, so you rush in, not giving him the space to draw the edged weapon. While he struggles, you take his head and bash it against your knee, leaping up to bring them together in the middle.

Barlow falls in a heap, and you go for his cutlass. But when you turn back, you see a trio of other pirates in the doorway, drawn by the commotion. It might have been better to wait until the ship was actually engaged in action, you realize. For then, a gunshot might have gone unnoticed. As it is, there's no way you'll take three bloodthirsty pirates on your own, and these men have no desire to see you bound and gagged. They'd rather break your bones and slit your throat.

THE END

Calypso

The fires set by the pirates are mercifully short-lived. Lush jungle (and further tropical squalls) help to quench the blaze; so too is your thirst for pirate blood slaked by the death of the pirate crew. You never learn the fate of the men who escaped in the jolly boat, but if they survived the journey in the small craft, their tales must have been such that all others should avoid your island.

The careened ship left behind provides a bounty with her stores of animals, dried foods, and supplies ranging from canvas, to iron and timbers. Even the ship itself can be broken down and used for a better shelter. The ship is far too large for you to sail alone, and even if you could, it's not like you'd want to.

This island is now and forevermore your home. You name it *Ogygia*, from the mythical island said to have kept Odysseus ensnared by the appeal of the Nymph, Calypso. The island provides, and lays claim to any sailors who might land on its shores—forever.

That's it! You've survived and thrived on a desert island. But there's plenty more to explore. *MAROONED* has three unique storylines (look for anchors, skull and crossbones, and the palm tree symbols) and over fifty possible endings. Maybe things would have worked out differently against the pirates if you had exposed Bullock's murderer? Or, what if you had boarded a different ship back in London?

Or, if you're finished, please consider leaving a review to help others find this book. It's an incredibly helpful and easy way to support the author (who thanks you in advance, and in third-person, no less!).

When you're done, don't forget to check out the other exciting titles in the Click Your Poison multiverse! You can also sign up for the new release mailing list, or check out James Schannep's blog for updates.

http://eepurl.com/bdWUBb
http://jamesschannep.com

Cannonade

⚓

"**Y**ou are addressing a superior officer!" Lieutenant Saffron chastises, in response to your criticisms.

"I'll be happy to address you as so, sir, after the battle. Until then, I have this broadside under my command, and I'll be damned if you're the reason we don't give as good as we get!" you reply indignantly.

Somehow, this rouses your men more than your earlier speech. Perhaps they see it as you sticking your neck out to defend them, but regardless, they're now fired up and ready to do their duty. The lieutenant shrinks away, knowing not to press the issue while an attack looms. The distant *crack* of musket fire reports from above decks, signaling the start of hostilities. The gun deck feels like a tinderbox—ready to blow.

Finally, the time for battle comes.

"Rear battery, fire!" the Captain issues loudly, which is relayed down to your command.

"FIRE!!!" you cry, signaling the last two guns.

The resultant explosion is unlike anything you've ever heard. As the cannons boom, your ears ring out, and the guns themselves slam backwards against their breech ropes. Seeing the several-ton weapons hurled violently backwards is a shock to the system, more so even than briefly going deaf from the cannon shot itself. But your senses soon return, and you ready the men for another round with commands of, "Swab the guns! Load cartridge! Shot! Now run out the guns!"

At this, the guns are cleaned, reloaded, and lined back up through the gun ports to be fired once more. Taking a moment to look through one of the unused gun ports, you see the behemoth ship bearing down on you still. Did those shots do *anything*? The order to "Fire as they bear!" is relayed down to your position. You swallow your fear, pushing the men (those within range of the approaching enemy ship) to fire the rear battery as often as they're able.

Then all hell breaks loose, as the Spanish return fire.

The gun deck explodes in a hail of splinters as cannon shot from the *Don Pedro Sangre* bombards your ship. Several men take splintering—yourself included, with a six-inch stake smashing into your right bicep. But you barely have time to feel that before the sailor next to you is blown apart by a direct hit to the ribcage. The pressure from the blast sprays viscera across the gun deck. It's complete carnage, with all the stunned seamen looking at the ranking lieutenant for an order. You don't even remember falling, but somehow you find your footing again and take charge.

"Lieutenant! Don't just stand there! Half your men need to take the wounded down to surgery. The other half can take their places on my guns! Prepare to return fire!" you shout.

Lieutenant Saffron nods, then splits his men fore and aft to the tasks assigned.

"FIRE!!!" you shout, signaling the rear battery once more.

The whole scene plays out again and again, and you tie off your arm to slow the bleeding, in-between commands. After what seems an eternity, a ceasefire is issued from above. The *Hornblower* has pulled away, and the enemy pursues the ship from the rear. Finally, you head down to Wycombe the surgeon to treat your arm.

You tell him to tend to you once the men with more serious injuries are dealt with, which leaves you waiting in his cabin until the wee hours of the night. The "splinter," as Wycombe calls it, is removed without issue, and your arm is bandaged. So long as it doesn't become infected, you're expected to fully recover and, best of all, keep the limb.

Finally, the adrenaline wears off, exhaustion sets in, and with a sense of pride keeping the pain at bay, you're able to get some sleep. Not much choice here:

Well done! You've survived your first battle at sea. But the Hornblower *isn't clear just yet. Get some much needed rest, and when you're ready....* Go to page 29

Caribbean Standoff

Now you're pointing your pistol at the man, reflexes sharpened by weeks of survival. The other pirates draw down on you, but no one dares fire. Rediker, for his part, simply laughs, then applauds. Whether he's applauding the spectacle or your bravado, who could say?

"Very well then, Saltboots. I've always wanted t'shoot in a duel, ya know that? Prove me mettle. I'd say we'd be about ten paces, wouldn't you?"

He draws his pistol and goes for the shot.

Crack! Before you even know what's happened, you've fired the flintlock, held these past few weeks for thoughts of revenge. The shot spent, you drop the pistol and produce the fifth of rum from your hip. Raising the rum, you say, "Here's mud in your eye."

Rediker falls to the beach, dead.

You drain the fifth, toasting to success and revenge, just as you've promised yourself. The shoreline erupts with more gunshots, first from Barlow, and then the other men follow suit. They all aim directly at you for revenge, and riddle you with holes.

Despite everything, this death feels a bit like victory, and you die with a smile on your lips.

THE END

The Carpenter

"**A**lways were a bloody liar!" Chips cries in response to your accusation. "Lying again, Saltboots! Don't believe a word-o'-it, Cap'n."

"Oh, I won't. Spare us the evidence, Saltboots. I know Chips be innocent."

"And how do you know that?" you say, taking the bait.

"Because a carpenter is far more valuable to this crew than a maroon. We're here careened, in case ye did not notice. And Chips'll have us float again, fast and sleek. You? Well, ye might provide a few hours of entertainment for the crew, but that's all. Boys, do what ye will with the castaway here. Just make sure there ain't no breath left when you're done."

The pirates leer at you with wicked grins. This won't be pleasant.

THE END

Carry On

⚓

"That's a dirty job, indeed. Top marks for volunteering!" Dalton says, with genuine appreciation.

You offer a salute and head down to the pump room. Wood is porous, and all ships take on water, no matter how tightly they're sealed. This accumulates in the ship's bilge, and the resultant "bilge water" must be pumped out, lest she rides low and collects drag, slowing the ship. Some water buildup is to be expected, but if you can clear out the excess, the *Hornblower* should see a boost in speed—which could be crucial in this chase.

It's backbreaking work, plunging and raising the handle again and again to pump the water out, but you're spurred on by an overwhelming sense of purpose. This is work that needs be done daily, but today is the first time that you truly feel like your doing so could directly save the lives of the crew.

After a grueling hour, you're relieved by the next shift and sent up to eat an early meal. Fine by you; that activity worked up quite an appetite!

The ship is abuzz with speculation pertaining to the Spanish warship now chasing your own frigate. Many of the men are keen to fight, even against a superior force. A frigate is more maneuverable than the larger man-o'-war, and Captain Longwick seems like a tactician who could use that to his advantage. The anticipation is the worst part—these sailors want to see what both he and the *Hornblower* can do!

The scuttlebutt is that the armory is to be unlocked, muskets issued, and stations taken. Each of the cannons is to be made ready for a possible fight. The excitement's getting to you too. Maybe it's time to get in on the action?

➢ Offer your keen eye as one of the snipers. Alone, aloft, and alienated from the cannon shot. Go to page 158

➢ Request a position on one of the gun teams. You've been training for this! Go to page 316

Castaway

One shot to end it, and rum for the courage to do so. That's the advice you were given, the advice for a murderer left to die and rot. But that's not the fate you deserve, marooned on an island for a crime you didn't commit. This won't be the end; can't be the end. For you, the single pistol shot will serve for revenge and the rum to toast your success.

They may have cast you aside, but this need not be a death sentence. One survives because they have a reason to survive, simple as that. It's a concept you've come across time and again in your studies—given a "why" to live, one can bear any "how."

For you, that reason will be to clear your name and see the true killer brought to justice.

Pocketing the rum and journal, and stowing the pistol in your waistband, you watch as the *Cooper's Pride* sets sail. Will Billy truly come back for you? Or, God willing, might some other ship happen by and rescue a sailor in need?

Neither will happen, however, if you don't survive this first night alone.

The sun hangs low on the horizon. Turning back, you see that this island must be at the start of the tropics. Broadleaf ferns lead into the jungle interior, and coconut trees dot the skyline. That's good. You may be deserted on this isle, but fortune favors you that it's not a *desert* isle. You'll find food here, and water.

There isn't much daylight left, but enough to start your preparations. What's the first priority?

> Shelter. The weather can turn sour at any moment and you need a "fo'c'sle" on your new home. Go to page 149

> Fresh water. Head into the interior of the island in search of something to drink besides rum. Go to page 319

> Fire. This was mankind's first invention, and a critical step towards taming the natural world. Go to page 145

Chaos

"Wh-what?" Rediker stammers.

"Go on, tell them, this is a mutiny!" you prod.

"Well, I mean, we got no love for Cap'n Bullock, but I never ordered ye t'kill the man!"

"At least not outright," Marlowe mutters.

"I'm confused. Who killed the cap'n?" Barlow asks.

That's when Billy arrives, demanding to know what's happened.

"It's a mutiny!" Joe says, backing away.

"Saltboots killed the cap'n," Chips adds.

"No, that's not true!" you say. "It *is* a mutiny, but I didn't kill the man. Someone in our number did. The mutineers. It's still a mutiny, and we are in charge!"

"Robin! Put these men in irons!" Billy commands.

"I'll not hang for this, damn you!" Rediker cries.

Then chaos erupts on the quarterdeck. Fists fly, and improvised weapons are used as bludgeons. More and more of the crew arrives by the second as word spreads, further increasing the carnage. Unlike a warship or pirate vessel, very few of the men are armed, but all are ready for a brawl.

Should you reach out for the captain's knife? You're considering this when a terrible blow strikes you between the shoulder blades, knocking you down. Rolling over, you see Chips raise one of his carpentry tools for another strike.

"Bloody murderer!" he cries, before becoming one himself.

THE END

Chart a Course

⚓

With the excitement of schoolchildren, you rush out with Cousin James up to the top decks to find the helmsman. The man sees your excitement plain as the stars in the sky, and grins to himself, but keeps his silence.

"Oh, come on! Tell us!" you say.

"If ye must know, have a look for yourself. Go on—where are we headed?" the helmsman asks, looking to the stars.

Cousin James studies the sky and you do too, but he's more experienced and shouts the answer. "West-sou'-west! But where to? Madeira? The Azores? Canary Islands?"

"Yes, the Canaries are Spanish-owned!" you supply.

"Indeed, but think… further," the helmsman says.

"The West Indies?" James says, trepidation in his voice.

"Aye, we're t'warn the Governors in the Caribbean of a Spanish plot."

Nodding thanks to the helmsman, you leave him be, discussing the possibilities with Cousin James. The West Indies, the Caribbean seas, and a Spanish plot!

"How very cloak-and-dagger," you say. "That's the haven of pirates, is it not?"

"Well, parts of it, anyway. Lots-o'-trade routes run through the West Indies, which draws in Brigands," he answers.

"Do you really think we'll see any?"

"You'd best hope not, Coz! The only thing worse'n a black flag would be a red one."

"A red flag?"

"A black flag wants only booty, but a red flag wants revenge. No quarter to be given," he says solemnly. "Come on, then, I'm beat."

Truth be told, you're exhausted as well, but your head spins with thoughts of pirates, gold chests, treasure maps, and adventure. Not much choice here:

➢ *Get some rest, and dream of daring rogues and walking the plank.* Go to page 311

Cheap/Thrills

Billy shakes it off good-naturedly. "Well, if you're afflicted by a chronic lack of coin, ye could always set sail like your cousin! Ask Jimmy Saltboots here for tale-o'-his first night a'sea."

"Jimmy... Saltboots?" you say, trying it out.

"Though greener than your hometown hillsides, I knew he'd have a sailor's life yet, ain't that right, Jimmy?"

"Not for me, Billy. I ain't never goin' back. I have a lifetime's tales to tell. But tonight, I only want the tail!" At that James downs the rest of his drink, scoops up his lovely companion, and carries her into a back room like a Viking raider might carry a prize after plunder.

"Don't s'pose you'd wanna take his spot on me ship?" Billy asks half-heartedly.

Though you know it's rhetorical, you take a moment, looking around at the bar and the life of a seaman by extension. All you see are a bunch of men living life like this night might be their last. In the rear, there's a man smoking from a hookah pipe who's so covered in tattoos you almost can't distinguish him from the patterned wallpaper. Other seamen lounge with still more women and drink.

Another few men play dice, exchanging coin between throws. They make eye-contact and with a nod, offer you a place at the table. Care to give it a go?

➢ Stay at the bar and say, "You're kind to think of me, Billy, but I shall simply wait to deliver my cousin home, whether he's ready to leave the seafaring life or not." Go to page 240

➢ Go join the gamblers and say, "Sorry, Billy. I think I've chanced upon a different way to earn some coin while I wait for my cousin." Go to page 318

Chips, Ahoy!

The ship's carpenter was a man who kept to himself, mostly. But after the death of the sailors in the storm, he opened up. Chewing on a hardtack biscuit, a fishing line over the edge in hopes of finding something more flavorful and easier to sink his teeth into. And during that time, he chewed on his own superstitions.

"Saw Saint Elmo's Fire," Chips said, as if to the night air.

"What's that?" you replied.

"Jacques, the crimped man who went overboard. He saw it the night before. Called it a *corposant*, but t'were the same. A bad sign, that. Worse omen still for he that spots it. And look what happened!"

"That's enough!" Captain Bullock had reprimanded, before continuing on his rounds.

After a few minutes, Chips continued, "I saw a sign m'self. Out on the seas, clear as day, were a boat. Not a sailing ship, but a boat, one with oars. They was rowing, but never came closer. Called out, I did. Ahoy! Sometimes people are lost, even found way out here. It's possible, is all I'm saying.

"Yet not a soul so much as looked up to answer me. Hailed several more times, as much for me own waning sanity. Ahoy! But all they did was row. Rowing, rowing, never coming closer. Unnatural, that. It had to be Charon's boat, d'ya see? Waiting for Jacques t'come aboard. The man fell over and the rower disappeared. Satisfied t'have his manifest filled, the ferryman left us be."

"Chips! Did I not tell you to stow such talk?" Bullock roared, making his way back.

"Aye, Cap'n!" Chips called back sharply.

"If I hear any more such superstition out of you, I'll cut your bloody tongue out and throw it overboard. Might do you some good, damn you. A carpenter needn't a tongue to do his work."

"Aye, Cap'n!" Chips called again.

That seemed to satisfy Bullock, who left. Chips took the threat to heart, and didn't speak up anymore, but kept his eyes trained on the inky waves, mind racing and seeing hobgoblins in the dark, no doubt.

Superstition can spoil a man's mind, rob him of his senses. Seamen are by nature a superstitious lot, and made them cast a Jonah overboard many a ship over the years. Could something he saw or heard have driven Chips to murder?

The link seems tenuous, at best. He was the first to arrive and accuse you, after all. Likely as not, if the man had truly been bewitched into committing murder, he would have felt justified and confessed.

No, if the carpenter had a real motive, it remains a secret.

> What about Robin? What secrets might the tattooed gunner have held?
  Go to page 279

> What about Joe? Was there any secret the bosun might kill to protect?
  Go to page 73

> That's enough for tonight. Best to take your mind off things and enjoy the warmth of the fire. Go to page 320

Cleanup Crew

⚓

Down in the ship's magazine, you find Cousin James stacking cartridges to redistribute the spent ammunition stores, likely preparing for an imminent resupply. The gunner, Monks, counts cannonballs, marking down the result on parchment; so you wait at the entry, not wanting to interrupt.

At length, he feels your presence and looks up. "Well? Whaddaya need?"

"Hello, Mr. Monks. Just wanted to check on my cousin, is all."

"Just Monks," he corrects, then looks back to his mate. "Go on, I can finish up."

"Many thanks," James says, wiping his brow and heading out to join you. James leads you to the nearest water cask, dips in the drinking gourd, and takes a long draw. But rather than looking sated, his face puckers and he says, "Ugh, thank God this'll be refreshed soon."

"Along with all that spent gunpowder…" you say, thoughts returning to the previous night's battle.

"Aye, have ya got your hearing back yet?"

"What?"

"I said, have you—" he starts, catching himself at your grin. "Bastard. Glad t'see ya made it through your first blood-letting."

"There were a few times I feared I might not," you confess.

The Master-of-Arms happens by before James can reply, butting in with, "Ahoy there, ya two idlers. Come and put your hands t'use while flappin' your gums."

Following the man, he leads you to the surgery, the boards outside of which are tacky with drying blood. "Go on then, clean 'er up!"

The Master-of-Arms leaves, and you find a bucket with Cousin James. Kneeling in the muck to scrub, you say, "Sorry. Guess I should've left you in the magazine."

"Eh, job needs doin'. You make for finer company than that grouch of a gunner. Honestly surprised he let me go, I am."

Continuing the chit-chat, you scrub the remnants of your fallen comrades off the planks, using the conversation as a way to keep your mind off of what's collecting underneath your fingernails. Talk inevitably goes to home, then back to thoughts of the war.

"Ya made it through the first battle, coz. Hard part's over!"

Your eyes drift past your cousin, into the surgery and the men laid up in various states of bandaging. The surgeon, Wycombe, steps out and peers down at you.

"There's more inside, if you've acquired a taste for it," he says.

"Sir…?" you reply.

"No? Go on, then. You've nearly finished. I imagine the captain will look to make good on his promise of victory rum."

"Let's go see!" James says, hopping up to leave.

And indeed, Captain Longwick has removed any limitations on beer and grog, and restored the right to rum. As if they fear the Master and Commander will soon change his mind, the men imbibe like they've been left on a desert isle for days,

43

only to finally find a spring. The way they gulp it down, those fears might prove to be a self-fulfilling prophecy.

You toast to His Majesty's health, taking your part in the revelry.

"Let's get some air above deck," Cousin James suggests.

The men, in various states of drunkenness, sing and dance, play cards and other games, jostling and joking in every berth of the ship. A fight breaks out, and though it's quickly subdued, the quarrel doesn't escape the attention of the officers up on the quarterdeck.

"It's been a while since they've been allowed to let loose, sir," Lieutenant Dalton says.

"Yes. Looks like the men might need to burn off some of this… enthusiasm," Captain Longwick replies.

"Aye, sir," Mr. Midshipman Magnus says from the other side. "Could rally 'em about for a Sailor's Hornpipe? Or Sling the Monkey?"

Noticing you eavesdrop, Dalton says, "Something we can help you with, Landsman?"

Curiosity getting the better of you, you reply:

- "Sorry to interrupt, but I must ask: Is there really a monkey onboard? One that we might… sling?" Go to page 190
- "Begging your pardons, sirs, but what exactly is a Sailor's Hornpipe?" Go to page 51

Cold Compress

⚓

As storm clouds continue to roll in, the night grows darker and darker. The few lamps on the ship only illuminate the most important instruments, lest the wooden ship risk catching ablaze. But that also means you're able to find a hidden corner to sit for a moment. Exhaustion takes over, however, and you don't even realize you've fallen asleep until you awaken with the shock of cold water. Full immersion; you're drowning!

You gasp for air, reaching out to swim, only to smash your knuckles against the wooden beams of the ship. James stands before you, holding a bucket, from which he merely splashed you awake with seawater.

"Bloody fool!" James cries. "Lucky 'twas me that found ya. Watch's up; did ya sleep clear through eight bells?"

"Oh, no. I fell asleep?" you say dumbly, finding your feet and a stiff, sore body.

"If ya get yourself killed, coz—do me a favor—take me with ya! Otherwise, no way I'll ever live with m'self after getting you into this mess."

You're about to reply when Lieutenant Dalton raises the alarm. "Up! Every soul, and nimbly, for God's sake, or we all perish!"

"Up into the maintop! Take in the topsail!" Mr. Magnus adds.

Lightning flashes, with the dreadful crack of thunder only an instant behind. The heavens open. Sheets of rain dump onto the ship, like the Almighty Himself thought your cousin left the job of dousing you unfinished.

"Not you," James commands. "You're not ready for this, coz. Stay down!"

He begins to climb up, fearless. Part of you wants to prove yourself, to jump up and do the same, but part of you thinks to the words of Shakespeare's Falstaff, "The better part of valor, is discretion." Maybe James is right?

Though as the wind rips across the bow so frightfully, loud enough that the men can't even hear themselves shout, you think instead of Shakespeare's *The Tempest*; The Bard didn't know the half of it.

What will it be?

➤ Climb the mast. Do your part! Go to page 223

➤ Watch and learn, young one. Go to page 220

Cold Pressed

⚓

Rushing forward with indignity as your ally, you confront the two men. "How dare you plot my demise! Have you no sense of honor? What scoundrels, here in the dark of night, seeking to undo your fellow shipmate!"

"Watch your tongue, or by God ye'll find yourself joinin' Neptune's Fishguard!" Magnus shouts back, matching your indignation with his own.

"I will simply not be addressed like this!" Dalton says, trading glances between the two of you. "Mr. Magnus, please instruct the Ward on how to properly address a superior officer!"

Then the Lieutenant marches off. Magnus watches him go, and finally turns back with a cruel grin. He removes a dagger from the sash about his waist and steps forward.

"Just you and me, ya motherless cur. Know why he left us 'lone? *No witnesses.*"

The man means to murder you! Your hands, previously used only to hold a quill, now ball into fists as if that were the most natural thing in the world. Still incensed, you rush him, but he makes to cut and you duck back. Magnus swings at the open air, left unbalanced, open for counterattack.

At this, you crack his skull with a full left hook, then go again with the right, knocking the Dutchman senseless. He stumbles forward with a wild swing of the knife and you move away to let him past. With your back now towards the side rail of the ship, you watch as he shakes his head, rights himself, and lunges again with renewed ferocity.

Trapped between the sea and Magnus's dagger, you have no choice but to wrestle for control of the weapon. The Dutchman presses forward on steady legs, but you stumble away under the momentum of the swell when the ship lurches from the approaching storm.

A scream announces Magnus's fall overboard.

One second, you're fighting for your life, the next there's a splash and the fight is over. The Midshipman disappears into the sea as lightning arcs across the sky and a terrible thunderclap hits the ship. The waves pull the *Hornblower* across the sea at incredible speeds. He's simply… gone. Swallowed by the sea.

Even in the gale-force winds, you hear the hammer on flintlock pistol click into place. Hands raised, you turn around to see the Master-of-Arms.

"Would you shoot me in cold blood?" you ask.

"Of course not. You're to stand trial for the murder of Mr. Magnus. I just saw ya push him overboard."

"That's not what happened!"

He grins. "M'word against yours, seein' as how Magnus ain't here to have his say."

➢ Surrender, await trial. The truth shall set you free. Go to page 162

➢ Rush him, wrestle the pistol free. Go to page 185

Conspiracy Theory

More and more of the crew arrive on the quarterdeck, an audience held just outside the late Captain Bullock's cabin. Rediker, Barlow, and Marlowe stare you down from the periphery, so—with literal blood on your hands—you simply try to sow the seeds of doubt.

"There's more to this than a simple killing," you say. "This is all part of a larger plot, the first step in a mutiny! I don't know if the plan was to make me appear to have killed the captain; I don't know if the rogues are that cunning. I only know there are those amongst us in the crew who have plotted Bullock's demise, and I swear I do not count myself amongst their numbers."

Billy arrives, demanding to know what's happened.

"Saltboots murdered—" Chips starts.

"No! That's a lie!" you protest.

Joe steps forward. "Cap'n Bullock's dead, that ain't in dispute. But there weren't no witnesses. You're the captain now, Billy. What should we do?"

Billy looks towards you, doubt in his eyes.

> Appeal to his emotion. Hasn't Rediker long been a troublemaker? He must be the murderer! Go to page 262

> Appeal to his reason. What possible motive could you have? There must be an investigation! Go to page 163

Convincing Performance

Falling to the jungle floor, you play "dead." Not moving, not resisting. Then you play "food" and are eaten.

Playing dead only works on a false charge. Leopards don't give false charges.

This is the end of your adventure.

THE END

Cypress

⚓

You move forward cautiously, the Master-of-Arms' shouts growing louder. Soon you see his outline; he paces in the dull lamplight before another sailor who shrinks from chastisement. It's quickly made clear what this is all about.

"You call yourself a Carpenter's Mate?" the Master-of-Arms mocks. "Never seen such shoddy workmanship! Give me one bloody reason I don't have ya re-assigned as cook's mate, *Christ Almighty*!"

"Please, sir. I'll learn me trade, I will!"

"Aye, ye learn or we sink!" the other man growls.

The ship suddenly lurches under rough seas and several of the woodworking implements slide across the deck. The carpenter's mate scrambles to collect them, but the Master-of-Arms just steps aside, letting the tools scatter.

"Even more worthless than the Captain's new Ward! What would ya have t'offer the Cap'n for that, eh? Nonsense position if e'er I heard-o'-one. Why dontcha both just 'fall over' and do us all a favor?"

An iron tool slides across the deck towards your feet.

➤ Ignore it, go back to your duties. It's not your place to interfere with the ship's discipline. Go to page 305

➤ Give it back, make a friend. The man knows he needs to improve, there's no need to be cruel. Go to page 266

➤ Take the tool and threaten the Master-of-Arms with it. That's the only language a bully speaks. Go to page 84

Daedalus

This group looks at you as if you're some kind of albatross; a portent of ill-omens. So be it. No one gives you any commands or bothers you with their superstitious chatter, so you're free to wander—mentally and literally—the decks of the ship.

As England disappears, you head up to the bow, straining your eyes to see France across the channel. The *Cooper's Pride* cuts through the water like a dart, bringing to mind your studies of the famed inventor Daedalus. Perhaps most well-known for creating the labyrinth, but also credited with inventing the angled bow upon which you now stand. Still, his Cretan labyrinth couldn't have been any more isolating than the sea itself. For who wouldn't be lost upon a horizon of nothing, save for blue-to-blue, as far as the eye can see?

Yet the state of this voyage, seemingly doomed to be spent in isolation with a tyrant captain, reminds you of still another Daedalian legend. That of Pasiphae's wooden cow, constructed so she could finally, truly love the perfect bull Poseidon had birthed from the sea. Perhaps you too were smitten by an ill-conceived love of the briny deep, and now find yourself trapped in your own wooden contraption, left to the whims of an ornery Bullock.

Hours pass with dour thoughts and roughening seas, which threaten to turn your stomach even more than your own negativity. Finally, eight bells sound, signaling that your watch is over.

"Get some sleep, ya lot!" Marlowe commands. "Eight more bells, then 'tis supper, and back to it. So ya better get your shuteye while 'tis on offer!"

The afternoon was more draining than you expected—mentally and physically—so time in the hammock could be exactly what you need.

"Up! All hands! Up, or we perish!" the cry comes, shaking you from your slumber.

How long were you asleep? It's impossible to tell, and in the commotion, it doesn't much matter. Now that you're on your feet, you feel the violent rocking of the ship that the hammock had countered. You rush up with the crew, ready to lend a hand to prevent the threat of death.

Thoughts of seasickness are replaced by sheer terror when you reach the open air. Lightning arcs across the sky with the dreadful crack of thunder only an instant behind. The sea rollicks like an open flame and foams upon the deck—beating her with great waves, threatening to pull all asunder.

One such wave nearly knocks the ship on her side, and a man who was up in the rigging of the mainsail is thrown into the sea. You recognize him as the third crimped sailor, the one in a white-and-blue striped shirt.

"Man overboard! Jack's gone in!" the sailor Marlowe cries.

Billy throws a rope, but when it hits the water, it disappears into the inky sea, and now he watches with a sort of helpless indifference as the sailor struggles for his life. It's clear the man has no idea how to swim and will soon drown.

➤ No time! Dive in and help crimped Jack back to the ship. Go to page 101

➤ Say a prayer for the poor seaman; nothing else you can do. Go to page 196

➤ Tie a length of rope around your waist and leap in! Go to page 164

Dance Party

⚓

"**W**ell, I'd say the fact that you have to ask is reason enough," Captain Longwick replies. "Assemble the Hornpipe."

"Sailor's Hornpipe!!!" Magnus bellows.

The ship's crew gives three *hurrahs!* in response, leaving you to wonder what you just got yourself into. The drunken sailors gather before the mainmast in a formation you've not yet seen. As your first clue into the nature of the Hornpipe, you see sailors appear with various musical instruments: a fiddle, a flute, and something hand-cobbled resembling a tambourine.

"Should we see if Argyle wants to use his bagpipe?" Lieutenant Dalton asks.

"Do so, and I'll have you thrown overboard," the captain replies. "What's the difference between an onion and a bagpipe? Why, no one cries when you cut open a bagpipe."

The musicians begin and the sailors gathered in formation anchor their hands on their hips, then begin wildly kicking their legs about in a dance. Next, they cross their arms in the air in front of their chests, then jump-squat and kick all over again.

"Go on, then, Landsman! A Sailor's Hornpipe ain't that complicated. Give 'r a go!" Magnus shouts down to you.

You join about in the frolicking dance, kicking and leaping about with abandon. After the Hornpipe, the musicians play other tunes and you spend an easy evening with the seamen drinking, dancing, and singing. It's a cool evening, which feels good after working up a sweat from the dancing.

➤ After a night full of drink, I think I'll hit my hammock. The ship appears to be spinning… Go to page 146

➤ I think I'll sleep out under the stars tonight. No sign of clouds, and what a great night it was! Go to page 146

The Darkest Timeline

⚓

Once the English flag replaces the pirate black, the Spanish warship fires her guns in salute. If there's an enemy more hated than the English navy, it's an English pirate ship.

Cousin James died of his wounds before the battle was finished—you weren't even afforded a chance to say goodbye. The only consolation is that you'll see his murderer tried and hanged. The *Cooper's Pride* is placed under your command, the rogue called Rediker made your prisoner, and the honor of sailing this ship back to London as her captain bestowed upon you.

Knowing James died for your sake always stays with you. Though you'll go on to a prestigious career in the Royal Navy, there is no joy in it. Never again are you close to another living soul; only to duty. Married to the sea, for only the sea can match the cold, dark depths in your heart.

It's Homer who can best sum up the rest of your days:

> *No one of the Achaeans labored so much as Odysseus labored and achieved, and for him the end was grief, and a sorrow that is never forgotten; for his sake, though gone so long, for we knew not whether he was ever alive or dead.*

That's it! You've survived and thrived in the world of a midshipman. But there's plenty more to explore. *MAROONED* has three unique storylines (look for anchors, skull and crossbones, and the palm tree symbols) and over fifty possible endings. Maybe things would have worked out differently against the pirates if you had you known James would join the attack? Or, what if you were a pirate yourself?

Or, if you're finished, please consider leaving a review to help others find this book. It's an incredibly helpful and easy way to support the author (who thanks you in advance, and in third-person, no less!).

When you're done, don't forget to check out the other exciting titles in the Click Your Poison multiverse! You can also sign up for the new release mailing list, or check out James Schannep's blog for updates.

http://eepurl.com/bdWUBb
http://jamesschannep.com

Deal with the Devil

Leaving the ship in the hands of the Bosun, you quickly follow Rediker to the Black Market. From the looks of it, your companion is acquainted enough with Boston to navigate his way directly to its criminal underbelly; you don't ask just how it is he came to this familiarization.

Weapons are sold here, of course, as well as unlicensed moonshine, opium and other narcotics. Prostitutes offer their services as you pass, and several men idle about, either waiting to be paid as hired muscle, or using said muscle to rob any errant outsiders foolish enough to wander into the Black Market alone, for curiosity's sake.

With one hand on your pistol, you continue on.

Once Rediker finds the establishment he was looking for, you head inside to conduct business. It's a more of a saloon than a pub; a stage is set for dancers, though none work at this early hour. Still, the house is packed with gamblers and boozers; a man soon arrives with drinks. After finding a booth in the corner, you get down to business right away.

"I understand you lot're looking to sell your wares," the man says in a strange colonial accent.

"Aye, that be the way-o'-it," Rediker answers. "Found a derelict ship, and managed t'save the cargo 'fore she sank. Salvage rights and all."

"Of course, of course. And the ship's manifest?"

"Lost to Davy Jones, I'm afraid."

"Isn't that always the way? In that case, I can offer seventy percent of market price."

"We'll settle for fifty, if you drop what you're doing and send men to collect now," you offer.

The merchantman's eyes grow wide. "In a hurry, are we?"

"Indeed. And we'll take our business elsewhere, if that will speed things up."

Rediker puts a hand on your leg under the table to slow your pace, but the merchant nods.

"No need for that. I'll send them over now."

"Thank ye kindly," Rediker says. "I can draw out a list-o'-cargo so we can tally payment."

All is agreed, hands shaken, pen and parchment fetched, and the finer details ironed out. There's some commotion around the stage as the house prepares for their next show. Noting your attention, the merchantman reveals the purpose.

"Slave fights starting up soon. Once I remit payment, we'd be happy to give you a discounted rate on a bet. Just pick your boxer and let me know."

The merchantman rises from the table to find your payment and you watch as several musclebound Africans are paraded into the room. They wear scars from previous brawls and are shackled, like men on the way to the gallows.

"Slave fights?" you mutter.

"Aye. Many a man 'board a ship might gamble on rat fights, or cocks, if they be lucky enough to have a good pair. They be uppin' the ante here, t'be sure, though I confess I have no taste for such barbarity. Some men, abused by masters and mates, pay t'see another man bloodied in turn."

The merchant returns with several satchels of coin. "Payment, based on your manifest. Though you'll kindly wait here until we've retrieved the cargo."

"Place me stakes on that big buck, third from the left," Rediker says as he slides one of the coin pouches back across the table.

The merchant takes the coins and leaves once more. Rediker downs his drink.

"Thought you didn't have a 'taste for such barbarity'?"

"That there be like a tip, Cap'n. Little extra grease t'ensure all the parts move smoothly."

A pair of slaves are unshackled and led into the ring. The Africans look intoxicated, though it might be a mixture of substance and bloodlust. From the whip scars on their bare backs, you can be sure they've been coerced into this life one way or another.

Very little is said before the fight begins. The slap of meat on meat and the crack of bone on bone is enough to turn your stomach. This might be the most violence you've seen thus far in your brief career as a pirate.

"Just can't watch this," Rediker says, shaking his head.

"Agreed. Can we leave yet?"

"I'll say our goodbyes if you're ready, Cap'n."

"Do it."

Rediker rises from the booth, removes his pistol, levels it at ringmaster of the fights and fires off his shot. The explosive *crack* stops the fight and all eyes look towards you both. That's not quite what you were expecting!

"Any man here wants a new life for himself, come join us on the *Cooper's Pride*. But ye must strike first t'be free. Ship's setting sail directly, so make up your minds *toot sweet*," Rediker says. Then, turning back, whispers, "Best be on our way, Saltboots."

He scoops up the coins while you ready your pistol to cover the escape. A full riot starts in the saloon, slave rising against master, and drunken gamblers using the excuse to try to rob the house and reclaim any losses. It's complete chaos. The merchant's hired muscle is so overwhelmed that you make it to the doors without trouble.

"Billy Greaves, damn his blood," Rediker says, exiting.

You step out, expecting to see the mate in the flesh, only to find fifty uniformed men marching down the wharf to arrest Captain Saltboots and the crew of the *Cooper's Pride*. Most hold muskets at the ready, and the rest carry iron shackles to help transport your men to the gallows.

"*Hostis Humani Generis*," the Reverend begins his remarks. The man is jowly, his white powder wig parted down the center, curls raised to either side. He struts in his black cloak before your crew, the magistrate, and the gathered crowds beyond the gallows, lining the near shore and perched atop neighboring Broughton Hill for a better view.

The Reverend continues, "Enemies of all mankind. Nothing good can be asked of thee, save the lesson to others by your death. I will take your final admonitions, for though you are condemned to hang by the laws of man, prithee ask for the Lord's mercy on your eternal souls. Jeremiah 31:20 tells us, '*I will surely have mercy on them, saith the Lord.'* And now, in the last moment of your lives, if you do truly repent and believe in the Glorious Redeemer unto the saving of thine souls and the pardon of all thee sins, ye shall be saved forever and ever. Amen."

"Thank you, Reverend Mather, as always," the magistrate says. "These brigands are indeed condemned for actions most piratical and felonious in the murder of their captain and the capture of his ship. They put their honest shipmates in corporeal fear of their lives and deigned to sell these ill-gotten gains for profit. You may each take a moment now to repent for your souls and to say any final words."

Then all goes silent.

The gathered crowd, hundreds of people, wait with hushed and eager anticipation for the pirates' last words. The magistrate and reverend simply wait. The hangman stands at the ready.

"Wine," Rediker says, clearing his throat. "Awful parched, I am."

The magistrate nods and an underling runs to fetch a bottle. This buys you a few minutes to compose your thoughts.

- Do not repent. Not many are offered the chance to go out with dignity, so make your last words count. Go to page 173
- Repent. It has been known to happen that the governors and magistrates offer pardons from time to time. There's still a chance! Go to page 294

Death Sentence

"You don't know the first thing about me, Billy," you say. "And as for the *Cooper's Pride?* Well... she's my ship now."

Then you raise the pistol and shoot the man. Smoke blooms from the muzzle and the *crack!* of gunfire echoes through the alleyway. Billy staggers back, clutching his ample gut, where the shot struck home. Then he falls to the ground.

Window shutters swing open, showing the grisly carnage to half a dozen witnesses, all uniformed military men. The building next to you, as it turns out, is the Admiralty Court building. That must've been Billy's destination, and now the Royal Navy sees what you've done.

"Murderer! Sound the alarm!" one man cries.

The next window over, a Royal Marine in signature redcoat uniform produces a rifle, and you take off running before the soldier has a chance to fire. The alleyways provide protection as you sprint back towards the ship.

An alarm bell rings out, and shouts of mustered troops spur you on. Billy took so many twists and turns through the alleyways that you find yourself lost—navigating only by the sounds of seabirds at the port and the distant smell of salt in the air.

Finally, you make it back to the wharf and the *Cooper's Pride*. Joe the bosun is here, supervising the final unloading of the goods, shaving with a razor as the lad often does to calm his nerves.

"Bosun!" you cry between heaving breaths. "Has Rediker returned?"

Joe simply points up to the ship. You make to hurriedly board, but the hulking gunner Robin emerges, blocking your path. It's a fair guess he'd like to know of Billy's fate.

"He—I'm sorry, Robin. Billy left you and the ship. But there's a place here, should you want it."

"Cap'n!" comes Rediker's cry from aboard the ship. "Goods sold as ordered, and I even gotcha a new crew. How's that for a day's work?"

He waves forward those standing behind him. A dozen new faces appear at the prow. Several Africans look down at you, bloodied and feral, fresh from a brawl, as well as a handful of ne'er-do-wells—likely out-of-work sailors. They gleam with golden-hooped piercings and leer with lusty grins, swaying under the influence of alcohol.

➤ "I think not! Get those men off my ship. I'll choose my own crew, thank you very much!" Go to page 126

➤ "Fine! But we must make sail, and with haste. Up anchor! Shove off! Loose all canvas for the wind!" Go to page 128

Decompressed

⚓

Suppressing a belch, you stumble sideways as the ship lurches violently. Seawater sprays up the side and the realization hits you with certainty—you're going to be sick. Though the swell pushes starboard, you're closer to the larboard, and you run against the ship's momentum in hopes of getting to the rail before losing your dinner upon the decks.

Just as you rush to the edge, that momentum shifts again, and suddenly you're sent sprawling. With a massive hit, you slam into the larboard edge, and, head over heels—you're over the side. In a twist of vertigo you reach out, but are rewarded only with splinters in your fingertips.

Haven't got your sea legs yet, otherwise you'd be used to the push-and-pull of the ship in rough weather. Instead, you hit the water's surface with a splash of seawater and panic. In your shame to be seen getting sick, you weren't seen falling overboard, either. You're swept out to sea, soon only a speck in a vast ocean, never to be seen or heard from again.

THE END

Deliberations

"Don't ye dare move," Chips says.

"If what ya say 'tis true, we'll get t'the bottom-o'-this soon enough," Joe agrees.

More and more of the crew arrive on the quarterdeck, an audience held just outside the late Captain Bullock's cabin. Rediker, Barlow, and Marlowe stare you down from the periphery, making your blood run cold, while Billy rushes inside the cabin, demanding to know what's happened.

"Billy! We're too late," you say.

Billy looks to Rediker, who stares back defiantly.

"Saltboots claims t'have found Bullock dead," Joe says.

"No! The man was alive!" you cry.

"This is ridiculous!" Chips cries. "Ye got the man's blood on your hands. That which spilled it, killed it."

"Give me a blessed moment t'collect me thoughts," Billy says.

He heads deeper into the Captain's cabin, searching for anything of possible significance. Watching as he goes, you note the same clues as Billy. He finds a wine goblet fallen to the floor, lifts it, sniffing the crystal. Dabs his fingers on the carpet beneath the glass, rubs them together.

"Dry," he says. "Must've spilt hours ago, but why not pick up the glass?"

Playing the detective, he continues on over to the Captain's desk, where he sets down the wine goblet. Everyone crowds the entrance to the Captain's cabin, trying to spy a bit of the investigation.

"Don't nothin' look missing. Man's sea chest is still locked tight. Wait! What's this, then? A page, torn out of the Cap'n's log! Today's entry. See if Rediker or those two men has the page."

"Me?!" Rediker cries, indignant.

Chips, Joe, and Robin search the men, but turn up nothing.

"Search Saltboots!" Rediker says. "The murderer's there, plain as day!"

Chips searches you roughly, and Joe does the same with a lighter touch. They find nothing, which, of course, comes as no surprise to you.

"'Tis the Captain's own knife," Billy says, crossing the room and examining the murder weapon.

He stands and steps back out to the quarterdeck, the crew moving with him. His face frowns with concern, and he tugs at his muttonchops as he ponders the crime. After an excruciatingly long silence, he finally speaks.

"I want to believe ya, Saltboots, but there weren't no one else here. Ya said so yourself, the man were alive when ye found him. I seen enough men bleed out t'know, ya ain't got long with a wound like that one. Few seconds at most."

➢ "It was Rediker and the others. A mutiny! I don't know how they did it, but God knows it's true!" Go to page 262

➢ "I swear it wasn't me, Billy. Don't condemn an innocent without proof, I beg of you!" Go to page 119

Depressed

⚓

James shuffles along with the rest of the "recruits" in a hangdog manner, wind gone from his sails, so to speak. He doesn't even acknowledge you when you join him by his side.

"James, do you know what will happen next?" you ask. "Are we to be taken to the ship this very moment and set sail before we can notify the family?"

Finally, he looks up at you. Maybe it's the anticipation in your voice; a mix of terror and excitement. "I thought the life-o'-a-seaman were behind me. And now look at the pair-o'-us. Oh, coz. I'm so, so sorry I gotcha into this," he laments.

You can see the future weighing on him, and you don't want to further his burden, so you say, "I am responsible for my own actions, cousin. I'm happy to serve on the same vessel together."

He looks at you in a queer way, as if he's not sure if you're being genuine. Then a flash of inspiration glints in his eyes. "You *are* the honorable sort. Perhaps… yes… *yes!* When we're brought aboard the ship, I want you to try to get into the Midshipman program. That'd make you a petty officer, or at least one in training, and by God it'd save ya from at least half the dangers a seaman faces."

"Cousin—" you start, but he continues at a newly frenetic pace.

"You must! Please. I gotcha into this, at least… this way ya might make something of it. They probably won't like it, as most Midshipmen're the children of close friends to the Master and Commander, but don't take no for an answer. You're educated, pure-o'-heart, and hard-working. They will see!"

Rather than replying, you take a moment to consider his words. If you were to get a billet as a Midshipman, you might indeed be able to "make something" of this assignment. But you would almost certainly be separated from your cousin if you join the officers' ranks. He awaits your answer with eager anticipation.

Will you do it?

➢ No. I want to learn to be an able-bodied seaman from the ground up, like James. I will keep my mouth shut and accept whatever assignment I'm given.
Go to page 288

➢ Yes, of course. James has been to sea, perhaps not in the Royal Navy, but still, his advice must be sound. I will be a Midshipman! Go to page 87

Depths of Despair

Once the helmsman changes the ship's course, it's clear you've made the warship change tactics. No longer do they fire warning shots at you, but rather full volleys.

"It's too shallow!" Rediker cries, but your orders are set.

The *Revenge* heads into the interior of the island, hoping the inlets will provide some protection. And indeed, this course does prove too shallow for the warship to follow, but it also proves too shallow even for your light-on-the-water merchant-man-turned-pirate.

With a sickening crash, the ship smashes into a reef, dragging your newly cleaned and careened bottom over the rocks. *Crack-crack-crack!* sounds out like a barrage of musket fire as the planks of your hull snap across the reef, one-by-one.

You've sunk her, captain. That much is certain. Dashed upon the rocks, like so many hapless sailors who came before you. What's worse, from the mouth of the bay, the British Warship further pummels you with cannon fire while you're helplessly perched atop the rocks.

At least you won't be going to prison.

THE END

Derelict

⚓

When action stations are called, the crew moves about with the same frenetic intensity as if they're bracing to fight against a hurricane. And indeed, each sailor has a role to play if a warship is to be any threat at all. You really should be down with the gun crews, as assigned, but with 200 seamen rushing all over the ship, it's easy to get lost in the crowd.

Mustered with a boarding party, you're given a musket and cutlass and told to await orders for hostilities to begin. Though you're not privy to Captain Longwick's plans, it's clear the Master and Commander has something in mind as the ship heads into coastal waters. The smaller pirate ship has the advantage in the shallows, so he must have a good reason for the maneuver.

The drummers beat out the cadence of war and the HMS *Hornblower* sails into action. Then the whole ship rocks as the starboard guns roar out below. The pirate ship is clearly out of range. Was that a warning shot? Is the captain hoping they'll surrender? Then, as the pirate crew turns away from a shallow bay and follows the coast towards deeper seas you realize he was trying to shape their course. And it's worked!

The *Hornblower* follows the pirate ship along the convex bend of the coast, until another ship is revealed from around the curve. A Spanish Man-o'-War, not too different from the last you've seen. She's moored in this hidden inlet, and the pirate ship dares not sail into her. This is an unexpected tactical wildcard—neither ship is allied with the Dons.

Will Captain Longwick continue the approach with the Spanish ship just beyond? It appears so, despite this new player being a much more dangerous foe. The man's of a singular mind and intensity, it would seem.

The *Cooper's Pride* turns, facing perpendicular to your approach. Then the pirates let loose a broadside of their own. The cannonballs smash into the prow, sending a hail of wooden splinters across the deck, but they have only a handful of big carriage guns. The pirates are outclassed, outgunned, and soon to be outmanned.

"Boarding parties!" the order comes, signaling you to be ready.

The *Hornblower* turns to meet the smaller vessel, side-by-side, coming to a near standstill for boarding—but not before letting loose a devastating broadside from the starboard battery. It's hard not to feel left out; that was your gun crews.

"Fire!" comes the command, and your new firing team discharges their muskets at the pirate crew.

Then the order for full attack comes, almost instantly drowned out by the battlecries of the sailors charging into battle. The musket fire was simply to give cover, and now you move forward with cutlass, ready for the fight.

You've grown much stronger these last weeks at sea. More capable with your hands and confident in their abilities. With the bloodlust of battle welling up inside, you rush the pirates, saber swinging with wild ferocity.

It's like a kind of dream, like you're watching someone else do all this fighting. And fight you do—like a lion. The pirates are large, fearsome, and musclebound. Covered in jewelry, fine leathers, and tattoos. But the ship is just as filthy as they are under this façade and they lack the discipline for a cohesive attack.

The pirates might actually be better individual fighters, but it's a not to be a fight of individuals. The sailors rush over the scoundrels with pure numbers and with these brothers at your side, you slay villainous rogue after villainous rogue.

"Cap'n Rediker, look out!" a mustachioed man shouts as you approach.

The pirate captain, one who wouldn't have been distinguishable as such from the rest of the crew without this forewarning, turns to face you. He has a red skullcap, a pierced eyebrow, and fire in his eyes. You try to think of something witty, some *prepare to die like a dog* sort of statement, but it's the blood-soaked cutlass that does your talking for you.

The pirate captain, rather than turning to cross swords with you, simply removes one of his four flintlock pistols with his other hand, draws back the hammer and dispatches you with all the attention he would give to putting down a rabid dog. Probably best you didn't call him one, to be honest.

Captain Rediker doesn't give you a second look as you stumble back, clutching the gut wound. It's another pirate, in fact the man who warned the captain, who finishes you off.

The last thoughts that go through your mind are something like, *they have pistols? How is that possibly fair?* Well, it's not. But that's what you get for bringing a sailor to a pirate fight. Though you did die for king and country, if that's any consolation.

THE END

Die Hard Pirates

The pirate crew leaves their looting, instead taking the Portuguese crew as plunder. Pistols aimed, knives to necks, the crew is held hostage as a desperate bid for negotiations with the Spanish. Soon, they are right up alongside your ship, looming over the *Revenge* by at least another deck height, if not two.

"English pirates, no?" the Spanish captain calls.

"These men are our captives. Turn, sail away and we will not harm them," you reply coolly.

"Drop your weapons now, and we shall not sink your ship."

"Do you doubt me? We will not hesitate to kill all these innocent men, if provoked."

The Spanish captain shrugs. "That many less Portos in the world."

You swallow hard. How to reply to that?

"I am commissioned to hunt pirates." The captain continues. "If you will not yield, I will be forced to sink both ships. A larger bounty if I bring you alive, to be sure, but I see pirates on both these vessels. Two sunken pirate ships will work just as well."

Looks like the Spanish are just as happy to spill Portuguese blood as your own. The only choice left is whether to go down in a blaze of glory, or to surrender and be hanged… or worse.

THE END

Dig Your Grave

This pit has been here for quite some time, as evidenced by just how hard the earthen walls are. The mud and rock are densely packed, but after some effort, you pull some loose. The floor of this natural well is a soup of mire after the recent storms and you can use that to soften the walls.

As the hours tick by, you make little progress. Bringing the dirt off the walls forms a thicker sludge on the ground, but one that your feet and legs sink down into. Looks like it will be quite some time before you've displaced enough earth to stand upon it.

After you get to a certain point, gravity starts to help out. You pull a particular stone or dirt clod and whole sections of the wall collapse. With these keystones removed, the rest follows.

Then you dislodge a particularly large rock and a huge sheet of dirt slides down into the well. Far too much, in fact. It slides down like an avalanche, burying you beneath before you have a chance to climb on top.

You're crushed beneath the earth, unable to move, barely able to breathe. And here you will remain, buried in a grave you've dug for yourself.

THE END

Doesn't Add Up

"Look, there's the killer's knife!" you say, pointing to the evidence on the floor.

Chips rushes inside the captain's quarters with Joe, searching for signs of the real killer… but the cabin is completely empty. No one hiding in the wardrobe, under the bed, nor beneath the desk. It's totally clear.

"That's impossible!" you cry. "I heard—he was alive when I came to the cabin. The killer must still be here!"

The search is renewed, reviewing the same spots over and over, but to no avail. More and more of the crew arrive on the quarterdeck, an audience held just outside the late Captain Bullock's cabin. In desperation, you pull at candlesticks, check behind paintings, press against the books on the shelf.

"There must be some way. A hidden door or compartment."

"D'ya take us for fools?" Chips cries. "Ye got the man's blood on your hands. That which spilled it, killed it."

Rediker, Barlow, and Marlowe stare you down from the periphery, while Billy rushes inside the cabin, demanding to know what's happened.

"Saltboots murdered—" Chips starts.

"No! That's a lie!" you protest.

Joe steps forward. "Cap'n Bullock's dead, that ain't in dispute. But there weren't no witnesses. You're the captain now, Billy. What should we do?"

Billy looks towards you, doubt in his eyes.

- Appeal to his reason. What possible motive could you have? There must be an investigation! Go to page 163
- Appeal to his emotion. Hasn't Rediker long been a troublemaker? He must be the murderer! Go to page 262

Double Up

Argyle swallows hard and turns to his ledger. Wycombe couldn't care less as he slaps more coin on the table to give it another go. But Monks is fuming. The cannon and cutlass tattoos ripple with tension just below his skin as he slides the coin pile your way.

Another win! You now have more coin than you know what to do with. The three men glower at you, though they're willing to keep going if you are. They place their bets, then turn to you.

If you want to say no, enough excitement for one night:

➢ Collect your winnings and return to the bar to wait for Cousin James. Go to page 233

Or let it ride! The winning choice has been randomized, and the outcome of these choices may or not be the same. Play the dice/coin game again, or simply pick your luck of the draw:

➢ Heads on the coin toss, or a one, two, or three shown on the die. Go to page 8

➢ Tails on the coin toss, or a four, five, or six shown on the die. Go to page 308

Down the Hatch

The gin burns on its way down and you cough hoarsely in response, much to the amusement of the hooch-hardened clientele of the tavern.

"Second one'll be easier," Spence promises.

"I think that might be the last one," you croak, still sputtering fire.

"Now, now, mind the rules. Here, take your medicine now, and sip it this time, while I tell ye of your good cousin."

Heeding her advice, you sip at the second glass of gin. It does go down much smoother this time, though not as easily as it might if mixed with tonic water and lime. Unfortunately for you (and for sailors plagued by mosquitos and scurvy), that would be an anachronism, as the famous "G&T" won't be in popular use for another century.

"Jimmy told any and all who'd listen that he wasn't bound back for a ship, but that he wasn't bound for Bucks, neither," she says, using the diminutive for Buckinghamshire. "He had his drinks like a man spending his last night upon the earth, and like most men, looked to spend said night with a buxom lass at his side."

"He found a girl and they left together?" you ask, finishing the drink.

A gruff, mutton-chopped sailor joins the bar at your side. By way of introduction, he says, "Jimmy Saltboots always were of a romantic nature. Give the pair-o'-us a round, on me, Spence."

The barkeep pours while you get a look at your new companion. He's well-dressed for a seaman, at least by your limited experience, though his garb holds tightly to a frame expanding with recently added weight. His grey whiskers are stained rust-red around the mouth from habitual tobacco use.

"Thank you, Mr....?"

"Call me Billy, mate of the *Cooper's Pride*, the ship that paid Jimmy's wages until tonight," accepting and raising his glass, he continues, "Clink and touch, then drink your hooch!"

His thick seaman's accent makes the toast rhyme, and you follow his motions: touching glasses together for the clink, tapping them against the bartop for the "touch," then downing the gin. It doesn't even burn this time.

"So, where's Jimmy now?" you ask, directing the question to the pair of them.

"Eh, engaged in congress, as ye might well imagine," Billy answers.

"I don't kiss and tell, nor share the exploits of others. Bad for business," Spence says. She starts pouring another two drinks and Billy looks to you.

"Customary t'buy a round if one's bought for ya," he says.

The gin makes this decision for you, and you nod, sliding a pair of coins forward from your collection to the growing pile that belongs to the house. You clink glasses with Billy once more, though without benefit of the toast this time.

"I don't know what ole Jimmy was goin' on about, you're not so bad," Spence says.

"What's that supposed to mean?" you ask, head swirling from so much of the powerful liquor.

"All he ever wanted was a good time with a good English girl," she says, smiling. Then goes to pouring another round.

"That's all any man could want! How 'bout a shanty, boys?" Billy cries.

As the rest of the sailors crowd the bar, Spence pours drinks for the lot of you, and your coins disappear with your cares. With the gin passed about, Billy starts off lyrically with, "When I was a little boy, so my mother told me."

The men reply in a droning sing-song chant, "Way haul away, we'll haul away Joe!"

Billy continues to lead the chorus with, "That if I did not kiss the girls, my lips would turn all moldy."

"Way haul away, we'll haul away Joe!" they cry, and getting the hang of it, you join in about halfway through the refrain.

"I worked the seas so long as I pleased, not knowin' what I was missin'."

"Way haul away, we'll haul away Joe!"

"Then I sets me sails afore the gales, and started in a-kissin'."

"Way haul away, we'll haul away Joe!"

"First I met a Yankee gal, but sh'was too fat and lazy!"

"Way haul away, we'll haul away Joe!"

"Then I met an Irish gal, but she was bloody crazy."

"Way haul away, we'll haul away Joe!"

"Next I court a Frenchie gal, but sh'was too free an' easy."

"Way haul away, we'll haul away Joe!"

"But now I have an English gaaaaaal, and sure she is a daisy!"

"Way haul away, we'll haul away Jooooooooooe!"

Everyone draws out the last line, then cheers and downs their drinks, offering a boozy kiss to the English girls on their arms. So it is that you drink the night away, forgetting about both your obligations and your cousin. Not much choice here:

Wake up the next morning and face the consequences of your actions. Go to page 93

Dragged Down

The jaguar is initially thrown off-guard when you shout out, the beast's ears back and tucked down for the offensive. But when you start up the tree, that shifts the creature's behavior into full predator mode. Jaguars are exceptional climbers. With a single bound, the jungle cat claws into your trousers and rips you from the tree. You're tangled together and the jaguar roars out as you fall.

What should you do?

> Play "dead." The jaguar is asserting dominance and will lose interest if I don't fight back. Go to page 48
> Fight back! Aim for the head with punches and kicks while protecting my jugular as best I can. Go to page 261

Dressed to Kill

Captain Vasco de Ferro of the *Dos Santos* was a man of fine tastes and distinction, if somewhat pretentious. Raiding his cupboards, you find dozens of bottles of rare and vintage port wine. The cabin itself is lined with oil paintings by masters of their craft and a sculpted bust in the man's own likeness. In his wardrobe are garments made of black Italian leather, crimson Chinese silks, and bone-white French lace. The top shelf holds a half-dozen tricorn hats with full, luxuriant feathers, stored in boxes.

And then there's what must have been his prized possession. Most likely a family heirloom: a military saber, with a gilded handle and a sharp gleaming blade. The sheath is black as death, with golden ringlets to hang the weapon at your side.

When you emerge from the cabin, it's in style. Primarily clothed in black leather to aid in combat, you've got the flourish of a crimson blouse with a clean, white cravat. Bullock's dueling pistol hangs from a silken sash, next to one taken from Ferro's collection, and his saber swings at your side. Your former captain's knife is tucked into knee-high boots, while your fingers are now protected by silver rings. With regal plumage, a velvet-lined tricorn hat gives an additional two feet of stature.

All eyes find their way to you—Captain Bloodbeard has been reborn yet again.

"Make for New Providence," you say.

Port Royal was once known as the wickedest city in the West Indies. To polite society it was "a receptacle of vagabonds, sanctuary of bankrupts, and a close-stool for the purges of our prisons"; it was considered by the civilized world to be "as sickly as a hospital, as dangerous as the plague, and as wicked as the devil."

Now, that dubious honor goes to New Providence Island, known as the Republic of the Pirates. If Justice looked the other way in Port Royal, New Providence went so far as to be the one that blinded her. So it's the safest harbor money can buy.

Rediker convinces the crew that the bulk of the prize money should go towards outfitting the *Deleon's Revenge* for future conquest. Though you doubled your armaments once you took the guns from the *Dos Santos*, you've still got a ways to go before you need not fear a ship-of-the-line.

As Bloodbeard's reputation spreads through the alehouses and brothels, more men are eager to join your ranks. A merchant ship of this class would normally hold 15-25 crewmembers, while a pirate crew on the same ship might swell to ranks of 75-85. Rediker chooses the fiercest from among the new pirates, as well as those with valuable skills, but you're confident that he's no longer plotting to vote you out.

The men who sailed here from Boston, not wanting to get left behind, spend their wages on weapons and clothing. Not a single one of your regulars opts to stay in New Providence.

Soon the ship is refitted and you have a fearsome pirate crew ready to for action. Best not to disappoint them. Where to, Captain Bloodbeard?

➢ Let's find an informant and pay to learn of a rich target. A small investment for a larger prize! Go to page 168

➢ Let's set sail and come what may! The world is ours for the taking. Go to page 17

Dudderidge

There's a moment of silence. Of shock. But then the men laugh, howling like animals, their heads thrown back, shrieking with laughter sent up to high heaven.

"Saltboots has gone mad on the island!" Marlowe cries.

"Where be Dudderidge, anyhow?" Rediker asks.

"In the kitchen, like always. That cripple never did leave his berth, save for killin' Cap'n Bullock, that is!" Barlow says, renewed laughter.

Then they all laugh.

And laugh, and laugh, and laugh.

And then they kill you.

THE END

Dumbstruck

So... that's a myth. Lightning strikes the earth roughly 40-50 times per second, or about 1.5 billion hits per year. If lightning were to really only strike a single spot once, we'd have stopped having lightning altogether eons ago, for want of a place to strike.

Instead, the truth is: if a particular target is appealing to lightning, it's struck over and over again. And what if a person were to stand directly in such a spot?

CRACK!!!

THE END

Duplicity

How did a seventeen-year-old boy from the Indian subcontinent get to be the bosun on an English merchant ship? From his youth, to the way he always dry-shaves on deck even in the roughest seas, to the way he practically glides across the deck on the surest feet in the crew—your bosun was an enigma.

Until you learned Joe's secret.

There could be no doubting his skill as a sailor, nor the bosun's proficiency in piping out the orders given by the captain, but it's certainly odd to rise to a rank of such prominence as a lad, especially one who hails from foreign shores.

If you didn't know any better, you might have suspected a lust for power and further advancement could have led Joe to any length, perhaps even to kill. Sure, the captain's knife was found covered in blood, but that could have been a ruse, could it not? Joe's razor seemed indelibly sharp; capable of a dry shave that left the bosun's face silky-smooth and without so much as a nick or a blemish.

At least, that's how it had appeared.

The first clue was a few weeks back, when one of the lashings came free on a starboard carriage gun. A loose cannon is a terrible danger aboard a ship, as the gargantuan slabs of iron can crush a man unlucky enough to be caught between the gun and a mast or deck rail.

Joe was shaving at the time, walking the quarterdeck while doing so (as was often the case), when the call of "loose cannon!" came from the ship's waist. The bosun leapt into action, dropping the razor in an instinctual bid to secure the lashing before the carriage gun could truly roam free.

The razor blade fell right down on top of you, but when you put up your hands to shield yourself, the shaver simply bounced off you, clattering to the deck. Picking the blade up, you learned there was no edge to the razor whatsoever. Duller than a butter knife; a razor in name only.

Joe's eyes had shot open when he saw you test his razor, and he quickly ordered you to help secure the cannon, leaving an open palm to demand the return of his blunt instrument.

Why shave with a false razor? Did he want to appear older, capable of growing coarse whiskers like the burly men in his crew? Such an odd and fascinating quirk.

That led you to watch the bosun more carefully. You quickly realized how much Joe had kept apart from the rest of the men. Eating and sleeping alone, off in some corner. Never dressed in front of the others, washed, or went to the toilet when anyone else was around.

Such behavior had never seemed odd to you before, as a bosun is somewhat of a superior position. But your curiosity was raised and, well, you took to spying on him. It wasn't the kindest or most proper thing to do, following Joe when he answered nature's call. Not something you're proud of, certainly. But it is where you learned the truth—that he… *is a she*.

"You can't tell anyone," Joe had pleaded when she saw you had learned the truth.

"But who are you, really?"

"I'm still me, I'm still good ole' Joe," the bosun replied, but your look must have said it all, because she went on, "I told the crew my name was Yousefah, which sounded enough like 'Joseph' to earn the nickname 'Joe.' But the truth of it is, my real name, my birth name, is Akademi. My father was a high-ranking official in service of the Emperor, but my mother, rather than shame him with only daughters, raised me as a boy. My older sisters would be married off, yet how could I? If I married, surely the secret would be revealed. So I was sent to sea, to become a man, and I did, in a sense."

"Does no one else know?" you had asked.

"Captain Bullock, but that is all. The captain values loyalty, and so he keeps my secret. You too, will have my loyalty and my gratitude if you'll only do the same. *Please*, you must not tell anyone."

And you did keep Joe's secret, but so much for his—*her*—loyalty. Did the bosun speak up when you were charged with Bullock's murder? Not a word in your defense. But… maybe Joe thought you truly were the murderer, and so feared you would reveal her true identity if she spoke out either way?

No matter. Joe's razor was not sharp enough to kill, and with Captain Bullock protecting her secret, she was loyal to the man. It couldn't have been the bosun who ended Bullock's life.

Indeed, thinking back, Joe was on watch beneath the night sky—just like you—when the gruesome deed was done. Who else might have held ill will against the late captain?

➢ What about Chips? Did the carpenter hold any ill will towards the captain?
  Go to page 42

➢ What about Robin? What secrets might the tattooed gunner have held?
  Go to page 279

➢ That's enough for tonight. Best to take your mind off things and enjoy the warmth of the fire. Go to page 320

Duty-Bound

⚓

You look away, back towards the open sea before you. Soon, it will be dark, and it's up to you to keep the *Hornblower* on a straight course from the time the sun has fully set to the time the stars can be read for navigation. Worse yet, it looks to be a cloudy night ahead, so you'll have to do most of the steerage by instinct.

With both hands on what's left of the wheel, you can feel the tug of the sea against the ship, and course-correct accordingly. But should you let her loose, free to list against the currents, you'll certainly lose your way.

That *crack* sounds on the wind again, and you take a wallop on the shoulder like you've never felt. There can be little doubt: you've been shot! But if the *Hornblower* can press on with a few splits in her hull, so can you.

The second marksman's attack is announced with the same *crack*. You take a hit right in the chest, only a few inches from the last wound. The gunshot burns fiercely, a great pressure as you try to breathe, but breathing is a luxury for cowards. You bravely keep hold of the helm.

"Shots fired!" one of the seamen shouts, finally recognizing the incoming fire.

"Return fire!" Captain Longwick commands.

Much louder exchanges of rifle fire erupt from behind as the sailors attack those in the Spanish crow's nest.

"Rear battery, fire!" the Commander issues.

As the cannons boom, your wrists grow cold as the blood pouring from your sleeves gets exposed to the crisp night air. Yet you hold your ground all the same.

Eventually, the firing from the ships goes quiet. You're relieved from your post, replaced by a new set of hands, and sent down to Wycombe, the surgeon.

"I can give your cousin something for the pain," Wycombe says, speaking to James about you. "But once sleep should come, I'm afraid that will be the end of it. The musket ball has penetrated the lung, bringing bits of uniform fabric inside. There are already signs of infection. I'm sorry, but there's nothing to be done. If you'll excuse me, there are others I must tend to."

Then Cousin James is by your side. "Did us proud, Coz. We're out of the worst-o'-it. You'll get a statue back home in Aylesbury, I'll make sure," he says, eyes glistening.

You fought bravely, but your adventure ends here.

THE END

Earning His Stripes

Carefully cupping the rum tot in your hands to protect it from both spillage and curious eyes (as, technically, you're supposed to drink when served, lest a seaman "store up" for a binge), you bring the gift down to the ship's hospital. In addition to serving as surgery and clinic for the infirm, this is Butch's cabin, though the man himself is presently absent.

Chips is here, consoling the wounded. Barlow and Rediker too. The young sailor who was flogged sits against a desk, as lying down in a hammock will be next to impossible with a flayed backside. Hopefully the rum will help.

"Never took ya for a rebel, Saltboots," Rediker says, noting the tot. "Ain't that against orders?"

"Captain ordered *Butch* not to give him anything for the pain. Never said anything about the rest of us," you say, handing over the rum.

Rediker nods his respect and passes the gift along. "There ya go, lad. Earned your stripes today. You're a tiger now!"

The young man gratefully downs the ration, then shakes his head. "I didn't even do nothing 'cept me duties. It were an honest mistake."

"Aye, 'course 'twas," Chips says. "Ya did nothin' wrong."

"Oh, ya did wrong all right." Rediker steps up. "Reminded the cap'n just how small a man he is, and a small man cannot abide by that. Needs t'make himself feel big, by makin' the other smaller still. But what he don't consider—is that you're stronger now, for the abuse. None fear the whip so much as he who ain't tasted the lash. But if that's the worst he can do, what's left to fear?"

"That's right. You're a tiger now, lad," Chips agrees.

Eight bells rings, signaling a change of the watch. The young sailor thanks the group for coming, then you all disperse and head up to perform your duties.

Even though the storms have subsided, the sky remains covered by a thick blanket of clouds. Once the sun has set, as now, that makes it increasingly difficult to navigate. The compass will generally keep the course, but there are strict orders for any seaman who makes a sighting of the stars to take note and report in to the captain, so he can compare with his charts and make a more accurate heading towards Boston. A discrepancy of even a degree could put you hundreds of miles off-course and mean a delay of several days or even weeks into port.

You're scanning the horizon for any astronomical signs when your eye catches several figures in the moonlight. It's a trio of men gathered near the bow, unusual in a severely undermanned watch. The three of them then head down into the hold, one by one, which is stranger still, as they now leave the bow unmanned.

➢ Surely they have good reason. Keep your watch. No good can come from abandoning yet another post. Go to page 205

➢ Best to trust a gut instinct, and this just feels plain wrong. Follow the conspirators down into the hold. Go to page 325

Easy Way

As a sailor, you're no stranger to the effects of alcohol. After all, your daily ration of drinking water has rum added to it to prevent the growth of algae inside the barrels. But that was diluted. This? A fifth of rum consumed all at once? With no freshwater whatsoever, and the sun beating down upon the sands of your island?

Intoxication sets in before you even finish the fifth.

That makes ending it all that much easier. The decision made, you just needed to take away any inhibitions that might've kept you on this mortal coil. Thoughts like, *Who really killed Bullock?* Or, *Will the killer simply get away with it?* Or, *Whatever happened to Cousin James?* Or, *Will anyone back home know what happened to me?*

Instead, finished with the rum, you bring the pistol up to your lips instead, a kiss to end it all.

THE END

Either Way

It takes quite a while to find the first game trail, but skills like this one will surely develop and grow easier with time. The grasses lilt towards the small, tromped-down path, trying to obscure it, but actually giving it a distinct pattern that you'll learn to recognize.

Game trails mean game, which means meat. Goat? Pig? Hard to say. Either way, you haven't seen any animals yet, so that might mean predators too. If the prey are hiding, then the game is afoot, so to speak.

Then you hear it—the telltale roar of water.

Rushing forward, you find a clearing with a great pond, fed by a waterfall. The source must come from somewhere up the mountain, and though it's no gushing river, it is more than a trickling brook. This water will sustain you!

Drinking straight from the waterfall itself, you taste the purest water you've had since becoming a sailor. Possibly even the best water of your life. Untainted by civilization, purified by the rocks and the motion of the waterfall, this is pure mountain stream water.

Well done! This source of water was an important find, and you mark it on your mental map as you head out to further explore the island. You'll want to find a better place for a more permanent shelter than on the shoreline. After last night's storm, you know it's too exposed to the elements out there. You'll certainly want somewhere close to this water source, and with a good view of the shore so you can watch for approaching ships. Somewhere elevated, perhaps.

So you start hiking to explore your island. And with the clouds rolling in, you'll soon get to see how the rest of the topography fares in a tropical squall. You're out in the open, hiking on a ridgeline with a perfect view of the coast where you were abandoned, when a "Boom!" from the heavens blasts apart a long-dead tree only twenty yards ahead on the trail.

A great thunderclap accompanies the lightning only a moment later, and the hair starts to rise on your neck. What should you do?

- Retreat to the waterfall and leap into the pond. The safest place is to stay lower than ground-level! Go to page 247
- Hurry to the exact spot where the bolt hit—lightning never strikes the same place twice! Go to page 72
- Dash back into a forested part of the jungle to find shelter under the trees! Go to page 298
- Immediately drop down, knees upon the trail and head bowed before the Almighty. Pray to be spared! Go to page 275

Empress of the Sea

⚓

Captain Longwick emerges in full uniform, his blue coat smart and tidy, buttons gleamed to a high shine. He places a hand against the mizzenmast and pauses, examining the wood grain as if this moment were shared by the ship and him alone. After some time, he nods approvingly, then paces—now appraising the crew, with his darkened eyes, in much the same way.

He cries out, "Welcome aboard the *Hornblower!* I'm not one for speeches, so I'll say only this. We set sail for Spanish waters. The enemy expects us, yet we are the superior seamen. Do your work as assigned, and victory will see the day. Fail to do so, and it's not only your life in your hands, but your brother Tars who stand to left and right of you. As such, I will tolerate nothing less than perfection. First night out, double ration of rum. After that—expect only to be rewarded for victory!"

The men cheer, the Captain departs, and the crew doesn't stand on ceremony. Someone calls, "Weigh anchor!" and the final preparations for leaving London begin. Other commands are bandied about, but you linger behind and watch land disappear with equal measures of excitement and dread.

As you move through the serving line for dinner, Cousin James comes to find you.

"Cousin, I'm the Commander's Ward!" you say, beaming.

"I know," he answers darkly, then continues in an urgent whisper, "The Master-of-Arms is none too pleased. I overheard him with a Midshipman, an oldster named Magnus. He's a bitter ole Dutchman, passed over for lieutenant too many times. They've got it out for ya, coz."

Before you can reply, Lieutenant Dalton shouts, "Ward! With me, on watch!"

"Go on," James says. "I'm opposite shift. I'll relieve ya in four hours."

Dalton escorts you through the ship and back above decks. Along the way he says, "You really should be eating with the junior officers. Fraternizing amongst common men is unsuitable for someone of your position.

"This ship is now your England; both homeland and monarch. Serve the *Hornblower* well, and she shall reward you in kind. But until you know her moods and temperament, it's best to stay out of the way and simply observe."

With a nod, you continue on to the top decks. The night is dark, with little to distinguish the sky from the sea. Maybe it's James's warning about the Master-of-Arms, or maybe it's that you haven't got your sea legs yet, but the same queasy feeling from yesterday's carriage ride rolls over you.

Dalton turns to an older man, white-haired, but somehow not as distinguished-looking. He's an older Midshipman, who greets the Lieutenant in a thick Dutch accent.

"Ward, this is Mr. Midshipman Magnus. You would do well to learn from his experience."

Magnus looks you over, gives a curt nod, then turns back to the Lieutenant and says, "Bad omen for a launch, sir. Rough seas ahead and no stars t'sail by."

"Let's check the barometric pressure, shall we? Ward, be so kind as to continue your rounds on the ship," Dalton says.

The pair of them walk off together, and your stomach swirls about in protest.

A familiar voice cries out from further down the decks as the Master-of-Arms berates some hapless seaman. You can't quite hear the words, but the tone of a disciplinarian is unmistakable. Cousin James's warning echoes in the back of your mind, curiosity getting the better of you. That double ration of rum might help for some courage right about now....

Where will your rounds take you?

➤ Follow Lieutenant Dalton and Mr. Magnus. If the Dutchman thinks ill of you, this would be the perfect opportunity to catch him expressing it behind your back. Go to page 11

➤ Go look after the Master-of-Arms. If he's making more enemies, perhaps it would be good to identify them as potential allies for the future? Go to page 49

Empty Promises

The Admiralty Court in Boston collects you for questioning, and then arrests the crew of the *Cooper's Pride*. Billy is true to his word, and gives an impassioned appeal to free not only you, but Robin, Joe, and Dudderidge the cook as well.

There's just one problem.

A common defense, as the defense solicitors explain, is to claim you were forced into piracy. That you had no choice and intended to escape as soon as you were able. That it was indeed only the captain and his quartermaster who were culpable.

The problem? *You're the captain.*

So... yeah. It's the gallows for you, Saltboots.

Your defense counsel does offer one last chance: An appeal for a pardon. Those who turn to the authority of the Governor of the colony can have their sentence commuted to something lighter than corporal punishment.

Will you grovel for your life?

> Yes! The Governor is an educated man, and you can use your final words to show yourself as a fellow scholar who merely got yourself into a terrible misunderstanding. Plead innocence and beg for mercy! Go to page 294

> No! Enough running from fate. These are your final words, etched into eternity. Say something eloquent but brief, for brevity is the soul of wit. Go to page 173

Equally Good

Though the jungle is thick and the terrain hazardous, with enough experience, one can read the topography as well as any map. That experience, for you, has only just begun, but you go into the wilderness with eyes open.

All this vegetation on the island proves that water is plentiful, and last night's rainstorm certainly proved that, but the water must collect somewhere. If you keep looking, surely you'll find it. The vegetation grows more lush and verdant, hinting of an area well-fed by water. The slope of the trek feels low-lying enough as well....

Then you hear it—the telltale roar of water.

Rushing forward, you find a clearing with a great pond, fed by a waterfall. The source must come from somewhere up the mountain, and though it's no gushing river, it is more than a trickling brook. This water will sustain you!

Drinking straight from the waterfall itself, you taste the purest water you've had since becoming a sailor. Possibly even the best water of your life. Untainted by civilization, purified by the rocks and the motion of the waterfall, this is pure mountain stream water.

Well done! This source of water was an important find, and you mark it on your mental map as you head out to further explore the island. You'll want to find a better place for a more permanent shelter than on the shoreline. After last night's storm, you know it's too exposed to the elements out there. You'll certainly want somewhere close to this water source, and with a good view of the shore so you can watch for approaching ships. Somewhere elevated, perhaps.

So you start hiking to explore your island. And with the clouds rolling in, you'll soon get to see how the rest of the topography fares in a tropical squall. You're out in the open, hiking on a ridgeline with a perfect view of the coast where you were abandoned, when a "Boom!" from the heavens blasts apart a long-dead tree only twenty yards ahead on the trail.

A great thunderclap accompanies the lightning only a moment later, and the hair starts to rise on your neck. What should you do?

> Immediately drop down, knees upon the trail and head bowed before the Almighty. Pray to be spared! Go to page 275
> Retreat to the waterfall and leap into the pond. The safest place is to stay lower than ground-level! Go to page 247
> Dash back into a forested part of the jungle to find shelter under the trees! Go to page 298
> Hurry to the exact spot where the bolt hit—lightning never strikes the same place twice! Go to page 72

Escape from Bondage

Despite holding no real ill-will towards you, Barlow ties the ropes tightly. A seaman's habits die hard, it would seem. But by straining against the bonds now, they'll be that much looser when you squirm free.

Your former shipmate binds your hands together behind your back, and your feet together at the ankles. Lastly, he adds a gag—a bandana set across your mouth and knotted behind your head.

"Don't fret, Saltboots. Good ole Red will lose those blue-backs by supper, and ye'll be back out with us. Ta-ta!"

With that, he's gone. Letting out that breath you've been holding, you feel the ropes slacken. Relax your muscles, and the effect is even greater. The ropes don't exactly fall off, but now at least you've got a chance.

Struggling against the bonds makes you sweat, which helps lubricate your skin against the tug of the hemp ropes. By bringing your fingers together in a conical point, you can slide your hands out, inch by inch, with each oscillation of your shoulders. One up, then the other. Closer and closer.

Finally, your first hand is free! After that, the second hand comes much, much faster. Then it's on to your feet. Slipping off your boots, you're able to get your feet free from the ankle ropes by pointing a toe and sliding away from there.

Cannon fire booms from above, signaling the start of hostilities. Boots clatter across the upper decks as the crew rushes from position to position. The pirate ship is under attack!

What should you do?

➢ Find a weapon. Time to fight off these pirates and help your liberators!
   Go to page 106

➢ Sabotage the ship. Drop the anchor and strike the sails! Go to page 259

Espresso

You pick up the tool—a twin-handled blade known as a cooper's hollowing drawknife. The two wooden handles are a deep brown, connecting to a central blade meant to drag fragments away from barrels and help shape them. The blade itself resembles something of a self-contained scythe.

Should certainly serve as a threat. Heart pounding and palms sweaty, you take the drawknife and move to intercept.

"Whatever mistake this man has made, surely he's been properly reminded not to repeat it in the future," you say.

"Well, well, well. One worthless tit done found the other, eh? Shipboard discipline's me purview, ya dunce. And whaddaya propose to do with that there drawknife, *Ward?*" he says, mockery turned your way.

"I suppose whittle you down to size, if you won't back down, sir."

His eyes grow wide. "Are ya threatening an officer-o'-the-watch? Drop it now, and maybe I'll see to it that you're only flogged for this and not *hanged.*"

The Master-of-Arms goes for the flintlock pistol on his belt. Your pulse quickens. Time to act!

➤ He won't shoot. Call his bluff as he calls yours. Raise the drawknife as a weapon, but hold your ground. Go to page 185

➤ He's close enough that you can definitely "disarm" him with the drawknife before he's able to draw. Go to page 208

An Example

Billy sighs, shakes his head, and mutters, "There's always one…"

The four sailors who share your predicament all look away, like they know something terrible is about to happen. The captain walks forward, shifting his cane from one hand to the next, clearly not using it for locomotion.

Without a word, he cracks you across the collar with the bludgeon. There was no windup, yet it's a brutal strike. The site burns with pain, and you instinctively roll for cover. He lands a second blow with the cane across your back, then follows up with a kick to the ribs. You gasp and wheeze for breath, unable to focus on anything save for the wooden planks of the ship.

"Sloth and idleness will not be tolerated!" the captain roars. "Yet I am a merciful master. Repent, pledge your obedience, and do your work as assigned. You've signed the papers, no use for morning-after thoughts here! Mr. Greaves, if you please."

Billy rolls you over, wiping your face with a cloth, wet and cool. "Ya had your say, yeah? We all know ye did the right thing, by honor. Now, simply make an oath to Cap'n Bullock. Mean your words and we'll see ya as honorable still. There's a good way out here; I'm tryin' to help ya."

The seaman seated next to you, a man in a red skullcap, nods his agreement and respect.

Robin lifts you to your feet, so you're once again facing Captain Bullock.

➢ Remain defiant, and say, "An oath spoken under threat of violence is no oath at all." Go to page 91

➢ Live to fight another day, and say, "Very well. I shall serve the *Cooper's Pride* with honor." Go to page 186

Exhausted

It's a rough night of fitful sleep, but sleep does eventually come. When you roll over to shift the pressures on your aching body, you hear sea birds shrieking and see patches of sunlight filter through gaps in your makeshift shelter.

Emerging to face the day, you find the shoreline wrecked with fallen tree branches and palm leaves. Looks like quite the squall last night. Indeed, you should count yourself fortunate that nothing fell atop your dwelling while you were inside.

Your stomach aches with hunger, and your mouth puckers with thirst. Sand clings everywhere, and your clothes are soaked through. While you are deciding what to put in your belly, might be a good idea to dry everything out—your clothes, journal, and pistol—in the morning sun.

Then what?

> The beach is littered with coconuts after the storm. There should be both something to eat and something to drink inside. Crack open a few, and call them breakfast. Go to page 111

> You didn't notice until the morning light, but there are several bushes thick with red berries nearby. A sailor's diet is long overdue on Vitamin C, and the sugars will help get you through the day. Go to page 290

> Looks like it's currently low tide, and the retreating sea has left several tide pools dotting the beach. Perhaps you can find some trapped fish, crabs, or mussels inside? Go to page 104

Express Yourself

⚓

You're marched back out to port with an escort of redcoat soldiers—Lobsters, as the sailors call them—past the docks that house the merchant vessels and off to a section where the ships-of-the-line reside. Huge command vessels, waiting to be filled full of military fighting men. There are smaller sloops and gunships too, looking fast and fearsome. England is readying herself for war against Spain, and these wooden ships and iron men are the tip of the spear.

Then there's the HMS *Hornblower*. Not the biggest in the fleet, but much larger than some. Timbers are newly scrubbed, pitched, and held tightly together; sleek yet powerful. She leans forward, ready to speed off as soon as her sails are unfurled. A colossal, carved figure from Norse mythology looms proudly at the bow.

The figurehead is a musclebound, bearded warrior, who holds an enormous ox horn as a trumpet that he's set to blow into eternally. It's so large that he needs both hands to hold the horn; biceps bulging from the effort just to hold the instrument in place. From your studies, you recognize the figurehead as Heimdall and the Gjallarhorn he'll use to signal the coming of Ragnarok—the end of the world.

"A frigate," James says, voice full of trepidation. "The workhorse-o'-the Royal Navy. We'll be sailing all over the seven seas on this tour, mark me words, coz."

Looks more like a Trojan Horse than a warhorse, by your lights. The ramp is extended and dozens of seamen bring supplies onboard. Your motley gang of recruits pales in comparison to the mighty beast of war. How many men does a frigate hold? 100? 200? Far more than the merchant vessels down the docks.

You're greeted by the Master-of-Arms, a fastidiously groomed sailor who doesn't bother with introductions further than his title. As each man passes, he gives them a position and a location to report. James is ordered to be the Gunner's Mate, but holds back, watching you explain your desire for officer training.

"Too old t'be a Midshipman," the Master-of-Arms replies. "Tell me your skills and I'll assign ye a proper billet."

"Sir," you protest. "I have a classical education—"

"Aye, do ya? Then how'd ya end up here, eh?" the man asks with a smirk.

"Look at these hands," you say, trying a different tactic. "I would much better serve the ship with my knowledge of geography, tactics, and—"

"I've heard enough. Our Midshipmen slots're already filled by the sniveling brats-o'-noblemen."

"Surely there is a way!" you protest, further trying the man's patience.

"You wanna plead your case to the Cap'n directly? Be my guest. Otherwise, fall in line, Landsman. We'll harden those hands soon enough. Now help us get these crates loaded up!"

> ➤ The Captain is a gentleman. He'll appreciate the gumption it takes to seek him out and will award me a spot within the officers' ranks. Go to page 98

> ➤ Get to work. Idleness will only make things worse. Go to page 133

> ➤ I've made a terrible mistake. I don't belong here! Sneak off the ship in the commotion of loading up. Go to page 204

Eye on the Prize

⚓

Dalton applauds your temerity and, after consulting his instruments, orders a heading of nor'-nor'-west. Having been at the helm several times in the last few weeks, you expertly steer the *Hornblower* onto the assigned course.

Once the ship has turned back, the wind catches in her sails, and you cut through the sea like a dart. In an open race, the Spanish man-o'-war wouldn't stand a chance in catching your frigate, but the winds are such that you're sailing across them, while the warship has a direct tailwind.

It's slow going, but the other ship steadily grows on the starboard horizon, doubling in relative size with each turn of the hourglass. Dalton is correct, it would seem. She'll be on you before nightfall.

Identified as the *Don Pedro Sangre*, the Spanish warship is now so close that you can hear the enemy calling orders in the breaths between your captain giving his own.

Longwick is ready for battle, as are the rest of the men. Cousin James and Monks the gunner have opened the magazine, and now the guns are loaded and readied. Those men not on a cannon team hold their muskets, anxious to open fire.

"Midshipman Ward, keep us on course, come what may," Captain advises. "If you drop steerage, we lose all speed and they'd certainly have us then."

A look across to the *Don Pedro Sangre* easily shows why. The *Hornblower* is a ship of 36 guns, formidable as part of a larger line of battle, but the Spanish warship has you outclassed. A third gun deck brings her cannon total to 74. You swallow dryly at the prospect of a direct fight.

"If we let the Dons rake us with a broadside, that would make for a short chase indeed," Captain Longwick says with classic British understatement. "But once we're under the same wind, we'll lose them. Lieutenant Dalton!"

Then he's off, leaving you alone with the steerage once again.

There's a slight *crack* on the wind, like someone trying to start a fire by striking flint. Curiously, one of the planks splits open a few feet in front of you. It's a small seam that appears, but that's an odd enough occurrence to merit notice. Treated wood typically can handle the expanding and contracting nature of the ship, and an eye-slit peering at you from the deck seems a bad omen.

Then that same *crack* sounds again just as a piece of the wheel shatters in your hand. The wooden handle simply bursts open from within, sending splinters across your chest. It's like someone lit a small pouch of black powder inside the handle, or… you look up, back at the *Don Pedro Sangre*, and suddenly it all makes sense. A pair of sharpshooters reload their muskets in the crow's nest.

They're firing on you!

> Stand your ground! Remember Captain Longwick's orders to hold course, come what may! Go to page 75

> Take cover! They've got a direct line of fire, and you clearly make an easy target out in the open. Go to page 167

Eye-Opening

Billy's expression falters, if only for a moment. Looking back at the figure of the captain, Billy tugs on his muttonchops, considering his words. Then he sighs and says in a low voice, "There ain't no justice nor injustice aboard a ship, sad to say. Here ye will find only two states: duty and mutiny. Mind that, and be governed by one law alone: All that ye be ordered to do, is duty—and all that ye refuse... 'tis mutiny."

Billy's somber words hang in the air while Robin cuts at the ropes binding the men and Captain Bullock approaches with his walking cane. The four "recruits" rub their wrists and their limbs after a long night spent bound up.

"Now go on, make your oath to Cap'n Bullock," Billy prods.

➢ "Very well. I shall do my duty, governed by honor." Go to page 186
➢ "It's not right, Billy. But I've signed your papers. I will say the oath." Go to page 186

Fall in Line

⚓

"Landsman, where do you think you're going?" the lieutenant asks, still in shock.

"To fight the bloody enemy," you reply.

Lieutenant Saffron makes no further effort to stop you as you cross to the rearmost starboard cannon, and the gun team you join simply nods in acknowledgment of your taking part. The midshipman in charge issues commands of, "Swab the guns! Load cartridge! Shot! Now run out the guns!"

At this, the guns are to be cleaned, reloaded, and lined back up through the gun ports to be fired once more. You look for the swab, but another seaman has that job. So you watch, waiting to see just which position you've inherited by stepping forward. When "Shot!" is called, all eyes look to you, so you load the cannonball into the breech. Though you're trained for swabbing the guns, these are all easy tasks that you've seen others perform dozens of times.

The order to "Fire as they bear!" is relayed down to your position and the team prepares for full combat, firing the guns as fast as they're able.

"FIRE!!!" the midshipman shouts.

The cannons explode with their deafening *KABOOM!!!* and the guns kick back against the breech ropes once more. Out of your usual position, you come within a hair's breadth of being knocked back by the enormous cannon. You're saved by a hand pulling you back at the last possible second, though you can't be sure just to whom it is you owe your life.

There's no time for thanksgiving, either, as the gun crew immediately prepares for another volley. "Swab the guns! Load cartridge! Shot! Now run out the guns!"

The only time the group pauses is to hit the deck when the enemy returns fire. The carnage is immense, and each barrage takes at least one of your comrades from the fight. You receive minor splintering, but nothing to prevent you from fulfilling your duties. The whole scene plays out again and again, and you tie off your arm to slow the bleeding, in-between commands. After what seems an eternity, a ceasefire is issued from above.

Captain Longwick comes to inspect the gun crews, with Lieutenant Dalton by his side, and says something, but your stare is distant, and you're half-deaf, with ringing ears. Captain Longwick departs and Lieutenant Dalton comes by to address you personally.

He says, "Orders are: no lights, and complete silence. We've pulled ahead of the *Don Pedro Sangre*, but the enemy is giving relentless chase. God willing, we'll lose her under cover of darkness. Now get some rest, we'll be on watch soon."

You're about to offer the usual sharp, "Aye, sir!" but stop just in time, giving only a salute.

Dalton nods, leaving you be.

Well done! You've survived your first battle aboard the Hornblower *and gave as good as you got. Now get some rest, and when you're ready....* Go to page 197

Falling Sickness

Billy shakes his head, clearly disappointed. But Captain Bullock looks right past you. He addresses the four men who were also crimped into service and says, "This, men, is why we always bring more hands than we need."

Then he pummels you with newfound ferocity. He was clearly holding back last time and now he beats you senseless with his full strength. You won't be much good to the *Cooper's Pride* with broken ribs or a fractured skull, but that's not the point of this display. You'll make a good tale.

The Legend of the Recruit Who Wouldn't Take the Oath.

It's a gruesome beating that ensures you're discharged from your obligation and returned to your home in Buckinghamshire. You'll recover after a month of bed rest, but you'll never be the same. No more translating Homer for you. Instead, you'll be spoon-fed mushy peas and read bedtime stories.

When people ask of your fate, the answer will invariably be, "Oh, such a shame. Got the falling sickness after a bad trip down to the Port of London."

THE END

Falling Star

It takes a considerable amount of core-strength to go spread-eagle up the well, so you'd better move quickly before you tire yourself out. The locomotion is an ungainly sort of gallop: left foot, left hand, right foot, right hand. It's a strange balancing act as you awkwardly scale the walls, but you do make progress. One hand, one foot. Other hand, other foot. Inches at a time.

Then you lift one foot to slide it upwards just as the grit beneath your opposite foot gives way. That foot slides out from beneath you faster than you're able to reposition it, and, with nothing to hold onto, you fall back down to the base of the well. The floor of this natural well is a soup of mire after the recent storms and you splash back into the muck, breath knocked out of you all over again.

Okay, let's try this once more:

➤ Leaning forward. Feet planted on at the rear wall and hands on the front, you can back slowly up. Go to page 172

➤ Try to dig your way out. By pulling down the earthen walls, you can make a ramp and climb to safety. Go to page 64

➤ Leaning back. With your shoulders and hands pressed on the wall and feet out in front, walking. Go to page 108

The Fear Merchant

The next morning, you awaken with a splitting headache and reach up to shield your eyes from the harsh light of dawn, only to find your hands are bound to your feet by ropes. Your stomach turns, and it feels like the whole world lurches continuously back and forth, back and forth. A hard, wooden beam digs into your shoulder blades, and your backside is numb from sleeping in this position of confinement.

Looking about, the first thing you notice are the four men who share in your predicament. Each has the look of a seaman, half still black-out drunk and the other half nursing head wounds. All five of you are bound together by your ropes. The next thing you notice: you're aboard a ship! A wave of panic rolls over you, and you realize that the world around you *actually is* moving back and forth with the swell of being afloat.

"Cut 'em loose, Robin!" a voice cries from somewhere out of sight.

A muscle-bound, heavily tattooed man does just that while you look for the speaker. It doesn't take long, for as he approaches he begins a monologue, "Me name's Billy, mate-o'-the *Cooper's Pride*, this fine ship upon which ye sit, and as as-o'-now, serve. I have papers 'ere, signed by yourself and the notorious Richard 'Spotted Dick' Martin. Dick is a crimp, a fear merchant if ever there was such a thing, and whatever debt ye find yourself in is now owed t'the *Pride*."

Billy tugs at his grey muttonchops thoughtfully, then adjusts his too-tight and ill-fitting garb. You start to protest, along with several others, but Billy interrupts, "Now, I know ye lot didn't volunteer for this, and I hate t'recruit this way, honest I do, but there's a war on and a shortage-o'-able-bodied seamen, so this's the way it must be. Hear me now: we're innit together. All in the same boat, as the saying goes. And 'tis legally binding, like it or no.

"Yet, take heart! You'll be paid a fair wage while at sea and come to earn your place among your brethren. Cap'n Bullock will take your oath-o'-obedience once I get ya t'make your mark on the contract with the *Pride*. We're headed t'Boston! Once formalities're over, I'll assign your quarters."

You glare at Billy, but before he makes eye-contact, your view is eclipsed by a Jerusalem Cross painted atop leather-tanned flesh. The tattooed seaman named Robin cuts your bindings and the newly unconstrained blood flow flushes a feeling of relief, if only for a moment. But when Robin moves on to the next set of ropes, you see Billy has been joined by a new figure.

This man is clothed in finery and lace, untarnished by the grit and grime of manual labor. The cravat tied about his neck is flawless, and a tricorn hat obscures his features beneath shadows. A wealthy merchantman, to be sure, but he holds his walking cane with deeply tanned hands so there can be no mistaking his mysterious appearance—this is your new captain.

"Mr. Greaves, I trust our new recruits are ready for their oath of obedience?" Captain Bullock says, addressing Billy formally.

Finding your feet, you look about and realize that you're still moored in port.

➢ Accept this new reality with quiet dignity. Try to fit in and learn before you make any moves. Go to page 186

➢ Cry, "I signed no such papers, nor will I sign anymore! I'll say no oath to no man! I don't belong here." Go to page 85

Fear the Unknown

Haunting, that's an interesting way to put it. These men are certainly superstitious, but they aren't cowards. You're able to walk just out of sight, nearly silently. After a few weeks in the jungle, you're much more adept at navigating theses trails than the men who tromp through the underbrush, hacking away at the vines and branches with their cutlasses.

But you're no native. Eventually, they perk up, having heard some twig or seedpod crack beneath your feet.

"What's that?" one of the pirates says.

They all listen for a long moment.

"Saltboots?" Marlowe says at length.

The men brandish their cutlasses, hacking ever closer to your spot hidden amongst the underbrush. One of the pirates, either by design or dumb luck, nearly slashes into you. Ducking back, you startle the man—and his fight-or-flight reflex is set firmly on the former.

He swings his cutlass at you with deadly intent, and you disarm the man in self-defense. It all happens so quickly, but before you know what's happened, you hold the man's cutlass for your own as he bleeds out on the jungle floor.

Crack! A pistol echoes, firing into the leaves only a hair's breadth away.

"Bring me that murderous bastard's head!" Marlowe cries.

The pirates give chase and you instinctively run, the whole gang after you. On an island, there's little room to flee, and should they find your shelter, you'll be at a decided disadvantage. What now?

➢ Find an ally. Lead them towards the jaguar's den. Go to page 148

➢ Use the terrain. Lose them down a ravine or into the natural well. Go to page 300

Feed the Beast

"Don't like sweeties, d'ya?" Dick says, tucking the tin away.

"I think I should go," you answer, trying to do just that.

Dick stays with you down the boardwalk, unshakable. "I agree! Only, maybe we're at odds with just where 'tis ye should end up."

"Leave me alone!" you protest, growing fearful. "I don't want your cake, I don't want your friend's transit service—I don't want anything to do with you!"

His eyes darken as he continues, "Guess we'll just do it the hard way. Port's full-o'-ships with manifests need fillin'. My calling is t'find aimless folk like yourself and help give your life some direction."

Another port-of-call for sailors awaits ahead, at the opposite end of the boardwalk, beckoning you to come closer with sounds of sea shanties and revelry. Surely, there must be some safety from this fiend in a public house!

You rush forward, Dick slow at your heels because of his crooked spine. A pair of sailors sway in their boots out front, clearly intoxicated. Their faces are bloodied and bruised from fighting, but beggars can't be choosers.

"Good sirs!" you say, "This man is pursuing me!"

They turn to see Dick, and your chest fills with hope when you see they hold no love for the man. Eyes narrowed, they square up.

"Bugger off, crimp!" one calls.

"I have no quarrel with ye lads," Dick says, huffing for breath. "Help me get this would-be deserter back in line and the next round at the alehouse is on me!"

That changes things. The pair of sailors now look at you like a meal ticket. Your hand gropes for your coin purse. You're not holding a great deal of cash, though maybe enough to buy some protection. But Dick must have encountered this tactic before, because he's ready for it.

He says, "On top-o'-that, I'm sure we could agree that whatever cash's held in there was lost in the scuffle, by fortune t'be found evenly split between your own two pockets."

That clenches it. You look around for support. No one in the tavern pays you any mind, but back towards London proper there's a patrol of town guard. If you call out for help, they just might hear you.

➢ Yes, that's what they're here for! Call to the guard. Go to page 118

➢ Dick has won the battle of wits. Your only real option is to fight. Go to page 322

Fire in the Hole

You let the Portuguese crew stew in the hold, simmering in their own fears and doubts, while Robin rigs up some grenadoes for the assault. The name comes from *granadas*, the Spanish for "pomegranate," due to the size, shape, and similarities to the seeds within.

As a precursor to the grenade, grenadoes are hollowed-out cannonballs, filled with shot, then lit by a fuse. Though these are the iconic image of a "bomb" used in modern-day cartoons, grenadoes are no joke, as you'll soon learn.

Robin brings one of these makeshift bombs, along with an external fuse to ignite when ready. You take the grenado, weighing it in your hand, then look to the hatch below. Murmured voices come from the hold, no doubt the Portuguese crew wondering when the assault might start.

Holding the explosive high to be ignited, all eyes on you, it feels a bit like you should be giving a toast. In a moment of inspiration, you say, "Had they surrendered, we'd wish them well. But they didn't—so they can go to hell!"

The pirates chuckle and Robin lights the fuse.

"Everyone, back to the *Deleon's Revenge*," you order. "Now!"

As they go, you drop the bomb down through the hatches, running hot on their heels back to your ship in preparation for the blast. You jump across the gap between the two vessels and—*KABOOM!!!*

Fire, smoke, wood, and viscera spray forth from the belly of the *Dos Santos* like the devil was a sperm whale breaking the surface of hell. Men scream and rush out of the hold, hoping to douse their burning flesh in the open air.

"Finish them off," you command.

Rediker leads the boarding party on the attack. It's a mop-up job, and there are a few fires left to extinguish, but there's almost no resistance, not anymore.

At length, Rediker reports in. "Christ Almighty. Absolute carnage. The master's dead, along with half the crew. But she'll float, so that half can limp home and call themselves lucky."

"And the prize?" you say.

"Massive haul, Cap'n. Sugar, indigo, cacao, tobacco, leather, silks, silver, gold, and jewels. Once we divide the shares, hell, I'd say each man just earned himself three years' pay! Not bad for a first-timer."

"Refit the ship first. Take their carriage guns, plus any weapons. Once the *Deleon's Revenge* is made stronger, the rest is profit."

"Aye, Cap'n. It'll take a few hours t'move all the cargo. Afterwards, shall we plot a course for New Providence to unload our ill-gotten gains?"

- ➤ "I'm going to go through the Porto captain's cabin to see what I can find. He was right, I need a manner of dress befitting the name of Captain Bloodbeard."
Go to page 70

- ➤ "'Twas a grand first catch, Rediker. Once we make sail, open the rum stores for the men. I'd like to make another toast… to the first of many! And the start of a prosperous partnership." Go to page 137

First Command

⚓

Lieutenant Dalton applauds your boldness and agrees to let you command the starboard guns—the side the Spanish will be approaching. You haven't a moment to lose in preparation. Typically, a midshipman would command only a single gun crew, while a lieutenant would oversee a group of such midshipmen, so to be given command of an entire broadside the first time the *Hornblower* sees action is a great honor, indeed. One you're determined to live up to.

The magazine is opened, where Cousin James and the gunner, Monks, offer cannonballs and gunpowder cartridges to be distributed. Ordering several of the younger sailors to act as "powder monkeys" to ferry these provisions, you ensure that your weapon teams will be well-supplied.

Though you don't have the luxury of standing idle and gazing about, word of the man-o'-war's approach reaches your ears nonetheless. The Spanish warship is identified as the *Don Pedro Sangre*, a first-rate ship of 74 guns. By comparison, the *Hornblower* has only 36, of which you command eight on the lower gun deck. A daunting prospect, to say the least.

"If the situation were reversed, we'd never dare," someone grumbles.

The men are clearly made anxious by the news. To reassure them, you say, "Fear not! We won't simply drop anchor and pound it out with a larger foe. Our duty is to keep the Spanish at bay long enough to reclaim the wind and outrun her."

There are more grumblings. Many sailors are still unsure, so you add, "But that doesn't mean we can't get some good licks in, right?"

The Lieutenant commanding the larboard broadsides, a young man named Saffron, whom you've had only a few encounters with, looks even more doubtful than the men under your command.

"We'd do better to put oars out these gun ports," he mutters.

- Ignore the man. Better yet, chastise him for weakening shipboard discipline. This is what these men have trained for! Your duty is to have these cannons ready for a broadside attack. Go to page 33

- It's true, if there were some way to speed up, you'd increase your chances of reaching the fleet alive. Perhaps there is something more you could do to help the *Hornblower* escape the man-o'-war? Go to page 114

First Impressions

⚓

The Master-of-Arms was clearly not expecting you to take him up on his offer. He demands your surname, and promises that he'll do what he can to personally watch your career—a threat so thinly veiled that, even with limited experience, you fear you've made an enemy of the man.

But, true to his word, he takes you to the Captain's quarters. After telling you to wait outside, he goes to announce your intentions to the Master and Commander of the HMS *Hornblower*.

"The Cap'n will see you now," the Master-of-Arms growls a moment later.

He tries to follow you inside, but a voice thick with authority says, "That will be all."

After the Master-of-Arms leaves, you step forward to face Captain Longwick, the Master and Commander of both this ship and your fate. Standing in the middle of the luxuriant cabin, he's younger than you might have expected, and his hair is coal-black, rather than the gray or powder-white of the current fashion. His eyes, deep-seated, and so dark you can hardly distinguish iris from pupil, move back and forth slowly, purposefully. As if hunting. You suddenly feel very much like the quarry.

Averting your eyes from his, you notice you're not alone. At the Captain's desk, another man sits, a quill poised in hand. He'd look just as gruff as any seaman if it weren't for the spectacles he wears. He stares at you over the rims of his spectacles, none too pleased to see you, and obviously finding your presence an interruption.

"That would be Argyle, my stenographer and cartographer. Behind you, you'll find Akuchi, my steward. And you would be my… what, exactly?"

Argyle nods in greeting at his introduction, then returns to work. You look back to see a well-dressed African removing the Captain's coat from a wardrobe. The steward then brings the coat around to Longwick and helps him don his formal uniform.

"I would be your Midshipman, sir," you say, trying to put on a brave face.

"I believe Geoff told you we are at our capacity of Midshipmen."

It takes a moment, but then you realize Geoff must be the Master-of-Arms. Looks like he's warned the Captain against your intentions.

"I would better serve you, serve the *Hornblower*, sir, as an officer candidate than as a Landsman," you say.

In the silence that follows, you tack on another "sir" just for good measure.

"*Each man delights in the work that suits him best,*" Captain Longwick muses, turning away to help Akuchi slide the officer's coat over his broad shoulders.

"*For the gods honor justice; honor the decent acts of men,*" you reply. After studying Homer's *Odyssey* for the last month, you'd more readily recognize the quote than you would the very ship upon which you now stand.

"Certainly weren't embellishing the education. Very well, if you took the time and effort to come convince me, I should think you'll continue to work hard aboard the quarterdeck of my ship," he explains. "Argyle, what do the manifests show?"

His recorder replies in a thick Scottish accent, "Midshipmen billets 're full, aye,

Cap'n. Though you yourself could always add another servant on the books."

"Excellent. I'll take this one on as a fosterling. Official title: Commander's Ward. Make it so."

"Th-thank you, sir! You w-won't regret this!" you stammer.

"Don't gush, Ward. I have enough toadies and lickspittles as is. If you're to join my officers' cadre, I'll need you challenging the veracity of my commands. No use comes from telling me how good a job I've done. Initially, I should like you to shadow Lieutenant Dalton, but first you'll need to speak with the quartermaster to be issued a uniform, and a fearnaught jacket. Do your best to live up to its name. Now then, I believe the men have mustered for my embarkation speech? That will be all, Ward."

You depart while Argyle scribbles your new position upon parchment and Akuchi offers Captain Longwick his commander's cap. As quickly as you can, you rush to find your new uniform and form up with the men on deck.

"So, you're the new Commander's Ward I've heard so much about," Lieutenant Dalton says. Word travels fast onboard, it seems. The man appraises you, but it's hard to read his reaction. Like one dog sniffing another, you look him over as well. He's fair-skinned and fair-haired, unusual for those who spend their days at sea. A twenty-year-old member of the gentry, bred to keep a stiff upper lip.

"I'm Lieutenant Dalton, your immediate supervisor and officer of the watch," he says, introducing himself with the traditional "left-tenant" pronunciation. "Tell me, Ward. What makes you so special that the Commander should pluck you from the press gang 'recruits' to join the ranks of the officers?"

You take a moment to consider an answer, looking out over the quarterdeck. Soon, the Captain will arrive to give his address to the crew—the whole ship is gathered awaiting his speech—but for now, Dalton wants to make small-talk.

➢ Play it close. Say, "In time, I should hope you'll see that for yourself, Sir. The Captain gave me an opportunity that I aim to make the most of." Go to page 250

➢ Confide in him. Say, "The Master-of-Arms barely gave me a second glance. If I would have left my fate to that man, I'd never have been given a chance such as this." Go to page 152

➢ Shine him on. Say, "It's not that I'm special, Sir. It's that none of us are. We are all but players strutting and fretting about war, wouldn't you agree?" Go to page 153

Fish and Chaps

Grinning like a fiend, James takes you under his wing as if he knew you'd come around the whole time. You walk together down the promenade, watching the spectacle. Nearby, fishmongers unload their catch for the Billingsgate market by throwing leviathan-sized prizes across the path, one man to the next, in a chain down the row.

"Stick close to me, coz, and keep one hand on your coin purse. If these men here can't sell it to ya, they'll happily unburden you in other ways. But then again, the pickpockets aren't nearly so bad as the press gangs and crimps."

"The *what?*" you say.

"You must've heard of 'em. His majesty's fleet's always in short supply-o'-good hands in time of war. And when they can't find good hands, well, any hands'll do."

"Surely, not," you say, examining your own smooth, student's hands.

"Don't look so worried," James chuckles. "They won't come snatch ya from your bed. But a drunk in port or a gambler down on his luck makes for easy pickin's, so the crimps are always on the lookout when a ship comes in. And whatever y'do, don't sign nothin' no matter what they tell ya 'tis."

"But what good would someone like me be on a ship?"

"I've worked with lads-o'-thirteen who managed to carry their weight. Hell, some of 'em might have even been lasses. Couldn't tell and didn't care, so long as they pulled their duties. And speaking of lads, lasses, and pulling duties, here we are."

James indicates the sign above the tavern, hand-painted and faded. SPENCER'S FREE HOUSE. With a fresh grin, he pushes the doors open like a man who owns the place, and swaggers up to the bar.

The interior is filled with the haze of smoke, barely illuminated by candlelight. You can hear the low murmurs of patrons, but you can't make out any of the figures within until your eyes have time to adjust.

The bar itself is brighter, illuminated by an oil lamp, amplified by a rear mirror. As you get closer, you see the figure manning the bar is, in fact, *womanning* the bar.

She stands at above average height, or perhaps her no-nonsense air gives the illusion of taller stature. She's anywhere between 40 and 50 years of age, dealer's choice. The barkeep shifts behind the counter, waiting to hear your order.

James speaks up, with exaggerated confidence, "You must be Lindy Spencer. I'm told Lindy's Ladies are the loveliest in London. We are but two lonely sailors looking for a good drink and someone t'share it with."

"Just in from port?" Her right eyebrow raises. "Both of you?"

"We have both indeed just arrived in port," you say, stretching the truth.

"Call me Spence. I can't claim the drinks are all that good, but they're cheap and in good supply, and they do what they say on the tin. And I happen to have a few friends who'll sit with you while you drink as many as ya please."

> ➤ "Just the not-so-good drinks for me, thanks." Go to page 112

> ➤ "No harm ever came from sitting together, and I could use a new friend!"
>   Go to page 109

> ➤ "Can I have a water? I'm the one responsible for getting us home."
>   Go to page 200

Fool/Hearty

You heroically leap into the surging seas and swim out towards the missing Jack. Adrenaline pushes you forward and, despite the resistance of baggy clothes, it feels like you skim across the surface towards the victim. In the darkness, you use the lightning flashes to try to locate the poor man, but there's no sign of him. The sea swells such that your only hope of finding him is to be at the crest of a wave when lightning illuminates the surface of the sea. You swim until your arms burn, and then—you swim some more.

Just as you're about to give up hope, there's a biting pressure and you're pulled under. No, not a shark. Jack has his claws dug deep into your flesh as he tries to climb *you* in order to stay afloat. Thoughts of heroism change to panic as you try to avoid assuming the role of victim. Still, he's incredibly strong and panicked himself; there's no reasoning with the terrified Jack.

Sadly, the buddy system will claim two lives today.

THE END

Footnote to History

What a disappointment this trip turned out to be! James was supposed to show up, regale you with tales of adventure over dinner, and then, as dessert, serve up the real juicy bits on the ride home. Tomorrow would be a day full of celebration, with a ball thrown in his honor! But, alas. You'll have to think of some excuse as to why you came home empty-handed.

Eventually, the family learns that James "enlisted" in His Majesty's Royal Navy the next morning and headed back out to sea. The savvier branches in your family tree, however, suspect the press gangs found him drunk and prevailed upon him to consider the needs of the realm over his own, but that will not be your cousin's legacy.

James goes on to be missing in action, and his legend grows to heroic proportions. A statue is erected for him in your hometown of Aylesbury. You, on the other hand, spend your life doing little more than reading about the exploits of others and dreaming of adventure. Perhaps, in another life…

THE END

Foreshadowed

Captain Longwick's mood darkens and a shadow creeps across his countenance as he replies, "The war is *here*, Ward. These are kingdoms; the seat of power. The colonies? At best, territorial skirmishes. At worst? A haven for pirates. Freebooters, buccaneers, privateers—call them what you will, but men of honor fight here, for King and country."

"The *Hornblower's* the fastest ship in the fleet, Captain! We'll be back before you know it," you say, trying to raise his spirits.

"This is your first posting, is it not? Soon enough, you'll see. The hours will be long and hot. Still, it won't be all bad. It gives me plenty of time to drill the men. And you? Well, there might not be a better time to study before the next promotion board convenes."

"Aye, sir. Do you really think I'd have a shot at lieutenant?" you say, taking the opportunity to change the subject.

"I think if you're seriously committed, I can lend you some pertinent books on the subject. The examination for lieutenant shouldn't be undertaken without due preparations."

"Aye, sir. Thank you, sir!"

➢ Captain Longwick is watching you carefully now. Accept his books and spend the evening studying to show him how committed you are. Go to page 263

➢ A night to celebrate, indeed! Head back to the *Hornblower* and toast to the events of the past, the gift of the present, and those challenges yet to come. Go to page 23

For the Birds

In Buckinghamshire, the early bird may have gotten the worm, but here on your island, the saying can be extrapolated for gulls and the fish trapped in tidepools. You'd have to get up pretty early to snatch any trapped sardines, for this is what these birds have eaten for eons.

Instead, you find an array of starfish, sea anemones, and tiny thimble-sized hermit crabs.

There are, however, a bed of mollusks that you can eat. Cracking the shells open with the butt of your pistol, you scoop out and eat the slimy morsel inside. The meal would certainly be better when cooked; something you'll keep in mind once you've got a fire going. In fact, you might do well to line your pockets with a few of these to have with dinner.

The meal leaves you with a great thirst, however, so you'd best look for a way to quench it.

> A quick mouthful from the tidepool should help keep thirst at bay while you look for fresh water. Go to page 25

> Try sucking on a pebble. Ancient wisdom says there's a hidden force at work that will slake your thirst. Go to page 9

> Open your mouth as you walk, flexing your tongue to "awaken" it. This will cure the dry mouth. Go to page 191

The Fortunate One

When you arrive at Captain Bullock's cabin, you find the door open. Stepping inside, you see the ship's master seated, a tablecloth draped about his chest, upon which lie several tendrils of hair. Standing behind the captain is a portly, clean-shaven man in the act of giving him a haircut.

"Sir, reporting as ordered—"

"Ah, there you are," the captain interrupts. "Am I to understand you're another Saltboots?"

"Aye, Captain!" you say, doing your best sailor impression.

"This man here is known as 'Butch.' He's our new surgeon. And now we've all met. Now then—"

"Surgeon?" you parrot back. The words contain more incredulity than you'd intended, which the captain clearly notices.

"Yes, we were just discussing his… unorthodox position. But a butcher who's lost his shop has more experience in carving meat than he does in cooking it, and I'm more in need of a surgeon than I am another cook.

"Now then, I can certainly see the family resemblance, Saltboots. But the reason I called you here was to take your measure, as it were. Young James lied about his age and experience when he came aboard, in spite of which he earned his place. I know the men don't ever much like their captain, but I liked your cousin, I confess. A hard worker who didn't talk back. Still, it's not my role to be liked. I am not your friend, you understand. Perhaps it's better if you came to see me the way young James did, which I should think is more like a father. What do you say?"

"*Arghhh!!!!!*"

The crashing sound and the piercing scream which follows infiltrate the cabin and make your blood run cold. Butch snips off a lock of hair he shouldn't have and the captain jumps to his feet, flinging off the tablecloth. The three of you rush out to see the commotion, where the screaming continues still.

A pallet of cargo was dropped onto the right leg of one of the new recruits, whose name you don't recall. Once crimped, now crushed.

➤ Rush down to help lift the cargo off the poor soul. Go to page 139

➤ Stay here behind the captain; maybe lift your jaw up off the deck instead. Go to page 179

Freedom Fighter

There are no locks where you were stored, like so much cargo. After all, cargo doesn't get up and walk away if it's properly tied down (or in your case, tied *up*). Which means you're free to move about the ship with ease. Captain Rediker ordered Barlow to deal with you, but the rest of the crew is engaged in something a bit more serious—a fight for their lives.

When you emerge above decks, you see the full scale of the action. The Royal Navy ship fires a steady barrage of chase guns, which blast splinters across the bow, but the newly careened *Deleon's Revenge* (né *Cooper's Pride*) is a much faster vessel.

The problem is, she's sailing into a trap.

The English ship pursues Captain Rediker until he sails around the coastline of another small island, where a Spanish Man-o'-War awaits. Is this the ship the pirates were hiding from? Did the English captain know this, and trap the vessel intentionally? Or is it simply the worst possible coincidence?

You'll be able to ask him yourself, soon enough.

Finding himself between two enemies, Rediker shouts orders for evasive action. But that lets the English warship catch up, toss grappling hooks, and board.

Meanwhile, gunfire pounds in and out from all sides. The *Revenge* takes the worst of it, but gives back as best she can. Carriage guns, swivel guns, *grenadoes* (handheld bombs), muskets, and pistols. It's a deafening barrage, and men fall in droves.

You pick up a fallen pirate's cutlass, slashing at the ones on the defense. You hit them in the back, when they least expect it, but these are men who fight without honor.

Finally, the Royal Navy boards. *Crack!* A young lieutenant fires his pistol right into your chest.

Dropping the cutlass, your hands go to your chest as you gasp for breath. Your eyes widen at the realization that this is a mortal wound. Didn't the Royal Navy Lieutenant know you were trying to help? Most likely not, as you were probably difficult to distinguish from the rest of the pirate crew in the action. One man's freedom fighter is another man's terrorist, after all.

THE END

Fresh-faced

The four groups disperse, and you join your watch to meet some new comrades. An old salt you'd met when hanging hammocks below introduces himself as Marlowe, leader of the watch. Two more common tars greet you with mumbles and nods of approval when you tell them you're the ship's new Saltboots.

The crimped man assigned to the watch wears a long-sleeved blue-and-white striped linen shirt with a handkerchief tied loose about his neck. He has rosy cheeks and a head of short, black curls.

"Jacques Goudron, a pleasure, I'm sure," he says with a thick French accent.

"You're a Frog!" one of the sailors cries in response.

"I am French, *oui*. But according to *le capitaine* as, ehh, Jacques were found at a port *Anglais*—English port—he can be made to work as an English man."

"S'pose that's true enough," Marlowe laughs. "Welcome aboard, Jack! Bad luck for ya, but good for us if you're worth your salt. Now then, we're the first larboard watch, and I have me traditions, if you'll follow."

Marlowe picks up a single cannon shot from its spot resting in a nearby brass monkey, and the group follows to the mainmast. Here he produces a silver coin and turns to address the group. He holds the coin up to the mast, ready to strike it with the cannonball to drive it home.

"Here we pay the angels for safe passage!" he starts loudly.

"What the devil do you think you're doing to my ship?" Captain Bullock cries from the quarterdeck.

Everyone freezes, fearing the power of the captain's ire. He hurries over, not even bothering to tap his cane against the deck as he comes. The crew snaps to attention at the captain's approach. "I said, 'What the devil do you think you're doing?'" Bullock repeats.

"T-t-tradition, sir," Marlowe stammers.

"It's bloody superstitious nonsense; I'll not having you damaging the mast."

"But sir, 'tis always been done!" Marlowe protests. "Every seaman here knows. Those who don't pay tribute, they—"

"I take no stock in the reports of illiterate men. Don't make me repeat myself now. If you want to appeal to a higher power, *pay me* for your safe passage. It's this hand which holds your lives."

Captain Bullock puts out his palm, which Marlowe stares at as if it might bite him. At length, the sailor gives up his coin, his shoulders slouching in defeat. The captain suddenly spins on his heels and hurls the silver out into the sea.

And then the ship's master is gone.

"A bad omen, that is," Marlowe grumbles. The other sailors nod in solemn agreement. Then Marlowe brightens. "Must be why God blest us with another Saltboots in the watch. Jimmy were good luck, so long as ye weren't his mate. Don't get too close t'this one, Jack Frog!"

➢ Leave the man to his superstitions. If he thinks you're good luck, that's good enough. Go to page 50

➢ Ask Marlowe, in no uncertain terms, what he means by this. Go to page 150

Friction

With your backside against the cold earth, you have a much larger surface area pressed against the sides of the well, so it's not as easy to slip. Additionally, having your feet out in front adds leverage, and that additional pressure also helps prevent slippage.

You press your back off the wall with your hands to make progress, but that still leaves four points of contact in place. When you move your feet, most of your body is against the wall as an anchor.

It's slow going, inch by inch, but eventually you make it up the side and out of the pit. Once free, you dust yourself off, stretch, and let out a sigh of relief. It's nearing sunset, so you head back to camp, revive the fire, and enjoy a meal from the remaining food stores scavenged from the island.

One might think such a trying ordeal would leave you exhausted and ready to fall into a deep sleep, but the opposite proves true. You're electrified by these near-death experiences and are wide-awake into the night. Naturally, your thoughts turn back to the *Cooper's Pride*, and the near-death experiences you had aboard. Surely the captain's murderer was close enough that you were almost killed as a witness when you found the body. Lurking in the shadows, watching, waiting.

Letting you take the blame.

But who was the killer? Rediker, Marlowe, and Barlow had grudges against the captain, while Robin, Chips, and Joe were nearest to him. Yet, try as you may, it's been difficult to decipher what motive they must have had. And if the true killer wasn't one of these shipmates, that leaves only Billy, the cook, or the surgeon. What do you know about these three?

➢ Think back to your time with Billy Greaves, the Mate and right-hand man of Captain Bullock. Go to page 140

➢ Rack your brain over what odd occurrences happened near Dudderidge, the sea cook. Go to page 227

➢ Revisit the memories of Butch, the former butcher employed as the ship's surgeon. Go to page 28

➢ Simply stare up at the stars—the same your shipmates presently sail beneath—until you fall asleep. Go to page 252

Friends in Low Places

"God must have been a sailor, for He built a port on every coastline, and every port-town is Heaven on Earth," James says. Then, rubbing his hands together like a gambler hoping to score big, he adds, "We're in for a treat tonight, coz. My treat. Two gins, Spence."

"A man in the company of a lovely lady gets his cups filled for half-price," Spence offers.

"Very well, make that two each!" James replies, slapping a palm on the bar. When the first pair of drinks is poured, he slides one your way and toasts, "Here's to mothers and sweethearts—may they never meet!"

The gin burns on its way down and you cough hoarsely in response, much to the amusement of the hooch-hardened clientele of the tavern.

"Second one'll be easier," Spence promises.

James seems not to notice, especially since a young courtesan comes to sit next to him. She's small, pert, and fit. His new friend wears a petticoat, clean and neat, though loose in several suggestive places. She laughs and wraps her arms around his.

The seat next to you creaks as someone sits down. You turn to see another young woman, this one made up to look like a farmer's daughter, and perhaps she was once. She runs a hand over your shoulder and leans forward to display her ample bosom, but her eyes grow wide once she actually gets a good look at you.

"Not quite what you expected?" you say at length.

"I'm sorry, only, well, I'm used to seamen is all," she says, without any hint of irony.

In your posh riding clothes, Sunday best to meet Cousin James, you certainly cut quite a different figure than the rest of the tavern's clientele.

"Not a bad thing," she says, wrapping an arm around and cuddling close. "Tender lovers are the best sort."

You down the second glass of gin, barely feeling the sting this time, and examine yourself in the mirrored back wall of the bar. Before you can get a good look, your new friend takes your cheek in her hand and turns you to meet her intense stare. She looks longingly in your eyes, and offers a coy smile.

"Not for me, Billy. I ain't never goin' back!" James cries, breaking the moment. I have a lifetime's tales to tell. But tonight, I only want the tail!"

You look back to see an older, mutton-chopped sailor blustering good-naturedly at your cousin's opposite side. He says, "Come now, Jimmy. When ya joined the *Cooper's Pride*, you stopped being James Landlubber and began your life as Jimmy Saltboots."

"Billy, ya always was a fair mate, so I'll not insult ya now by air'n me grievances. Join me instead in a toast: Here's to Spencer's Free House. Where there's many a lass, and many a glass, and never'a stormy sea."

James toasts with Billy, clinking glasses and tapping them on the bartop. James downs the rest of his drink, scoops up his lovely companion, and carries her into a back room like a Viking raider might carry a prize after plunder. Billy then takes his seat next to you, shaking his head.

"Don't s'pose you'd wanna take his spot on me ship?" he asks half-heartedly.

A tug on your sleeves brings your attention back to your lovely companion. In the low, dusky light of the bar, her eyes shimmer.

"Don't s'pose you'd rather take me someplace more private-like?" she asks.

- Take the farmer's daughter in for a roll in the hay. You and James will have quite a few family secrets to share after tonight, no doubt about that. Go to page 256
- Cast a glance back in the mirror and ask yourself, "What are you doing?" Tell her it was nice meeting her and pay her for her time, but part company. Go to page 240

Get Cracking

The fact that coconuts are on your island is perhaps a bigger blessing than you realize. The green, new coconuts are filled with vitamin-enriched water, while the brown husky fruits are filled with a fatty "meat" that serves as your island's superfood.

The shells are quite tough, but no match for a rock or the butt of your pistol. Flintlocks are known to be unreliable, so such pistols are also designed for their club-like secondary uses.

The coconut is both filling and nutritious, so long as you eat a few. You could live solely on this fruit and want for nothing, save variety. A green coconut holds roughly 12 ounces of liquid, while the brown coconuts have about 500 calories each. You also get minerals such as potassium and lauric acid, which provides antibacterial and antiviral properties to bolster your immune system.

Great choice; a breakfast of champions. Where to next? Though you can certainly survive off the coconut water, it might be worth finding a source of fresh water on the island for cooking, cleaning, and other uses. Now that you've had a good morning meal, you've got the energy to go for a hike.

What's the best way to find a source of fresh water?

> Seek a low-lying part of the island near broad-leaf vegetation. That's a natural spot where you're likely to find ponds or streams. Go to page 82
> Look for animal trails and see where multiple paths converge. They need fresh water too, and they've discovered the island's secrets long ago. Go to page 78

Get Thee to a Ginnery

"As promised, first round's on me!" James says cheerfully.

This gets the attention of several sailors in the eaves of the tavern. Emerging from a thick haze of smoke, they swarm towards the bar. Did he really mean he's buying the whole tavern a round? Spence, the barkeep, raises her right eyebrow as if asking that same question.

James seems not to notice, especially since a young courtesan comes to sit next to him. She's small, pert, and fit. His new friend wears a petticoat, clean and neat, though loose in several suggestive places. She laughs and wraps her arms around his.

The seat next to you creaks as someone sits down. You turn to see an older seaman with muttonchops. Spence pours him a drink while you look him over. He's well-dressed for a seaman, at least by your limited experience, though his garb holds tightly to a frame expanding with recently added weight. Getting a closer look at the man, you see his grey whiskers are stained rust-red around the mouth from habitual tobacco use.

"Buyin' for all your former shipmates, Jimmy?" the man asks.

James looks about as if considering his predicament for the first time.

"A man in the company of a lovely lady gets his cups filled for half-price," Spence offers.

James addresses the seaman next to you. "Know what, Billy? I'm retired, so why the hell not? Give us a song and we'll drink to it on me!"

"Aye, but let's wet our whistles first!"

The sailors all cheer, and Spence pours gin in as many glasses as there are men. James's courtesan appears most pleased with his generosity. You take your glass in hand with the others, and down it when they do the same. The gin burns on its way down and you cough hoarsely in response, much to the amusement of the hooch-hardened clientele of the tavern.

"Second one'll be easier," Spence promises.

"Customary t'buy a round if'n ya get one bought for ya," Billy says, giving you an elbow.

You respond:

➤ "Sadly, I am unaccustomed to these traditions, and lack the coin for such generosity." Go to page 41

➤ "They say what goes around, comes around. Sing us a good one—I'm buying!" Go to page 269

Getting the Axe

Rushing forward, you scoop up the axe and follow the more senior seaman into action. If education serves, the idea here is to lessen wind resistance, lower the ship's center of gravity, and thus reduce the imminent risk of capsizing.

It's only a quick scramble up, one that you successfully make with a great deal more ease than expected, but you shouldn't be too surprised: the rigging is designed to be traversed. Once aloft, you hack away at the foretop with the axe, while the able seaman does the same from the opposite side.

A truly gargantuan wave crests over the bow, shaking the whole ship and snapping the mast like it was a mere pencil—and taking the two of you with it. The other sailor is pulled overboard, but you're crushed between the mast and the side of the ship; the fury of the sea instantaneously snuffing the life from your *terrenum corpus*. The ship is saved, with the pair of you as the sacrificial offering to Poseidon.

THE END

Giving Chase

⚓

"You know what? You're absolutely right, Lieutenant. What good are you, standing over at the larboard broadside without an enemy to face?" you say.

"I beg your pardon?" Lieutenant Saffron says, blinking with surprise.

"No good at all, I'd say. Come on, then. Take the starboard broadside. You're the senior officer here."

"Well, yes, I suppose that's right," he says, crossing the gun deck. "Men, are you ready?"

Exchanging places with him, you size up the larboard gun crews before finally ordering the men to abandon their posts, "With me! Let's go." They look about, unsure, so you press on with, "What, would you rather just stand there, guns limply in hand, staring out at the open ocean? Let's go! We've got an enemy to defeat!"

Now they follow you, though you're just as unsure what motivated this sudden swell of madness within you. After a few moments, you find yourself back at the magazine, addressing Cousin James.

"Cousin, we've got a superior force chasing us. What've you got to slow them down?" you ask.

James ponders this for a moment, then his eyes brighten. "If we hit their sails with bar-shot, that might do the trick."

"Load us up."

Monks, the gunner, comes forward. "Cap'n give orders?"

"I'm here with his authority," you say, somewhat stretching the truth.

"Hit 'em with the chase guns," James elaborates. "A well-placed hit with bar shot and you could just take out a sail or two."

The gunner and his mate then distribute the bar shot—in essence, a pair of cannonballs connected by a long bar in the center—and wish you Godspeed. The sounds of distant musket fire and the boom of the starboard broadside announce that hostilities have begun without you. Hurrying, your men haul the munitions and follow you up to the main deck and the chase guns at the stern.

The enormous man-o'-war pounds at the rear starboard side, but you wait patiently. Armaments like bar-shot have precious little range... but that patience pays off. Soon, the *Don Pedro Sangre* sinks back for direct chase, hoping to steal the *Hornblower*'s wind by blocking your ship with her own superior size. Not this time.

"FIRE!!!" you shout.

The trio of chase guns boom out in a deafening report, each cannon flying back against a breech rope in response to the enormous power from the shot. In the waning light, it's difficult to see the effect of the attack, so you order the men to swab the guns to prepare for a second volley.

But, then it's clear something has happened. The enemy sailors rush to the bow, and your own men cheer out in realization: you've severed the rigging at the bowsprit! This has knocked the jibs loose, taking the wind from their staysails and slowing the enemy.

The crew of the *Don Pedro Sangre* rushes to repair the damage, but perhaps this is just the lead the *Hornblower* needs! You've got the attention of your Master and Commander, that's for certain. Captain Longwick appears demanding to know who gave the order to fire chase guns.

"No-one, sir."

"*No-one?* Midshipman Ward, I'd thought you were on the starboard broadside?"

"Aye, sir. I was, but I had Saffron take my place. I figured…"

"I can clearly see what you *figured!*" Captain Longwick shouts, looking over the remaining bar-shot. His deep black eyes blaze with intensity, matching the glow of the darkening sky. But then the edges of his mouth twist into a devilish grin and he says, "That's a hell of an initiative, Ward! Keep that up and you've got a bright career in front of you. Lieutenant Dalton!"

Then he's off, further preparing battle stations, leaving you alone with the gun crews. With the ship sinking back, there will be no need to fire the chase guns tonight, so you dismiss the men to get some rest. You'd likely do well to do the same yourself.

Not much choice here:

Well done! You've survived your first battle at sea. But the Hornblower *isn't clear just yet. Get some much needed rest, and when you're ready….* Go to page 29

Go Down with the Ship

It's your die/do moment. The African pirates emerge from the hold with shrieking battle cries, ready for action. Robin leads the gun teams against the Royal Navy, which only returns fire with their swivel guns—their larger carriage guns would blow you out of the water, and it's clear they mean to take you alive.

"Cap'n!" Rediker cries. Turning back, you see him point to a fuse, which leads down into the hold.

"What's the meaning of this?"

"Say the word, and we take the bastards with us. Whole ship is ready t'go."

Without response, you turn back to lead the fight. Royal Navy officers storm the decks of your ship, leading their own into action. You fight like a tempest. Cutlass-slashing across the nearest enemy sailors, pistols discharged in the intervening gaps, one by one. You keep a half-dozen of the flintlocks on your person, tossing the spent weapons aside with each shot fired.

It's grisly combat, but the sailors continue flooding in, in seemingly endless numbers. Outmanned four-to-one, they steadily push you back until it's clear: you've lost the fight. In a way, the *Cooper's Pride* really did die with Captain Bullock. Now the *Deleon's Revenge* will go down with Captain Bloodbeard.

"Rediker! Do it!!!" you shout.

He ignites the fuse, which quickly retreats below decks as it sizzles. Seconds later, there's a bright flash—you're dead before you can even process the blast. You go down as the costliest pirate-boarding action in history. That is to be the legacy of Bloodbeard.

THE END

A Good Ribbing

Without another word, you turn and flee, rushing past Rediker and Barlow as they pull at the cordage to bring in the jib.

"Oi! Where the bloody hell d'ya think you're goin'?" Rediker shouts as you pass.

"T'the privy, I'd say! Our Saltboots's scared shitless!" Barlow calls in reply.

They both have a good laugh at your expense and continue in their task, despite the deluge that threatens to wash them overboard.

You head down inside, battered about by the rolling of the ship as you go. The hold is relatively dry, warm and inviting, though there's even more screaming down here as the sows squeal in horror. Eschewing the animals, you delve deep into the cargo, hoping to wedge yourself tightly into a safe spot.

There's a great crack as the ship lurches again; one of the ties breaks loose—sending several full-sized water casks careening towards you. No time to move; you take one of the barrels in the chest, ribs snapping under the blow. Another water cask slams into you, then another, and another until you're crushed to death.

THE END

Good Town Company

Hollering at the top of your lungs, you sprint towards the town guard.

Calls of "Lily liver!" and "Run, Nelly, run!" and "Go to the Town Rats, you weasel!" and "What a dandy!" fill the air behind you as you go.

"What's this, now?" one of the pair of guards asks as you arrive.

"Yeah, what's all the hullabaloo?"

"Those men thought to assault me!" you protest.

"There, there, you're safe now. Tell us where you're staying in London and we'll make sure you make it back safely. That's enough excitement for one night, I'm sure," the second guard says, comforting.

"Well," you admit, sheepishly. "I'm not staying anywhere in London."

"Poor planning," his partner offers. "But I'm sure we can find you an inn."

"I don't have money for that. I can't even afford a carriage anymore."

With a sigh, the first guard says, "Then I suppose we'll just have to put you up for the night."

"Really? You'd do that?" you say, somewhat dumbstruck by their kindness.

"Well, of course! In fact, we're required to by law, ain't we?" he replies.

"That's the way of it," his partner agrees. "Ever since the Vagabonds Act was passed back in 1597, we've been giving a free holding cell to any and all vagrants."

"Vagrants!?" you protest, but it falls on deaf ears.

Not much choice here:

Go directly to jail, do not spend $200 on a place to stay, and await your sentencing!
Go to page 188

Governor of the Island

Billy nods as you explain yourself, then holds up his hands to silence the murmurs of the crew. "What Saltboots says be true—we don't know for certain who killed Cap'n Bullock. All can be said, the man 'tis dead and there weren't no witnesses."

"Billy, come now—" Chips starts before Billy continues.

"That'd be Cap'n Greaves now, bless my soul. Never thought the day'd come and God knows I'd rather it hadn't. And, well, that's what I'm sayin' here, Chips. God only knows what happened, or why. So leave Justice to the Almighty, we must. As men-o'-the *Pride*, we can't prove this one way nor the other, and I won't condemn an innocent, but won't let a murderer roam free neither. That leaves one solution as I can see it. We'll make Saltboots here the Governor-o'-the first island lacking habitation we come across."

Until now, his words have been directed at the gathered crowd. The men solemnly nod, and at length, Billy—Captain Greaves—turns his gaze towards you.

"Marooned, in a word. If innocent ye be, God will provide," he says.

Then Billy motions and Robin clasps you in irons.

"Land ho!" the cry comes, three days later, letting you know the time has finally arrived.

It's Captain Billy Greaves himself who comes to release you from confinement. He throws a conspiratorial glance over his shoulder, allowing your heart to entertain the fleeting notion that he might free you. Then Billy speaks in a low whisper.

"I believe ya, Saltboots... but me hands be tied. Do what ye can to survive on the island, and for my part, I'll try t'discover the true killer. If the Almighty favors us both, I'll come back for ya on our return journey."

Before you can respond, he steps aside and Robin arrives to escort you to one of the jolly boats. This time crawls by wordlessly, as the pair of you are hoisted down into the waters and Robin rows you ashore.

As he rows, you stare at the island as it grows in size. The shores are made of soft sand, a thick tree-line abutting right up against the surf. It's hard to grasp the scale of the island from down in the jolly boat, but the center appears to rise into a hillock or small mountain.

Do what ye can... Billy's words echo in your mind as you look towards the prospect of surviving all alone in the wilderness.

The boat makes landfall, the sudden stop jarring you from foreboding thoughts. It's been over a month now since you left the earth and took to the sea, and a feeling of vertigo washes over you as your world suddenly stops swaying in tune with the sea.

Robin helps you out, unclasps your irons, and hands you your leather-bound journal, a quill, and a pot of ink. "Last will and testament, for those might happen by."

Then he offers a pistol. You look the weapon over, wondering just what he intends.

"One shot, to end it," Robin says, and, passing a fifth of rum, adds, "And for the courage t'do so."

Then he pushes the boat back into the sea, leaving you alone—Governor of the Island.

You look at the pistol in your left hand, bottle of rum in the right, trying to comprehend the final words spoken to you. Does the man think you a murderer? Is this his way of dispensing justice? Or was this a mercy? Does he know of untold horrors lurking in the forest?

- No. I will survive this ordeal. I am innocent and I will prevail over this tribulation. Go to page 38
- Better a quick death than starvation (or worse). Down the rum for courage, then.... Go to page 77

Gravesend

"All hands! Up anchor! Ahoy!" the bosun calls, and men rush out like a colony of ants surging forth from the earth. So it is that they swarm the capstan, and push her 'round to weigh anchor.

The *Cooper's Pride* is loaded with manufactured goods ready to sell in the New World, hopeful to return with her belly full of raw, exotic treasures. If all goes well, you should be halfway across the world and back in less than half a year's time.

If all goes well.

"Ain't ye part of *all hands*, Saltboots?" Billy calls, pointing your way then to the capstan.

Offering a clumsy, "Aye!" you rush over, man one of the beams and push the nautical equivalent of a millstone, raising the anchor cable with each turn of the wheel. Once that's finished, more commands are bandied about, but they might as well be uttered in Greek for all you can understand. Actually, given your education, you'd likely understand Greek better than this Sailor's Pidgin!

But the rest of the seamen heave to and pull at the rigging, adjust the sails, and get the *Pride* underway. You help where you can, offering extra muscle on ropes or holding *this* in place while *that's* tied down.

Before you know it, the ship is on the move, gliding atop the River Thames with an effortlessness of locomotion you've never felt on land. Why, yesterday's carriage ride was downright barbarous compared to this ethereal slip across the damp.

The *Cooper's Pride* sails through Westminster, His Majesty somewhere beyond. Then the Temple and York Buildings glide past. The ship continues, unrestrained by the shoreside aristocracy, cruising beyond the Admiralty Office; where they're certainly conspiring to press more men into service at this very moment. The Tower of London stands starkly on the horizon, almost as if appraising the merits of your journey.

The streets and narrow lanes of the sailors' neighborhood of Wapping in London's East End passes by, offering sights of gin, ale, and music houses interspersed with shops, markets, and workshops. Then your view darkens as you pass the gallows. Blackened, decaying, crow-ravaged corpses hang in iron gibbets—a gruesome reminder of the punishment for breaking maritime law.

"All hands, cease!" Captain Bullock commands. "Cast your eyes ashore! See these brigands? Launched into eternity for piracy, felony, and mutiny. You'd best do well to remember the rewards for such fraternity! To swing in the open air for all to see."

The *Cooper's Pride* continues in solemnity, past Greenwich and the Prime Meridian, and beyond the Royal Naval College and those plotting war against Spain. Finally, London disappears after the township of Gravesend, and so too the last vestige of the River Thames, before it becomes the English Channel and the open sea.

"Aye, Gravesend, a right name as e'ery sailor knows," a seaman named Marlowe grumbles, low.

"But is it grave-*send*, for us today? Or graves-*end*, for those who return only in memory?" Rediker asks.

"Are those me only options?" Barlow replies with a wily grin.

"All right, ye lubbers! Enough loafin' about," Billy cries. "Form up into the watch, so I can add our new recruits t'the rounds! We do four watches here aboard the *Pride*, active and rest, larboard and starboard. Bell rings every half-hour, so at eight bells, your four hours are up!"

The men separate into four groups and Billy adds the crimped sailors brought aboard with you—Rediker, Barlow, and now only one other—a man in a white-and-blue striped shirt—one to each watch. In this way, those malcontents forced into service are separated amongst the trusted crew, outnumbered three to one.

That leaves just you. Swallowing the first signs of seasickness, you await assignment. It would make the most sense to add you to the fourth group, but more likely, Billy knows you lack the skills necessary to make a difference, so he simply calls, "Saltboots! You'll switch about weekly 'til ye learn the ropes. Go on, then, step to the first group, meet your chums, then back to work, ya louts! The *Pride* won't sail herself t'Boston!"

The thought of the vast oceans between England and the colonies swirls your stomach, but you try not to let it show as the sailors look your way. It's not like you know any of them, though there is a familiar face in each group. So… which of the watch will you join first?

➤ The group with Barlow. He's Rediker's man, and might have something to say. Go to page 16

➤ The group with the "other" crimped sailor. Time to meet some new faces! Go to page 107

➤ The group with Rediker. Something tells me I should keep an eye on him. Go to page 292

➤ The group with the tattooed hulk, Robin. Could be worth getting on his good side. Go to page 293

The Great Compromise

"I need you both, dammit all!" you say, hoping the unfamiliar swear will resonate with the seamen. "We need all hands to get this ship sailing."

The *Cooper's Pride* groans, further listing as if to emphasize the point.

"Ya heard the Cap'n!" Billy cries.

"Go on, ya louts!" Rediker adds to his loyal men.

The crew runs back to their stations to regain control of the ship. By some miracle, it would seem, you got the two parties to work together to right the ship in the nick of time. The *Pride* sways violently for several minutes, even once the men take control of her steerage. That was too close.

Captain Bullock's body is thrown over the side, with those who so desire given the opportunity to say a few words of respect. The mood is tense aboard the ship, and you fear another mutiny could arise at any time. To celebrate your survival, Billy suggests opening a few more rum casks. A decision Rediker seconds, only adding a further suggestion, that the casks instead be the late Captain Bullock's private brandy selection.

Neither of them partake that night, but it does much to increase the crew's morale after such a trying day. It will be a tense journey, if it's to be a journey brought to fruition at all.

"Twelve-mile lighthouse!" Billy calls, pointing out the landmark and handing you the spyglass.

You've nearly arrived in Boston. Being short-handed has left little time for further dissent among the ranks, and truth be told, having the least-experienced sailor serve as captain was a blessing to the ship. You gave Dudderidge the cook free-rein to give the choicest provisions to the crew these last few weeks, so that the stores are nearly barren by the time you arrive in port. Case in point was just this very morning, when Dudderidge gave you a cup of coffee so foul you spat the first sip in a spit-take.

"What the bloody hell is that?" you had asked.

"Coffee. Moreover, burnt toast steeped in hot water, Cap'n, which 'tis a bit like coffee," the cook replied.

"How, pray tell, is this supposed to be *anything* like coffee?"

"Looks a touch like coffee, if ya squint."

Presently, Castle Williams appears on the horizon, signaling only three miles to your destination. The great fortification raises a pinnacle flag in greeting, but your eyes are drawn to the cannons upon the mighty walls. If they knew what you really were—a pirate in the eyes of the law—they would not offer so friendly a reception.

The *Cooper's Pride* sails beyond the fort, past a narrow channel, before entering the great wharf of Boston Harbor. Hundreds of ships navigate in the shadows of the fort, from great man-o'-wars to numerous schooners and tiny dinghies.

Though not quite as grand in scale as London, Boston is impressive in her own right. Everything seems new, and growing. The port is large enough to merit its own Admiralty courts; the merchants who made this boomtown into a success must be cunning businessmen indeed.

"Billy and Rediker will come with me to shore, whereupon we shall discuss the sale of goods," you say.

"Cap'n, a moment?" Rediker replies.

For this private chat, Rediker ushers you inside the captain's cabin, where he grabs a pair of dueling pistols. For a moment, your heart rushes with adrenaline, but your spirits are becalmed once more when he simply hands you one of the pistols.

"The merchants' suspicions oughta be aroused when Bullock don't show. Like as not, some company man's already prepared to reload the ship for London. We need t'sell these goods on the black market and make for a quick turnaround 'fore we're found out. Still, the black market brutes could be just as perilous as the authorities. Best we take care."

"Good thinking," you say, stowing the pistol in your waistline.

Rediker hesitates, then adds, "I don't know if ye truly killed Bullock… but I hope ye did. If not, there still be another murderer aboard this ship. I'll not ask if it be true—and don't tell me! For we need the men's fear-o'-you and their trust-o'-me. They respect what ya did; freeing us-o'-Bullock, the tyrant. Yet fear only goes so far. With me as your quartermaster, and my trust in ye, they'll in turn trust that ya have their best interests in mind still, for future voyages."

"Future voyages?" you ask.

"Aye. D'ya think a man like Billy Greaves will just let us live in peace should we return t'London? We're marked, surely ya can see that. There ain't no normal life waiting for us. We're pirates now, Saltboots."

Before you can reply, there are a series of loud knocks upon the cabin door. Without waiting for an answer, the Bosun opens and darts inside.

"Cap'n! We've docked—" Joe starts.

"Excellent."

"No! Billy's jumpin' ship!"

The fear on the Bosun's face is clear. If Billy means to sneak away… what does that mean for the rest of you?

> Appoint Rediker as quartermaster, have him sell the cargo. You've got to stop Billy! Go to page 301

> Forget Billy. He's got no heart for this business. Help Rediker sell the cargo, and leave with haste! Go to page 53

Gun Runner

There can be no mistaking their intent; the larger English warship is chasing you. As if the intercept course weren't obvious enough, she's used her signaling flags to ask you to slow. Thinking the point was missed, they're now firing on you as they give chase.

"Warning shots, Cap'n. Aiming wide," Marlowe reports.

"Steady, man. We'll lose her in the shallows."

"There!" Joe reports. "An inlet, Cap'n."

He points towards a bay. Does it go through? Many of these islands have outcroppings where you could lose the warship. If only you'd had more time to familiarize yourself with these shores. *CRACK!* The ship shudders with the impact of cannon shot. Several others splash in the water nearby.

"Final warning..." Barlow grumbles.

Now what?

➤ Into the inlet! They can't follow; it's too shallow. Go to page 60

➤ Follow along the coastline. Full sail! We'll lose them around the bend. Go to page 255

Hang Separately

Rediker appears downright flabbergasted at your order. The would-be pirates upon your deck lose their devil-may-care attitudes and look to their recruiter with equal measures of shock.

"Cap'n, a word," Rediker says at length.

"No time! Get these men off my ship. Go with them if you must, but the *Cooper's Pride* is leaving without these ruffians. Joe! Robin! Prepare us for departure."

The Bosun and Gunner get to it, the former piping out commands on his whistle and the latter untying the ship from the wharf and ordering your skeleton crew back aboard. Rediker, however, stands stock-still, as if struck dumb.

"Didn't you hear me, Rediker?"

"Aye, Cap'n... Only ya appointed me your quartermaster, which means I speak for your crew. By all rights, we get a say in this next voyage. Ya ain't even told us nothin' 'bout where we're headed! Not a man here wants t'go back to London, I can say with certainty."

"Don't think I don't know what you're doing, Rediker. You found a dozen new hands to supplement the dozen already aboard, hoping I'd be too willing to increase our ranks after the near-fatal voyage here."

"Of course, Cap'n—"

"But once we were at sea, you'd hold a new vote for captain, isn't that right? And with those new loyal dozen, and your men already on the *Pride*, it would be no contest," you say. Rediker can't even look you in the eye, so you continue, "You new men, I don't know what Rediker promised you, but he did so without the authority to back up his word. Get off my ship!"

In unison, two dozen eyes grow wide, then the men scatter—jumping off the ship with haste. Several plunge straight into the harbor, while others slide down lengths of rope or nimbly hop from crate to crate to disembark with speed.

"That's right. Good," you say, nodding to mask your surprise at how enthusiastically they followed the order.

Not knowing what else to do, you turn back to nod at Joe and Robin, only to find fifty uniformed men marching down the wharf to arrest Captain Saltboots and the crew of the *Cooper's Pride*. Most hold muskets at the ready, and the rest carry iron shackles to help transport your men to the gallows.

"*Hostis Humani Generis,*" the Reverend begins his remarks. The man is jowly, his white powder wig parted down the center, curls raised to either side. He struts in his black cloak before your crew, the magistrate, and the gathered crowds beyond the gallows, lining the near shore and perched atop neighboring Broughton Hill for a better view.

The Reverend continues, "Enemies of all mankind. Nothing good can be asked of thee, save the lesson to others by your death. I will take your final admonitions, for though you are condemned to hang by the laws of man, prithee ask for the Lord's mercy on your eternal souls. Jeremiah 31:20 tells us, '*I will surely have mercy on them, saith the Lord.*' And now, in the last moment of your lives, if you do truly repent and believe in the Glorious Redeemer unto the saving of thine souls and the pardon of all thee sins, ye shall be saved forever and ever. Amen."

"Thank you, Reverend Mather, as always," the magistrate says. "These brigands are indeed condemned for actions most piratical and felonious in the murder of their captain and the capture of his ship. They put their honest shipmates in corporeal fear of their lives and deigned to sell these ill-gotten gains for profit. You may each take a moment now to repent for your souls and to say any final words."

Then all goes silent.

The gathered crowd, hundreds of people, wait with hushed and eager anticipation for the pirates' last words. The magistrate and reverend simply wait. The hangman stands at the ready.

"Wine," Rediker says, clearing his throat. "Awful parched, I am."

The magistrate nods and an underling runs to fetch a bottle. This buys you a few minutes to compose your thoughts.

➢ Repent. It has been known to happen that the governors and magistrates offer pardons from time to time. There's still a chance! Go to page 294

➢ Do not repent. Not many are offered the chance to go out with dignity, so make your last words count. Go to page 173

Hang Together

Joe and Robin untie the ship from the wharf and make for departure, the bosun piping commands on his whistle while the gunner hefts the last few crates of victuals to resupply the ship. It was a hasty stopover, without time to collect much more than fresh water, and you'll need more provisions as soon as you've cleared the harbor.

The veteran crewmembers snap to and help get the ship to sea, but the new pirate crew idle about. You turn towards Rediker to admonish him for his recruits, but there's no time.

"Cap'n, looks though we may have company," the older sailor Marlowe says.

You turn back, only to find fifty uniformed men marching down the wharf to arrest Captain Saltboots and the crew of the *Cooper's Pride*. Most hold muskets at the ready, and the rest carry iron shackles to help transport your men to the gallows.

"Rediker! Get these men moving!"

Rediker nods, turns and shouts, "Hard-o'-hearing? Shove off! Man the capstan! Barlow, a pirate shanty t'get us under way, if ya please!"

His mustachioed mate obliges with a sing-song, "*Yo-ho, yo-ho, a pirate's life for me. We pillage, plunder, we rifle and steal. Drink up, me hearties, yo-ho. We kidnap and ravage, delight in their squeal. Drink up, me hearties, yo-ho!*"

The soldiers on the wharf line up in clean ranks, the first kneeling and the next row aimed over their shoulders, muskets readied as commands are called.

"Gunner! Prepare to return fire!" you cry. "A full broadside onto the wharf!"

Robin looks your way as if hoping he's misheard. Rifle fire peppers the ship, taking two of the new recruits with the first volley. That gets him moving. Having lost a pair of their comrades, the new pirates look back to the wharf with menace and eagerly help the gunner to the task.

"Fire at will!" you command.

The pair of larboard carriage guns roar out with a deafening *KABOOM!!!* And slam back against their restraints with incredible power. The cloud of gunpowder dissipates, allowing you to see the resultant carnage. Robin's aim was true, and the wharf now lies in splinters, the men scattered like so many pins on a bowling green.

"Three cheers for Captain Saltboots!" Butch the surgeon cries. "Hip-hip!"

"Hurrah!" The crew supplies in unison.

But before they can start the second volley, Joe leaps forward with, "Cap'n, the fort! We'll never make it!"

It's true. Castle Williams looms, large like a mountain, standing mightily between the harbor and the open seas. You can hear the grinding of metal on stone as the soldiers at the fort hastily reposition the cannons to sink your ship.

"There! Pull us alongside that schooner!" you cry, singling out a merchant vessel already on its way out to sail. "Put her between us and the fort!"

Marlowe offers a steady hand on the helm, guiding the *Cooper's Pride* up against the merchant while Rediker and his new recruits throw grappling hooks to pull the ship ever closer. Robin mans one of the swivel guns, aiming it directly at the terrified merchant captain, should he get any funny ideas to suddenly change course or drop anchor.

"Steady, man, and you'll live to see supper!" you cry out.

The ploy works wonderfully. Castle Williams finds itself unable to fire upon your escape, for fear of collateral damage, and soon you're out of the harbor and ready to make a clean getaway.

"Release that ship! Make all sail!" you cry.

And the *Cooper's Pride* is underway once again.

"Cap'n, what course?" Marlowe asks, once the commotion of the moment has finally settled. It's a good question, one that you take a moment to consider.

Rediker steps forward, speaking loudly for all to hear, "Well, we done finished the plan t'Boston—and got out by the skin-o'-our teeth. By rights, the crew should vote on what's next to come…"

"I see. And vote on a captain to lead on the next journey as well, I suppose?" you say, seeing the writing on the wall.

Barlow clears his throat. "Saltboots did well freein' us-o'-the tyrant, Bullock. But were a landsman only two months hence. Talks fancy like a ship's master, yet knows the least 'bout the ship."

It's said in an odd, stilted cadence so that you can be sure the line was re-hearsed. This usurping of power was well-planned, probably from the very day you stepped in and altered Rediker's ideas for mutiny. Now the would-be master and commander begins his own well-rehearsed monologue:

"Aye, and we'll always be grateful, Saltboots. But inspiring gratitude ain't the same as leadership. No one here wants t'go back to London, ye can lay t'that. Men-o'-fortune are free t'make our own destinies, but we need articles t'live by. We need to sort these laws much as we should sort shares for prizes, and injury pensions for good men made lame fighting for their brothers. We can't drift t'the back-o'-beyond without aim. We need a cap'n with experience in such matters."

That leaves an empty silence until Rediker turns to Barlow, clearing his throat.

"Oh, right. Eh… served on a privateer, did ye not, Rediker?" Barlow says, catching his cue.

"So I did, lad. And I'd be honored t'be entrusted with this responsibility here and now."

"Would you have us be privateers then, Rediker?" you ask, pivoting off his talking points.

"Indeed, not! Why let a bureaucrat in London dictate what prizes we take? We no longer sail the *Cooper's Pride* for King George. We sail under the banner-o'-King Death! I say we raise the black flag on a newly christened ship—the *Deleon's Revenge*—t'claim eternal glory, Spanish gold, and live like kings ourselves!"

"Huzzah!" the new recruits cry in unison.

But the old crew still see you as their captain, and wait for your response.

➢ Say: "Very well, you've convinced me, Rediker. You have my vote for captain." Go to page 231

➢ This is your ship! Give your own impassioned appeal for captain. Go to page 170

Half-Empty

The barkeep gives you a nasty look, but you've paid your tab and there is no short supply of sailors willing to accept the drink on your behalf. Once settled, you offer a curt nod and turn to go. With your eyes fully adjusted to the dull candlelight of the tavern, you give another desperate scan, but see no sign of James. One older seaman watches you go, tendrils of smoke from a hookah pouring from his nostrils and swirling about his grey muttonchops.

Out front, the driver has disappeared. "The rapscallion!" you shout in frustration. Though you shouldn't be too surprised. He told you you'd need to pay him to stay, and he didn't much want your fare to begin with.

"Cursing like a sailor already," a familiarly dour voice croaks.

You turn back to see Spotted Dick, the hunched and scabbed man you avoided last time around the port. It looks like he was waiting for you.

"Getting awful dark out," he continues, looking up to the sky for emphasis. "Far past the hour that business conducted above-board should be concluded, wouldn't ya say?"

"I'm afraid I no longer have fare to give your cabbie friend," you say. "Not if I should want supper too, and I think that's where I should head now. So I'll bid you—"

"Not so fast! Why, what else is friends for if not t'be there for us in time of need? If 'tis a bite t'eat that ya need, you're lucky to have found me!" he cries, coming closer.

Dick removes a bread tin from his cloak, peels back the lid, and offers you a look inside. It's a traditional pudding, a cake of suet mixed with dried fruit, which, as a Brit, you recognize immediately.

"Spotted dick?" you say, calling the dessert by name.

"The best you'll ever taste! How else d'ya think I got me nickname?" he asks, scratching at one of his multitudinous sores without a hint of irony.

He holds the tin out in offering, and you're surprised to feel your stomach grumble with hunger. Haven't eaten since breakfast, after all.

➤ Sure, why not? If it's the best I'll taste, I can placate the man, thank him, and be on my way. Go to page 176

➤ Best not. The man is clearly a rogue. Who carries a tin of spotted dick and calls himself the same? Go to page 95

Half-Full

"**A** *refund?* Carriage drivers don't give refunds!"

"But you didn't take us home!" you protest.

"I'm willing to, by God, it's you who's refusing the bloody fare. I'm trying to do you a favor here, but you're so blind to the situation, you can't see the nose at the end of your own damnable face."

Reflexively, you try to look at your nose, going momentarily cross-eyed. Then you shake your head, huffing with impatience. "I'm trying to do what's right as a matter of course. If you'd take all the money I have in the world and leave me penniless, at night, then you're no better than the brigands that stalk these planks!"

The driver recoils. You can tell you've wounded the man, and you're moved to apologize, but before you can he digs into his coin purse. He tosses a small satchel your way and yells, "Half! I'm taking the other half as payment for services rendered. Not least of which is scaring off that crimp 'twas skulking around following ya. If you're to be a fool, let it not be on my conscience that you'd end up a dead one for lack of coin. Best-o'-luck!"

Then he snaps his reins and the carriage starts away into the darkening night. You watch him go, weighing the significantly lighter coin purse in your hand as he disappears.

"Your cousin James wouldn't happen to be known as Jimmy Saltboots, would he?"

Turning, you see the mutton-chopped sailor who was looking at you in the tavern now standing at the threshold of the doors. He's well-dressed for a seaman, at least by your limited experience, though his garb holds tightly to a frame expanding with recently added weight. Getting a closer look at the man, you see his grey whiskers are stained rust-red around the mouth from habitual tobacco use.

"Do you know where he is?" you ask, suddenly hopeful.

"I can do ya one better. I know where he was, and I know where he's headed still."

"And I suppose you'll want the other half of my coin to tell me, that it?"

"No, nothing of the sort. I'm an honorable soul, or so I try to be, like yourself. I just want to tell ya, and maybe you'll do me the favor of hearing my offer to help further, by the by."

After a moment's consideration, you say, "I make no promises, though I should like to hear what you know about Cousin James."

The man nods, stepping out from under the tavern roof and looking up to the night sky before turning his attention back to you. "If it pleases, call me William Greaves while we're here on land, though I'm best known as Billy, mate of the *Cooper's Pride*. Ya see, 'twas that ship your cousin set sail with last time she was a' port. Jimmy were a good lad, ready to work hard and earn his keep. Took to the sea like a dog just learned that his whole life, well, he'd really been a seal all along.

"Of course, certain… events… can weigh on a young man his first time at sea. When half your chums become chum, or an oasis port brings the other half to desertin'. See, 'tis a lonely life, when all's said and done. If he were here, now, Jimmy would tell you he's done with life as a Jack Tar, but what he's soon to learn is that once the sirens call ya out t'sea, that they never truly let ya be. He'll have his share of drink and lays, but by end-o'-week he'll be back on the briny fields of destiny, if you'll pardon an old sailor his romantic notion of things."

"So… you don't really know where he is," you say.

"We're all lost souls, caught between the Devil and the deep blue sea."

You take a moment to ponder Billy's words, his reference to Homer's *Odyssey* and the sirens not lost on you. That's the kind of coincidence that those who believe in it would call "fate."

"I said I'm the mate-o'-the *Cooper's Pride*. So it is that we have an opening or two on board, if ya wanna take Jimmy's spot. She's a decently fast ship, tight as a drum—and ready to be filled with treasures. Cap'n Bullock's a fair and honorable man, too, and good, honorable seamen are in short supply. The position comes with a pay advance, of course, which many find helps ease the woes of the family left back home."

You're overwhelmed by the unexpected offer, and your thoughts stray from your cousin, if only for a moment. You, a sailor? You've dreamed of adventure for so long…

"Where's she headed?" you ask, wistfully.

"The American colonies," Billy answers with a knowing twinkle in his eye. "I'm offering you a chance t'see a whole new world."

Taking a moment to consider, you finally say:

- "Sign me up! James won't be the only adventurer in the family. I'll need a ream of paper and a goodly sized bottle of ink to draft a letter home, and to keep a journal of my days at sea." Go to page 267

- "You're kind to think of me so, but indeed I do try to do the honorable thing. In this case, I must find my cousin, whether he's ready to be found or not." Go to page 239

Hard-Pressed

⚓

It's backbreaking work, but the other men are happy to have your help, so long as you don't get in the way. You start by taking small crates or sacks of sundries meant for the stores. Then you offer your hand to share the larger loads. By the end of it, you're aching in places you didn't even know a body had muscles, but the seaman give a nod of thanks and you're treated—more or less—as an equal, if only for a few hours. The work leaves you exhausted, proud, and with a mighty thirst.

The group eventually disperses, and you're issued a hammock (as well as a uniform of utilitarian linen clothing), and sent to the front of the hold to find a spot to hang it. This is communal living, with hammocks hung every few inches apart. The men down here all have their own sea chests; a foot locker for goods stored beneath their swaying beds. Looks like you'll have to pick one of those up when you can. Cousin James is within sight, just down the row, hanging his own hammock, so you find an opening nearby.

"I'm beat," you complain, muscles shaking as you try to mount your bedding. James helps, and you see his forearms are newly tattooed with his initials, cut and filled black with gunpowder.

"Weren't me choice," he explains. "If the ship's magazine should blow, they can identify which parts belong to what man."

"All hands on deck!" someone shouts before you can reply. "Captain's address."

You follow the sailors up top, find a place near the mizzenmast, and await the arrival of the Master and Commander of the HMS *Hornblower*. And... you wait.

There's some grumbling from the men, having to muster just to wait on the Captain, and your own aching muscles grumble of their own accord. Then a rapid pressure change falls over the quarterdeck and the men go silent before snapping to attention. You follow suit. Best not to stick out.

"Cap'n on deck!" the Master-of-Arms shouts.

Captain Longwick emerges in full uniform, blue coat smart and tidy, buttons gleamed to a high shine. He's younger than you expected, and his hair is coal-black, rather than the gray or powder-white of the current fashion. His eyes, deep-seated, glitter like black pearls. He paces, though deliberately. Coupled with his dark, soulless eyes, he gives the impression of a Mako shark on the constant hunt for quarry.

"Welcome aboard the *Hornblower*! I'm not one for speeches, so I'll say only this. We set sail for Spanish waters. The enemy expects us, yet we are the superior seamen. Do your work as assigned, and victory will see the day. Fail to do so, and it's not only your life in your hands, but your brother Tars who stand to left and right of you. As such, I will tolerate nothing less than perfection. First night out, double ration of rum. After that—expect only to be rewarded for victory!"

The men cheer, though you can't be sure if they're truly excited to be hunting the Spanish or simply fulfilling their duty to cheer after a Captain's speech. Most likely, they're cheering for the double ration of rum.

The Captain leaves and the men don't stand on ceremony. Someone calls, "Weigh anchor!" and the final preparations for leaving London begin. Other commands are bandied about, but you linger behind and watch land disappear with equal measures of excitement and dread.

In addition to rum, which is poured by a half-gill tot and diluted with water into a half-pint measure, you're issued a gallon of beer. Both of these libations are intended to keep longer than a barrel of fresh water might, and lacking that, at least make scum palatable once it turns.

Muscles aching from the day, the rum and beer goes down easily. Too easy, in fact. Cousin James notices your empty jug at dinner and addresses you wryly. "Coz, the time for that's behind ya. A gallon's supposed t'last ya 'til tomorrow's supper!"

Before you can reply, a shout dampens your thoughts. Only when it comes again do you realize he's talking to you. "I say, Landsman! With me, on watch!"

"Go on," James says. "I'm larboard watch, opposite shift. I'll relieve ya in four hours."

You nod and rise to join the officer of the watch. A little unsteady, and not just because you haven't got your sea-legs under you just yet. The man appraises you, but it's hard to read his reaction. Through the boozy haze, you look him over as well. He's fair-skinned and fair-haired, unusual for those who spend their days at sea. A twenty-year-old member of the gentry, bred to keep a stiff upper lip.

"I'm Lieutenant Dalton, your immediate supervisor and officer of the watch," he says, introducing himself with the traditional "left-tenant" pronunciation. "As a landsman, your duties on watch include the literal one—that is, keeping a watchful eye for signs of sail, rocky outcropping, or anything unusual, really—but moreover, you're a part of the general upkeep of the *Hornblower*, intended to help preserve the ship's course and maintain the highest possible speed. As the newest and greenest recruit onboard, however, your first assignment is to watch and learn. If anyone asks you to do something, you do it. If not, you stay out of the way. Is that clear?"

During his speech, the pair of you walk through the ship and back above decks. The night is dark, with little to distinguish the sky from the sea. The same queasy feeling from yesterday's carriage ride rolls over you. Perhaps, with some luck, your green pallor won't show in the cloudy moonless night.

"Aye, sir!" you say after suppressing your bile.

Dalton turns to an older man, white-haired, but somehow not as distinguished-looking. He's an older Midshipman, too old for his rank, which makes him an "oldster." He greets the Lieutenant in a thick Dutch accent.

"And how are we looking, Mr. Magnus?" Dalton replies.

"Bad omen for a launch, sir. Rough seas ahead and no stars t'sail by."

"Let's check the barometric pressure, shall we?"

The pair of them walk off together and you take a cautious step to follow, but your stomach swirls about in protest. It's not just the too-much rum and beer, though that certainly didn't help. Can't deny it any longer: you're not just drunk, you're *seasick*. Not the best start to a new career in the Royal Navy….

➢ Rush over to the side to spew while no one is here to witness such an event. Go to page 57

➢ I need to rest, just for a minute. Lieutenant Dalton did say I should stay out of the way unless ordered. Go to page 45

Hatchet Job

Robin takes one of the boarding axes and smashes it into the wooden door, tearing a gash and sending splinters flying back. He alternates blows with the largest of the African pirates, a former slave who calls himself Freeman. The pair of giants breach through the door in no time.

"Make them wish they'd never resisted," you say.

"Bloodbeard's revenge!" Rediker yells.

The pirate crew rushes inside with ferocious cries, echoed back by horrified screams. The clang of metal against metal adds its own screeching to the fray, and pistol fire adds its own roar above all. Whether it was Rediker's or the Portuguese captain's, time will tell.

After a few violent minutes, the fighting stops.

You hold your pistol at the ready, afraid as to which side might be the first to emerge. Breath held with anticipation, a man emerges and your adrenaline spikes, but it's your very own Bosun, Joe.

"The ship is yours, Captain," Joe says, heaving for breath.

Walking inside the dark interior, the smell of death is overwhelming. Men writhe in pain at your feet and the corpses you step over hold more familiar faces than not. Losses were heavy on both sides, it seems. At the end of the corridor, the enemy captain stands defiant, held captive by Rediker and his men.

"You now have what you wanted. Please. Spare the rest of us," the man says with a thick Portuguese accent.

"What I wanted, was no resistance," you say. "I will spare the rest of your men."

"I have a wife. Children."

"And were you a good father?"

"W—what?"

"Were you a good master to these men? Did you treat them fairly?"

"Of course!" he cries.

You look past the captain to his men. Most look away at your gaze, but a youth with tears in his eyes and purpled bruises shakes his head "no." At this, several others also shake their heads. This man was a cruel master, a tyrant, perhaps even worse than Bullock.

"Glad to hear it," you say. "All I ask of you, then, is to give a toast to your captors."

"A toast?" the terrified man parrots back.

"A toast—to Bloodbeard!"

The men quickly produce a grog cup, fill it, and hand it to the captain. He looks uncertain, but you offer a smile and nod. "Go on. Drink up. All of it."

"To Bloodbeard!" he toasts.

The captain brings the cup to his lips and leans back as he drinks deeply. At this, you signal to Rediker, who slits the man's exposed throat. The captain sputters and spits, falling back.

"To Bloodbeard!" Rediker yells.

"Hurrah!" the men cry.

Blood sprays for a few sickening moments, then the captain falls, dead.

"Sign the articles, join Bloodbeard's crew, and you'll sail as free men!" Rediker announces.

Once the inventory is finished, Rediker reports in, "Massive haul, Cap'n. Sugar, indigo, cacao, tobacco, leather, silks, silver, gold, and jewels. Once we divide the shares, hell, I'd say each man just earned himself three years' pay! Not bad for a first-timer."

"Refit the ship first. Take their carriage guns, plus any weapons. Once the *Deleon's Revenge* is made stronger, the rest is profit."

"Aye, Cap'n. It'll take a few hours t'move all the cargo, but we should be full up. Afterwards, shall we plot a course for New Providence to unload our ill-gotten gains?"

"Do it!" you say.

➢ "'Twas a grand first catch, Rediker. Once we make sail, open the rum stores for the men. I'd like to make another toast… to the first of many! And the start of a prosperous partnership." Go to page 137

➢ "I'm going to go through the Porto captain's cabin to see what I can find. He was right, I need a manner of dress befitting the name of Captain Bloodbeard." Go to page 70

Haven on Earth

It's time for a celebration! While you've been a pirate in the eyes of the law for the better part of a month now, this first true act of piracy has cemented your reputation as Captain Bloodbeard, scourge of the seas. Now you'll toast rum with your crew and sail to New Providence, famed haven of the Brethren of the Coast.

Though the current watch is sober, the rest of the crew are far from it. Butch the surgeon stumbles about the quarterdeck, murmuring a song to himself. As he gets closer, his melody grows louder. "Have a drink, and t'hell with care! Be gone, dull care, I prithee, be gone from *meeeee!*" he sings, drawing out the final note until his voice cracks.

"Cheese it, ya lout," Rediker says. But it is a celebration of merriment, is it not?

So you ask, "Who here can give us a *real* song?"

Butch looks contrite and mutters curses under his breath, but the rest of the crew remains silent, looking from man to man. Then Joe clears his throat and starts, "Oh, I love a girl across the water." It's a clear, ringing, angelic tenor that catches the attention of all on the ship.

Rediker smiles at recognition of the song and replies with the refrain, "Way, hey, roll and go!" and the rest of the crew joins in as the chorus, *"And we rolled all night and we rolled all day, gonna spend my money on Sally Brown."*

"Sally Brown is a bright mulatto," Joe continues.

"Way, hey, roll and go!" Rediker echoes.

"Well she drinks dark rum and she chews tobacco," Joe sings.

"Way, hey, roll and go! *And we rolled all night and we rolled all day, gonna spend my money on Sally Brown!*"

"Goin' down to Nassau t'see Miss Sally," Joe begins the next stanza.

"Way, hey, roll and go!"

"Oh, yeah, when she sees me she won't dilly-dally."

"Way, hey, roll and go! *And we rolled all night and we rolled all day, gonna spend my money on Sally Brown!*"

"She's lovely up aloft and she's lovely down below," Joe sings.

"Way, hey, roll and go!"

"She's lovely 'cause she loves me, that's all I want t'know."

"Way, hey, roll and go! *And we rolled all night and we rolled all day, gonna spend my money on Sally Brown!*"

The shanty finished, the crew cheers and downs their drinks, and continues the celebration late into the night.

Port Royal was once known as the wickedest city in the West Indies. To polite society it was "a receptacle of vagabonds, sanctuary of bankrupts, and a close-stool for the purges of our prisons"; it was considered by the civilized world to be "as sickly as a hospital, as dangerous as the plague, and as wicked as the devil."

Now, that dubious honor goes to New Providence Island, known as the Republic of the Pirates. If Justice looked the other way in Port Royal, New Providence went so far as to be the one that blinded her. For you, it's the safest harbor money can buy.

Rediker convinces the crew that the bulk of the prize money should go towards outfitting the *Deleon's Revenge* for future conquest. Though you doubled your armaments once you took the guns from the *Dos Santos*, you've still got a ways to go before you need not fear a ship-of-the-line.

As Bloodbeard's reputation spreads through the alehouses and brothels, you find more men eager to join your ranks. A merchant ship of this class would normally hold 15-25 crewmembers, while a pirate crew on the same ship might swell to ranks of 75-85 men. Rediker chooses the fiercest from among the new pirates, as well as those with valuable skills, but you're confident that he's no longer plotting to vote you out.

The men who sailed here from Boston, not wanting to get left behind, spend their wages on weapons and clothing. Not a single one of your regulars opts to stay in New Providence.

Soon the ship is refitted and you have a fearsome pirate crew ready to for action. Best not to disappoint them. Where to, Captain Bloodbeard?

➢ Let's set sail and come what may! The world is ours for the taking. Go to page 17

➢ Let's find an informant and pay to learn of a rich target. A small investment for a larger prize! Go to page 168

Helpless

You rush down to the man's side, Captain Bullock hot on your heels. Billy arrives on the scene at the same time, but when you reach out to lift the load, your hands are swatted away by the captain's cane.

"Leave him be! Any who tries to help this scoundrel, I swear by God I'll bury you down under there with him!" Bullock roars, before turning his ire on the hapless victim. "Oh, you bastard. Think I don't know what you're doing? I pay the crimp for your debt, and you try to abscond by injury! I'd wager you think you're entitled to a disability pension too? You bastard. You won't get a single penny, do you hear? Not a single penny! Mr. Greaves, get this coward off my ship and file a claim against him for damaging our cargo. Bosun! Get us underway as soon as he's gone, before any of the others try the same."

With that, Captain Bullock turns his back on the man and signals for Butch to return with him to his cabin. Billy waves you forward, and now you help lift the great load. You only need a few inches before the poor sailor pulls the remainder of his wrecked leg from under the remainder of the wreckage. Following the mate's lead, you help the man up and off the ship.

A shrill whistle sounds and the other sailors rush to muster above decks. At your hesitation, Billy says, "C'mon, Saltboots! That there's the Bosun's call!"

Not much choice here:

Head on back to see what the call means. Go to page 121

Herring

Indeed, try as you might, you cannot think of any particular grudge or secret that Billy might hold against Captain Bullock. But not all murders are premeditated. Perhaps this was a crime of passion, or even an accident of sorts. If Billy were to be implicated in such a thing, there's only one set of memories you need concern yourself with: where was Billy Greaves on the day of the murder?

That'd be the same day as the flogging of the boy, and the whole crew was made to be present for that grisly event. Once things had settled down and the men sent back to their watches, what had Billy been up to?

Dealing with the fallout of mail day.

As the day prior had been a mail day—in which another ship had delivered a parcel of postage—the men were likely in a state. Most news a seaman receives from shore is of ill portent, and that leads to a sort of tunnel vision, where every event could be construed as a bad omen. On mail days, sailors skulk about their duties, foul moods simmering together to make a stew of negativity on all decks. This could have spilled over into the following day, and many of the crew likely credited the bad omens to the flogging itself.

Billy himself was in a foul mood the day of the murder, though not because of the flogging. Had he received a nasty letter in the post? Or was it simply the burden of cleaning up after everyone else ate the bad news stew?

"How'd this happen, Butch?" Billy said when they had spoken after the flogging.

"I dunno, Billy. That's why I called ya here."

You'd been heading up towards your night watch when you'd heard the voices coming from the surgery—which was both the ship's hospital and the surgeon's quarters.

"Tell me what ye saw."

"Nothing, Billy. I weren't here. Went up to speak to Cap'n Bullock, as ordered. And when I returned, I found it like this—smashed open and all sorts of vials of God-knows-what stolen from the pharmaceuticals."

"And what did Captain Bullock want with ya?"

"Well… that there'd be a private issue, Billy. A letter about me late wife, God rest her soul. Settling of affairs back in port."

Staying back and out of view, you peered in through the open door. Butch's medicine cabinet was broken; smashed open, glass everywhere. As for the boy who received the flogging, he lay sleeping, knocked insensible by pain killers.

"And him? What'd he see?" Billy asked.

"Slept straight through, from the looks-o'-it."

"Didn't Bullock order against medications?"

"Well… maybe 'twas the Christian thing to do," Butch said, rubbing his chin thoughtfully. "Better yet, maybe 'twas the thief that smashed my cabinet and took the laudanum t'give the lad?"

"Which was it, then, Butch?"

"How the bloody hell should I know? Said I weren't here!"

"Christ. Now I got a poppy-head amongst the crews. Get this cleaned up, find a secure place for the rest-o'-them medicines, and I'll see what I can't do t'get this sorted."

Seeing Billy about to leave, you hastily left the corridors yourself, heading above decks before your shift on watch. If there were a thief onboard, perhaps there's more to this than a simple killing. Had Bullock caught the thief? Who would have stolen medicines from under Butch's nose? If the order to have the surgeon report in to the captain's cabin had been relayed, the thief could have known the medicine cabinet would be unattended.

"Look at Red's herring!" Barlow shouted when you reached the top deck. "Hot damn, Red! Herring!"

Rediker had been fishing over the side, and now held a herring as his prize.

These two clearly had no idea what was going on below decks, though you weren't much more informed. There must be some clue you're missing….

➢ Rack your brain over what odd occurrences happened near Dudderidge, the sea cook. Go to page 227

➢ Revisit the memories of Butch, the former butcher employed as the ship's surgeon. Go to page 28

➢ Simply stare up at the stars—the same your shipmates presently sail beneath—until you fall asleep. Go to page 252

Honor Bound

James marches determinedly down the muddy promenade, despite your pleas for him to wait just one confounded minute. Thinking rashly, you tromp after him, grab him by his arm, and spin your cousin around on his heels.

His sharp eyes look to your hand upon his arm, then slowly up to your face. He releases the handle of a dirk at his waist—which, truth be told, you never even saw him reach for—then takes your hand in his own. James's skin is rough and calloused, fingers firm as wood, with a grip strength that would rival a winch.

"Never, ever, take hold-o'-a seaman like that if ya value these fingers," he says, prying your hand off himself and holding it up for inspection, as if you'd never seen your own fingers before. "Most would gut ya 'fore they took the time t'look ya in the eye, understand me?"

"I don't intend to deal with any rogues, save for yourself," you say, mustering your coolest tone. "Aunt Margaret entrusted me with enough coin to see you fed and returned home, and enough oath-swearing to ensure I'd discharge my duty with haste."

"Oaths you've sworn are not mine to uphold, coz."

James spins back around and continues on his way.

"So you will not return?" you call after him. "Shall I tell your mother of your refusal? Or should I grant her the mercy of saying you'd never arrived at port at all?"

He turns back, exasperated. "I arrived *early*, or did ye not notice the sun shines still? If you're bound and determined t'buy me a steak-n'-ale pie and load me into a carriage, go procure those things whilst I take a moment to wash the salt off me soul. Don't I deserve a sailor's welcome from a wench before I'm forced to endure an Englishman's welcome from his mother?"

Seeing you hesitate, he adds, "Or come, let me buy you a drink while I'm still in a cheerful mood. But I swear by all the virgins, Mary or otherwise, if ya come between me and my shore leave one more time, I'm bound t'forget we're related."

➤ Let him have his fun while you find a carriage. Best James feed his baser natures while you're out of sight and can still claim plausible deniability when Aunt Margaret grills you later. Go to page 265

➤ Don't let him out of your sight! If the cost of keeping your cousin at your side is enduring a shot of sailor's rotgut, so be it. Go to page 100

Hospitable

⚓

Dalton commends your choice, noting, "Not many have the stomach to enter the surgery unbidden."

Then he leaves you to it, moving about on his own rounds. The pathway to the surgery is sticky with drying blood, and you order the first sailor you come across to find a mop and a friend and see to it. Then you head inside.

The air is warm and humid, and there's an earthy stench, like month-old garden compost. A dozen men lie about in various states of treatment, while the only one on his feet is the surgeon himself—Wycombe.

"And?" he says, not looking up from his current patient.

"And what?" you reply.

"And what do you require of me?" Wycombe sighs out.

"I've only come to check on the wounded."

Now he looks up at you, as if he's only now decided you're worth noticing. He appraises you, keeps his findings to himself, and turns back to his work. "Help yourself."

Practically every man has a bandage of some sort, most from wooden splinters from the cannon barrage. A few have limbs tied off completely, the ends mangled by battle and bound back together by the surgeon. Then there's a man you recognize from one of the gunner teams, skin ashen, eyes grey. His stomach opened, the viscera inside congealing.

"I thought you were here for the wounded?" Wycombe asks, suddenly at your side.

"That's right," you say.

"That man's dead," the surgeon offers.

"What's he doing here?"

"Wasn't bothering anyone until recently." There's a glaze over Wycombe's eyes, pupils the size of saucers. He adds, "I suppose he's awaiting a funeral. If you'd like to help with the others, trying to stave one off, that might be a better use of your time."

You nod and Wycombe bids you follow. There's a seaman with a distorted stump of a foot who groans in a fog of pain. The surgeon informs you that he'll need to saw off a clean end for the man, and asks you to hold the sailor down while he does so. You pin the man's arms by his side and Wycombe gives him a leather strap to bite onto. The surgeon nods, and you return the gesture.

Then Wycombe saws away just below the knee.

The seaman cries out muffled but ferocious animal growls, bucking about in agony. You manage to keep him held down, and it's a clean cut. As Wycombe tends to the newly exposed flesh, you watch the freshly poured blood seeping between the planks of the floor, and find you're panting for breath.

"Don't look away!" Wycombe shouts with sudden passion. "Remember that man's face, Midshipman Ward. This is the true bounty of war. If God and His Majesty see fit to make you a commissioned officer, I pray you carry this moment with you throughout your command."

You look at the surgeon with new eyes. He doesn't fight the battles, yet he's always the closest to the dead and dying. Unable to find the words, you simply nod in response, and spend the rest of the afternoon helping in the surgery. Speaking with those despairing, feeding those unable to do so themselves. Sopping up the spilt bounty of war where you can.

➤ This has put me in a somber mood. As an officer candidate, it's my duty to learn how to best prevent carnage like this in the future. I'll spend the night studying. Go to page 263

➤ I could use a drink after this. Surely Captain Longwick will re-open the rum stores to toast our escape from the enemy. Time to celebrate life! Go to page 23

Hubris

It's tempting to use the pages of your journal for kindling, but no—this will hold the only record you were here! The first task is easy enough. You gather dead and dry driftwood and the fibrous husks of coconuts and tree bark peelings to use as kindling. Once gathered and stacked in such a way as to protect the fire pit from the wind (while giving enough space for the fire to breathe), you simply need to ignite the pyre.

Taking the rum bottle, you try to focus the sunlight into a beam of concentrated light and heat. But, alas, the waning sun of evening does not provide enough light for this technique. Perhaps you could strike the correct type of rocks against one another to send a spark into the kindling? It's likely there are some to be found in the interior, but out here by the sandy shore, you're not given much.

Looks like your only option left is friction. Rubbing the driftwood together eats at the flesh on your hands, but after the time on the ship spent hardening them against the ropes, they're up to the task. All it takes now is time and patience.

The sun sets without any hints of fire, and all you have to show for your efforts are warm pieces of driftwood. You're starting to fear you may be going to sleep hungry, thirsty, exhausted, cold, and disappointed.

That thirst makes you think of the rum, which in turn makes you think of the pistol. The *flintlock* pistol! In a sudden burst of inspiration, you remove the shot and powder, careful to rest the components in a bowl-shaped scrap of wood rather than lose any on the beach—you'll need this weapon one day.

The flintlock mechanism works by literally striking a piece of flint, which creates a massive spark. So all you have to do is hold the pistol near the kindling, cock the hammer, and pull the trigger. Flash! The sparks leap into the kindling.

When the first tendrils of smoke curl from the driftwood, you jump up and shout out with joy. Then you gather your senses and breathe the breath of life into the fire, helping the spark grow into a flame, growing it amongst the rest of your kindling. The process only takes a few seconds until you've got yourself a roaring fire. You carefully reload the pistol and store it back into your waistband. Best not to use that trick too many times, or you'll wear out the mechanism.

Sitting back, you enjoy the warmth of the fire. Though you have an empty belly, you feel a sense of accomplishment. Until the first drops of rain patter down from the heavens. The fire hisses at the assault, and the flames strike back, licking higher into the sky. The rain grows into a deluge, sheets of water dumped atop your island.

"Why?!" you shout. But fire cannot survive the onslaught, and soon you're soaked through. Like Prometheus, you've been punished for bringing fire into the world. Now, in the freezing rain, it's tempting to use that fifth of rum to peck at your liver; Zeus's punishment would feel like a blessing here, if only for a few moments.

No, you won't succumb to the temptation. You push the thought from your mind and instead, look for a place to hide from the brunt of the storm. But where?

- ➢ Beneath a coconut tree. The broad leaves will provide some protection, and I can rest against the trunk. Go to page 307

- ➢ Do what you can with the rest of the driftwood. Some of the husks are big enough to lie under. Go to page 277

Hungover

⚓

You awaken the next morning with a muster to the main decks. It's to be a funeral for the men lost in battle. The crew is gathered, and the fallen are laid out near the edge, ready to be dropped into the sea.

Every single one of the faces of the dead are familiar, despite this being a ship full of nearly two-hundred other men. Faces you'd seen at the water cask or in line for chow. Faces you'd hauled rigging with or scrubbed the decks beside. Faces you'd heard making jokes, singing shanties, or damning the storms.

Those faces are still now, white as marble.

The dead lie upon their hammocks, nearly sewn into them—the only bit that remains exposed are those faces. The last step will be to sew them up completely, with the final stitch sewn through the nose to ensure that they are truly dead and not just insensible.

Captain Longwick says a few words, but all you can hear is the sea. Birds caw and waves rush against the hull of the ship. When the eulogy is complete, that final stitch is sewn and the men are flung over, sent into a watery grave.

The last act of kindness and remembrance is an auction of the men's gear. Their best mates bid much higher than any set of trousers or leatherbound book or corncob pipe is actually worth, for the profit will be sent back to England as a final gift of pension to the men's families.

So too does this speech become muddled to your ears. You hear nothing but the creaking of the ship. Indeed, the only words you hear are Homer's: "Beware the toils of war; the mesh of a huge, dragging net, come to sweep up the world."

"Ahoy, there, Landsman!" a voice finally breaks through your subconscious. It's the Master-of-Arms calling out to you. He says, "Nice of ya to join us back here in the land-o'-the living! We're making landfall. There's wood to be chopped and water to be pumped."

➤ Go out in search of a good spring. You haven't had a clear drop to drink in weeks. Go to page 278

➤ Join the team chopping wood. With all the repairs to the ship, you'll need a fresh resupply. Go to page 327

Hunted to Extinction

"Leave the prize! Make all sail!" you command.

And the panic sets in. Half your crew, if not more, is deep inside the Portuguese merchantman rifling through her cargo when the orders come. How long will you give them to make it back?

In the rush to flee, the boarding platforms simply fall into the sea. The grappling hooks are severed, rather than detached. Men leap from the Portuguese ship back to the *Deleon's Revenge* and with the Spanish warship approaching, some men are indeed left behind.

But those are the lucky ones.

"She's a bloody pirate hunter!" Rediker shouts.

"Fire rear guns!" you command.

That's when the first shots from the Spanish warship boom forth, smashing into your comparably tiny ship and battering the crew with wooden splinters from the blast. And they're gaining still.

It was too late from the get-go. The Spanish ship had the wind while you were at a complete stop. By the time you reach your full speed, they've already caught you. The only choice left is whether to go down in a blaze of glory, or to surrender and be hanged… or worse.

THE END

Hunter

The pirates give chase through the jungle, hot on your heels, slashing their cutlasses as they go. None fire their pistols, for it would be a waste of the flintlock's single shot to discharge the weapon without a clear line of sight.

Lithe and swift, you manage to pull slightly ahead of the men. This frenzied run soon brings you to the jaguar's lair. Here, you hide nearby, claiming a stone the size of a small cannonball. Once the pirates come close, you hurl the projectile into the jaguar's den, drawing the men closer with the clatter, and the beast out of the cave at the same time.

"Over here!" Marlowe hisses to the others, leading them inside.

A great animal yowl sounds out, followed by the screams of men and the rapport of pistol fire. The jaguar sprints off into the jungle, but not before killing two of the pirates—Marlowe and another man. In the commotion, you're able to take them from behind and kill the others.

Claiming a pistol off the fallen pirates, you now stalk the rest of the men, armed to the teeth. They respond in kind, setting fire to the underbrush of your island. Soon, only Barlow and Rediker remain—and you've got a pistol for each man.

The flintlock you've been carrying all these weeks is the one you save for Captain Rediker. Stepping from the underbrush, they turn to face you, faces full of surprise. Out here, on the very beach you were abandoned upon, only the three of you stand living.

➢ Fire at Rediker first—he's the bigger threat. Go to page 189

➢ Fire at Barlow first—savor the victory. Go to page 315

A Hut of One's Own

The first night's dwelling won't be much more than that—a dwelling. Like an animal nest, you need a "human nest" in which to sleep. Having a comfortable abode is something that can come later. For now, priorities are two-fold. First, somewhere protected from the elements, and second, somewhere out of the way of curious neighbors.

What can you expect to find on this island? Lions, tigers, bears? *Cannibals?* You don't know what's out there yet, so it's best they don't know where you are, either.

Collecting small downed trees and large branches, especially those with natural forks, as well as palm leaves and fibrous husks that you can twist into cordage, you get to work. A raised or protected area to post your shelter would be ideal, but you make do for tonight.

Fortunately, your experiences with the ropes and rigging of the ship, as well as with assisting Chips the carpenter now come to bear fruit on your first night alone. The forked branches of wood serve as a nice frame for the makeshift hut, which you layer with palms and smaller branches to make the roof.

The sun has long since set, but still you continue making the dwelling as secure as you can. When the rain starts in, you're glad you did so. The heavens open in a deluge, and while your shelter isn't water-tight, it's better than you could've hoped for.

Lying inside, your own body heat is enough to insulate; such as it is, the hut is small enough that not too much heat escapes. You could swear you can hear someone or *something* walking around out there, so you keep as silent as death. Maybe it's just the sounds of the storm and your imagination conspiring against you?

The pistol digs against your side as you try to sleep, but you keep it close lest the storm spoil the gunpowder. The idea of revenge, of justice, is the one thing keeping you going right now. But who could have killed Bullock? He was slain by his own knife, in his cabin, so the killer couldn't have gotten far. Moreover, who might have had a motive to kill the captain? There was a page missing from the ship's log—that cannot be a coincidence.

Then it occurs to you: you kept your own log all this time. Since your journal faithfully recalls a month spent with these seamen, you might actually know them well enough to ascertain their motives. Perhaps if you think hard enough, the answer is already there, waiting in the recesses of your memory! At the very worst, it should help keep your mind off the storm and whatever's "out there."

You start with the most obvious suspects. Three men in particular, thick as thieves, come to mind:

- Marlowe, the oldest sailor on the ship. Go to page 281
- Rediker, the ringleader of the crimped men. Go to page 166
- Barlow, the mustachioed man always at Rediker's side. Go to page 181
- Actually, no. Best way to keep my mind off things will be just to get some rest. Go to page 86

Icarus

"Every seaman here knows," Marlowe says.

"Well, I do not. And I should like you to explain yourself, lest I take offense!"

"No offense intended, honest. Nothin' bad never happened to Jimmy, nor those on watch with him. Only, he had two chums that he got on with—those were the only two that we lost on the whole voyage! He took that second man's loss harder than most, and kept to himself after—and we ain't lost no more men. So, ya see, he's a good-luck charm! So long as ya don't get too close…"

"Flew too close to the sun…" you mutter.

"That's right! Some sun is good, course, but Jimmy was like too much-o'-a good thing. Left out in the sun, ye go mad."

"And what if I'm not like my cousin?"

"Aye… but what if ye are?" he counters, wily-eyed.

Can't argue with that. The conversation over, Marlowe goes about assigning watch duties, which for you starts off with uncoiling and recoiling rope. It's a menial task, leaving you plenty of time with your own thoughts. You try to imagine Jimmy—Cousin James—out alone for two years with his only friends in the world dead, with the other crewmates saying he was the cause of their misfortune. Then you try to imagine being avoided from the start.

Eight bells sound, signaling that your watch is over.

"Get some sleep, ya lot!" Marlowe commands. "Eight more bells, then 'tis supper, and back to it. So ya better get your shuteye while 'tis on offer!"

The afternoon was more draining than you expected—both mentally and physically—so time in the hammock could be exactly what you need.

"Up! All hands! Up, or we all perish!" the cry comes, shaking you from your slumber.

How long were you asleep? It's impossible to tell, and in the commotion, it doesn't much matter. Now that you're on your feet, you feel the violent rocking of the ship that the hammock had countered. You rush up with the crew, ready to lend a hand to prevent the threat of death.

Thoughts of seasickness are replaced by sheer terror when you reach the open air. Lightning arcs across the sky with the dreadful crack of thunder only an instant behind. The sea rollicks like an open flame and foams upon the deck—beating her with great waves, threatening to pull all asunder.

One such wave nearly knocks the ship on her side, and a man who was up in the rigging of the mainsail is thrown into the sea. You recognize him as the third crimped sailor, the one in a white-and-blue striped shirt.

"Man overboard! Jack's gone in!" the sailor Marlowe cries.

Billy throws a rope, but when it hits the water, it disappears into the inky sea, and now he watches with a sort of helpless indifference as the sailor struggles for his life. It's clear the man has no idea how to swim and will soon drown.

➤ Tie a length of rope around your waist and leap in! Go to page 164

➤ No time! Dive in and help crimped Jack back to the ship. Go to page 101

➤ Say a prayer for the poor seaman; nothing else you can do. Go to page 196

Ill-Presentiment

⚓

Seizing the opportunity to vent your frustrations, you continue, "They're expecting more than they rationally should, yet trying to undermine any chances I have to get the hang of things. I swear, cousin, you were right that they've got it out for me, only I don't know what to do!"

The pair of you take your supper in a relatively abandoned corner of the mess. As the days have gone by, the common tars have started to avoid you as if you yourself were an omen of ill-foreboding, so it's easy to find a spot alone.

"I feel partly responsible. 'Twas my suggestion ye took, coz. I didn't know jumpin' the chain would make ya such a target," James says after you're seated.

"If they gave me a fair shake, I could prove myself. I know I could!"

"You're as likely t'find a fair maiden aboard as you're t'find a fair supervisor!" he says, trying to lighten the mood. "Hell, take me. Day in and day out, I slave for this curmudgeon of a gunner, calls himself 'Monks,' but he's anything but. While I scour my flesh with sulfur, coal, and saltpeter, he just gambles with the surgeon and recorder!"

Somewhere in your sleep-deprived memory, an image of the ship's recorder rises to the surface. "The Scotsman? Argyle?"

"That's the one! Lord knows they're in the ship's magazine right now, rollin' bones."

"The Captain turns a blind eye? I thought gambling was strictly forbidden?"

James shrugs. "I doubt he knows. Who goes to inspect the magazine but the gunner?"

After a moment, you reply,

- "Who should inspect the magazine, indeed! I'll not go down without a fight, cousin. And you've just given me a most brazen idea…." Go to page 248

- "Bunch of bastards, the whole lot. I'll just work harder, prove them wrong. Then I'll be a fair and honorable officer, you mark my words." Go to page 217

Impresario

For a telltale moment, the lieutenant's eyes narrow after your response, but then he recovers to a more detached, hard-to-read expression. This leaves you with nothing more to go on than an indication: Dalton will remember that.

"It's best that you came to me with these concerns, Ward. Geoff was a crusty old seaman for a long time before he became a petty officer, and he retains that gruff sense of duty. I understand how it might rub you the wrong way, but that's simply the way he is, I'm afraid," he says at length. "Just make sure you come to me first from now on. That's how the chain of command works, you understand. If you have a problem, we needn't trouble the commander with every little trifle."

He waves his hand about as if any problem you might encounter would be no more of a nuisance than a housefly. Then a rapid pressure change falls over the quarterdeck and the men go silent before snapping to attention.

"Cap'n on deck!" the Master-of-Arms shouts.

Not much choice here:

Follow suit and snap to attention. Best not to stick out. Go to page 79

Impressionist

⚓

For a telltale moment, the lieutenant's eyes narrow after your response, but then he recovers to a more detached, hard-to-read expression. This leaves you with nothing more to go on than an indication: Dalton will remember that.

"No, I would not agree. I would not agree one bit! And if you think that way about your new duties, well, I should say you might need to re-evaluate your chosen career," he says at length. "Just make sure you come to me first from now on. That's how the chain of command works, you understand. If you have a problem, we needn't trouble the commander with every little trifle."

He waves his hand about as if any problem you might encounter would be no more of a nuisance than a housefly. Then a rapid pressure change falls over the quarterdeck and the men go silent before snapping to attention.

"Cap'n on deck!" the Master-of-Arms shouts.

Not much choice here:

Follow suit and snap to attention. Best not to stick out. Go to page 79

Impressive!

⚓

You need to accomplish two tasks: Chiefly, you must fire the first shot. Once blood has been drawn, the duel is over, and if the Master-of-Arms were to line up a shot and fire after being hit, it would be treated outside the confines of the duel as attempted murder.

Secondly, and more importantly, you must hit the man.

If you miss, he'll be able to take his time and carefully aim his own shot. Not an outcome that favors your odds of survival. Luckily for you, he's not a particularly thin man. What's more, he must have survived other duels in the past, because he stands with shoulders square and legs spread like a man unafraid.

The ship sways, throwing off any real chance for accuracy. Still, you aim for the midsection, picturing his navel as a bulls-eye, and squeeze the trigger. The burst of sparks that comes from the flintlock force you to squint and turn away, but a loud *twang* tells that—unless by some miracle you hit his belt buckle—the shot went wide and hit some iron implement on the ship.

When you open your eyes again you see only a plume of smoke between yourself and the Master-of-Arms. With certain dread, you know you've missed your one shot; a shot made all the more difficult by your unfamiliarity with both firearms and the sea beneath your feet.

It feels like an eternity, but after a few moments the spent gunpowder dissipates, and the Master-of-Arms stands before you, *unarmed*.

You've shot the pistol right out of his hand! All eyes look to you with astonishment, and it takes every ounce of self-control not to let your own jaw hit the deck.

"The Ward's a bloody dab hand with a flintlock!" Mr. Magnus says, voice full of awe.

"A real crackerjack shot," the ship's surgeon adds, shaking his head in disbelief. "Didn't even see the need to draw blood, bless you."

"Geoff, do you yield?" Captain Longwick asks.

The Master-of-Arms looks you over with new eyes and you stare back with a cold countenance, not wanting to dispel the notion that you're a ringer with the pistol.

"Aye, sir, I do," he says at length.

Cousin James is over the moon when he hears of your victory. You have a reputation now, and as your cousin, he's given a wide berth, accompanied by nods of appreciation from the rest of the crew. At recognition of you, however, the men of the ship touch their brow in salute as they would a full-fledged officer.

Supper that night, though truly no different, is the best meal you've ever eaten. Men toast to the crackerjack of the HMS *Hornblower* and Lieutenant Dalton dares not chastise you for eating your meal out amongst the common sailors.

Captain Longwick summons you to his cabin after you've finished.

"Ward, at ease. I was hoping you'd like to join me for a glass of port," he says, taking a seafoam-green glass bottle and pouring the deep red wine into two crystal cordial glasses.

"Aye, sir. Thank you," you say, taking your glass.

"Do you know why they call it 'port' wine?"

"Because it's from Portugal," you answer.

His look shows the question was rhetorical, so he ignores your response, raises his glass in toast and continues, "Because port reminds us why we fight: For England's exports and imports, foreign ports and home ports!"

"Here, here," you say, then share your drinks together.

"That was a hell of a thing you did today."

"Thank you, sir."

"That wasn't entirely a compliment. Geoff offered his resignation as the Master-of-Arms, and Mr. Midshipman Magnus requested to be transferred to a new ship along with him. Whatever bad blood was between you three, well, they're afraid of you now. And I find myself short two officers." The Captain looks you over, trying to gauge a reaction, before going on. "The open Midshipman billet is yours, should you still want it."

"Yes, sir! Thank you, sir!"

"Tut-tut, don't be too hasty. The offering comes with a catch. The men hold a great deal of respect for you now, I'm told. And the same can't be said of our former Master-of-Arms or your predecessor, which I suppose means I owe you a debt of thanks. Even so, should you accept this promotion, I ask for your word of honor: no more duels. It simply wouldn't do to have you throw your weight around every time there's a disagreement with another officer. You'll have to learn to work with the others. Do we have an accord?"

"Yes, sir. Of course, sir," you say, still shocked by the day's turn of events.

"That will be all, then."

You salute and turn to leave, but he stops you. "Oh, one more thing. I was rather fond of those pistols before you ruined the one. I do believe you owe me a new set."

"Aye, sir!" you say, unable to keep the grin off your face.

Outside the Commander's Cabin, Lieutenant Dalton awaits. He approaches with some trepidation, wringing his hands together nervously.

"Good evening, Ward. I... I would be honored if you would continue on my watch this evening," he says.

You let the moment hang in the air, so he continues, "I realize I may not have gauged your full potential, and for that I am truly sorry. I do hope you'll give me another chance. I should like us to be friends."

Remembering your promise to try to work well with the other officers, you say, "Of course, Lieutenant. I shouldn't think you'll underestimate me again, only now, it's Midshipman Ward."

Not much choice here:

Go about your duties with a new lease on life. Well done! <u>Go to page 218</u>

In Good Hands

"Yes, I suppose we'd best tell the carpenter to get started. I understand he's apprenticed at the shipyard; building them from the ground up, as it were. He's the expert, Ward. If he says it must be done a certain way, that's the way it shall be done," Dalton orders.

"Very good, sir," you reply, then salute and head off to find the carpenter and his mate.

The carpenter is a stout, serious man called Woody. Whether his name is coincidentally Woodrow, or if it's a none-too-creative carpentry nickname, you can't say. Instead, you inform Woody that the time has come to repair the ship and ask what he needs to accomplish the task.

He inspects the damage first, prioritizing the sites by their likelihood of springing a leak. While his mate fetches the tools, the carpenter has men bring up the extra timbers kept down in the stores. In a wooden world, the carpenter is often one of the most valuable hands on the ship. Highly skilled, his position can mean the difference between sailing and sinking.

Taking Lieutenant Dalton's advice to heart, you stay out of the way and simply observe. Woody replaces the badly damaged wood with custom-fit timbers, while his mate beats old rope known as "oakum" to fit an initial seal. By the by, Dalton comes by to inspect the scene himself.

"How goes it, Midshipman Ward?"

"Woody has it fully under control, sir."

"Indeed. If the other men knew their duties half as well as he, well, this ship could sail herself. Humbling, isn't it?"

"Aye, sir. I've got much to learn."

"That feeling never leaves, even as an acting commander. And it shouldn't, not in any officer worth their salt. Always strive to better yourself."

You simply nod, continuing to watch. Perhaps your scholar's habits will serve you well aboard a ship after all. If there's one thing you know how to do, it's how to better yourself.

"Seeing as how Woody has the situation under control, I suppose we'd best get to scrubbing," Dalton says. "Captain Longwick won't even recognize the *Hornblower* once he's back!"

The "we" the lieutenant refers to are, in fact, the common men. Not an officer's place to scrub the deck, even if that officer is only a candidate midshipman. But as you watch the seamen scour the decks, it's with a renewed sense of pride. Soon, the captain will return, and when he does…

- It's time to celebrate! Hard work pays off, and toasting with the men is that very payoff. Captain Longwick promised to open the stores for victory, and the day has arrived! Go to page 23
- Time to better myself! As an officer candidate, it's my duty to learn everything one can about the workings of the ship. I'll spend the night studying. Go to page 263

Inner Circle

The Red Kites native to Buckinghamshire may have circled in search of prey, but the birds on your island circle for a different reason. Once you make it to the interior of the island where they flit and fly, you see that they're taking turns diving down to skim off the water's surface for a drink—of fresh water! The birds only just barely touch the water, as if they're evading a predator. When you burst from the trees, they scatter in response.

Rushing forward, you find a clearing with a great pond, fed by a waterfall. The source must come from somewhere up the mountain, and though it's no gushing river, it is more than a trickling brook. This water will sustain you!

Drinking straight from the waterfall itself, you taste the purest water you've had since becoming a sailor. Possibly even the best water of your life. Untainted by civilization, purified by the rocks and the motion of the waterfall, this is pure mountain stream water.

Well done! This source of water was an important find, and you mark it on your mental map as you head out to further explore the island. You'll want to find a better place for a more permanent shelter than on the shoreline. After last night's storm, you know it's too exposed to the elements out there. You'll certainly want somewhere close to this water source, and with a good view of the shore so you can watch for approaching ships. Somewhere elevated, perhaps.

So you start hiking to explore your island. And with the clouds rolling in, you'll soon get to see how the rest of the topography fares in a tropical squall. You're out in the open, hiking on a ridgeline with a perfect view of the coast where you were abandoned, when a "Boom!" from the heavens blasts apart a long-dead tree only twenty yards ahead on the trail.

A great thunderclap accompanies the lightning only a moment later, and the hair starts to rise on your neck. What should you do?

- Dash back into a forested part of the jungle to find shelter under the trees! Go to page 298
- Retreat to the waterfall and leap into the pond. The safest place is to stay lower than ground-level! Go to page 247
- Immediately drop down, knees upon the trail and head bowed before the Almighty. Pray to be spared! Go to page 275
- Hurry to the exact spot where the bolt hit—lightning never strikes the same place twice! Go to page 72

Into the Crow's Nest

⚓

The offer to volunteer is one that's readily accepted, perhaps too eagerly. You're handed a musket and told to climb the mizzenmast. The sharpshooters assigned to the other two masts are not so keen to take on the duty, and you wonder if you might have offered yourself in haste.

"What're ya waitin' for?" Midshipman Magnus asks. "Grab Brown Bess and give me regards t'the gulls!"

It's a high climb to the top, but that's kind of the point. From up there, you'll have an unobstructed line of sight on the enemy crew when the fighting begins. With *Brown Bess* slung over your shoulder, you head to the top.

Once you arrive, you learn why the others didn't want this assignment. It's not the size of the mast that matters, it's the motion of the ocean beneath. You're on the tip of an inverted pendulum, in a sense. The rocking and swaying of the ship is amplified because of your distance from the source. A larboard dip of the hull a few feet into the sea turns into a dozen yards swaying through the sky from up here. It's enough to give even the most seasoned sailor seasickness. You do your best to keep your eyes to the horizon line, but seasickness arrives nonetheless.

The sun has nearly set by the time the enemy warship arrives. And she's a big one; a first-rate man-o'-war, much larger than the fifth-rate frigate you ride upon now. Your orders are to wait until the firing has begun, then pick and choose your targets as you please. As you await the inciting of hostilities, you look for the most favorable targets: the helmsman, cannon teams, and swivel-gun operators are all obvious choices, but perhaps you'll even spot the Spanish *Capitan* himself.

With a distant *crack,* the opening volley of musket fire has begun, so you ready your weapon. You've got a clear line of fire on the helmsman, and line up on the wheel to take aim. With a squeeze of the trigger, the musket snaps off a deafening report, but the swaying of the mast throws off your shot: it's a miss.

Time to reload and try again.

A gigantic stridency of explosions tells of cannon fire, but that comes from down below in the gun decks—there's little you can do to affect that from up here; which is exactly the point of keeping the gun crews below. As the enemy ship gets closer, you try for another shot. This time you let the swaying of the mast line up your shot for you—*crack!*—a direct hit to the helmsman, who staggers off, gripping his left shoulder.

Several enemy sailors point upwards, and suddenly you see a collection of muskets aimed your way. Taking cover on the opposite side of the mast, you reload your weapon once again while the rear of the mast sings out with hits from musket fire. Adrenaline courses through your veins, and you blindly return fire from behind cover, reload, and repeat.

Before long, day gives way to night; carefully chosen targets change to just aiming at lanterns or muzzle flashes. Once you've expended all of your ammunition, it's time to head back down. Stepping off the rigging after the climb, you find you're surrounded by darkness. So it gives you quite the start when you're practically assaulted by Lieutenant Dalton.

"Not a word, Landsman!" he hisses. Then, in an urgent whisper, he continues,

"Orders are: no lights, and complete silence. We've pulled ahead of the *Don Pedro Sangre*, but the enemy is giving relentless chase. God willing, we'll lose her under cover of darkness. Now get some rest, we'll be on watch soon."

You're about to offer the usual sharp, "Aye, sir!" but stop just in time, giving only a salute.

Dalton nods, leaving you be.

Well done! You've survived your first battle aboard the Hornblower *and gave as good as you got. Now get some rest, and when you're ready…*. Go to page 197

Jamaican Me Crazy

Billy swallows his pride, knowing full well that while four men stand behind him, another dozen now stand in opposition. Rediker doesn't seem to realize the precariousness of the situation, however, and so stands tall—emboldened by the new position of power.

"Saltboots, I'll need ya t'be me second-in-command. On a pirate vessel, there be no first nor second mates, only a quartermaster who speaks for the crew. You've spoken for us all by inciting the mutiny, and now by putting your trust in me. Will ye continue t'do so?"

You nod, accepting the new position, while Billy fumes.

Rediker continues, "We sail for Jamaica! There, we can offload this cargo t'men who know how t'make plundered goods disappear—"

"Jamaica!" Billy cries, unable to hold his tongue. "Ye can't claim a simple mistake or accident now, this be a capital offense—we'll all hang for this!"

This incites unrest in the crew, and Rediker puts up his hands to silence the group.

"What ye don't understand, Billy, is that the mistake was yours to begin with. Men like Bullock and yourself, masters and mates, bein' so harsh on sailors—that's the true capital offense. We resisted a brutal captain? That's mutiny, aye, and the punishment is t'be hanged. Then should we turn pirate? Well, we'd be hanged. And if I were t'kill ya now in cold blood? Hanged, of course. But I only have the one neck, ya see. Sentence me t'the gallows once and I become a free man until the day I die."

The ship starts to list, such as it is that no one is steering her. With the crew simply idling, there's real danger that the *Cooper's Pride* could turn against the wind, hit a bad patch of seas, and capsize.

"All hands! To stations! Back to work, or we lose the ship!" Rediker commands.

"Aye, cap'n!" comes the unified call, for the captain's best authority is the face of danger.

Rediker proves capable of navigating to Jamaica, which was nearer than continuing on to Boston. He even seems to form a grudging respect for Billy, so that the former Mate comes with the two of you to port to negotiate the trade deal.

All goes smoothly—until business is concluded and a Spanish platoon captures your crew. They knew right where the *Cooper's Pride* was moored: an otherwise secret and secluded cove. That is to say—they must have been tipped off.

"Only thing the Spanish hate more'n pirates is English pirates," Billy says, joining the ranks of the Spanish. "Didn't take much convincing t'sell the lot-o'-you into slavery."

As it turns out, life as a slave in the Spanish mines is worse than any condition a ship could hold. Though you try to escape, the rest of your life is brutish and short.

Gracias, Billy. *Hijo de puta*....

THE END

Joe

"How d'ye figure that, Saltboots? I were the one sent ya t'get the Cap'n. Do ye think I slit the man's throat, then went out to make celestial navigations while he bled out?" Joe says.

"Always were a bloody liar!" Chips cries in response to your accusation. "Lying again, Saltboots! Don't believe a word-o'-it, Cap'n."

"I know your secret, Joe! And I bet this crew of lusty pirates will be thrilled to hear it!" you say.

Joe's eyes grow wide, and the young Bosun flies into action. Pistol drawn and—*crack!*—shot fired before you can speak further. Some secrets are worth killing for, it seems, even if Joe wasn't the one to murder Captain Bullock.

You fall to the ground, choking on your own blood, unable to speak or breathe. At least you'll die quickly.

THE END

Judge Longwick Presiding

You're held in the brig overnight while the *Hornblower* weathers the storm, offered a decent meal for breakfast, then brought up on decks before an audience of your peers. Captain Longwick, Master and Commander of this ship, also serves as judge, jury, and executioner in times of war. If you had not only just yesterday embarked on a new voyage, you might be held in the brig until you could stand trial before the Admiralty High Courts. Alas, that's not to be.

Longwick wears his full uniform, hat pointed broadly, saber jangling at his side. The man listens as the evidence against you is presented. The witness testimony is understandably brief. After some time, he steps forward to make his remarks.

"Shipboard discipline is the tar that keeps the Royal Navy bound together. If we do not rule ourselves, these Spaniards will gladly take up that mantle for us. When one amongst us is murdered, the most heinous crime that can be committed, we must act swiftly and righteously. And so it is with the authority of my posting on this ship, an authority granted me by His Majesty the King and by the Lord God Almighty, that I sentence the accused—whom I find guilty—to be hanged by the neck until dead."

That's it. No appeal, no further investigation.

There's plenty of rope to tie you up with, and ample beams from which to hang you. The sentence will be carried out without delay. The only choice left is whether or not to look your cousin in the eye one last time, or to die looking out to sea.

What'll it be?

THE END

Jury's Out

"Give me a blessed moment t'collect me thoughts," Billy says.

He heads deeper into the Captain's cabin, searching for anything of possible significance. Watching as he goes, you note the same clues as Billy. He finds a wine goblet fallen to the floor, lifts it, sniffing the crystal. Dabs his fingers on the carpet beneath the glass, rubs them together.

"Dry," he says. "Must've spilt hours ago, but why not pick up the glass?"

Playing the detective, he continues on over to the Captain's desk, where he sets down the wine goblet. Everyone crowds the entrance to the Captain's cabin, trying to spy a bit of the investigation.

"Don't nothin' look missing. Man's sea chest is still locked tight. Wait! What's this, then? A page, torn out of the Cap'n's log! Today's entry. See if Saltboots has it tucked away!"

Chips searches you roughly, and Joe does the same with a lighter touch. They find nothing, which, of course, comes as no surprise to you.

"You see! It couldn't possibly have been me!"

"Unless ya ate the page!" Chips says.

"Hush now," Billy says, crossing the room and examining the murder weapon. "'Tis the Captain's own knife."

He stands and steps back out to the quarterdeck, the crew moving with him. His face frowns with concern, and he tugs at his muttonchops as he ponders the crime. After an excruciatingly long silence, he finally speaks.

"I want to believe ya, Saltboots, but there weren't no one else here. Ya said so yourself, the man were alive when ye found him. I seen enough men bleed out t'know, ya ain't got long with a wound like that one. Few seconds at most."

> Deny the murder, of course. You didn't do it! Beg him to be merciful long enough for you to prove your innocence. The truth will set you free.
> Go to page 119

> They wish to paint you as a villain? So be it! Claim you killed Captain Bullock, and that any who trifle with you will be next. Their fear will keep you safe.
> Go to page 194

Keelhauling

Despite the commotion aboard the ship, you're able to fit a rope around your waist tied tightly with a generic knot. The able seamen scrambling across the decks and climbing about the rigging could probably offer dozens of different knots for the task, but they're a bit tied up with tasks of their own.

You heroically leap into the surging seas and swim out towards the missing Jack. The heavy hemp braids of the rope are water-logged and sodden, slowing your progress. In the darkness, you use the lightning flashes to try to locate the poor man, but there's no sign of him. Still, you swim in vain, hoping he might find either you or your rope. You swim until your arms burn, and then—you swim some more.

Exhausted, you take a minute to catch your breath. Looking back towards the *Cooper's Pride*, you see the ship lurching ever closer. On deck, it was near-impossible to see which direction she was being buffeted across the seas, but it's clear now—she's coming right for you!

You cry out for help, hoping Billy or someone will pull the rope up for you, but to no avail. They're trying to save the ship, not just you. The *Cooper's Pride* is right upon you now, and you duck down beneath the waves in an effort not to be battered by her keel. Your only chance is to swim the width of the ship and come up on the other side of it.

Sweeping the water aside with renewed frenzy, you stroke your way through the cold ocean. You've made it to the midpoint when you feel sudden resistance; the rope pulls taut. That's as far as you can go! A realization that fills you with panic. You're trapped under the ship, pulled up against the keel by the rope, barnacles and other marine growths now tearing at your flesh.

The rope! You scramble to untie it, but the hemp has expanded in the water and you cannot possibly pull yourself free. If you'd have known how to tie a better knot, you might have slipped free and avoided this scenario, but truly, your first mistake was leaping into stormy seas in the first place.

THE END

Keep Calm

⚓

Orders are bandied about in organized chaos; disparate parts brought together like an orchestral performance composed of a cacophony of shouts, bosun whistles, and sing-song chants or sea shanties. Chiefly among these orders is to "Let out reefs!"—with the nearest available sailors assigned to the task at hand.

Mr. Magnus spots you and cries, "Landsman, the foresail!"

Quickly, you help the other sailors adjust the lines to the foresail, letting out the canvas to full capacity. The sails were brought in—*reefed*—for cruising speed, but now you're full speed ahead and need all the wind you can muster.

Your hands move deftly and competently. It feels good to be carrying your own weight in chorus with the other men, and the work keeps you singularly focused—which is also good, considering that this is an effort to forestall the approach of a much larger warship.

Once this task is completed, the Midshipman cries, "Stuns'ls!"

In response to this order, you climb the rigging up to the yardarm to release the studding sail. This extra canvas billows over the sides of the ship, adding much needed surface area to help harness as much wind as is possible. For a few vertiginous moments, you hang out over nothing but the sea, but you complete the job competently and return to the deck.

"Aye, well done, Landsman! You'll be a canvas monkey yet! Now get some tack in your gullet, 'tis set to be a long night indeed," Magnus orders.

"Aye, sir!" you reply, before heading below for some chow.

The ship is abuzz with speculation pertaining to the Spanish warship now chasing your own frigate. Many of the men are keen to fight, even against a superior force. A frigate is more maneuverable than the larger man-o'-war, and Captain Longwick seems like a tactician who could use that to his advantage. The anticipation is the worst part—these sailors want to see what both he and the *Hornblower* can do!

The scuttlebutt is that the armory is to be unlocked, muskets issued, and stations taken. Each of the cannons is to be made ready for a possible fight. The excitement's getting to you too. Maybe it's time to get in on the action?

- Request a position on one of the gun teams. You've been training for this! Go to page 316
- Offer your keen eye as one of the snipers. Alone, aloft, and alienated from the cannon shot. Go to page 158

Kept Private

You know Rediker as an instigator, a troublemaker. The whole crew knew this. He would be the obvious choice, of course, but did he personally hold a grudge against Captain Bullock? Thinking back to the early days of the voyage, there might have been a clue right away.

Rediker had served as a privateer on board a ship called, fittingly enough, the *Doomsday*. Officially commissioned by the Crown to hunt down Spanish ships. Like being a pirate, but legal.

Rediker himself hadn't advertised this fact, but it bubbled to the surface soon enough. A man on a privateer gets treated far better than one crimped into a merchantman's service. Like pirates, privateers work on a "no prey, no pay" share system, so there's more of a sense of equality amongst the ranks.

Captain Bullock had made sure Rediker knew he no longer lived in that world. He received a tongue lashing as soon as the master learned of Rediker's history, as if that were enough to condemn the man. But, perhaps his desire to repeat that history was?

The captain offered constant verbal barbs. "You're not a privateer anymore, you're mine now!" was a common refrain. It was like he hoped to get a rise out of Rediker. It was really a dare. Bullock wanted the man to act out, to give him an excuse to really discipline him.

But Rediker never gave him the satisfaction. This, of course, infuriated the captain all the more, but there was nothing he could do about it.

Had Bullock finally discovered something to use against Rediker? Could that be what he recorded in his captain's log? Or did he simply push Rediker past his breaking point by constantly reminding him that the world of fair wages and equal treatment was only in his past? If it ate away at Rediker enough, he could have determined to mutiny and bring back egalitarian rule through piracy. He could have convinced someone on that ship to murder the captain.

Regardless, one thing was true: Rediker may have been plotting against Bullock, but he was below-decks when the gruesome deed was done. So whose hand might have been on the knife?

> - Marlowe—the old sailor was the third pea in their pod. But why? What ills did he bear Captain Bullock? Go to page 281
> - It could certainly have been Barlow. What motive might have the mustachioed sailor held? Go to page 181
> - That's enough for one night. Time to get some sleep. You'll need your energy for tomorrow. Go to page 86

Knot so Fast!

⚓

Ducking back, you're sheltered by the rail, the mast, and the ship's wheel itself. It's much harder for the enemy to get a shot on you while you're cowering from sight, but you've also just disobeyed a direct order. And, what's worse, with no one steering, you'll soon lose all headway. If you stay here, the *Hornblower* is certain to be overtaken by the Spanish warship.

You may be down, but you're not out. You're not giving up, you're just not offering yourself up as an easy target. *Think, damn you!* If only there were a way to steer the ship without putting yourself out in the open. Looking around, a burst of inspiration brings a plan to mind.

A coil of extra rope, waiting to resupply the rigging in time of need, should serve nicely. Grabbing the rope and quickly fashioning a Perfection Loop, you create a handle of sorts—an open loop knotted at the end. At mid-length in the rope, you create a second loop. Yes, that will do!

Darting forward, you loop the end over a handle at the 10-o'clock position of the wheel, and the second loop over the 2-o'clock position. A *crack!* sounds out as the sharpshooters fire, but you slide back just in time. The shot hits the wheel rather than you, and you're able to keep the ship on-course by tugging on the ropes from a covered position. It's not as good as standing at the wheel, but it's much better than abandoning the helm altogether.

"Shots fired!" one of the seamen shouts, finally recognizing the incoming fire.

"Return fire!" Captain Longwick commands.

Much louder exchanges of rifle fire erupt from behind as the sailors attack those in the Spanish crow's nest.

"Rear battery, fire!" the Commander issues.

Looking back, you see the sharpshooters shrink away under your shipmates' counterattack, so you stand back at the wheel to make the necessary course corrections. Keeping a wary eye up over your shoulder, ready to duck back at a moment's notice and use the jury-rigged rope steerage, you keep the ship at the proper heading.

Captain Longwick comes by, sees your setup and glares at you with narrowed eyes before uttering, "Clever…" and continuing on. Somehow, that didn't seem a compliment, but you make peace with the idea and continue to steer under less-than-mortal danger.

Eventually, the sky grows dark, and the firing from the ships goes quiet. You're relieved from your post, replaced by a new set of hands, and sent down to get some sleep.

Not much choice here:

Well done! You've survived your first battle at sea. But the Hornblower *isn't clear just yet. Get some much needed rest, and when you're ready….* Go to page 29

Knowledge is Power

The harbormaster accepts your bribe and smiles broadly through rotten and missing teeth. "Ye seeks an easy catch, eh? I can do ya one better! There be a Spanish warship spotted in these waters, just past Cuba, said t'hail from Maracaibo. A pirate hunter called the *Elige tu Veneno*. Do yourself a favor and set course for Bermuda and stay on the leeward side-o'-the islands t'steer clear. Find your prey there, where she'll be unprotected."

Thanking the harbormaster, you make sail. Though his advice proves sound enough to keep you free of the pirate hunters, you don't find the whereabouts of any merchant ships, either. Likely, they're sticking close to the very protection that you seek to avoid.

"Cap'n, shipworm done set in. We've gone overdue for a careen," Chips the carpenter reports a week later.

Rediker agrees that this is as good a time as any, so you order the ship to find an island to careen upon. Wooden ships naturally rot over time, a condition that's exacerbated in warm Caribbean waters. To combat this, it's common for ships avoiding port authorities to beach themselves on an island where the hull can be scrubbed and repaired. Once finished, she'll be as fast as she's ever been.

A suitable island will provide a refill of your fresh water stores and perhaps even fresh meat from local goats or pigs. What's more, you can finally have the name "Cooper's Pride" removed from the ship and "Deleon's Revenge" painted in its place.

A suitable island is indeed found shortly, and upon seeing its shores, you can't help but feel a pang of familiarity, Déjà vu, like you've been here before in another life. The shores are made of soft sand, a thick tree-line abutting right up against the surf. It's hard to grasp the scale of the island from atop your ship, but the center appears to rise into a hillock or small mountain.

Shaking off the odd feeling, you order the crew to make landfall and refit the *Deleon's Revenge*.

Another week passes, and you find yourself back in familiar waters in search of prey. It's not long until you hear the call of "Sails!" and emerge to the quarterdeck to get a better look.

"Raise the black!" Rediker cries.

"Belay that order. Let's get a good look at her first," you say.

"Aye, Cap'n. What colors should we fly? English?"

You nod, then take the looking glass for yourself. The bloom of canvas and wood is only slight on the horizon, but they make from open seas towards the coastline you now sail along. She's a large vessel; of that there can be no doubt. The Spanish warship? If so, you're no safer flying the English flag than you would be flying the black. Whoever it is, they've spotted you—for they sail on a direct approach.

At length, you make her out. She's a warship, all right, but one of His Majesty's Royal Navy. If they think you a simple merchant vessel, their intercept course is certainly odd. If they know you to be a pirate—perhaps even after word of your escape from Boston—that would explain her trajectory.

"An English frigate," Rediker confirms after you show him the looking glass.

"Ship-o'-that size has at least three times our guns," Marlowe adds. You can be sure his calculation includes those guns you've added in these last few weeks.

"I ain't made for a prison," Barlow says.

"Me neither, mate. Comes to that—we'll take them down with us," Rediker says.

The crew look to you for orders.

➢ "Helmsman, run us along the coast. Big warships aren't made for the shallows. If they want to chase us, they'll have to risk running aground." Go to page 125

➢ "Steady. Half the crew into the hold. Get blankets and cover the remaining crew. We'll see if they'd like to board a ship quarantined for plague." Go to page 258

Laid to Rest

"You're right, Rediker," you say. "Your man Barlow, too. I couldn't agree more."

Rediker stares back dumbly, blinking with disbelief. "Well... good. That settles it, then?"

"Not quite. You're right about ignoring those in London. The English plunder the Indies for spices and tea. The Dutch take from the dark continent, looting the very Africans themselves," you say, to pointed looks from the former slaves now on your ship. "The Spanish ravage the natives of the Americas, filling their ships with treasure. The French do the same, pillaging the New World for delicacies. And we? Well, I say we take from them all!"

Many of the crew nod and mumble assent, but you're just getting started.

"Barlow, you're certainly right about my experience. Rediker undoubtedly knows more than I do about running a ship. But tell me truly, Rediker, how were these new men recruited? Did you tell them that you were an excellent bookkeeper, with fair and just pirate articles? Or did you entice them with tales of the mutineer who slit a terrible captain's throat from ear-to-ear, leaving the tyrant with a beard of blood?"

You pause briefly, allowing Rediker a sheepish, "Well..." before you continue.

"Few knew Edward Teach, but who among you hasn't heard of Blackbeard? They're one and the same! But it's the legend itself that instills fear in the hearts of seamen. When facing a larger-than-life persona, merchantmen will gladly give up their stores rather than confront a living devil.

"So go on, then. Put it to a vote. Should we sail under Jack Rediker and know that our hard-fought plunder will be distributed fairly by equitable articles? Or will you follow a captain who strikes fear in the very soul of my enemies to become a scourge of the seas yourselves—pirates renowned for hunting Spanish men by day... and French women by night?"

This last bit you leave with a grin, which gets lusty chuckles from the men. Now that you've got them, you finish with, "I say we take from them all, or offer a blood-beard in return!"

A slow chant starts by one of Rediker's African recruits, quickly picked up by the rest of the crew: "Blood-beard... Blood-beard... Blood-beard!"

It's unanimous. More than that, it's a new identity.

"Don't misunderstand. I value you, Rediker, and your knowledge. Come! Help me draw up Captain Bloodbeard's articles for the *Deleon's Revenge!*"

You pump a fist in the air and get a mirrored "Hurrah!" from many in the crew. At length, the crew's cheering dies down; the bosun pipes them back to work. Rediker joins you in the cabin.

"At least we have a clever Cap'n," he concedes.

"Rediker, you must swear not to try something like this again. Rather, let us work together, grow rich together, then we can part ways as allies and friends."

The man sighs, then nods. He spits in his hand and puts it out for a shake. "Make me your quartermaster, Cap'n Bloodbeard, and I swear t'serve both ye and the ship as best I can."

After shaking on the accord, you set up the articles that will govern your future lives as pirates. In the process, you share brandy and chat into the late hours of the night.

The next morning, you're awoken to shouts of, "Sails!" A rush of excitement brings you out to the quarterdeck to see for yourself. Spotting the bloom of white on the horizon, you reach out for the spyglass to get a better look. She's a merchant ship! What luck!

"*Dos Santos*," you read the painted name on the stern. "Spanish?"

"Portuguese, from the make," Marlowe replies.

"Helmsman, plot a course to intercept. Quartermaster, ready the men for action. Our first catch of the day."

Rediker takes up his role as Quartermaster, commanding the pirates to prepare for boarding. Robin readies gun teams, and soon, every hand is up on deck, itching for action. Barlow arrives with two bolts of cloth, one red and one black.

"Flags, Cap'n," he says. "I only just finished the Jolly Roger. Should we fly the black?"

"Red means no quarter given. Black says we'll play nice if they surrender," Rediker explains. "Seen men jump ship at the sight-o'-red, which can be useful. But we can always recruit more crew from the black. That'd be my recommendation, Cap'n."

Your orders?

> Fly the English flag! Let's wait until we're right up next to her before showing our true colors. Go to page 13

> Fly the red! The dread pirate Bloodbeard leaves no survivors! Go to page 199

> Fly the black! All we truly want is the loot and plunder. Go to page 283

Landslide

From this position, you get to watch the floor of the well become steadily further away with each step you make up the sides. It's a strange balancing act as you awkwardly scale the walls, but you do make progress. One hand, one foot. Other hand, other foot. Inches at a time.

Then you lift one foot to slide it upwards just as the grit beneath your opposite foot gives way. That foot slides out from beneath you faster than you're able to reposition it, and, with nothing to hold onto, you fall back down to the base of the well. The floor of this natural well is a soup of mire after the recent storms, and you splash back into the muck, breath knocked out of you all over again.

Okay, let's try this once more:

- Try to dig your way out. By pulling down the earthen walls, you can make a ramp and climb to safety. Go to page 64
- Leaning back. With your shoulders and hands pressed on the wall and feet out in front, walking. Go to page 108
- Like a starfish. With your arms and legs spread on opposite walls, you can totter your way up. Go to page 92

Last Will

A bottle of wine is opened, but only those deemed in charge—that is, yourself and Rediker—are offered a glass. Hierarchy and propriety must always be honored, it seems, even when punishing a pirate crew. As the Captain, you're allowed to go first.

"I repent of nothing," you say, raising the glass in a toast. When you drink the wine, the notion of *honey-sweet wine* and Homer comes to mind, so it is Homer's words that flow from your lips. "There is no creature on earth feebler than that of man, for he thinks that he will never suffer evil… there is a time for words, and a time for sleep."

Then you down the rest of the wine.

Rediker raises his glass in a toast, saying, "I have but one regret, and 'tis not starting The Life sooner. If ye want a lesson from me, I'd pray it thus: that masters-o'-vessels not use their men so severely, as many do, which exposes men t'great temptations."

With that, a rope is strung about your neck, prayers uttered, and the platform falls out beneath your feet to leave you swaying in the breeze.

THE END

Letter of the Law

"Aye, legal it may be!" Chips says, ire getting the best of him. "So be it the hangman's never tried for murder, neither."

"Some dogs'll lick the master's hand no matter how many times he beats 'em," Rediker snarls back.

"Oh, you bastard. Think a Letter-o'-Marque made ye a big, tough man, did it? Not so tough no more, is ya?"

"Gentlemen, please!" you try, but the nearest sailor puts his hand on your shoulder to keep you out of the dispute.

"Sometimes the law recognizes the value of a man. Other times, well, men resort to natural laws," Rediker proselytizes.

"Only law out here be Cap'n Bullock, and 'tis that man's nature ye should concern yourself with!"

"Go on, then, toadie up t'your master and report me mutinous talk!"

Chips slowly shakes his head. "I'll not make it so easy for ya. Want a flogging? Earn it yourself! Until then, this here be the first starboard watch, and I'll only concern meself so much as ya perform your duties. Even King George don't own the thoughts in a man's head, so long as that be where they remain."

The tension finally seems to be subsiding. Rediker gives the slightest nod. "Of that, Chips, we are of one mind. What duties would ye have me perform?"

Chips' face sports a wicked grin. "Decks need scouring. Me professional opinion, that is. Grab some holy-stone and get to scrubbing. Saltboots, think ye better join Rediker in his task."

Scrubbing the decks leaves your hands raw and bloody. Rediker attacks the task ferociously, taking out his frustrations upon the *Cooper's Pride*. Doesn't seem like he has any more to say on the matter, and he keeps his distance. Still, this isn't a simple punishment but a necessary task; after four hours, the deck is smooth and unblemished by splinters or signs of rot. A healthy ship is a happy ship.

Eight bells sound, signaling that your watch is over.

Chips arrives, appraising your work. "That'll serve. Eight more bells, then we fill our bellies and take our next watch. Get some time in the hammock while ye can."

The afternoon was more draining than you expected—both mentally and physically—so time in the hammock could be exactly what you need.

"Up! All hands! Up, or we all perish!" the cry comes, shaking you from your slumber.

How long were you asleep? It's impossible to tell, and in the commotion, it doesn't much matter. Now that you're on your feet, you feel the violent rocking of the ship that the hammock had countered. You rush up with the crew, ready to lend a hand to prevent the threat of death.

Thoughts of seasickness are replaced by sheer terror when you reach the open air. Lightning arcs across the sky with the dreadful crack of thunder only an instant behind. The sea rollicks like an open flame and foams upon the deck—beating her with great waves, threatening to pull all asunder.

One such wave nearly knocks the ship on her side, and a man who was up in the rigging of the mainsail is thrown into the sea. You recognize him as the third crimped sailor, the one in a white-and-blue striped shirt.

"Man overboard! Jack's gone in!" the sailor Marlowe cries.

Billy throws a rope, but when it hits the water, it disappears into the inky sea, and now he watches with a sort of helpless indifference as the sailor struggles for his life. It's clear the man has no idea how to swim and will soon drown.

➤ No time! Dive in and help crimped Jack back to the ship. Go to page 101

➤ Tie a length of rope around your waist and leap in! Go to page 164

➤ Say a prayer for the poor seaman; nothing else you can do. Go to page 196

Let Them Eat Cake!

You scoop up the spotted dick from its tin, custard dripping from the base, and shovel it into your mouth. Salivating at the prospect of the treat, your tongue is greeted by the fatty goodness of a pudding so rich, it melts in your mouth. Only the dried fruits give a need to chew. There's a metallic tinny aftertaste, but you pay that no mind. It was stored in a tin, so that seems only natural.

Spotted Dick watches as you devour his eponymous treat, smiling and pantomiming for you to eat more. "Good, innit? Don't be shy, polish'er off. There ya go. Best ya ever had!"

It is quite good, insofar as spotted dick goes, and the sugary fat goes straight to your head. The rush leaves you lightheaded, tongue tingling and lips numb. When your fingers start going numb too, you start to panic.

"Oh, don't worry, that's just me secret ingredient!" Dick croons with laughter. "The *ether* helps keep ya docile as a newborn calf that's found mummy's teat for the first time! And while ya suckle away blissfully in dreamland, that's when I pen ya up inside a ship and collect me shepherdin' fee."

Your legs go like jelly, only serving to cement his metaphor that you are not much more than a veal cutlet waiting to be processed.

Vision blurring from an overdose of ether, you lose consciousness.

Wake up, little sea cow, maybe you'll find greener pastures atop the emerald waves?
<u>Go to page 93</u>

Letting it Slide

Both men look to you, bringing their glares with them.

"Well, Saltboots. Allow me to educate ya," Rediker says. "Ship's watch be how the common Tar earns his pay and spends his day; it's grueling, backbreaking work. This way ye find yourself hungry enough t'eat the rotten, meager rations and tired enough t'sleep on schedule in a kennel that wouldn't be fit for dogs."

"Aye, so it be, but 'tis our lot, and best that we not waste any more-o'-Cap'n Bullock's time with idle chat," Chips adds.

"And what would ye have us waste it on?"

Chips' face sports a wicked grin. "Decks need scouring. Me professional opinion, that is. Grab some holy-stone and get to scrubbing. Saltboots, think ye better join Rediker in his task."

Scrubbing the decks leaves your hands raw and bloody. Rediker attacks the task ferociously, taking out his frustrations upon the *Cooper's Pride*. Doesn't seem like he has any more to say on the matter, and he keeps his distance. Still, this isn't a simple punishment but a necessary task; after four hours, the deck is smooth and unblemished by splinters or signs of rot. A healthy ship is a happy ship.

Eight bells sound, signaling that your watch is over.

Chips arrives, appraising your work. "That'll serve. Eight more bells, then we fill our bellies and take our next watch. Get some time in the hammock while ye can."

The afternoon was more draining than you expected—both mentally and physically—so time in the hammock could be exactly what you need.

"Up! All hands! Up, or we all perish!" the cry comes, shaking you from your slumber.

How long were you asleep? It's impossible to tell, and in the commotion, it doesn't much matter. Now that you're on your feet, you feel the violent rocking of the ship that the hammock had countered. You rush up with the crew, ready to lend a hand to prevent the threat of death.

Thoughts of seasickness are replaced by sheer terror when you reach the open air. Lightning arcs across the sky with the dreadful crack of thunder only an instant behind. The sea rollicks like an open flame and foams upon the deck—beating her with great waves, threatening to pull all asunder.

One such wave nearly knocks the ship on her side, and a man who was up in the rigging of the mainsail is thrown into the sea. You recognize him as the third crimped sailor, the one in a white-and-blue striped shirt.

"Man overboard! Jack's gone in!" the sailor Marlowe cries.

Billy throws a rope, but when it hits the water, it disappears into the inky sea, and now he watches with a sort of helpless indifference as the sailor struggles for his life. It's clear the man has no idea how to swim and will soon drown.

➢ Say a prayer for the poor seaman; nothing else you can do. Go to page 196

➢ Tie a length of rope around your waist and leap in! Go to page 164

➢ No time! Dive in and help crimped Jack back to the ship. Go to page 101

Life Sentence

You slowly release the hammer on the pistol so it's no longer cocked, then lower the weapon and stow it in your waistband once more. Billy's shoulders sink with relief and he steps forward.

"Go on then, Billy. I have business at port, so we'll amicably part ways."

"I knew ye were a good sort, I did."

"But… you could've just asked, you know. Might be I would've even left you with a pension to live out your days here in the colonies."

He tugs at his muttonchops thoughtfully, then says, "Come now, Saltboots. The pirate's life ain't for 'ole Billy, but I'm a sea dog until the day the good Lord sees fit to take away me fitness for seafaring, and ya can lay down t'that. I aim t'find me a good, honest ship and earn me place aboard. Come with me! Vouch for ya, I would. Maybe ya got in over your head? How's about a second chance, eh?"

➢ Take him up on his offer. He's right. You *are* in over your head. It's never too late for a fresh start! Go to page 81

➢ Refuse. You've got a ship of your own. Why volunteer to lick the boot of some new tyrant? Go to page 270

Listless

You stand, shocked and waiting to see what can be done for the man. Billy arrives on the scene, but it's too much weight for one man to lift. Captain Bullock turns to Butch, asking, "Could he still work? Can you save his foot?"

"Best I could do is cut it off," the surgeon says with a shrug.

The crimped sailor hears this reply and a new batch of wailing erupts.

"You want to keep your broken foot, then take it with you—get off my ship!" Captain Bullock cries. "If this was an accident, I'll not have a man so incompetent in my employ. If this was malicious, to shirk your duty, I'll not clear your debt due to injury, oh no! Breaking your body so as not to break your word, eh? What a fiend. Mr. Greaves, get this coward off my ship and file a claim against him for damaging our cargo. Bosun! Get us underway as soon as he's gone, before any of the others try the same."

With that, Captain Bullock turns his back on the man and signals for Butch to return with him to his cabin. Billy waves you forward, and now you help lift the great load. You only need a few inches before the poor sailor pulls the remainder of his wrecked leg from under the remainder of the wreckage. Following the mate's lead, you help the man up and off the ship.

A shrill whistle sounds and the other sailors rush to muster above decks. At your hesitation, Billy says, "C'mon, Saltboots! That there's the Bosun's call!"

Not much choice here:

Head on back to see what the call means. Go to page 121

Loose Lips

"Ye won't find many in Boston friendly t'deserters," one of the sailors warns.

Rediker shrugs. "'Tis already a prison sentence we face, innit? Worse yet, this here be a jail ye can drown in."

"Oh, they don't aim t'lock ye up. The pride-o'-Boston is her gallows." This silences the man's impunity, for a moment. The sailor continues, "Just be careful when he's in a state. If the Cap'n ain't happy, ain't nobody happy!"

"Surely, if he were that bad, ye wouldn't agree to another voyage with him as master," Barlow, the crimped, mustachioed seaman chimes in.

The first man shakes his head. "I've sailed under worse tyrants. Truth is, we thought it best t'sign up fast and avoid the press. No offense."

"None taken," Barlow and Rediker say in unison.

"Cap'n Bullock's a right wanker, no denyin' it. But he mostly keeps to himself and Billy runs the ship day-to-day, thanks be t'God."

They hush themselves at the sound of approaching footsteps, but it's only the second pair of crimped men arriving, and the idle talk continues unabated.

"I'm Marlowe," the experienced seaman says at length.

You make a mental note not to confuse Marlowe with Barlow as the rest of the men introduce themselves, ten more common tars in total. Then you do the same, adding, "Admittedly, this is my first time aboard a ship. My cousin James sailed into port with the *Cooper's Pride*, though you might know him as Jimmy Saltboots."

A broad grin stretches over Marlowe's face. "Jimmy were our good-luck charm! Why, as long as ye wasn't mates with Jimmy, nothin' bad could happen t'ya. Glad t'have another Saltboots aboard, but keep your distance."

So he's saying… Jimmy was good luck so long as you weren't his friend? That doesn't bode well for your companionship over the course of these next few months! Your mind scrambles for a way to say that you're not your cousin, and that his luck has nothing to do with your own.

"Red's got the luck-o'-the Devil himself!" Barlow says, interrupting your thoughts. "Already escaped the hangman once, what with a letter-o'-marque."

"You were a pirate?" the words escape your lips.

"*Privateer.*" Rediker's eyes narrow, and he shoots a glare at Barlow. "Aye, we hunted the seas of the Spanish main. But the letter's expired, so return to London we must and here ye find us now."

The other seamen look at Rediker in a new light, but before anyone can speak further, they hush at the sound of footsteps. This time it's Billy, the mate.

"Ho, there, Saltboots! Cap'n Bullock wants a word. Get a move on! The rest of ye, look lively, we still got cargo t'be loaded before we can set sail! C'mon now!"

Not much choice here:

Best not keep Captain Bullock waiting… Go to page 105

Love Story

Barlow was one of the sailors crimped into service at the same time you joined up with the *Cooper's Pride*. He'd arrived with Rediker, and was by the other man's side day and night, following him like a lost puppy. The mustachioed man never struck you as particularly bright; not the kind who could orchestrate a murder where he would vanish from sight. But what he lacked in intellectual prowess he made up for in loyalty. But is pure loyalty reason enough to kill?

This reminds you of a time, the day before the murder, in fact, when you came into contact with another ship that had departed from London bearing letters. It's common, as you learned, for ships to carry mail for those with whom they might cross paths.

Rising Phoenix—that was the name of the ship. It sticks out in your memories because you yourself received a letter from home. The *Phoenix* had caught a favorable wind to catch the *Pride*, though that was the only favorable aspect of the encounter.

The letter from home informed you that Cousin James had been pressed into the service of His Majesty's Royal Navy. Right now, even, James likely sails for King and Country in the war against the Spanish.

As much as your own family was angered, hurt, or even in shocked disbelief of your going to sea, Aunt Margaret was a tempest at your failure to bring your cousin home. She had arranged a marriage for James; a favorable pairing with the daughter of a magistrate that Maggie claims to have spent all of her social currency in arranging. But without him back in Buckinghamshire, the match was surely to fall through, and Aunt Margaret to spend the rest of her days in squalor.

"You're a buggerer!" Captain Bullock had cried, lowering his own letter.

Barlow stiffened at the accusation, but did not meet the master's gaze.

"I'll have no abnormals in my crew. Look at me, man! Your captain is speaking, Barlow!" Bullock had continued, circling around to chastise Barlow. "What I hold here, is nothing more than a dire warning against your queer tendencies!"

"Cap'n, I dunno whatcha heard—" Barlow had started.

"Heard? What I've read—in plain black-and-white, inked by a captain whose word I trust—is that you and that damnable Rediker were caught sharing a bunk. By multiple witnesses!"

Barlow gaped, but was unable to respond. As for Rediker, the man was down in the fo'c'sle at the time, getting his rest between watches.

"It ain't true," Barlow managed at length. But you could see it on the man's face, the plain truth of the accusations. He and Rediker had been more than just friends, it seems. Perhaps still were.

"I don't want to hear you deny it, Barlow. Your sins may burn you in hell yet, but while you still walk this earth, you are mine to command by rights. What I want to hear is your solemn oath that there'll be no buggery aboard my ship! Swear it, you bastard!"

"Aye, Cap'n. I swear it," Barlow said, tears in his eyes.

The captain's own eyes narrowed, lingering to look over Barlow and see if the man were sincere. He must've thought he'd sufficiently frightened the seaman, for

Bullock left the encounter at that and stormed away.

The crew who'd witnessed the outburst had looked away; pretended not to hear, and let the issue drop. As for yourself, it seemed at the time that unless unfounded—the truth of it—was that Barlow truly did love Rediker.

You'd heard of the proclivities men would engage in when far from shore, so paid it no mind. But now, in light of the Captain's death... was it reason enough to kill? If Bullock had further discovered the men in a moment of passion, he could have threatened punishment or legal actions in Boston. Men had been hanged for less.

Barlow would have certainly had a motive; that much is clear from your reminiscing. The page missing from Bullock's log could likely implicate Barlow and his affections. But did he have opportunity to commit the crime?

Thinking back again to the conspiracy of men in the moonlight, that fateful final watch before you'd discovered Captain Bullock in the final moments of his life. One of the three figures, upon further reflection, had moved in a peculiarly familiar way.

He moved like he was following a companion he'd do anything for. Like he was following the man he loved. Barlow had gone down into the hold before you discovered the murder, there can be no doubt. So if he had acted against Captain Bullock—his was not the hand that held the knife.

Who else might have hated the master and commander of the *Cooper's Pride* enough to kill?

- Rediker himself, obviously. Think back to what you know... could his have been the hand on the knife? Go to page 166
- Marlowe—the old sailor was the third pea in their pod. But why? What ills did he bear Captain Bullock? Go to page 281
- That's enough for one night. Time to get some sleep. You'll need your energy for tomorrow. Go to page 86

Lucky

As the roll of the dice would have it, you win! You're still getting the hang of the game, and yet, Monks slides a heap of coin over to your side of the table, muttering, "The Lord giveth…"

"And this be how we choose to spendeth," Argyle agrees, noting the scores in his ledger.

"Can one not boil down all of life to a fifty/fifty split? Everything that can be can also *not* be. Riches, poverty. Love, hate. Life, death. The fates toss dice, and always play double-or-nothing at sea," Wycombe notes, eyes fluttering from his opium high.

Something sticks with Monks and he cries, "That's right. Gotta give us a chance to win our money back—double'r nothin'!"

If you want to say no, enough excitement for one night:

➢ Collect your winnings and return to the bar to wait for Cousin James. Go to page 233

Or let it ride! The winning choice has been randomized, and the outcome of these choices may or not be the same. Play the dice/coin game again, or simply pick your luck of the draw:

➢ Heads on the coin toss, or a one, two, or three shown on the die. Go to page 308

➢ Tails on the coin toss, or a four, five, or six shown on the die. Go to page 66

Marlowe

"Have ye gone mad? Or were ye just always daft?" Marlowe says in response to your accusation.

"He was with me in the hold, planning a mutiny, when the deed were done," Rediker says.

"Ah-ha! I've just got you to admit to mutiny!" you say, pointing a finger back at him.

"I think too many meals of coconuts have gone and made ye just plain nuts, Saltboots," Rediker says, tapping his own head for emphasis. "Of course I admit the mutiny! I'm captain-o'-a pirate crew!"

Then they all laugh.

And laugh, and laugh, and laugh.

And then they kill you.

THE END

Master-of-Arms

⚓

Tendrils of smoke curl about the barrel of the Master-of-Arms' flintlock pistol. Somewhere in the back of your mind the enormous *Crack!* of the gunpowder shot registers. Your chest tightens. Breathing becomes difficult, and then you taste copper as you try to inhale through a lung that's flooding with blood.

You've been shot!

The Master-of-Arms smirks with satisfaction and brings his pistol back into resting position; elbow cocked and flintlock pointed skyward. What did you expect? His name is the "Master-of-Arms," after all, and now he's just proved it by serving up a fatal gunshot wound.

THE END

Master of Fates, Captain of Souls

The captain puffs up and paces before the crimped men and yourself, deliberately tapping his cane before each step, despite no limp to compensate for. The ruffles of his garb, as well as his own strutting, make him look somewhat like a rooster inspecting a henhouse.

The cock of the walk, as they say.

"If I'm to be favored by fortune," he starts, "And the lot of you are to do your work as assigned, without giving me any vile troubles, this will be our only interaction for the duration of the voyage. You are by all rights mine to command, but the law sees fit that you'll be fed, clothed, sheltered, and even paid for the privilege."

Captain Bullock has the look of a man who's the Admiral of his own imaginations. Putting on the airs of a military man, despite his uniform of civilian finery. Perhaps he truly was once a Naval Officer, passed over for promotion, only to take the fast-track to command via hiring on as the master of a merchant vessel. Or, perhaps he knew himself better than to seek a commission in the first place, harboring a secret shame of cowardice, and now plays at military commander here on the *Cooper's Pride*.

"But there's another law aboard this ship—and that is my word. You must act, without hesitation, at any order given. Failing to do so puts this craft in mortal jeopardy, and it is mine own duty to put down a wretched dog endangering the lives of a score of others."

He pauses, staring the group down for emphasis.

"Excellent. I do believe we are in accord. Now step forward, state your name, swear to follow my orders, and return to Mr. Greaves for assignment," Captain Bullock concludes.

The first man rises forward. He has a red skullcap, like the blue cousin James wore, a pierced eyebrow, and fire in his eyes. A troublemaker, to be sure. Yet it is with poised solemnity that he says, "Rediker, sir. You have my oath."

The next seaman, who wears a long mustache and a patch of whiskers just beneath his lips, steps forward. "I, Barlow, do solemnly swear t'do me duties, sir."

Captain Bullock looks to you next. Swallowing your pride, you swear an oath to the ship and her commander, then walk over to the mate, Billy Greaves, while the next two would-be-sailors say their piece.

"Don't look so low, now," Billy says. "Soon enough you'll learn 'tis the common tars who run the ship and Cap'n Bullock's only another part-o'-her t'be steered and managed. Your cousin Jimmy Saltboots survived, and you'll find you're a Saltboots too. Now here, take your hammock, slops, and head to the fo'c'sle to find your berth."

"My... what?" you ask, dumbly.

A grin parts Billy's muttonchops. "Hammock's whatcha sleep'n, slops whatcha wear, and the fo'c'sle—the *fore-ca-stle*—be where ye do it all." He exaggerates the syllables of "forecastle," which he had originally truncated like "folk-soul." You nod and he adds, "Just follow the other recruits. Monkey see, monkey do."

He shoves a stack of cloth against your chest, pushing you away. Billy has other preparations to get the ship ready to sail, and you can't be looked after like a lost child the duration of the voyage, so you follow his advice and join the seamen down in the fo'c'sle.

It's dark, crowded, and dank—a cellar, meant to store men. Those you've followed set their hammocks (which are simply a sheet of canvas big enough to lie in) mere inches from one another, for space here is at a premium. There are other sailors about, those who truly did volunteer, and they have chests set below their hammocks to store belongings. Hopefully you'll acquire one of those soon.

You stow your hammock in the same way as the other men, then change into your "slops"—loose-fitting breeches and a jacket meant for mobility and protection at sea.

While sorting his own meager belongings, the seaman in the red skullcap who called himself Rediker gives a sing-song chant, *"Oh, the times're hard, and the wages low. Leave 'er, Johnny, leave 'er. I'll pack my kit and go below; it's time that we did leave 'er."*

Many of the other sailors chuckle, but it's his companion, Barlow, who explains, saying, "We ain't even set sail yet and your singin' 'bout desertion?"

"I see ya met Cap'n Bullock!" one of the hired sailors cries out to a reception of guffaws.

Yet you fail to see the humor. Desertion is a serious crime, with serious consequences. Still, these men just woke up to find themselves consigned aboard a ship against their will; maybe a little humor is the best way to process this new reality?

➢ Idle talk will occur whether I hear it or not. I'll stay and listen to the way the common sailors speak. Go to page 180
➢ I'm keeping my nose clean and staying out of it! Time to head back up top for some fresh air. Go to page 304

Meet the Press

⚓

The next morning, you're marched out before the local magistrate and the High Court of Admiralty. It's an open-air public event, with a small crowd gathered to spectate. You watch as several young seamen types are brought out to join you; shocked by what you see in the face of the final man. Sure enough, it's your cousin James!

Mouth agape, you simply stare. You're too far away to speak to him, and he must not notice you, because he only looks ahead to the magistrate. This man wears a powdered wig and, now that all have arrived, begins his remarks.

"You all stand accused of various crimes against the crown. Vagrancy. Inciting a riot. Petty theft. Assault and battery. Property damage. Each of which is a blight upon this fine city that shall not be tolerated. Though, I am inclined to leniency. This is a time of war, as you should well know, and there is a mutually beneficial course set before us. His Majesty needs good hands to sail his ships, and you lot need discipline instilled into you. Defending the realm is a matter of duty! And so, by the authority of a wartime hot press, I hereby order your sentences commuted to the HMS *Hornblower*, under direct supervision of Captain Charles Longwick."

The crowd cheers and your head swims, unable to accept this new reality. You've just been pressed into the service of the Royal Navy! The magistrate continues his speech, but it's hard to concentrate on the man's words, truth be told, because it's all you can do not to call out to your cousin. James looks more distraught than ever.

Finally, the ceremony is over and you're led away from the court. Where are they taking you? Will you head directly to the ship? Just what is going on here?!

➢ Find your way to James. He'll know what's going on. Go to page 59

➢ Stay silent, stay in line. Go to page 288

Merciful

Crack! You fire the pistol and Rediker falls to the beach, dead.

The promise you made to yourself by carrying the flintlock all these weeks, finally fulfilled. Was Rediker the one responsible for Bullock's death and—by extension—your exile on this island? One thing is certain: as a pirate captain, he's certainly the most culpable now.

Barlow drops to Rediker's side, blubbering with emotion and cradling the dead man in his arms. This sudden outburst after weeks in isolation is more than you can handle, and you use the other pistol to put the man out of his misery, as much for his sake as for your own.

All is silent. It's over. A splash pulls your attention to the shore, where Dudderidge the cook and a few others launch the jolly boats out for escape. They must have seen the island aflame and decided to flee.

Watching them leave, watching the island burn, you remove the rum and uncork the fifth.

"To revenge," you say.

Go to page 32

Monkey Business

⚓

"You shouldn't have asked that question, Landsman," Captain Longwick says, gravely. Then he turns playful and shouts, "Because now you're to be the first monkey!"

"*Sling the Monkey!!!*" Magnus bellows.

The ship's crew gives three *hurrahs!* in response, leaving you to wonder what you just got yourself into. The drunken sailors gather a good deal of rope, and two of them scramble up to the top mast and thread it through the crosstrees. The other end is tied into a bowline loop, which you get to wear about your waist. There's no slack in the rope, but you're not lifted off the ground, either.

Lieutenant Dalton finds a piece of chalk, and draws a circle about your feet. Then he hands you the chalk. The men tie their handkerchiefs into knots, then wet them.

"Your goal, monkey, is to mark someone with that chalk!" Lieutenant Dalton cries out. "Once you do, they're the next monkey. And in the meantime, the men will try to baste you! You're safe in this circle, but you must emerge to mark an opponent. Good luck!"

The officers watch from the quarterdeck, while the other seamen swing their handkerchiefs about, ready to hit you with them. You lunge forward, striking out with the piece of chalk, but the men scramble away. The rope tightens, lifts you off the deck in a swing, and brings you back to your circle. Several seamen give a wet kiss of their handkerchiefs as you fall back.

Now you're getting it!

You run forward at an angle and launch yourself against the rope, swinging in a wide, fast arc. The seamen try to get you with their handkerchiefs, but drunkenly misjudge your speed and you manage to mark the carpenter's mate before swinging back into the circle.

"Well done, Landsman! We've got a new monkey!" Midshipman Magnus yells.

So goes the game of Sling the Monkey, and you make your own handkerchief ready for basting. Round after round, hours go by in laughter and fun. Drinks are taken between games, played on into the night, which ultimately turns to song and poetry, the men jovially celebrating the night. It's a cool evening, which feels good after working up a sweat from the games.

> I think I'll sleep out under the stars tonight. No sign of clouds, and what a great night it was! Go to page 146

> After a night full of drink, I think I'll hit my hammock. The ship appears to be spinning... Go to page 146

Mouth Breather

Ummm, what are you doing? Walking around with your mouth open and flexing your tongue? Okay... that succeeds in drying your mouth out even further. Having your mouth open exposes your membranes to the air, which dries them out. Breathing through your mouth (as opposed to nasal breathing) also dries out your mouth. And by flexing and moving your tongue about, you succeed in increasing the surface area exposed to the air, thus compounding the problem.

So, basically, you do everything in your power to dry your mouth further. Maybe stop doing that? Back to finding water, yeah? The birds on this island may have taken the fish from the tidepools before you arrived this morning, but if you pay attention, they can lead you to water. Mouth closed, eyes up.

What you see, when you stop to observe, are a group of birds circling inland and other large groups leaving the circle in a more-or-less direct path to some unseen destination. What does this tell you?

➢ The circling birds are probably just looking for dead/helpless animals. Head to their destination instead. Go to page 206

➢ Go to where the birds are circling. That's most likely where a reserve of fresh water will be found. Go to page 157

Moving On

⚓

Captain Longwick shakes his head and says, "Alive, of course. Putting a pirate to the gallows is the only deterrent we have. But if it's to be you or him, don't go down on your sword for a bloody pirate, Ward."

"Aye, sir," you say, before saluting.

Rushing below decks, you find your cousin in the ship's magazine, as expected. Word of the impending pirate battle has already flooded through the ship, and the *Hornblower*'s crew surges forth to action stations.

"Me old shipmates, pirates?" James says after you tell him the news.

"That's unclear. They've taken the ship, that much is true. As for the crew…"

"Bullock were a right bastard, I'll say at risk of speaking ill-o'-the dead. But Billy? Robin? Joe and Chips? Marlowe and Dudderidge… These were good men. If you're leading the attack, coz—count me in!"

"I'm sorry, James. Captain Longwick needs you here."

"That's right," Monks adds. "Call came for action stations. Get a move on, lad!"

"What can you tell me? Anything that might give a tactical advantage?"

He shakes his head in despair. "She always were a fast ship. Not prone to leak like this sieve. But the *Cooper's Pride* is no match for a warship; even a frigate such as this ought to overpower her."

Leaving Cousin James to prepare the ship's munitions, you head up to fight. He watches you go, clearly conflicted about the battle to come.

The drums beat for war as the *Hornblower* sails towards the pirate ship. The plan, insofar as you've been made aware of it, is to pin the *Cooper's Pride* up against the coast, without letting them slip through an inlet and escape into the shallows. You'll cut off the smaller ship, board her, and take the pirates with flintlocks and steel.

The cannons boom, making what could be considered a warning shot—but more likely is meant to shape the fleeing ship's course. It works, and the *Cooper's Pride* alters its course to flee further along the coast.

The *Hornblower* follows the pirate ship along the convex bend of the coast, until another ship is revealed from around the curve. A Spanish Man-o'-War, not too different from the last you've seen. She's moored in this hidden inlet, and the pirate ship dares not sail into her. This is an unexpected tactical wildcard—neither ship is allied with the Dons.

"Maintain course," Captain Longwick orders, belying nothing.

"Ready muskets," you say.

The pirates, realizing they're caught between two enemies, turn to the open sea just as Longwick had planned. Did he know the Spanish were taking roost here, or was this an unexpected boon?

Knowing they've been caught, the *Cooper's Pride* lets out a broadside, peppering the *Hornblower* with cannon fire and resultant splinters. Then the order comes to attack at will.

"FIRE!!!" you order, and the muskets discharge in unison. Not waiting for a reload, you draw your saber and shout, "Charge!"

The boarding party drops muskets and instead launches grappling hooks and walkways across the open sea, bridging the two ships. It's a ferocious and bloody battle from the start. The pirates are brutal fighters, but numbers are on your side. The sailors rush against the gilded barbarians, taking the others by sheer overwhelming force.

It's not as noble a pursuit as you might've imagined. No one is offering clever barbs and retorts while clashing cutlasses. Rather, men stab each other between the ribs and down along the spine when the opponents least expect it. The idea is to inflict as much damage as possible until the pirate captain surrenders.

That's when you spot him. He has a red skullcap, a pierced eyebrow, and fire in his eyes. He's not distinguishable from the rest of the crew, but you recognize a fellow leader of men when you see one. They fight in a circle radiating out from this man, keeping their trust in his leadership, ready for whatever orders he may give.

"Cap'n Rediker, look out!" a mustachioed man shouts as you approach.

"Surrender now, or your men all perish!" you call back.

The pirate captain, rather than turning to cross swords with you, simply removes one of his four flintlock pistols with his other hand, draws back the hammer and dispatches you with all the attention he would give to putting down a rabid dog.

"No!" comes the fateful cry, just as cousin James leaps and takes the bullet for you. It was your voice shouting out, for your cousin wasn't even supposed to be in the boarding party. Damnable fool!

Captain Rediker doesn't give you a second look as you rush to James's side. It's another pirate, in fact, the man who warned the captain, who comes to finish you off. Battering the man's sword away with renewed vigor, you run him through with the very next swipe of your own blade.

"Barlow!" the pirate captain cries out.

Now he's ready to face you. Or, so you thought. Instead, Captain Rediker dashes back and lights a fuse—the long tendril of which ignites and runs down below decks. Without another thought, you dash over, leap and slam your cutlass down upon the fuse; cutting the head off this fiery serpent just before it would retreat below decks.

Rolling to your side, you barely evade the cleave Rediker meant to stove your skull in with. His blade sinks into the wooden planks of the ship, and you offer a savage kick at the man while he tries to yank it back.

Rediker reclaims his saber, but stumbles back, allowing you time to regain your footing.

"Surrender!" you growl, sword pointed with menace.

The man takes a swing at you, and you parry the attack, returning with a slice across his forearm. He grunts in pain and backs away.

"Surrender!" you call again.

Now Rediker goes for a second pistol and you leap into action, bringing down the blade upon his wrist with an overhead strike. The man is disarmed—literally.

"Surrender!" you say for the third time.

"I yield!" the pirate whimpers.

Go to page 52

Murderous Pirate

"It's true! I killed Bullock! One slain to save many! The captain would've gotten us all killed before we ever saw English soil again—who among you hadn't wished him dead? Only you lacked the courage of your convictions!" The words flow out theatrically, as if playing a role, like you'd do with your cousins each summer—Odysseus or Julius Caesar or Macbeth—only now, actor and role become one.

"That weren't the plan," Barlow mutters before Rediker elbows him into silence.

"Why you're… you're…" Chips stammers. "You're a bloody pirate!"

"So be it!" Rediker cries, taking up a role of his own. "This is an act-o'-true piracy, a mutiny for the greater good-o'-all aboard."

Robin takes an aggressive step towards you, but Billy puts a hand on the hulking man's shoulder to keep him back. Rediker comes to stand next to you, his mate Barlow follows, and the older seaman Marlowe joins the pair at your side.

"Now what, Saltboots?" Billy asks. "Ye killed Bullock, what of the rest-o'-us? Are the four-o'-ye t'force us into a life-o'-piracy? I've had me a lifetime before the mast as a good, honest sailor."

"Honest sailor? Just look at ya, man! 'Tis clear ye eat that which would befit two men," Rediker chuffs.

Now Marlowe steps forward. "Come, gents. We've barely enough hands left t'steer the blessed ship. We must work together."

"Billy should be the new cap'n, by law," Joe speaks up.

"By law—ha! Only another tyrant like Bullock invokes such a defense; these merchants rob the poor under the protection of *law*. The merchant vilifies the freebooter, for a pirate is truly his better, as he plunders only under the protection of his own courage! Chips, these timbers upon which we stand, ya said they hail from Sherwood, did ye not? We could be a band-o'-merry men! Take from the rich t'give to the poor, and there ain't no poorer than a poor 'ole seaman!"

"Heed not this silver tongue, men," Billy says. "We know what's right!"

The crew begins a great confabulation, ready to come to blows. It's clear the sailors are divided, and they split themselves in the literal sense. Butch, the surgeon, comes to stand by Rediker while Dudderidge, the cook, folds his arms behind Billy.

Despite this, you can't help but notice, of the fifteen men before you—most look *your* way for guidance. You've taken credit for this mutiny, after all. It's likely you could sway the vote either way.

➢ Publicly endorse Rediker as captain. He has the right of it. This isn't admiralty law, this is natural law. The law of the jungle. Divine right, proving that all men are equal. Rediker is my man. Go to page 160

➢ Publicly endorse Billy as captain. By law, Billy should be captain. He knows the score now—how we deal with captains who betray the trust of their crew—and should be a fair leader accordingly. Go to page 203

➢ Put yourself forward as captain. If you've taken credit for the mutiny already, then why not lead the ship? With the hands looking your way for guidance, you could diffuse this tension and rise to the top. Go to page 26

Mutinous

"I've heard everything," you say. The men startle and jump to their feet. "And I want in. There can be no justice under Captain Bullock's reign, for his orders will get us all killed. We've seen the food and rum rations worsening while he eats fresh beef and drinks wine with every meal. Each loss in the crew puts us all at risk—we're slowly dying out here. Overthrowing the man is a responsibility. A sacred duty."

Although the words just spill out, they put the men at ease; you are welcomed into their company with eager handshakes and wide grins.

"Were ye not also on watch, Saltboots?" Marlowe asks.

Rediker nods. "We must move quickly, lest we're discovered. Saltboots, I'd wager Bullock least suspects yourself. Go to the Captain's cabin, tell the man ye have a star reading, and bring him out t'see. We lot will be waiting to throw the man overboard."

"That way it looks like an accident," Barlow emphasizes.

"Go! Make haste!" Rediker says.

Nodding your understanding, you rush towards the captain's cabin, trepidation and exhilaration swirling in your breast. Knocking on the door, you hear a muffled reply and a clattering from within. You knock again, and the door creaks open. Must not have been latched….

The door swings wide with a lurch of the ship, and Captain Bullock falls forward into your arms. He makes a hideous gurgling noise, crimson bubbles frothing from his lips. His body falls prone and the unexpected weight of the man brings you both down outside the cabin.

You roll the captain onto his back to find the source of the suffocation, only to see his throat's been cut! Completely severed, ear to ear. There's a bloody knife inside the cabin, lying only a few feet away. Captain Bullock continues gagging for breath, blood pulsing from his wound, then—with one more sickening gasp—the man expires.

A cacophony of boots clatter on deck as the crew rushes towards the commotion. The first to arrive is Chips, who looks aghast with horror. Here you are, kneeling over the body of Captain Bullock, the man's blood on your hands. Joe arrives only a few moments later; more and more of the crew appear by the second.

"What's happened here?" Joe asks.

"Saltboots… killed the cap'n," Chips says, ashen-faced with shock.

Rediker, Barlow, and Marlowe arrive, eyes wide with disbelief. This definitely wasn't part of the plan! But there's no use in closing the stable door after the horse has bolted. The captain is dead, that much is certain. What now?

➢ Take credit. "That's right. Bullock had it coming! We all know it. This is a mutiny and… I'm in charge." Go to page 194

➢ Look for a way out. "This is a mutiny, isn't that right, Rediker? Your men must've killed the captain." Go to page 39

Nightmare Scenario

Having woken only minutes ago, this feels like some sort of terrible dream of suffocation. Being held in place, unable to move. Jack flails a moment longer, then disappears into the briny depths of the sea. Your stomach swirls in protest, and not just because the sea batters the ship about; seeing a man simply disappear from the face of the earth twists your stomach with a vertigo worse than any seasickness ever could.

"Couldn't he swim!?" you shout.

Billy shakes his head, comes closer. "Why should a man want t'learn swimmin'? Rather sink straight down and not drag out the whole affair! If ye can swim, keep it t'yourself, Saltboots! Cap'n don't like sailors who can swim, lest they jump ship near shore!"

There's a great cracking sound from the main mast, and men shout swears that are muffled by the gale. Billy turns, and bellows commands at the ship's best seamen.

"Take an axe! Aloft with ya! Cut away the foretop mast! Loose the ropes at the bowsprit! Off with haste!" he cries.

The nearest able seaman doesn't hesitate, claiming an axe and climbing into the rigging. There's a second axe nearby, but no one rushes to join him. Great waves of water splash across the decks as the storm rages.

➢ Run down into the hold and take cover. Better to stay out of the way than get swept out to sea. Go to page 117

➢ Take the second axe and get climbing! Go to page 113

➢ Ask Billy how you can help. He's the mate, after all. Go to page 313

The Night's Watch

⚓

After a fitful few hours' sleep, you head up to join the watch. Though there's not much watching to be done—for the early morning brings with it a dense fog. It's a haze that glows with the promise of dawn, but the only indications that you're still on the same ocean as the night before are the lamplights from the *Don Pedro Sangre*, which illuminate your tail like fireflies in the distance.

Despite the orders for silence on deck and no lamplight allowed to illuminate the *Hornblower*, the enemy has stayed with you like a phantom. But it's the fact that *another* glowing haze now appears on the larboard side that truly sends chills up your spine. Another ship? Out here?

"The *Flying Dutchman*," one of the sailors whispers, referencing the famed ghost ship.

You look back, seeing the lights of the *Don Pedro Sangre* still visible behind the stern.

"Look, 'nuther still!" a second seaman hisses, pointing to the starboard side.

Indeed, more lights can be seen opposite, along with ethereal voices disembodied in the fog. Have the Spanish managed reinforcements? Were you surrounded in the night? It's not threat of ghosts that frighten you, but the very real prospect that you might soon be joining them.

Then, as if crossing some unseen barrier, you pass through the fog completely. So too, dissipates the fog of your misunderstanding. For it isn't the Spanish around you at all: you've met with the rest of the Royal Navy! Lieutenant Dalton rushes to orders, desperate to signal the fleet before the *Don Pedro Sangre* realizes the trap they're sailing into. He does so at the exact right moment, for the enemy follows into clear skies, but not before several British warships arrive to claim her as a prize.

Breaking the order of silence with the rest of the seamen, you hurrah at the sight of your countrymen, knowing that victory has saved the day.

"Well, then," Captain Longwick says, appearing on deck and looking most pleased. "I suppose I should go meet with the Admiral in accepting the Dons' surrender. Lieutenant Dalton, you're in command until I return."

➤ Volunteer to join the longboat and row the Captain across to see the flagship! Go to page 235

➤ What's Cousin James been up to in all this? Go see how he's fared as the gunner's mate! Go to page 43

Nine Lives Are Up

"**B**illy, you'll serve as my quartermaster, same duties as mate. Bosun, get me the cat! We need discipline to run this ship. The rest of you, back to stations!" you order.

But no one moves.

"Saltboots don't want us as free men," Rediker says. "Only wants to sit atop the throne now that 'tis empty."

"Keep up that talk and it'll be another dozen lashes. Bosun, the whip!"

"Long live Bullock the Second!" Rediker roars.

"Hip, hip!" Barlow says, raising a "Hurrah!" from most of the crew.

You've lost them.

The ship makes a sharp turn, sails snapping against a change in the wind. She's now sailing against the waves, and the *Cooper's Pride* rolls powerfully with each swell, back and forth like a pendulum—but increasing the arc with every sway. The crew all latch onto what they can; so violent is the turbulence that it's impossible to keep one's footing.

"Back to stations!" Billy cries.

"Damn your blood!" Rediker hollers back.

It's too late. The ship lurches painfully, and the larboard bow dips into the sea, pulling her down. Now the hand of Neptune grabs hold of the sails, pulling the *Pride* full over until the ship has capsized. There's no righting a ship out in the middle of the ocean, and nowhere to swim once she's sunk. Your only hope now is to drown before the sharks notice you.

THE END

No Survivors

Flying the red flag successfully gets the bloodlust going in your new pirate recruits. The old crew seem less pleased with the decision, but a captain's orders must not be questioned during battle. The crew of the *Dos Santos* appear even less pleased. They fire their guns as you approach, but as a merchant vessel, they have the same number of guns as the *Deleon's Revenge*—that is to say, six in total.

"Cap'n, they hit us on the water-line!" Chips reports in.

Generally speaking, it's best to fire right at your opponent's decks. This maximizes splintering and casualties, with the goal of sapping your foe's will to fight. This is where your guns are aimed to fire now. Cannon shot hitting below decks certainly damages the ship, but the men are up top during action, so this is generally seen as wasted shot.

Hitting right at the line between wood and water, however, serves one deadly purpose: to sink the enemy.

"Do what you can to patch us up!" you order the carpenter, and, turning to the rest of the crew, add, "Grappling hooks, let's board!"

Just as Rediker predicted, many of the crew on the *Dos Santos* leap overboard at your approach with the red flag. When faced between a choice of being hacked to bits or drowning, it makes sense. Theoretically, that should make things much easier.

The rest of the Portuguese sailors, however, are prepared to fight to the death. It's a gruesome fight, full of bloody carnage. Casualties are high on both sides, but ultimately your crew wins the day. Still, it was risky to go in full-tilt before you've become better armed than the average merchant vessel. They pummel you in this fair fight. It's a Pyrrhic victory—one so costly as to be nearly indistinguishable from defeat.

Your ship is sinking. The one you captured is in tatters, and you're down to half your crew, a crew who, after this battle, vote for a new captain. And no, it wasn't Rediker's idea. That man died in combat.

In a cruel twist on the "Captain always goes down with the ship" mantra, you're voted to be left on the *Deleon's Revenge* by yourself while the remaining crew limps away on the *Dos Santos*. But on the plus side, you'll go down in history as one of the most bloodthirsty pirates ever to sail the seven seas.

THE END

Not a Drop to Drink

Spence raises her left eyebrow this time, but doesn't protest. Instead, she pours James a glass of gin. The clear liquid swirls around the glass like the haze of the desert heat on its way to producing a mirage.

Then she pours your water. The glass shows particulates floating in the brown, translucent sludge, like something that might have been scooped out of the gutter two days after the last rain.

James seems not to notice, especially since a young courtesan comes to sit next to him. She's small, pert, and fit. His new friend wears a petticoat, clean and neat, though loose in several suggestive places. She laughs and wraps her arms around his.

The seat next to you creaks as someone sits down. You turn to see an older seaman with muttonchops. Spence pours him a drink while you look him over. He's well-dressed for a seaman, at least by your limited experience, though his garb holds tightly to a frame expanding with recently added weight. Getting a closer look at the man, you see his grey whiskers are stained rust-red around the mouth from habitual tobacco use.

The sailor eyes your bog water, shudders, then says, "Never known a sailor not to drink."

"I never said I was a sailor," you answer quietly.

"But I thought ya just arrived in port with your cousin?"

"Indeed I did. But I never claimed to have done so from aboard his ship."

"I'm just puttin' ya on!" the man laughs, slapping you on the back. "I know ya didn't sail in with him. I know you're no sailor, neither. See, me name's William Greaves, but when I'm at sea, folks just call me Billy, mate of the *Cooper's Pride*. Your cousin sailed with me by the name Jimmy Saltboots!"

At the name, James turns back. "Now, Billy, remember this is family. We don't tell sea tales in front-o'-wives, children, nor cousins neither."

"My lips are sealed, Jimmy! I was only makin' acquaintances."

"Jimmy... Saltboots?" you say, trying it out.

"Every adventurer needs a larger-than-life persona, surely your library at home taught ya that, coz!" James says and his courtesan laughs for him.

"More adventures await!" Billy offers.

"Not for me, Billy. I ain't never goin' back. I have a lifetime's tales to tell. But tonight, I only want the tail!" At that James downs the rest of his drink, scoops up his lovely companion, and carries her into a back room like a Viking raider might carry a prize after plunder.

"If 'tis for lack-o'-coin you ain't drinking, I'd be happy to buy a round for the cousin-o'-Jimmy Saltboots," Billy offers once James is gone.

"No, thank you. I aim to keep a clear head. I'm obliged to help cousin James make it back home this evening."

Billy gives a knowing grin, chuckles to himself, then goes back to his gin.

"Did I say something funny?" you ask, curiosity getting the better of you.

"Jimmy ain't headin' home. I know, I know what he said. But the sea don't let a man go so easy."

"Did something happen to him out there?"

"Certain… events… can weigh on a young man his first time at sea. When half your chums become chum, or an oasis port brings the other half to desertin'. See, 'tis a lonely life, when all's said and done. If he were here, now, Jimmy would tell you he's done with life as a Jack Tar, but what he's soon to learn is that once the sirens call ya out t'sea, that they never truly let ya be. He'll have his share of drink and lays, but by end-o'-week he'll be back on the briny fields of destiny, if you'll pardon an old sailor his romantic notion of things."

"So… there's no special reason he'd want to avoid home? No shame, nor secret? No reason to go out, but no reason to stay, something like that?"

"We're all lost souls, caught between the Devil and the deep blue sea."

You take a moment to ponder Billy's words, his reference to Homer's *Odyssey* and the sirens not lost on you. That's the kind of coincidence that those who believe in it would call "fate."

"I said I'm the mate-o'-the *Cooper's Pride*. So it is that we have an opening or two on board, if ya wanna take Jimmy's spot. She's a decently fast ship, tight as a drum—and ready to be filled with treasures. Cap'n Bullock's a fair and honorable man, too, and good, honorable seamen are in short supply. The position comes with a pay advance, of course, which many find helps ease the woes of the family left back home."

You're overwhelmed by the unexpected offer, and your thoughts stray from your cousin, if only for a moment. You, a sailor? You've dreamed of adventure for so long…

"Where's she headed?" you ask, wistfully.

"The American colonies," Billy answers with a knowing twinkle in his eye. "I'm offering you a chance t'see a whole new world."

Taking a moment to consider, you finally say:

➤ "You're kind to think of me so, but indeed I do try to do the honorable thing. In this case, I must deliver my cousin home, whether he's ready to leave the seafaring life or not." Go to page 240

➤ "Sign me up! James won't be the only adventurer in the family. I'll need a ream of paper and a goodly sized bottle of ink to draft a letter home, and to keep a journal of my days at sea." Go to page 267

An Offering

The next morning, you head down to check on your *swine before pearls*, as it were, only to find the animal no longer there. The hempen rope you made is cut and frayed, though if it's from a knife or chewed through by an animal, you couldn't quite say.

Did you really expect to leave a pig floating in a pond in the jungle and have it still be there the next day? It's certainly been eaten, and you'll likely not get another opportunity like this one for quite some time. Still, whatever ate the meat surely thanked their lucky stars.

Disappointed, you turn back to leave, only to come face to face with a jaguar.

Its golden fur glows tawny in the early light; black splotches break up the outline of the animal, even as it stares at you out in the open. Is this who's been following you these last few days? Likely so. What was once curiosity to size you up now very well may put you on the menu. What do you do?

- Stand tall, but slowly back away. Speak calmly. Say, "It's okay, I don't mean you any harm." Go to page 306
- Confidently walk towards the jaguar. Lock eyes to show dominance. Say, "This is my island now!" Go to page 287
- Scream loudly to frighten the animal and climb up into the nearest tree for safety. Go to page 69
- Shout, "Look, over there!" and then run in the opposite direction as fast as you can. Go to page 226
- Almost as if in slow motion, remove your pistol and shoot the beast. Can't get revenge if you're dead. Go to page 326

Oh, Billy!

Rediker looks truly wounded when you endorse Billy as captain. But, moreover, the rest of the crew looks relieved—including Rediker's co-conspirators. Uncertainty can be more terrifying than tyranny, and even if Billy was dining on the choicest foodstuffs with Captain Bullock, the men know and respect Billy.

The ship starts to list, such as it is that no one is steering her. With the crew simply idling, there's real danger that the *Cooper's Pride* could turn against the wind, hit a bad patch of seas, and capsize.

"Back to it or we all go down!" Billy commands.

The men return to their stations, leaving only Billy, yourself, and Robin on the quarterdeck.

"Ya didn't really kill Bullock, did ya, Saltboots?" Billy asks. "Oh, don't bother, I can see it in your eyes, mate. 'Twas quick thinking, lest we descend into madness. Robin, do us all a favor and wrap the captain for burial. We'll hold a service on the morrow."

Robin lifts Bullock like a sack of flour and takes the corpse away to sew the man into canvas. Billy throws his head in the direction of the cabin and bids you to follow. Once inside, he claims the captain's decanter, opens and pours the red liquid into a pair of crystal goblets, then hands one to you.

"Well done, Saltboots. Ya might've just saved the ship. When we get t'Boston, I'll see Rediker and the others hanged. Here's to you as a true seaman, and why 'tis we never say die!"

He toasts, and you share the drink with an echoed, "Never say die!"

"So who was it truly killed Cap'n Bullock?" Billy asks after you've both finished your drinks.

"I honestly don't know, Billy. It's like the man slit his neck himself."

Billy tugs at his muttonchops thoughtfully, and you clear your throat. The alcohol burns; must be that you're only used to diluted rum in your daily rations. But Billy notices it too, rubbing his own neck in response.

"This'd be some shite port wine. Personal stock? Ya can keep it—"

Then he makes a gagging sound and his other hand comes up to his throat. His face blooms red, then purple.

"Billy!" you cry. "Are you all r—"

Then you feel it too: your airways constricting as your throat expands. You can't breathe! In a desperate bid for air, you go for the bloody captain's knife on the floor, but Billy's own survival instincts kick in and he tries to wrestle the knife from your grasp. If only you can breathe again, you'll be free!

Through the pain, a dire realization comes through: Captain Bullock wasn't killed by his own knife… the man was poisoned!

THE END

Oppressed

⚓

Your naivety towards shipboard discipline speaks volumes. Do you think the Royal Navy is a stranger to those who would shirk their duties? Likely, as one of the newest "recruits," they were already watching you, expecting you to try something like this. You're easily caught and brought before the Master and Commander on the quarterdeck. Now what?

Captain Longwick is to make an example of you, it would seem. You're told to "kiss the gunner's daughter"—meaning, in this case, to bend over one of the long guns and drop your trousers. Then the Captain unfurls his cat-o'-nine-tails whip and proceeds to flog you violently. You think you're going to keep a stiff upper lip about it, but the barbs of the whip bite into your skin, pulling flesh away as they retreat for another round. Involuntarily, you scream out in tremendous pain. That only seems to make the commander's blood rise higher; he lashes you all the more fiercely.

What's worse is what comes after. The men of the ship now view you with suspicion. In a carefully rationed world, one who would merit extra attention without pulling their weight is a decided negative. So you get the worst helpings in the kitchen: rotting and festering food. The surgeon declines to look over your wounds, and soon they too rot and fester.

James tries to support you, sneaking food away, but you know if he's caught stealing, he'll share your fate, so you refuse your cousin's gifts. With your wounds preventing you from being able to sit or lie down, a lack of sleep seals your fate. A fever comes in less than a week. A week after that and you've fully wasted away.

Once you've expired, you're sewn into your hammock and unceremoniously dropped into the briny deep.

THE END

Out of the Loop

The men disappear on their errand while you continue the rounds, not letting imagination get the better of you. It's just as well, because only minutes later, there's a break in the sky.

"Saltboots! Impeccable timing. Come, record these measurements!"

It's Joe the bosun, manning the helm. He uses an astrolabe and records the constellations and their distance from the horizon. Once you're at his side, he starts reciting the measurements aloud so you can record them onto parchment. It's a frantic, excited pace, but you're able to keep up until he's finished reading the heavens.

"Make haste, then! Cap'n will want these numbers 'fore he notices the skies've cleared. Tread lightly, he's in one-o'-his moods."

Nodding your understanding, you rush towards the captain's cabin, trepidation and exhilaration swirling in your breast. Knocking on the door, you hear a muffled reply and a clattering from within. You knock again, and the door creaks open. Must not have been latched....

The door swings wide with a lurch of the ship, and Captain Bullock falls forward into your arms. He makes a hideous gurgling noise, crimson bubbles frothing from his lips. His body falls prone and the unexpected weight of the man brings you both down outside the cabin.

You roll the captain onto his back to find the source of the suffocation, only to see his throat's been cut! Completely severed, ear to ear. There's a bloody knife inside the cabin, lying only a few feet away. Captain Bullock continues gagging for breath, blood pulsing from his wound, then—with one more sickening gasp—the man expires.

A cacophony of boots clatter on deck as the crew rushes towards the commotion. The first to arrive is Chips, who looks aghast with horror. Here you are, kneeling over the body of Captain Bullock, the man's blood on your hands. Joe arrives only a few moments later; more and more of the crew appear by the second.

"What's happened here?" Joe asks.

"Saltboots... killed the cap'n," Chips says, ashen-faced with shock.

You shake your head, trying to find the words.

➤ Point out the knife and cry, "No! I found him like this! The killer must still be inside!" Go to page 65

➤ Tell them about the conspiracy of men you saw in the moonlight. Go to page 47

Out to Sea

Following the stream of birds, you end up on the leeward coast of the island. Turns out there's a natural bay on this side, with rocky cliffs that cup the sea in such a way as to provide a natural updraft for the birds. So many of them are attracted to this area because it's easy to glide in the thermals before diving down into the waves to hunt for prey.

But... no signs of fresh water. After this hike to a dead end, you're thirstier than ever. Better not make that mistake again. Where to this time?

➢ Back to the birds' preferred circling area. If they're looking for food here, they must be doing something else there. Like, drinking fresh water, hopefully. Go to page 157

➢ Look for animal trails and see where multiple paths converge. They need fresh water too, and they've discovered the island's secrets long ago. Go to page 78

➢ Seek a low-lying part of the island near broad-leaf vegetation. That's a natural spot where you're likely to find ponds or streams. Go to page 82

Overindulgent

⚓

"To my success?" Captain Longwick parrots back. "Did I sail the *Hornblower* myself? That might've proved difficult, what with my lone firing of the rear cannon battery to keep the Dons at bay. And how I had time to tend to the wounded, keep the pumps running, feed, arm, and clothe the men whilst I was simultaneously making repairs! No, Ward. Tonight I will toast to the crew, to their success. A ship is not one man, you'd do well to remember! If you should one day earn the King's commission as lieutenant, I should hate for an officer nurtured under my command to toast to their own successes!"

"Aye, sir. No, sir. Of course not. We will certainly toast to the *Hornblower* and our fine crew. I only meant as the Captain, you deserve recognition for leading us to victory, sir."

"Don't grovel, Ward. It's unbefitting an officer candidate."

"Aye, sir. Do you really think I'd have a shot at lieutenant?" you say, taking the opportunity to change the subject.

"I think if you're seriously committed, I can lend you some pertinent books on the subject. The examination for lieutenant shouldn't be undertaken without due preparations."

"Aye, sir. Thank you, sir!"

- Captain Longwick is watching you carefully now. Accept his books and spend the evening studying to show him how committed you are. Go to page 263
- A night to celebrate, indeed! Head back to the *Hornblower* and toast to the events of the past, the gift of the present, and those challenges yet to come. Go to page 23

Over the Precipice

⚓

You rush in and swing with the drawknife, hoping to knock his hand clear of the pistol. The ship lurches under the swell of the approaching storm and your aim is not so precise. The large, two-handled blade connects with the meat of the man, right at his neckline, and (true to its name) draws a huge ribbon of flesh away as easily as a butcher with salt pork.

Blood sprays like a fountain, and the cooper's mate screams in horror. The Master-of-Arms lets loose his own blood-curdled howl and tries all the more frantically to claim his pistol. You've come too far for that, so you swing and get the blow as originally intended—a cleaving hack to his wrist that will leave the man needing a hook for a hand for the rest of his life.

With so much blood loss, the rest of his life is only a few minutes. The Master-of-Arms falls to the deck, and you drop the drawknife next to him as the bloodlust wears off.

By now, you have the attention of the whole watch. Lieutenant Dalton and Mr. Magnus pull you away from the body, muttering something about a swift trial.

Await that trial from the ship's brig. Go to page 162

Over Your Head

James nods and you turn back to the bar, but your cousin spins back and plants his fist squarely against the phantom kisser's nose. With a terrible crack, the man stumbles back, and the tavern goes briefly silent. All eyes go to the four of you.

The other winds up for a drunken punch and you duck down from its path. James steps forward and socks him one right in the nose too. The whole tavern erupts into fighting; a powder keg that you just lit the fuse to. Glass shatters over heads, chairs crack against backs and shoulders, and fists generally let fly.

You back away, hoping not to get caught in the fray.

"Town rats!" someone yells.

"Press gang!" cries another.

"Run for it!" sounds the general refrain.

The commotion intensifies, and someone gets thrown through the front window. Several others are stabbed, beaten senseless, or bludgeoned to death around you. It's total chaos, but you can't find a way out.

James stands at the front of the tavern and is taken by the town guard when they storm the bar. Nothing you can do to stop it. Finally, a stampede of sailors looking to avoid the press gang crashes through a rear entrance, and with a heavy heart, you're swept away in the current.

The next morning, James stands before the High Court of Admiralty, along with many others. It's a public event, perhaps designed to instill order in the rowdier parts of London. The magistrate goes on about duty, telling all present that due to lack of volunteers, they're now pressed into service in His Majesty's Royal Navy. It's hard to concentrate on the man's words, truth be told, because it's all you can do not to call out to your cousin. James looks more distraught than ever.

What are you to do?

➢ Volunteer to join his ship! Your cousin needs you. Surely if they're this desperate for fighters, they'll allow you the concession of joining James's ship. Go to page 317

➢ Wait out the sentencing, then ask if he'd like you to deliver a note to his mother when you head back home to Buckinghamshire alone. Go to page 102

Parlay

☠

The Portuguese captain looks at his terrified men, then to the lusty pirate crew, and finally to you. He sizes you up, then says, "Times must be lean, when men of fortune wear rags. Very well, the ship is yours. I only ask that you leave us enough supplies to survive the journey."

You nod, then turn to Rediker. "Do it. It's best if we're known as a crew you'd want to surrender to. Leave them what they need to survive the trip home, take the rest. I'll entertain the Porto captain."

In a shockingly peaceable standoff, the crews don't move against one another, as the captain crosses over to the *Deleon's Revenge* and the pirate raiders move in to sack the *Dos Santos*.

Not wanting the captain to fret, you escort him into the cabin for a drink. In this way, he won't be able to see any transgressions committed by Rediker and the men against his own crew. Out of sight, if not out of mind.

"I am Captain Vasco da Ferro of the *Dos Santos*. I must admit, when I think of a pirate captain I imagined gold rings and silk and leather. You look like the hands aboard my ship."

"I'm Captain Bloodbeard of the *Deleon's Revenge*," you say, trying to remain cordial. "Let me offer you a drink. Brandy?"

He looks around at the selection and eyes Bullock's crystal decanter. He indicates his interest and you nod. Opening the decanter, he gives it a sniff.

"Port wine, no?"

"Couldn't say. Haven't tasted it myself."

"Your former master must have been a man of distinction. I myself have a magnificent palate for such things. I can tell you the region, even the year," he says pouring himself a glass and offering one to you as well. "So, Captain Blood… beard? Why do they call you this?"

"The men are fond of their nicknames. Last captain who gave me trouble, I opened his throat and gave him a beard of blood."

At this, Captain da Ferro's genteel attitude drops. "Please. I did not mean to disrespect. I—I have a wife. Children. This was to be my last voyage. We have a, a plantation de *açúcar. Meu deus, por favor.*"

The man is so terrified, his wits abandon him and he reverts to his native tongue.

"Relax, Captain. As I said, we only want the goods on your ship. You're in the safest place, here in my cabin. Now, please. Enlighten me on the origins of this port," you say, trying to bring him back to the present.

Captain Ferro nods rapidly, bringing the drink to his lips. Yet, he does anything but taste the fortified wine, gulping it down to calm his nerves. He makes a sour face at having chugged the port and sets the glass down, clearing his throat.

"I think this port has soured," he says, rubbing his neck in response. "Something else, please, this taste, it is—"

You go for the brandy just as he makes a gagging sound and his other hand comes up to his throat. His face blooms red, then purple. He starts clawing at his own neck, drawing blood.

"Captain!" you cry. "Are you all r—"

In a desperate bid for air, he goes for the captain's knife held at your waist, Captain Bullock's own knife—the murder weapon from that fateful night. So frenzied is Captain Ferro that he takes the knife before you can stop him, slitting his own throat.

Through the confusion, seeing a scene like *déjà vu*, a dire realization comes through: Captain Bullock wasn't killed by his own knife... the man was poisoned! Something in that port is a constricting agent, and now two men have opened their own throats in a misguided bid for breath.

At the sounds of the commotion, Joe and Robin burst into the cabin, ready to defend their captain. They quickly see that there is no need. Their shocked expressions go from the dead man on the floor, to you. What do you say for yourself?

➤ The man, Captain Ferro, he killed himself. Go to page 12

➤ Their captain insulted me, so I showed him why I'm called Bloodbeard. Go to page 268

Passive/Aggressive

Barlow ties the bonds tightly, though you make no effort to resist. He looks like he might say something, maybe apologize for the necessity of all this, but in the end he thinks better of it and remains silent.

You wait and calm your mind, sitting in the room where Barlow left you. It's not easy to get comfortable, with your hands bound behind your back, and after a while they go numb.

Cannon fire booms from above, signaling the start of hostilities. Boots clatter across the upper decks as the crew rushes from position to position. With any luck, the pirate ship will soon be boarded by the Royal Navy, and they'll rescue you once they deal with the crew of the *Deleon's Revenge*.

You wait, and wait some more. Men scream, gunpowder screams louder.

After some time, both go silent, and eventually you're discovered by one of the naval crew. Hooray, you've been rescued! Though your knight in shining armor doesn't see it quite the same way. Despite your gagged protests, the sailor makes no effort to free you from your bonds, but instead lumps you in with the rest of the captives.

Once you're handed over to the nearest colonial governor, you're similarly lumped in with those to be hanged. Though you plead your case with the magistrate, it falls on deaf ears. Too many of the pirate crew also claim to be forced into conscription, sailing under the black against their will. The Admiralty Court recognizes no such defense. Surely if they did, all save the captain could claim victimization.

As it stands, you're to be summarily hanged with Rediker and his whole crew.

THE END

Patronizing

⚓

"Eccentric?" Captain Longwick replies, with almost a hint of humor in his voice. "I take it you mean his playing at shovelboard. I don't know if that display was meant for his men or the Spanish, but I suppose he was trying to imply, subtlety and all, that the capture of the *Don Pedro Sangre* was barely worth his lordship's attentions. Still, the lesson you should take away, Ward, is that eccentricity is the luxury of powerful men. The same behavior displayed by a subordinate would be called madness, would it not?"

"Aye, sir."

"I've known Vice-Admiral Maturin all of my career. It's worth having a powerful, influential man as a patron who's invested in seeing you succeed. You'll need the same if you're eyeing a King's commission as lieutenant. And it wouldn't do well to disparage those patrons, no matter how far you've advanced in your career."

The words aren't spoken harshly, but the meaning is clear: Longwick didn't appreciate you putting him in the position of speaking ill of the Vice-Admiral, no matter how strange the man might be.

"Aye, sir. Do you really think I'd have a shot at lieutenant?" you say, taking the opportunity to change the subject.

"I think if you're seriously committed, I can lend you some pertinent books on the subject. The examination for lieutenant shouldn't be undertaken without due preparations."

"Aye, sir. Thank you, sir!"

➤ A night to celebrate, indeed! Head back to the *Hornblower* and toast to the events of the past, the gift of the present, and those challenges yet to come.
Go to page 23

➤ Captain Longwick is watching you carefully now. Accept his books and spend the evening studying to show him how committed you are. Go to page 263

Penniless

The interior of the tavern is filled with the haze of smoke, barely illuminated by candlelight. You stand at the threshold, blinking with wide eyes, willing them to adjust while your ears search out James's voice from the din of the bar.

After a few moments, shapes begin to materialize in the smoky lounge. A dozen sailors recline in the eaves, each with a woman or two for company.

"Has anyone here seen a sailor named James?" you try.

A few blank looks find their way towards you, then the men go back to their own business. A sinking feeling settles into your chest; you go to the bar in search of answers. The proprietor plants both palms on the surface of the bar and leans in to get a good look at you as you approach. Perhaps she also aims to disarm you with a double helping of cleavage, but you're in no mood to take the bait. Her right eyebrow rises inquisitively. Clearly, you're not her usual clientele.

"I'm looking for my cousin, James. He was coming in for a quick drink. I have a carriage waiting."

She shrugs. "You're welcome to look around."

"You haven't served him? He's about yea-high—"

"A drink? Hmm… a *drink*? Has someone bought one-o'-those in here? I don't rightly know. What'd that be like, pouring a drink? If only there was some way to *remind* me. My memory ain't what it used to be, ya see."

"I'm afraid I don't have any money," you say, picking up on the solicitation of a bribe.

Now her left eyebrow rises. "Then I'm afraid you are indeed a lost soul, and unwelcome here. Nothing personal, but if these sea dogs and scallywags starting thinking they can mill about without payin' for the privilege, well, my business is sunk. You understand, I'm sure."

You offer a curt nod and turn to go. With your eyes fully adjusted to the dull candlelight of the tavern, you give another desperate scan, but see no sign of James. One older seaman watches you go, tendrils of smoke from a hookah pouring from his nostrils and swirling about his grey muttonchops.

Out front, the driver puffs at his own pipe. He can't help but read the disappointment on your face and says, "The best way out of it, if ya don't mind me sayin' so, is t'give him a good clout on the ear, worst one you can muster, then offer him a double if he don't want to follow you back outside."

"I appreciate the advice, only he's not there. We agreed I'd be right back! I don't know where he could have disappeared to."

"I've got a few ideas," the driver says with a sigh. "Sailors at port are all the same. You want another piece of advice? Let me take you home. 'Tis getting dark out, and this is no place for good, wholesome country folk like yourself. I mean that kindly, mind you."

➢ No! You gave your word to return your cousin safely home. Thank the driver for his time, but ask for a refund on the fare. James is bound to turn up, sooner than later. Go to page 131

➢ Maybe he's right? If James gets himself in trouble, that's on him. You gave it a good try. It's time to end this foolishness and head back to Buckinghamshire. Go to page 102

Perchance to Dream

"Up! All hands! Up, or we all perish!" the cry comes, shaking you from your slumber.

How long were you asleep? It's impossible to tell, and in the commotion, it doesn't much matter. Now that you're on your feet, you feel the violent rocking of the ship that the hammock had countered. You rush up with the crew, ready to lend a hand to prevent the threat of death.

Thoughts of seasickness are replaced by sheer terror when you reach the open air. Lightning arcs across the sky with the dreadful crack of thunder only an instant behind. The sea rollicks like an open flame and foams upon the deck—beating her with great waves, threatening to pull all asunder.

One such wave nearly knocks the ship on her side, and a man who was up in the rigging of the mainsail is thrown into the sea. You recognize him as the third crimped sailor, the one in a white-and-blue striped shirt.

"Man overboard! Jack's gone in!" the sailor Marlowe cries.

Billy throws a rope, but when it hits the water, it disappears into the inky sea, and now he watches with a sort of helpless indifference as the sailor struggles for his life. It's clear the man has no idea how to swim and will soon drown.

➤ Tie a length of rope around your waist and leap in! Go to page 164

➤ Say a prayer for the poor seaman; nothing else you can do. Go to page 196

➤ No time! Dive in and help crimped Jack back to the ship. Go to page 101

Pitiless

Rushing inside the dim tavern, you call, "James? Oh, Cousin James?" to deaf ears.

You bump headlong into a dark shape your unaccustomed eyes can't quite make out. With a rude, "Hey, watch it!" you're given a hard shove and sent sprawling towards the bar. It's brighter up here, illuminated by lantern, rather than the dull candlelight of the eaves.

"You look lost," a feminine voice notes.

"So I've been told," you reply, dusting yourself off and straightening your clothing. "A congenital affliction, I'm afraid, though one I've only learnt of today."

"We don't get many… *refined*… customers, is all."

You look up to the barmaid, only to find a bar*matron*. She's pleasing enough to look at, though it's clear she's weathered many years' tenure behind this bar, the effect of which has hardened her features.

"I'm looking for my cousin, James. He was coming in for a quick drink. I have a carriage waiting."

"You're welcome to look around," she shrugs.

Tired of getting the runaround, you say, "That tactic doesn't seem to pay dividends. Perhaps if you supplied me with information on my cousin's whereabouts, I'd be the one paying you?"

"Lost, but not a fool," she replies, smiling. "That's good to hear. Elsewise I might be worried for your safety. Tell you what, buy yourself a drink and it might help loosen my lips."

"I thought the effect was intended for the one who imbibes, not the other way around."

"My bar, my rules. I'm the owner, by the way. Lindy Spencer, but call me Spence. That's another rule-o'-mine."

"Very well, pour me the same you served James," you say, bringing your coin purse up to the bar.

"Taste for the strong stuff must run in the family," she says, right eyebrow rising. "Though I'm afraid this hooch and the tale I have to tell will both leave a bad taste. Your cousin was here, sure enough. I know for certain because the first words from his mouth were, 'That damned cousin of mine will be the death of me,' and I can only assume there ain't two sailors with cousins searching for 'em."

Eyes fully adjusted to the dark, you look around, but see no sign of James.

"So he had a drink and left," you reply, leaving 'hoping to leave me behind' left unsaid.

Her left eyebrow goes up now. "Ain't touched your drink. That's bad manners, and I need to pour ya a second if you want to hear part two."

- "I appreciate the effort, but I'm afraid I must abstain." Pay the tab, then leave to search for James with a clear head. Go to page 130
- "Very well, a liquid dinner for me, then." Down the drink and nourish yourself on the ambrosia of information. Go to page 67

Precipitating Event

⚓

James looks deeply distraught, clearly knowing there's more to it than that, but all he does is give a squeeze to your shoulder before parting ways. After getting a belly full of food—the only source of energy the sleep-deprived can hope for—you head up top to start the night's watch. The evening is dark, but warm. Humid, with the threat of yet another stormy night.

"Have you studied Norie's *Epitome* much, Ward?" Lieutenant Dalton asks, handing you a copy of the book. "Do give yourself a refresher this evening. I should like to have a chat on a few key subjects after watch."

After watch meaning during your rest cycle, of course.

"Aye, sir!" you say, accepting the volume.

The full title is *The Epitome of Practical Navigation*, which is gilded upon the smooth, leather-bound spine just above the emblem of an anchor. You take the book, find a quiet spot illuminated by lamplight, nestle down into a makeshift basket of coiled ropes, crack open the tome—and immediately fall asleep.

You awaken with a start; half a dozen hands grope over your body. They're all common seamen, and you barely recognize the faces. The carpenter's mate is here, as is a corporal you've seen under the Master-of-Arms. What do they want with you? Are you dreaming?

"We told ya there'd be no more warnings," Mr. Magnus says. "Tried dousing ya in cold water, but it wasn't enough, eh?"

"A Jonas! Best tossed overboard!" the carpenter's mate shouts.

"Aye! The storm's been follow'n!" another sailor agrees.

"Come now, we ain't savages," Magnus says.

Then the Master-of-Arms speaks up. "That's right. Get a basket. If splashing water ain't workin', we'll just have to try *longer exposure*."

You're shoved into a metal birdcage, barely big enough to fit a person inside. A rope is fastened through the top and you're lowered overboard, just to the waterline. Every few seconds, the swell of the sea overtakes you, dunking you into the cold wet of the waves before bringing you back up again. It's all you can do to keep breathing.

"Ya can spend the rest-o'-the watch down there!" the Master-of-Arms calls down. "Should keep ya 'wake, I'd think!"

The mob disperses, leaving you to the whims of the sea. It's a terrible existence; the equivalent to waterboarding in the age of sail. So it comes as a mercy half an hour later when you catch a glimpse of Mr. Magnus sawing at the rope from above with his dagger. Soon, he cuts you loose.

Just like that, you sink down with Davy Jones, never to be seen again.

THE END

Present for Duty

⚓

Without the Master-of-Arms or Midshipman Magnus trying to sabotage your career (and with Lieutenant Dalton sufficiently subdued), you're able to proudly walk the decks as a Midshipman. No one forgets your roots, however, and the nickname "Ward" stays with you. Instead of your surname, you're addressed as Midshipman Ward. And, truth be told, you wear the title as a badge of honor.

Sevennight passes, each evening with wicked weather. Your digestive tract gradually empties itself of countryside finery (butter and milk and cheese), and is resupplied with hardtack and "Irish Horse" (coarse sea biscuits and salt-beef), which helps harden your constitution.

Then a fortnight goes by, finally without any seasickness, and with skies clearing up. As time goes by, you learn the rigging and the sails, how to spot and tell the difference between sandbars and reefs, how to splice lines, knots and their various names, as well as steering and navigating both the ship and the social world of the crew on it. You read many volumes on seafaring, while also learning to read the stars, the sky, the weather, and the mood of your commander.

In all, an idyllic time at sea. There's hard work, and plenty of it, but you're accepted as part of the crew now, and becoming a more valuable asset with every day that passes. So it is that when a full month goes by without sight of a Spanish ship, it's a blessing. Stronger, more confident, able to move about on sturdy legs, yes, all these things, but you're still unproven as a Naval Officer. Luckily for you, that chance is just on the horizon.

Presently scanning with the looking glass, you nearly pass over the bloom of wood and canvas; so unfamiliar is the sight of another ship at sea. But there can be no mistaking it: from the ink drawings you've studied, you know you're looking at an enemy warship.

"Sails!" you shout, lowering the looking glass.

"The Dagoes?" Lieutenant Dalton asks, before taking the telescope for himself. "By Jove, yes! Raise the Captain. We have a Spanish Man-o'-war in sight."

Excitement coursing through your veins, you do just that. Returning with the Captain a moment later, you stand by, excited to see just what his orders might hold.

After taking a look for himself, Longwick says, "They've spotted us. Note this position and make all sail back towards the fleet. We're to report the furthest vanguard of the Dons to the Admiral."

Dalton hesitates. "Captain, do you mean we're to outrun her? If we turn now, surely they'd see and get the jump on us. They have the wind; she'll catch us before nightfall."

"Then you'd better get us underway with haste, Lieutenant."

"Aye, Captain. Midshipman Ward! Chart a course, we're to outrun her and report back!"

Without a minute to spare, you leave them to set sail back towards home on an intercept course with the rest of the fleet. The pair finish their discussion out of earshot; Lieutenant Dalton offers a sharp salute, and Captain Longwick disappears back into his cabin.

Dalton turns and says, "God help us, Ward. They have a forty-degree lead on our course… There will be a bloody battle before we see the fleet again, mark my words."

That might be true, but this could also be the perfect opportunity to shine! After a moment, you reply:

- "Once the course is set, I'd like to command one of the broadsides. The guns will keep them at bay." Go to page 97
- "Lieutenant, leave the steerage to me! I'll pilot the helm and take us true." Go to page 88

Pressing Forward

⚓

The crew rushes forth, frenzied to brace the ship against the storm while there's still time. Yet the sight before you is another scene of chaos. The men move with extreme coordination—like a finely-tuned grandfather clock—each with their own part to play; perfectly set in their timing with one another. They swear terribly as they go, which to your nascent ears proves just as frightful as the storm.

Lieutenant Dalton notices and offers some insight. Shouting over the gale, he cries, "They swear to match the intensity of the storm! If they stop and kneel to pray, that's when you should worry!"

The surging seas are so bad, you spend most of the time hugging a bucket and emptying your stomach into it, but no one blames you for being green around the gills. Dalton even offers a kind word here, saying, "Mr. Magnus is one of our most experienced sailors and he tells me this storm is one of the worst he's ever seen."

Sevennight passes, each evening with wicked weather. Your digestive tract gradually empties itself of countryside finery (butter and milk and cheese), and is resupplied with hardtack and "Irish Horse" (coarse sea biscuits and salt-beef), which helps harden your constitution.

Then a fortnight goes by, finally without any seasickness, and with skies clearing up. You shadow as many of the able-bodied seamen as will let you, making sure you switch mentors regularly before trying anyone's patience too much. In this way, you "learn the ropes" both literally and figuratively.

You learn how to handle the rigging, where to stand and what to hold, how to bind the ropes together, splicing the hemp with hitches and knots, lanyards and lashings, connections and concoctions with names like *Cat's Paw*, *Sheep Shank*, or *Flemish Eye*. You learn the sails too: gallants and coursesails, topsails and jibs, studdingsails and staysails. You learn to furl, to loose, to shorten, to reef, to back and balance.

So it is that when a full month goes by without sight of a Spanish ship, it's a blessing. Stronger, more confident, able to move about on sturdy legs, yes, all these things, but you're still a fish out of water. Perhaps one that has figured out how to breathe air, but it'll be a while more still before you learn to walk.

No one would call you Jack Tar, but you're more than the would-be scholar who left London such a short time ago. For now, you're still known as Landsman, and you'll have to earn your designation of "able-bodied seaman" in time. Luckily for you, a chance to prove yourself is just on the horizon.

"Sails!" shouts Mr. Magnus, lowering the looking glass.

"The Dagoes?" Lieutenant Dalton asks, before taking the telescope for himself. "By Jove, yes! Raise the Captain. We have a Spanish Man-o'-war in sight."

Straining, you can just barely make out the hint of wood and canvas on the horizon. What you wouldn't give for a turn at the looking glass! Instead, you stand nearby, listening intently and splicing a length of rope so as not to appear in the way.

Captain Longwick arrives on deck, white shirt billowing. His ceremonial officer's coat hasn't been worn in weeks and his dark hair, overdue for a cut, flutters in the wind. With an open hand to receive it, he's given the telescope by Dalton.

At length, the captain lowers the telescope and says, "They've spotted us. Note this position and make all sail back towards the fleet. We're to report the furthest vanguard of the Dons to the Admiral."

Dalton hesitates. "Captain, do you mean we're to outrun her? If we turn now, surely they'd see and get the jump on us. They have the wind; she'll catch us before nightfall."

"Then you'd better get us underway with haste, Lieutenant."

"Aye, Captain. Mr. Magnus! Chart a course, we're to outrun her and report back!"

Captain Longwick takes another long study from the looking glass, then adds, "Double the men pumping the bilge for maximum speed. We'll lose them under cover of darkness. Not a single lantern to be lit after sunset, nor a match for a pipe. Have the cook serve early, then extinguish. Once fed, prepare gunners and load the guns, open the armory and set snipers. If they hope to catch us... we're going to make it costly."

Lieutenant Dalton offers a sharp salute, and Captain Longwick disappears back into his cabin. Dalton turns, ready to relay the orders. From what you've seen these last few weeks, this could be the perfect opportunity to shine!

➢ Volunteer to lead a team into the pump room. The Captain listed this as his first priority! Go to page 37

➢ All sails is quite the task and requires as many hands as can muster. Await your orders here. Go to page 165

Pressure Point

⚓

You stay hidden, watching and waiting to see what else they'll say. Lieutenant Dalton checks the barometer again just as the first few drops of rain start to splash against the deck. There's a sudden swell in the seas, and the *Hornblower* lurches in response—as does your stomach.

But it's your heart that leaps into your throat when you hear, "Just what the bloody hell d'ya think you're doin'?!"

Both Dalton and Magnus look back towards the voice. When you turn, you see it's the Master-of-Arms standing behind you.

"Performing my rounds," you say, trying to sound nonchalant.

"I'll be damned if ya are! You were *spying* on these men!"

"I was doing no such thing! I was performing my rounds, as ordered."

"Like hell. Your intents be easier t'see than that of a shark drawn to the sounds-o'-battle!"

"What's all this, Geoff?" Dalton asks. "What exactly is going on here, Ward?"

➢ Tell these men you think you got off on the wrong foot and want to start over. Say, "Gentlemen, please. This is all just a misunderstanding!" Go to page 305

➢ Perhaps there's another way out here. If you challenge him to a duel, he'll have to back down! Say, "This man is calling me a liar! I demand satisfaction!" Go to page 309

Pressurized

⚓

You grab hold of the rigging and hoist yourself up. Even with exhausted muscles, adrenaline spurs you on, higher and higher. Rope over rope, you climb. The wind whips with a ferocity you've never experienced before, and though the fibers cut into your soft hands, you're happy to have the extra grip against the incredibly fierce storm.

After you make it sufficiently high enough, you look around and feel a sense of accomplishment. You've really pushed your way up here!

But... now what?

As a Landsman, you haven't been trained for this. You don't know what to do next. So... looks like you're clinging. You could try calling out for help, but no one would hear you way up here, shouting to match the storm. Besides, everyone else is busy securing the sails. Can't have them tearing in the gale-force winds.

That's it! You need to help loose the sails, right?

You pull at the knots, but unfamiliar with those too, you have a rough time getting them to budge. Finally, one of the connections goes limp and the rope lashes out again and again, like a whip in the wind. Part of the rigging, newly free, sweeps out and knocks you clear.

You fall, taking the fastest way back down to the deck. A thunderclap sounds with a great *crack!* and you smash back onto the ship with a terrible crack of your own to echo the storm. Luckily for you, that break in your spine means you didn't feel this otherwise painful death.

THE END

Prestige

⚓

"Well, well, I didn't realize we had nobility in our manifests! Might ye have a ring I can kiss, your lordship?" the Master-of-Arms says, taunting.

"That… that isn't necessary," is all you can think to say in reply.

"Well, thank God Almighty for that!" he laughs.

"I only mean to say, that I might better serve in a capacity befitting my education."

"Too good t'be a common Tar? That ye might be, but midshipmen don't show up with the press gang, no matter how posh they'd be who sired ya."

"Sir, I really must protest," you protest.

"You wanna plead your case to the Cap'n directly? Be my guest. Otherwise, fall in line, Landsman. We'll harden those hands soon enough. Now help us get these crates loaded up!"

➤ Get to work. Idleness will only make things worse. Go to page 133

➤ The Captain is a gentleman. He will appreciate the gumption it takes to seek him out and will award me a spot within the officers' ranks. Go to page 98

Presumptuous

⚓

Before the Master-of-Arms has a chance to shoot, you turn to offer him only your profile as a target, lock your elbow, aim between his eyes, and squeeze the trigger. The burst of sparks that comes from the flintlock force you to squint and turn away, and when you open your eyes again you see only a plume of smoke between yourself and the Master-of-Arms.

It feels like an eternity, but after a few moments the spent gunpowder dissipates, and the Master-of-Arms stands before you, unharmed.

You've missed him!

The head offers only a very small target; a shot made all the more difficult by your unfamiliarity with both firearms and the sea beneath your feet. It was one in a million, really, and those betting on the outcome of your duel adjusted their payout odds accordingly.

The Master-of-Arms is now free to take his shot, unobstructed by time or the need for haste.

➢ Pray for a miracle. Go to page 185

➢ Think skinny thoughts. Go to page 185

➢ Watch the man line you up in his sights. Go to page 185

Prey Upon

As this is not a domestic jaguar (not that those even exist), it finds your pointing gesture meaningless. However, when you start to run, that's a signal it can pick up on. Jaguars are not known for attacking humans, but a fleeing animal strikes a chord with the predator on an instinctual level. The jungle cat sprints after you as you tromp through the woods, catching you easily and bringing you down with a practiced tackle.

Pound for pound, the jaguar has one of the most powerful bites of any living feline, which makes quick work of your spine and skull.

THE END

Proving Ground

Dudderidge had been a kindly sea cook. A man of about thirty, who hobbled around on one good foot, the other having been ruined by some long-ago accident. The wound looked like that inflicted by a crate drop, or perhaps a foot smashed by a horse while on shore leave, or maybe even a combat wound from an old engagement. Truly, you couldn't say—and no explanation was ever volunteered.

Still, the man had always done fairly well with what he was allotted in his kitchen. The joke aboard many a merchant vessel is that there's only one qualification needed to be a sea cook: you can't know the first thing about cooking. Dudderidge broke the mold in this way. Yet even if the man were secretly a gourmand, he wasn't afforded the ingredients to really show off.

Your memories of Dudderidge are primarily that of standing in line for chow and a simple, "Here ya go," uttered before he'd slop a scoop down on your square food tray.

Three times a day; three square meals. There were only a handful of times you saw the sea cook outside of his kitchen, and only one time you saw him in a mood other than jovial. In fact, he was outright panicked. Outraged. Like a hot kettle set to boiling.

Something had been bothering you prior to this reminiscence. Deep down, you knew the way that feral jungle pig died felt oddly familiar. Now that you're thinking back to your time on the *Cooper's Pride*, you can recall why. Dudderidge had been in his foul mood the day a prized sow had been found dead. But it wasn't just the loss of future meals. There was something else, too....

"Christ almighty! Short-o'-fresh meat as it is!" Dudderidge moaned. "Butch, what in the bloody hell happened here?"

"Why ask me?" the surgeon shot back.

"Ain't ye the one who found it?"

"Aye, got a dead pig, same as I told Billy. Here, see for yourself."

"What's wrong with the damned thing? Ain't ye the ship's surgeon?"

"Only because there already were a cook. Spent me whole life butchering dead flesh; what do I know about *why* they die?"

"Stow the sob story. I just need t'know if we can eat it, is all. Blessed thing looks poisoned," Dudderidge said.

"Or strangled," you had added.

That got a look from both men. But it truly did look that way, the way the flesh was swollen around the animal's throat. Spittle made a foam around the snout and mouth. You'd have to be a monster to strangle a hog of that size. Even Robin might not have been up to the task.

"Disease. I'd be sure of it," Butch said, all at once.

"Disease? Christ almighty!" Dudderidge had shot back, throwing his hands up.

"Could ye be mistaken?" Billy asked. He was silently watching the pig hitherto. But now he let his concerns be known. "Diseases mean quarantine…"

"Well… no need for that. Yes, 'tis disease. But not one that can be caught by men, so take comfort there. Best we toss it over straightaway."

And that had been the end of that. Still, there's something about this memory that feels, well, familiar. Maybe if you keep digging through the recesses of your mind, the truth will bubble up to the top?

- Think back to your time with Billy Greaves, the Mate and right-hand man of Captain Bullock. Go to page 140
- Revisit the memories of Butch, the former butcher employed as the ship's surgeon. Go to page 28
- Simply stare up at the stars—the same your shipmates presently sail beneath—until you fall asleep. Go to page 252

Puffy

Like little floating rocks, these fish even puff when you miss, filling themselves full of air and allowing an easier second attack. It takes a few stabs with the spear to get the hang of it, as the refraction of light shifts where you perceive the fish to be versus where they actually are, but eventually, you're able to catch a meal of rock-shaped fish.

Making a great feast from your bounty, you eat like you truly are the monarch of this small island. It all goes down swimmingly. Huzzah!

That is, until the toxins set in. Fish like these are some of the deadliest known to mankind. Known to you a little too late, it would seem. Your face and neck expand, much like those pufferfish. Then paralysis sets in and you die slowly, lying near your camp.

THE END

Push Your Luck

"Whaddya mean ya ain't got no more coin?!" Monks the gunner yells.

"Ya wagered double your loss, and thus owe twice what ye placed in the pot last round," Argyle says, as if you simply don't understand the math.

"I don't know what to say. I got carried away."

"We wasn't playin' for fun. You'll pay, damn you!" Monks says, slamming a fist on the table. The commotion brings the attention of the rest of the bar.

"Spence, in your tavern, what pray tell, happens to a gambler unable to settle a debt?" Wycombe asks, appealing to authority.

"It gets settled outside," she says. "Either by the press gangs or by a beatin', aggrieved party's choice."

"Who says it can't be both?" Monks asks, glaring at you.

"Now, gentlemen, wait, please. I'm sure we can come to some accord."

"It can't be both," the surgeon explains, almost detached, "Because if you beat a debtor too badly, they lose value to the press."

Before you even know what's happened, Monks has you lifted from your chair and escorts you outside. You desperately look for any sign of James, but he's nowhere to be seen.

"Sadly, I don't think it possible to work off the debt before we next set sail," Argyle says.

"The three of you were pressed! You wouldn't want to see me pressed, would you?" you reason.

"True enough. Let's beat the tar right outta this cheat," Monks says.

"We won't press you," Wycombe says to three sets of shocked eyes.

"You won't?" you say, wincing in preparation of a beating.

"No need. That man there is a crimp." Wycombe says, pointing.

Turning, you see a haggard-looking man. The boils on his flesh make James's scars look angelic by comparison. Hunched in such a way as to hide his great height, perhaps even from a long ago mis-healed wound. Presently, he grins at you through a maw of chipped and missing teeth.

"You ain't no Londoner, nor a sailor," a harsh voice croaks out.

"I'm not! I'm no good to you!" you cry.

"No problem at all. I can sell a debtor into civilian service," the man says, speaking to the trio of seamen. "I'll pay ya half'a what this one owes."

"Half!" Argyle calls. "I don't intend to get robbed twice tonight!"

"Curse your blood, crimp," Monks agrees.

Wycombe steps forward. "Do it. Otherwise we're left with nothing but whatever cuts you intend to get on your knuckles, and I'd just as soon not sew anyone up just yet."

"Let me get just one good lick in," Monks says.

"Suits me," the crimp says.

Your luck, it seems, has finally run out. Not much choice here:

Wake up the next morning and face the consequences of your actions. Go to page 93

Put to Vote

"You're right, Rediker," you say. "Your man Barlow, too. I couldn't agree more."

Rediker stares back dumbly, blinking with disbelief. "Well... good. That settles it, then?"

"I suppose, but we still need to vote on where we're headed, don't we?"

Now he grins. "If it were up t'me alone, I'd say we set sail for the West Indies. Loot a fat merchantman flush-o'-New World booty on the way, then offload in New Providence, where we can have the... *port experiences* we missed out on in Boston."

Several of the pirates grunt in the affirmative at the euphemism.

But it's Marlowe who speaks up. "I support your bid for Cap'n, Rediker, I do. But the Caribbean's a terror. I heard tale-o'-zombies on those isles. Men made slaves by *voodoo magic*. Then there's yellow fever, shipworm, hurricanes and—"

"Bloodthirsty pirates?" Rediker finishes. "Aye, there's a reason for that. More inlets and islands than stars in the sky. We can strike from nowhere and be gone again 'fore we could ever be caught. 'Tis a tropical paradise, man! Voodoo zombies? Ha! If there are slaves t'be found in the West Indies, they'll be liberated by the *Deleon's Revenge!*"

Now the African pirates cry their support. Marlowe seems unconvinced, though he drops the issue.

"All in favor-o'-Cap'n Rediker leading us t'riches?" Barlow says.

"Aye!" comes a mighty roar.

"And all in favor-o'-sailing for New Providence, plunder, and well-rigged women?" Rediker asks.

"Aye!!!"

"Sails!" comes the cry from the watch the next day.

"Just a slaver," Barlow says, handing the spyglass to Captain Rediker.

"Slaver?" several of the crewmen mutter, spreading the word. The African pirates seem keenly interested in this new discovery.

"The *Amazing Diamond*, eh? Helmsman, pull us up alongside her!" Rediker orders.

"Cap'n?" Marlowe says from the helm.

"Ya heard me orders, Marlowe! We need food and water. We need more guns and crew—she's got 'em!"

"She's a bloody fortress!"

"Aye! Mayhaps we need a new ship, too! Action stations!"

"I'll not pilot us into the mouth-o'-hell," Marlowe says, releasing the wheel.

"Cap'n has full say during battle, damn you! Barlow, raise the black. I'll take the bloody helm if you're too lily-livered!"

Rediker takes the helm, while Barlow unfurls a bolt of black canvas. As he raises the flag, you see the design chosen for the *Deleon's Revenge*: crossed cutlasses form the frame of an hourglass, with a death's-head encapsulated in the upper chamber and a crimson drop of blood falling like sand into the lower chamber. The warning here is three-fold: time is limited, and should the enemy resist, he risks bodily injury, or even death.

At sight of the approaching black flag, the *Amazing Diamond* opens fire. Wooden splinters blast across the ship, but Captain Rediker continues his approach undaunted. Your ship fires back, but the merchantman only has a handful of guns to the dozen or more firing back at you. The carnage is immense, and you soon see firsthand why Marlowe refused his orders.

"Cap'n, they hit us on the water-line!" Chips reports in.

"Abandon ship! Take the enemy as prize!"

The pirates throw grappling hooks at the galleon, which floats half as high again as the *Deleon's Revenge* out of the water. Armed with cutlasses, they climb aboard for the attack.

"Free those in chains! They'll join us in our fight!" Rediker cries, cocking his pistol at the ready before joining the climb himself.

With the *Revenge* sinking, you've little choice but to climb the fortress and join the assault.

The pirate crew is greeted with shocking defenses. In order to resist a slave insurrection, ships like this one are built to defend not only attacks from without, but attacks from within as well. There's a huge barrier erected between the main decks and the crew on the quarterdeck. And what's worse, the swivel guns are aimed not seaward—but at the middle of the ship.

These guns fire now at the attacking pirates, with brutal efficiency. Those who survive make to scale the barrier and find the slaver captain, but the crew slashes at them from above, maintaining the high ground.

It's a brutal attack, one you're unprepared for with your small guns and smaller crew. These sailors are terrified at the thought of a pirate attack, and now revel in fending off your blundering attempt at plundering.

A slave ship would indeed make for a grand pirate vessel, and history has a few examples where this really occurred, but those pirates were hardened crews, better armed and better prepared.

Rediker's eyes have proved bigger than his stomach, and it's clear now he bit off more than he could chew. With a sinking ship being the only place to flee, you're left to the mercy of the slaver crew—a notoriously merciless bunch. They live their lives throwing dead and dying human cargo overboard and beating the living into submission; what tenderness could you possibly hope for now?

THE END

Quit While You're Ahead

Or, while you still have a head. Win or lose, these sailors are dangerous men, made more so by drink. Probably best to walk away while you can and wait for your cousin.

So you sit by the bar nursing a gin, lost in a half-drunken translation of Homer. *Oh for shame*, you start, or is it *How shameless?* Hmmm. Perhaps either could work, so you continue with, *mortals blame the gods, for it is said evil comes from gods, but it is mortal men, rather, who by their own recklessness do earn sorrows by their deeds...*

A chorus of "Hurrah!" rocks the tavern and breaks your thoughts. When you look up, you see that Cousin James has returned. He's practically glowing, with a smile that threatens to wrap all the way around his head.

"Cousin! Come, let's continue our revelry elsewhere," he says, leaning in for confidence with a whispered, "Not much more we can do in this tavern, eh?"

Back outside, the sun has set and the moon now dominates the night sky. Despite the biting cold of the riverbank after dark, you feel warm and content. But that'd be the gin talking. In fact, it speaks for you now, getting wistful as you say, "What a life you lead, cousin. Excitement, adventure, romance, and brotherhood."

"Beware and take care, ye would-be seamen. Though two-hundred set sail, less'n fifty come in," James replies, lyrically. "Don't get ahead-o'-yourself, coz. 'Tis a hard and dangerous life. One I'm done with, truth be told."

"Really? But how can you go back to Buckinghamshire after seeing Barbados?"

"You don't find many old sailors," James replies, somber. "I aim to retire while I can. Now come, I've lost my taste for gin. Let's have a good English ale, shall we?"

Another port-of-call for sailors awaits ahead, at the opposite end of the boardwalk, beckoning you to come closer with sounds of sea shanties and revelry. This one, from the sign out front, calls itself THE BLOW HOLE.

"Another brothel?" you ask.

"No, just a pub. Why? What makes you think that?"

"Never mind," you say, looking once more at the sign before heading inside.

It's a rowdy group, singing and carousing. That somber tone still infects James's voice as he orders ale; you can tell his memories weigh heavy on his conscience.

"Did you... lose many friends?" you try.

"Not many, no. Good mates are hard to come by. Best mates, even more so. I only lost just the one, coz. Like a brother. Maybe more than that, I dunno. I loved that man, I did," he replies, then taking the ales, toasts loudly, "To Johnny. There's old ships, and new ships, and ships lost at sea. But the best ships are friendships, so let's drink t'you and me."

James's voice cracks at the end and his eyes glisten, if ever so slightly.

"To Johnny," you say, then clink your tankard against your cousin's.

As you're drinking, a nearby sailor scoffs, "What a coupl'a ninnies."

His friend puckers a fake kiss. "More like buggerers. *C'mere Johnny, oh Johnny,*"

> Punch him right in that kisser. Teach him for disrespecting the dead, and your cousin to boot. Go to page 22

> Tell your cousin they're not worth it, and offer to buy the next round. Go to page 209

Rabbit

You turn and run, heading down past the tavern, hoping to lose the men in the twists and turns of the alleyways. Unfortunately, you must not have done much hunting in the countryside, otherwise you'd know that fleeing prey only stirs up the blood of a predator.

The men sprint after you, howling not only in your imagination. These sailors spend all day every day on their feet, climbing ropes and heaving equipment, while you're more accustomed to a drawing desk or a fainting couch.

The first thing you feel is your feet fly out from under you as you're tackled to the ground. They wail on you, using you as a release for their frustrations.

"Show you who's fool!"

"Like that? Have 'nother, ya Nelly!"

"Dandy bastard!"

You're beaten savagely, left facedown to drown (somewhat ironically, in a port) in a puddle of muck. Not the noblest final resting place.

THE END

Rank Has Its Privileges

⚓

Jumping to the front, you're able to secure a spot on the longboat. Once it's lowered into the water, Captain Longwick gives the order to row, and the small craft glides smoothly under the power of your strokes. A dozen questions flutter in your mind as you row towards the enormous first-rate ship of the line, the supersized HMS *Rochambeau*.

While the Spanish warship *Don Pedro Sangre* dwarfed the HMS *Hornblower*, the flagship is as impressive as they get. The pride of England—even if she is a prize from the last war fought against the French. The longboat crewmen hail out to the sailors aboard the *Rochambeau* and a rope ladder is thrown down.

Captain Longwick starts up, and you make to follow, but one of the other sailors tugs on your breeches to pull you back with a call of, "Sit down!"

"Aren't we to board?" you ask.

"Aye, Landsman. An' there ye'll be served fine English roast beef and ale pumped straight from the cask!" another seaman cries, voice thick with sarcasm. The other sailors get a good laugh at your expense.

"Did ye forget your shore rigging? We're t'meet with all the finest ladies-o'-society!" another says, barely able to get the words out before bursting into another round of laughter.

"We're really to just wait in the boat?" you ask.

"Of course not," the eldest seaman says, straight-faced. The others quiet down and look to him, but then a broad grin breaks across his face and he continues, "But first they gotta call, 'Ho! Landsman on deck!' t'hail your arrival!"

The longboat rocks about in the sea under the thrashing belly-laughs.

"Hardy har-har," you say, crossing your arms and looking out to the open sea.

The longboat sits moored to the warship for several tedious hours, during which time the sailors intermittently try to revive the long-dead joke about the Landsman Who Wanted to Meet the Admiral, but mostly they spend that time napping.

At length, Captain Longwick returns, looking rather perturbed. You want nothing more than to know what happened aboard the ship, but you've learned your lesson and don't press the issue. Perhaps a midshipman could have accompanied the Master and Commander on this errand, but certainly not a common Tar.

Once back aboard the *Hornblower*, Captain Longwick addresses Lieutenant Dalton, which is about as close to the scuttlebutt as you'll get.

"Captain Longwick, the ship is yours. You'll find we've already begun repairs from our action at sea. Nothing else to report," Dalton says, offering a salute.

"Excellent. We'll need to finish repairs and resupply before our next assignment. We're to head to the West Indies and deliver word of the Spanish plans in the Caribbean. But that can wait until tomorrow. For tonight—I believe I promised rewards for victory? Remove any limitations on grog and open up the extra rations of rum."

The men, in various states of drunkenness, sing and dance, play cards and other games, jostling and joking in every berth of the ship. A fight breaks out, and though it's quickly subdued, the quarrel doesn't escape the attention of the officers up on the quarterdeck.

"It's been a while since they've been allowed to let loose, sir," Lieutenant Dalton says.

"Yes. Looks like the men might need to burn off some of this… enthusiasm," Captain Longwick replies.

"Aye, sir," Mr. Midshipman Magnus says from the other side. "Could rally 'em about for a Sailor's Hornpipe? Or Sling the Monkey?"

Noticing you eavesdrop, Dalton says, "Something we can help you with, Landsman?"

Curiosity getting the better of you, you reply:

- "Begging your pardons, sirs, but what exactly is a Sailor's Hornpipe?" Go to page 51
- "Sorry to interrupt, but I must ask: Is there really a monkey onboard? One that we might… sling?" Go to page 190

236

Rats in the Cargo

The hammocks sway as the rollicking of the ship increases. You must be headed out into open seas, for the vast ocean pushes the *Cooper's Pride* nearly to her side with each undulation. The fact that the hammocks move in tune with the ship is a mercy, so it's almost like you're not rocking at all, but rather the ship rolls around you. Closing your eyes helps maintain this illusion.

But when the floorboards creak, you sneak a peek towards the source. Just as you suspected! Barlow slinks away, on tip-toes no less, silently weaving through the sleeping men.

Trying to match the creaking of his steps to mask your own, you step off your hammock and follow the man down into the hold. The ship's swaying gets to you, but you swallow your bile and continue on.

Barlow moves down past the stores of wine and rum (an obvious spot to steal away to) and past the chickens and dairy cows. It's not his stomach that leads him away, that much is clear. He takes a lantern hanging from a beam and uses it to light his path. You'd never imagined it would be so dark below decks, but without sunlight, lamplight is all you can hope for. You'll have to follow close, lest you trip and reveal yourself.

"Ah-ha, there ye are! Knew I'd find ya down here…" Barlow says to some unseen partner.

Leaning close, eyes straining in the darkness, you're unable to make out his fellow conspirator. Realizing that the other half of this clandestine rendezvous might be able to see *you* in the lamplight, you duck aside. The ship lurches at the exact same moment and you knock over a bucket as you're scrambling for footing. Should you run? Hide? Leap out with a roar?

"Over here, c'mon out," Barlow calls out. Gritting your teeth, fists balled for a fight, you reveal yourself. "So… ye heard it too, eh?"

Barlow holds up the lantern, temporarily blinding you. Then you see that he holds a small black kitten in his other arm, tucked against his chest.

"I got ears like a…" he trails off, blinking. "Well, somethin' that hears good."

Perhaps you've overestimated the man's wit and cunning.

"Think I'll call him either Cap'n Kiddy or Bartholo-meow Roberts."

"Bartholo-*meow*?" you parrot back.

"Black Bart, on account-o'-his fur. Maybe small now, but give'm a bit-o'-milk and he'll be a rat-catcher yet, mark me words. Say… ya wouldn't report a man for an act-o'-charity would ya, Saltboots? This little one needs me help."

Bart gives a pitiful mew to punctuate the point.

"I'm not one to begrudge a kitten his milk. Your secret's safe with me, Barlow."

"Aye, knew ya was a good sort, I did. Best we get back to the fo'c'sle 'fore we're noticed absent."

Indeed. And the way the ship is swaying, you can't get back into the hammock's equilibrium soon enough.

✧ ✧ ✧

"Up! All hands! Up, or we all perish!" the cry comes, shaking you from your slumber.

How long were you asleep? It's impossible to tell, and in the commotion, it doesn't much matter. Now that you're on your feet, you feel the violent rocking of the ship that the hammock had countered. You rush up with the crew, ready to lend a hand to prevent the threat of death.

Thoughts of seasickness are replaced by sheer terror when you reach the open air. Lightning arcs across the sky with the dreadful crack of thunder only an instant behind. The sea rollicks like an open flame and foams upon the deck—beating her with great waves, threatening to pull all asunder.

One such wave nearly knocks the ship on her side, and a man who was up in the rigging of the mainsail is thrown into the sea. You recognize him as the third crimped sailor, the one in a white-and-blue striped shirt.

"Man overboard! Jack's gone in!" the sailor Marlowe cries.

Billy throws a rope, but when it hits the water, it disappears into the inky sea, and now he watches with a sort of helpless indifference as the sailor struggles for his life. It's clear the man has no idea how to swim and will soon drown.

➢ No time! Dive in and help crimped Jack back to the ship. Go to page 101

➢ Tie a length of rope around your waist and leap in! Go to page 164

➢ Say a prayer for the poor seaman; nothing else you can do. Go to page 196

Ready, or Not

Billy nods, though it's clear he doesn't appreciate your sense of honor in this regard. "Take care-o'-yourself, but be warned. The longer ya linger at port, the more likely you're t'end up pulled out t'sea."

He disappears back inside the tavern, and you continue your search for James.

Another port-of-call for sailors awaits ahead, at the opposite end of the boardwalk, beckoning you to come closer with sounds of sea shanties and revelry. Another tavern, as can plainly be heard all the way across the promenade. With no other leads, you make your way down the river banks towards the tavern light like a moth to a flame.

This one is called THE BLOW HOLE, which would be a real waste of a name if it weren't another brothel as well. But you can sense a different atmosphere as you approach. Open windows, through which you hear men shouting.

Just as you arrive, a sailor comes flying from the alehouse and into the muck at your feet. The doors burst open, with a trio of other men engaged in fisticuffs. Two of them quickly get the better of their foe and knock him flat on his back, next to the barroom Icarus lying before you.

Do they need your help? Before you can decide, they get to their feet. A testament to the numbing effects of alcohol, no doubt. The pair watch their adversaries head back inside, then turn their attention to you.

"Bloody hell ya lookin' at?" one cries out, wiping the blood from his nose.

"Some kinda Nelly?" the other asks. "Buy us a drink, then?"

He laughs, but his friend takes it seriously. "You're right! This town'd be nothin' without brave men like us, so how's 'bout a little thanks?"

They slur their words, eyes measuring you hungrily. You back away, uttering, "Truly, you have my thanks. I'll just be on my way to go get a cask. Wait here."

"This dandy takes us for fools," blood-nose says.

"Just 'cause a man works with his hands, he still has a brain," his partner protests.

You look around for support. No one in the tavern pays you any mind, but back towards London proper there's a patrol of town guard. If you call out for help, they just might hear you.

> ➤ Yes, that's what they're here for! Call to the guard. Go to page 118

> ➤ Fight the men. That's the only language they understand. Go to page 299

> ➤ Run for it! Half as much as not, the hare manages to outrun the hounds. Go to page 234

Rebuffed

"I can see it in your eyes," Billy says. "Same as Jimmy's when he first signed on. Y'may not know it yet, but you're a Saltboots too."

"And I prefer if you'd figured it out sooner than later," Spence interjects. "Drink, lad, or lass. Paying customers only."

"My intention is only to wait for James," you say, your mind still half-considering Billy's words.

Now her left eyebrow rises. "Then I'm afraid you are indeed a lost soul, and unwelcome here. Nothing personal, but if these sea dogs and scallywags starting thinking they can mill about without payin' for the privilege, well, my business is sunk. You understand, I'm sure."

"You're kicking me out?" you ask with surprise.

"Go buy yourself a supper," she says, shaking her head. "No man wants to walk out that door to see he's kept someone waiting. Come back when Jimmy's through with his welcome home. Here, I'll give you the name of a place serves up a decent steak-n'-ale pie."

You look to Billy for support, but he simply shrugs as if to say, "Not my tavern, not my rules."

Back outside, the sun has set and the horizon holds a red glow.

"Somethin' I can help ya find?" a harsh voice croaks out.

Turning, you see a haggard-looking man. The boils on his flesh make James's scars look angelic by comparison. Hunched in such a way as to hide his great height, perhaps even from a long ago mis-healed wound. Presently, he grins at you through a maw of chipped and missing teeth.

"I should think not," you say. "Just off to find supper before I conclude my business at port. I'm afraid I haven't any alms to give to the poor..."

The haggard man glowers and says, "Got a business partner waiting on ya?"

"Precisely," you lie, sensing the way out.

"Best-o'-luck with it," he says, clearly wishing you the opposite fate.

You're not sure what that was all about, though your instincts say it was one of the unsavory characters who might be hanging around port that James warned you about. Happy to be free of him, you hurry off to find your meal.

That steak-n'-ale pie was quite good, but your hand looked practically naked without a tankard in it, and your throat was left dry without a frothy *something* to wash the flaky crust down with. Still, best to keep your head clear while you're on your own.

Back outside, the same haggard-looking man hunches in the shadows a block away. He starts forward, but recoils at the sight of something behind you. When you look back, you see a pair of town guards patrolling the streets. Sensing the safety of their presence, you say hello. They note your provincial clothing with concern.

"Far from home at a late hour, ain't ya?" one asks.

"Sure feels that way," you confess.

"There, there, you're safe now. Tell us where you're staying in London and we'll make sure you make it back safely. That's enough excitement for one night, I'm sure," the second guard says, comforting.

"Well," you admit, sheepishly. "I'm not staying anywhere in London."

"Poor planning," his partner offers. "But I'm sure we can find you an inn."

"I… I need to find my cousin."

"And where might this cousin be?"

"He…" you start, then think better of admitting his use of a brothel. "I don't know where he is."

With a sigh, the first guard says, "Already sleeping soundly, I'm sure. You can find him in the morning."

"Don't you worry, we'll put you up for the night," the other adds.

"Really? You'd do that?" you say, somewhat dumbstruck by their kindness.

"Well, of course! In fact, we're required to by law, ain't we?" he replies.

"That's the way of it," his partner agrees. "Ever since the Vagabonds Act was passed back in 1597, we've been giving a free holding cell to any and all vagrants."

"Vagrants!?" you protest, but it falls on deaf ears.

➢ Go directly to jail, do not spend $200 on a place to stay, and await your sentencing! Go to page 188

➢ Get out of jail free. Make a run for it and lose the town guards in the alleys! Go to page 284

Red Crossing

⚓

There are some men beyond saving. The one obliterated by a cannonball isn't even in few enough pieces to count. Another has a two-foot wooden beam buried in his abdomen, his face ashen, and crimson on his lips.

But there are others you *can* help. One nearby sailor shattered his kneecap when struck by the flat side of a piece of debris. Helping the man up, you wrap his arm over your shoulder and help him walk.

Another reaches out and you pull the man to his feet, offering your other side for support. Blood pours from his left leg, and you soon realize that his foot has been completely blown away. He too might be beyond saving, but damned if you won't try anyhow.

"Where do you think you're going?" Lieutenant Saffron demands.

"Sir, taking these two to surgery."

"You can't abandon your post!" he says, clearly too stunned to think rationally.

"Aye, sir. I won't be gone a minute. You've got the larboard broadside covered for me, don't you?"

He looks back, so you continue on before he can protest further. The ship is complete chaos, but there's a clear path to the surgery. It's marked by drips of red, which quickly become a river as you drag the bleeding wounded down to surgery for help.

Wycombe, the ship's surgeon, quickly examines the two you've brought him. "Christ Almighty. You've got to tie off limbs like that one! What's wrong with the other?"

"Me knee!" the sailor groans.

"Keep off it, stay out of the way. I'll see to you after I sew up the bleeders."

"Somethin' for the pain, please."

"No. Get him out of here!"

Wycombe goes to work tying a tourniquet for the man missing a foot, and you help pull the other wounded sailor from the surgery. Finding him a quiet place to sit, you rush off to find others to help. And there are plenty. More cannon shot is exchanged as fast as the crews can reload, creating freshly wounded seamen with each enemy hit.

At length, the night goes dark, the *Hornblower* pulls ahead of the *Don Pedro Sangre*, and a ceasefire is ordered. Captain Longwick comes to inspect the gun crews, with Lieutenant Dalton by his side, and praises everyone for working through the terror. Then he orders the viscera mopped up.

"And Lieutenant Saffron—quick thinking, by having your gun crews tend to the wounded. Well done!" Captain Longwick says, praising your superior.

Saffron gives a slight glance your way, but then salutes and says, "Aye, sir. Thank you, sir."

He doesn't give you a second look.

"Bastard," one of the other seamen growls. The men know the truth of it, even if you won't get credit for it with the Master and Commander of the ship. Captain Longwick departs and Lieutenant Dalton comes by to address you personally.

He says, "Orders are: no lights, and complete silence. We've pulled ahead of the *Don Pedro Sangre*, but the enemy is giving relentless chase. God willing, we'll lose her under cover of darkness. Now get some rest, we'll be on watch soon."

You're about to offer the usual sharp, "Aye, sir!" but stop just in time, giving only a salute.

Dalton nods, leaving you be.

Well done! You've survived your first battle aboard the Hornblower *and gave as good as you got. Now get some rest, and when you're ready....* Go to page 197

Rediker

Interesting choice, Dear Reader. Not sure if you just weren't paying attention during all those campfire ruminations, or if you're trying some sort of bluff, but here's how it plays out:

"The killer was none other than... Rediker himself," you say.

There's a moment of shocked confusion, then a smile breaks over Rediker's face.

"Of course it was me," he says.

"Wait... what?" you reply.

"I orchestrated the whole thing, from day one. Killed Bullock without so much as arousing suspicions. And then? I took his ship for meself and now sail as Cap'n Rediker, the most fearsome pirate t'ever sail under the black. It's that very same cunning, Saltboots, that makes these men follow me t'the back-o'-beyond."

He's taking credit! Trying to look more the pirate to his men. Well, that backfired.

"But can't have ye revealing me secrets t'the civilized world, can we?" Rediker says, then with a flick of his head, he sends his most bloodthirsty men after you.

THE END

Red Rum

"The murderer was the ship's surgeon—Butch," you say, before going on to relate your recollection of the events on the *Cooper's Pride* that led to this suspicion. All listen silently as you detail the moments leading up to the crime, their eyes darting from you to Butch and back again, hanging on every word.

Once you've told your tale, the focus turns entirely to the accused. From the look on his face, you can be certain you've uncovered the truth. At length, the man sighs, looks down, and then slowly nods his head. As he confesses, you take the rum from your hip and drink to justice for spilt blood.

"Aye, 'tis true. Was my hand that ended Bullock's life, though it were his own that spilled the blood. Poisoned, made to choke, and slit his own throat in hopes-o'-drawing another breath. I never knew the man would do such a thing, but it made so none suspected my hand, so…." Butch shrugs with a calloused sort of nonchalance. "Remember that dead sow? How the hog looked strangled? Well, that were just practice; trying t'get the right concoction at the right dose. I smashed the cabinet in the surgery, 'cause I thought once ye lot knew the cap'n were poisoned, that would send ya down t'me. But I never needed the excuse, as it turned out."

"But why? Why kill the captain? That's the one detail I never could discover," you say.

Butch reaches inside his blouse, removing a small section of parchment, folded into quarters. As he unfolds the note, you realize he's holding the missing page from the captain's log! Rediker motions and Barlow snatches the page from Butch's grasp, giving it to the pirate captain to read.

"Discovered a man amongst my crew to be that of a convicted killer. Known as 'The Butcher of Bicester' by local authorities; these same men who informed me that the surgeon on my ship was wanted for *uxoricide*—the murder of his own wife. I am to deposit this 'Butch' with the Admiralty Court of Boston at my arrival, which it will surely give me great pleasure to do with haste," Rediker reads.

"You kept the page?" you say, incredulous.

Butch shrugs again. "The cap'n wrote that right in front-o'-me, dictating aloud as he did so. Showing off his power. Ain't so powerful now, is he? Well… I s'pose 'tis a trophy-o'-sorts. *The Butcher of Bicester*—who would believe it? Me, famous! That oughta show her too! Oh, she had it comin'."

"I believe that would be *infamous*. And now I believe what you have coming, as it were, is to be taken into irons, or perhaps left on this island in my stead. Seeing as how the sentence is rightfully yours, I will happily relinquish it," you say.

Rediker chuckles, starts to laugh, and soon the others join in until it's a boisterous chorus of guffaws. *Buahahaha!* and the like. Hearty pirate laughter.

"We all be murderers now, Saltboots!" Rediker says. "Bloody thieving pirates, every last man. Ya think we'd turn one-o'-our own over t'face *justice*? There is no justice, save for what we carve out for ourselves. If we want our thirty pieces-o'-silver, we'll damn well take 'em."

"Besides, only offed his old lady," Marlowe says with a shrug.

"That's right. Ain't poisoned none the rest-o'-us, have ya, Butch?" Barlow adds.

"Not yet!" Butch laughs, getting in on the joke.

And the boisterous laughter begins anew.

"Oh, come now, don't fret, Saltboots!" Rediker says. "Butch's still one-o'-us, but ye did indeed prove your innocence. We'll take ya with us and drop ya off at the next civilized port we find. Never let it be said Cap'n Rediker ever killed who didn't have it coming."

"Just like me wife!" Butch adds, furthering the piratical merriment.

That was about the best outcome you could hope for, seeing as how you are dealing with bloody thieving pirates, after all. Now that you've gotten to the bottom of things in the *Case of the Mysterious Captain Murderer*, the crew focuses on getting to the bottom of their ship—the careening of the hull, for which they are moored here.

You show them where the fresh water lies, along with the best food stores, helping to expedite the process of refitting the ship. Then they put you to work scrubbing. Chips orders a few of the planks replaced completely; others are vigorously treated with brimstone and tallow. Soon the ship is cleaned and treated—free of worms, barnacles, and mollusks—once more as seaworthy as she ever was.

Careening complete, the pirates take to sea. Truth be told, you missed floating along the waves, and it feels good to be out among sailors again; even if they are bloodthirsty pirates. Though that good feeling is to be short-lived.

"Sails!" comes the call.

"Spanish? Did that bloody warship find us?" Rediker asks.

"Aye, warship, Cap'n. But she's English!" the watchman calls back.

"Damn our rotten luck," Marlowe says.

Rediker shakes his head. "We'll have t'lose 'em in the inlets. Stay close to shore. King George's dogs ride too low to follow along the reefs and sandbars. Barlow, secure Saltboots here into the hold before our honest shipmate gets any ideas-o'-aiding the Crown."

Barlow nods, then takes you roughly down below to be tied up in case of action.

- Once you're alone, fight him off! Barlow's thin as a whip, and you're now a hardened survivalist. Go to page 31
- Resist, but slightly. Flex, take a deep breath, then squirm your way free of these bonds once he's gone. Go to page 83
- Don't resist, but as soon as he's gone, remove the gag and call for help once the action starts. Go to page 257
- Make no resistance. Stay put, rescue will come at the hands of His Majesty's Royal Navy. Go to page 212

Reflecting Pool

Dashing back through the jungle, tripping over roots and vines, thorns tearing at your clothes, you make it back to the freshwater pond with all the grace of a stampeding wildebeest. Performing a cannonball leap into the center of the pond, you create quite a splash, but once the waters settle, you realize that you indeed have not been struck dead by lightning.

It worked! But, well, you were only sort of right. While the pond is situated in a lower-lying area than the ridge, and thus is less likely to attract the attention of Zeus's bolts, jumping into the pond itself didn't really help. If anything, it's made things worse, because now your head is the tallest object in the water.

And the second tallest is swimming right towards you.

Crocodylus acutus, the American crocodile. It would seem your flailing about has set off the predatory instincts of this riparian reptile, and since you acted like a wounded animal, the crocodile responds in kind.

With your own lizard-brain kicking into high gear, you make to swim back out of the pond, but you're a few hundred-million years behind the evolutionary power curve on this one.

THE END

Representation

⚓

James looks at you, knowing you're up to something dastardly. Heading him off, you say, "Best if you don't know what I've got in mind, cousin. Only do me a favor before you walk away, and drop your key to the magazine."

Your cousin simply stares at you for a moment more. Maybe it's the wily look in your eyes, or maybe it's the bags beneath them, but after another beat he turns, presses his palms against the table, and gets up to walk away. There, left behind next to his plate, sits his gunner's mate's key to the ammunition stores.

Taking the key, you head down to the magazine. You should be mustering for watch right now, but you have a few precious minutes before the first bell sounds. If anyone were to ask what you're doing skulking around below-decks, why, you're just taking the initiative! Familiarizing yourself with your ship, like a good Ward.

As you make it down to the magazine, you hear voices behind the locked door. This is it! You slowly turn the key, not wanting to alarm them, but truly—they have no other exit.

When you open the magazine, the scene is set perfectly. Cannonballs, musket shot, gunpowder; everything as expected. But also, three chairs around a crate with coin and dice on the surface. And three guilty parties seated *in flagrante delicto*.

The ancient mariner across from you seems to be the leader of the bunch, a clean-shaven bastion of civilization amongst these brutish men whom you make out as Wycombe, surgeon assigned to the HMS *Hornblower*. The gruff man on your left has several facial scars and two tattoos: a cannon along one forearm, and a cutlass on the other. He'd be the man your cousin called "Monks," the ship's gunner. To your right sits Argyle, the bespectacled ship's recorder. He's the only one who looks at you with recognition.

"Ward? What in the bloody hell're ya doin' down here?" he says.

"Before we go any further, gentlemen, know that I have measures set in place should I suddenly 'disappear.' Should you choose to silence me with violence, the Captain will certainly soon learn the truth of it all," you bluff, the words flowing from some unknown muse. "Know also that I have no ill-will against you three, only I'm in a terrible predicament and I see no other means out. So, should we agree to terms, you can trust this is the end of it, as far as I'm concerned. You have my word of honor."

"The devil are ya blatherin' about?" Monks asks.

"It's plain to see," Wycombe answers for you, with cool nonchalance. "We're being blackmailed for our vice. Go on, then, what are your terms?"

As it turns out, the three hold no great love for either the Master-of-Arms or Midshipman Magnus. They simply want to roll their bones in peace, and you don't ask much in return for letting them do just that.

After you've struck an accord, the men are true to their word. Cousin James is no longer to be treated as a workhorse, but that's simply the icing on the cake. Your main course comes from Argyle himself. Once he's finished his agreed-upon part of the bargain, you're summoned to the Captain's quarters.

◇ ◇ ◇

Argyle steps out, gives you a stern look, and says, "I don't doubt these men deserved this fate. Nor do I think of your maneuver as anything other than a desperate measure. Just know: we are not allies. Nor should you want me as an enemy."

Before you can reply, the Captain cries, "Ward!" and Argyle leaves. Best not to keep your commander waiting any longer. Once you enter and the formalities are dispensed with, you're placed at ease.

Longwick offers no small talk. He launches right into, "My summoning you here, Ward, isn't entirely a compliment. Argyle has re-evaluated the books and it looks like I don't have room for a Ward after all."

For a panicked moment, you think the recorder has betrayed you, but the Captain continues, "What's more, Argyle tells me our Master-of-Arms is overdue for reassignment to a larger vessel and Mr. Midshipman Magnus must be transferred with him. So now I find myself short of two officers. "The open Midshipman billet is yours, should you still want it."

"Yes, sir!"

"Only this is a provisional promotion, with a strict initial probationary period. I've heard the grumblings and scuttlebutt in regards to your recent performance, yet Argyle has assured me you can handle this. I trust his judgment, but you must prove yourself capable in my eyes. You'll need to learn to work with the others if you want to keep the title of Midshipman. Do we have an understanding?"

"Yes, sir. Of course, sir," you say, still shocked by the day's turn of events.

"That will be all, then."

You salute and turn to leave, unable to keep a grin off your face. Outside the Commander's Cabin, Lieutenant Dalton awaits. He approaches with some trepidation, wringing his hands together nervously.

"Good evening, Ward. I... I would be honored if you would continue on my watch this evening," he says. You let the moment hang in the air, so he continues, "My uncle—that is, Wycombe, the ship's surgeon—tells me I may not have gauged your full potential, and for that I am truly sorry. I do hope you'll give me another chance. I should like us to be friends."

Remembering your promise to try to work well with the other officers, you say, "Of course, Lieutenant. I should think we'll get on much better as friends, only now, it's Midshipman Ward."

Not much choice here:

Go about your duties with a new lease on life. Well done! Go to page 218

Repressed

⚓

For a telltale moment, the lieutenant's eyes narrow after your response, but then he recovers to a more detached, hard-to-read expression. This leaves you with nothing more to go on than an indication: Dalton will remember that.

"Indeed, we shall see, Ward. Indeed we shall," he says at length. "Just make sure you come to me first from now on. That's how the chain of command works, you understand. If you have a problem, we needn't trouble the commander with every little trifle."

He waves his hand about as if any problem you might encounter would be no more of a nuisance than a housefly. Then a rapid pressure change falls over the quarterdeck and the men go silent before snapping to attention.

"Cap'n on deck!" the Master-of-Arms shouts.

Not much choice here:

Follow suit and snap to attention. Best not to stick out. Go to page 79

Rescued

As fate would have it, Cousin James is indeed aboard the warship, which you come to learn is called the *HMS Hornblower*. He was pressed into service the very same day that you began your journey on the *Cooper's Pride*.

Your cousin vouches for your honor, which helps get an audience with Captain Longwick, Master and Commander of the ship. The story you tell is a fantastic one, but Butch still carries the fateful page from Bullock's log, thus verifying your account. Of all aboard, you alone will *not* be tried for piracy.

Instead, you sail home to London as a guest, during which time you pen your memoirs. This eventually forms the basis for *Marooned by Pirates*, a bestseller and a seminal work on the subject of both island survival and the story of freebooters, inspiring future generations to spin the seafaring yarn.

You'll be knighted; as much for your derring-do and role in helping capture the pirates as for your status as a great novelist. You retire back to the Buckinghamshire countryside and, along with your cousin, live out the rest of your days in comfort as a local celebrity.

That's it! You've survived and thrived on a desert island. But there's plenty more to explore. *MAROONED* has three unique storylines (look for anchors, skull and crossbones, and the palm tree symbols) and over fifty possible endings. Maybe things would have worked out differently had you been a member of the pirate crew? Or, what if you had boarded the HMS *Hornblower* back in London?

Or, if you're finished, please consider leaving a review to help others find this book. It's an incredibly helpful and easy way to support the author (who thanks you in advance, and in third-person, no less!).

When you're done, don't forget to check out the other exciting titles in the Click Your Poison multiverse! You can also sign up for the new release mailing list, or check out James Schannep's blog for updates.

http://eepurl.com/bdWUBb
http://jamesschannep.com

The Return

The following days and weeks on your island pass almost peacefully. Learning the land like a child at play, you soak up every detail. Where foodstuffs grow, what game trails the pigs use, how to avoid the jaguar, and when a storm might arrive. You fortify your shelter to the point where it's water-tight and warm in the night.

It feels harmonious, this return to the natural world. You're accepted as a part of the island, and even the flora and fauna adapt to accommodate a new resident. You even manage to forge a crude sort of ink, so you're able to journal your thoughts (and suspicions) once the small bottle runs dry.

Presently idling about the freshwater inland pond, your thoughts drift away, carried as if by the spray from the waterfall up and out of the jungle. What might have befallen your shipmates? Did they make it to Boston? Did Billy learn the nature of Captain Bullock's murder, as promised? And what of Cousin James? Could he have made it back to Buckinghamshire, with the rest of your family?

Then a great thrashing from the water draws your attention back to the present. A crocodile, jaws snapping open and shut, only inches from your legs. But as you lurch back reflexively, you realize the crocodile is moving *away* from you—being dragged backwards.

On the opposite bank, the jaguar pulls the crocodile out of the water by its tail. The croc thrashes again, trying to free itself, but in only a few quick seconds the jungle cat pulls the reptile from its riparian home and digs its fangs deep into the crocodile's neck. The saurian predator goes limp, dead.

The jaguar makes eye-contact with you, almost as if to say, "You're welcome," and slowly drags its kill off into the verdant foliage and beyond. Panting for breath, you rise to your feet and back away in the opposite direction.

When you turn to go, you see a view of the distant shoreline—and a ship. It's the *Cooper's Pride*! Careened on her side, the merchant vessel is beached, ready to be cleaned and repaired. That means the crew will remain on your island for at least a few days. Looking back towards the pond, you can't help but think of the scene that's played out as an omen of sorts.

What should you do?

> Creep down to the jungle's edge and spy on them. Much has likely changed these few weeks. Go to page 302

> Go announce yourself. Surely they remember you're here; no point in beating around the bush. Go to page 271

Return Trip

The haggard man glowers and says, "Got a business partner waiting on ya?"

"Precisely," you lie, sensing the way out.

"Best-o'-luck with it," Dick says, clearly wishing you the opposite fate. "And do make sure t'pay ole Dick a visit once it's all concluded."

You nod, then continue on, pausing to look over your shoulder every few paces. At first, Dick watches you, but eventually he disappears into the shadows and you continue around the corner onto the cobbled London streets.

As luck would have it, the first sight you're greeted with is that of a carriage. In fact, the very same one from your arrival! The driver stuffs his pipe at a tobacconist's shop while his horse chomps on dinner from a sack of oats.

"'Ello, 'ello," he says, grinning upon recognition. "Couldn't find that cousin of yours?"

"No, I did. He's down at the port tavern."

"No surprises there," the driver chuckles.

"I'd like to pay fare for our return journey."

The driver's cheery nature drops. "Sorry, Guv. I was looking forward to a night in London. 'Fraid I'm off the clock."

Your heart jumps into your throat just thinking of your other taxi options back at the port.

"Please. This place is crawling with unscrupulous characters. Truth of it is, you're the only one I trust," you say. The driver thinks it over, not nearly convinced, so you add, "I'll pay double for your trouble."

That extra money was intended for dinner, but after the number the ride up here did on your stomach, you doubt you'll miss it anyway. At length, the driver nods in agreement, though from the look on his face, you can't help but think part of his reasoning is due to pity.

"Thank you. If we can just go collect my cousin from the tavern, we'll be on our way."

The trip back down to the river banks is mercifully short, and you exit the carriage with haste.

"Hold on there," the driver says. "If you want me to wait, I'll need your fare to keep me company. I'm either on the clock or I ain't, if ya take my meaning."

You hesitate. Paid in advance? That's all the money you have in the world right now. It's not that you don't trust him, but being left penniless at the Port of London seems like a risky move. Still, your own words echo inside your head: *You're the only one I trust.*

What'll it be?

> Yell, "I won't be a minute!" then run inside before he can protest.
> Go to page 216

> Give the driver the money. He'll wait for you. Maybe shake his hand, just in case.
> Go to page 214

Robin

Interesting choice, Dear Reader. Not sure if you just weren't paying attention during all those campfire ruminations, or if you're trying some sort of bluff, but here's how it plays out:

"The killer was none other than… Robin," you say.

There's a moment of shocked confusion, then a smile breaks over Rediker's face.

"Seeing as how the man's final words, just before I ran him through, were, 'Ain't no rest for a murderer. Ye will rot, Rediker. In this life or the next.' He didn't take kindly to our mutiny, even less so when we hanged Billy from the yardarm. He were a company man, through and through. So I think I can safely say there's about as much veracity in your statement as a pickpocket in port offering t'return your belongings out of the goodness-o'-his heart. Are ye thinkin' us for fools, Saltboots? We shall see who has the last laugh. Boys, do what ye will with the castaway here. Just make sure there ain't no breath left when you're done."

We shall see who has the last laugh, indeed.

THE END

Rock and a Hard Place

The helmsman sails along the convex bend of the coast, hoping to lose the English warship along the curve. The Royal Navy stays close, but the geographical advantage helps slightly—until from around the bend comes sight of another ship.

"Sails!" Marlowe cries the obvious.

It's a Spanish warship. The pirate hunter *Elige tu Veneno*, no doubt. Even though you're not flying the black, Spain is at war with England—this is not a good turn of events.

"Make for open seas!" you cry.

But it's too late for that. The Spanish open fire just as the English warship catches up from behind. You're pinned between the two behemoths, with no way out, save for down into the murky depths of Davy Jones's Locker.

THE END

Rollin' on a River

Your first time with a woman turns out to be an illicit affair at the Port of London. If someone told you what this day would hold when you woke up this morning, surely you would have taken this soothsayer for mad.

And still, you don't even know her name. Maybe it's better this way. You can remember her fondly as an almost mythic character in your life's story rather than, well, as a whore. She can be your Helen of Troy, the face that launched a thousand tiny ships. While she may not be quite a beauty to write an epic ode to, together you embark into the night.

Loose lips may sink ships, but they can also send you floating on cloud nine, if you'll pardon the flow of cliché. Let your imagination set sail, Dear Reader! Your courtesan shows you routes to pleasure that take you to the edge of ecstasy and back again.

Once your allotted time has expired, you wander back out into the tavern to cheers and hurrahs from the sailors. You blush, but accept the praise like a returning hero. Billy, James's mutton-chopped chum, buys you a drink to toast your having docked at port for the first time.

Sipping on the gin, your head swims with the carnal rush still coursing through you. Taking time to appreciate the moment, you look around the tavern.

Billy goes back to some cushions in the rear, where he shares a hookah pipe with a man so covered in tattoos you almost can't distinguish him from the patterned wallpaper. Other seamen lounge with more women, and sadly, one sailor already entertains the very same girl now etched onto your heart.

Another few men play dice, exchanging coin between throws. They make eye-contact and with a nod, offer you a place at the table. Care to give it a go?

➢ Luck, be a lady tonight! Why not continue your good fortunes? This will surely be a night to remember. Go to page 318

➢ No, just sip at the gin and await Cousin James's return to the tavern. Go to page 233

Rotten Luck

Barlow ties the bonds tightly, though you make no effort to resist. He looks like he might say something, maybe apologize for the necessity of all this, but in the end he thinks better of it and remains silent.

Though you're unable to free yourself from his expertly tied sailor's knots, the gag is another story. Sure, it's pulled tightly against your jaw, wedged back and forcing your mouth into an agape grimace, but it's not fool-proof. A human face is soft and flexible.

Rubbing your face against the wall, the gag slowly pulls down over your chin.

Cannon fire booms from above, signaling the start of hostilities. Boots clatter across the upper decks as the crew rushes from position to position. With any luck, the pirate ship will soon be boarded by the Royal Navy, and they'll rescue you once they hear your shouts.

So shout you do, hollering at the top of your lungs. "Down here! Help! Prisoner! *HELP!!!!!*"

Eventually, your ragged cries have paid off; the door flings open. Marlowe enters, his face bloodied and with a glare to beat down the devil himself.

"Brought this bad luck on us, Saltboots. You're a bad omen, ya are. We had nothing but fair weather and good plunder 'fore we brought ya aboard, Jonas! Always knew befriending a Saltboots were bad luck. Cap'n Rediker should have left ya on that island. S'pose it's up t'me to set things right. Make ya an offering t'Neptune or the Almighty, whomever might accept."

Then he brings his cutlass forward, spilling your blood with one brutal swipe.

THE END

The Ruse

Half the pirates hide down in the hold, as ordered. These are mainly the former African slaves, as their presence as free men aboard a supposed English merchant vessel would raise even more questions. The other half cover their fine pirate garb with blankets, doing their best to look like downtrodden plague victims. It doesn't take long before you start to sweat under the thick blankets, with the Caribbean sun beating down upon you, giving the appearance of a feverish countenance—which should help the ruse all the more.

"Hello, there!" calls the cry from the warship. "We are His Majesty's Ship the *Hornblower*. I say, is this Captain Bullock's *Cooper's Pride*?"

They've heard of your old captain? Well, that's some rotten luck.

"Bullock is dead! Plague! We are under quarantine!" you shout back.

There's a long silence while the British officers discuss this turn of events.

"They ain't buyin' it," Marlowe grumbles.

"Stow that talk," you snap back.

It's a tense few moments, so much so that you hardly dare to breathe.

"Why was the ship re-christened *Deleon's Revenge*?" they call back at length.

"Damn," Rediker grumbles.

"Bullock's dying wish," you say, trying to keep the doubt from your voice. "Once the plague set in. He—he wanted to die with his ship, in a sense."

"Drop anchor, we're coming on board." Apparently that wasn't what they wanted to hear.

"Do not! We're very ill! Very contagious," you say.

They don't reply, only continue their preparations for boarding.

"The jig is up," Marlowe says. "What now, Cap'n?"

"Raise the black!" you cry, knowing that this might initially panic the enemy, buying you precious time. "Then…

- "…retreat into the hold. I've got one trick left." Go to page 303

- "…call the rest of the men out! Fire cannons! We'll not go without a fight!" Go to page 116

Saboteur

Sneaking out of the hold, darting out of sight anytime a group of pirates happens by, you come across the ship's magazine. There's a long fuse coiled into a collected mound of explosives; the other end grows like a vine up and out of the grating towards the sun above decks. How curious.

Studying the munitions, it suddenly occurs to you—the ship has been rigged to blow! If someone were to light that fuse from above, the *Deleon's Revenge* would explode from inside, killing all aboard. Clearly Rediker does not intend to be taken alive.

Well, unfortunately for him, that is precisely your intent. Ducking inside the magazine, you find an old knife which must have regularly been used by the gunner as a tool. It's not the sharpest blade, but it's good enough to saw through a fuse. Just to be safe, you slice through and separate a good three feet from the rest.

That should stop the trap from springing. But as you hold the fuse in hand, you're given another idea for how to best sabotage the ship. Moving quickly, you pile together a mound of explosives of your own, rigging a smaller version of the trap. Once you've made your bomb, you deftly carry it towards the pump room.

All it takes is to light the fuse from the nearest oil lamp, then—bombs away!—you throw the explosive into the pump room and run for it. The resultant *BOOM!* is somewhat muted by the sounds of combat from above, aided by the fact that the pump room is in the lowest recesses of the ship. Hopefully, there weren't too many sailors operating the pumps at the time, but now the newly careened hull should be leaking like a sieve.

But there's more to be done. Out on the top decks, you see the pirates fully engaged in battle against the Royal Navy. In fact, the British are nearly on top of the *Revenge*! Maybe you can help slow the ship further?

Engaged in battle, the pirates barely notice you. They don't anticipate an enemy in their ranks before they've been boarded, so you're able to remove the brace from the capstan and drop anchor without detection. Then you take the gunner's knife and saw at the lines holding the sails. All that seaman's know-how you learned at sea now comes to use as you deliberately cripple the ship. The first sail flaps loose in the open breeze after you saw your way through the ropes.

"Saltboots! Ya right bastard," Rediker calls out.

Not a bad run; destroying the pumps, cracking the hull, dropping anchor, and removing a sail—all before getting caught. You'd love nothing more than to cross cutlasses with Rediker, but well, he's the only one with a cutlass. And four pistols, to boot.

Instead, you flee from the pirate captain, dashing across the ship as grappling hooks launch through the air from the Royal Navy ship, grabbing the *Deleon's Revenge* in order to board her. One of the pirates makes to hack loose the nearest such line, so you plow into the man, tackling him from behind and launching the unsuspecting rogue out into the sea.

"I bring ya aboard me ship, rescued from bein' marooned, and this'd be how ye repay me?" Rediker calls, pursuing you still.

Rising from the move, you continue to flee. Rediker brings his full attention on you, chasing you the length of the ship, from stem to stern. Finally, you're cornered. Rediker holds his cutlass in one hand, a pistol in the other.

"Should have left ye t'rot, but I'll remedy me errs directly. Say your prayers."

"You may want to heed your own advice, *fiend*," a gentlemanly voice cries out from behind the pirate captain.

Rediker turns back and you get a good look at your rescuer He's fair-skinned and fair-haired, unusual for those who spend their days at sea. A twenty-year-old member of the gentry, bred to keep a stiff upper lip. A lieutenant in the Royal Navy, no doubt, with a contingent of fighting sailors at his back. He holds a pistol aimed at Rediker, who now raises his hands in defeat.

"Damn your blood, Saltboots," Rediker growls.

"Saltboots? Wouldn't happen to have a relation; young lad goes by the name of Jimmy?"

"You know my cousin James?" you reply, dumbfounded.

"We shall see," the lieutenant replies, then adds to one of his men, "Fetch the gunner's mate."

<u>Go to page 251</u>

Savage Stomp

Kicking, punching, resisting however you can, you fight off the jaguar. It lays its claws deep into your flesh, turning your clothes to ribbons. Yet, you survive. After landing a few blows to the beast's head, it retreats into the jungle. Prey doesn't normally fight back.

The creature might think twice before attacking you again. Though you came close to death, part of you feels like king of the jungle. You just survived a jaguar attack!

Granted, that could just be today. You're still best to keep a roaring fire at night and look over your shoulder as you hike through the jungle. And watch your footing—nothing screams, "I'm prey!" like falling and flailing. Just ask that little piggy.

Although this final lesson you'll have to learn the hard way.

You're hiking through the jungle, looking for signs of a larger pork population, when the underbrush goes out from under you. Falling into darkness, you lash out for a handhold, but just too late. You slam down at the base of a natural well. It's not a manmade trap, for there are no spines at the bottom. Still, the fall was incredibly painful and it's pitch-black down here.

Anything broken? You don't think so. Regardless, it's best to take a moment to catch your breath before finding your way back out. What's the best way out of a natural hole?

- Like a starfish. With your arms and legs spread on opposite walls, you can totter your way up. Go to page 92
- Leaning back. With your shoulders and hands pressed on the wall and feet out in front, walking. Go to page 108
- Leaning forward. Feet planted on at the rear wall and hands on the front, you can back slowly up. Go to page 172
- Try to dig your way out. By pulling down the earthen walls, you can make a ramp and climb to safety. Go to page 64

Scapegoat

You point the finger at Rediker and his conspiracy, hoping to take the pressure off yourself.

"That's a bloody lie!" Rediker cries.

"I saw you out in the open, conspiring mutiny!"

"Tryin' t'save your own skin, that's all this is! Chips saw ya lay down the body-o'-the man ye killed, ain't that right, Chips?"

"Aye, true enough," Chips reluctantly agrees.

"And where exactly were ya, Rediker? At the time the killin' took place?" Billy asks.

"I were down inspecting the hold. Hell, maybe I stole me an egg from the hens. Flog me if ye must, but a murderer I am not."

"I were there, I can vouch," Barlow says.

"Same here," Marlowe agrees.

"That's a double alibi," Rediker says. "Last hand t'see the Cap'n alive is standin' there covered in his blood."

"Enough!" Billy roars.

That buys a moment's silence, which Joe finally breaks. "Cap'n Greaves—as that is your title now—consider this point: when we make landfall at Boston, the Admiralty should want t'know what happened with Cap'n Bullock. Be that as it were, ye should have a suspect ready t'hand over. Let the courts in Boston handle things from there."

Billy's brow wrinkles and he looks at you with genuine regret. But that doesn't stop him from ordering you placed into irons.

No further evidence comes from any subsequent investigations, which likely aren't performed anyhow. With two less hands to work the ship, it's lucky that the men remember to feed you meals. You'll spend the rest of the voyage in isolation, as well as your time in Boston. The trial will be brief—a formality, really, leading towards your sentencing to death for committing a murder most foul.

THE END

Scholastic

⚓

Partway through your studies, Captain Longwick returns, but you're so engrossed in the books that you don't even notice the Master and Commander's presence.

"I admire your temerity, Midshipman Ward. I don't want to dampen such enthusiasm, but I had hoped you'd join the officers for a celebratory dinner. No, no. Stay seated. Don't let me tempt you away from your studies. I shall have my steward bring a selection of books from my personal library. The very ones I used on my examination for lieutenant. I don't imagine you'll have a chance to meet the promotion board until after we return from our next mission, so there's plenty of time, but it's always good to let out canvas when the winds of inspiration blow, eh?"

Thanking the captain for his kindness, you excuse yourself to continue reading. Perhaps a single night of celebration would have been prudent, but no matter. Now you'll be seen as a go-getter with upper-management written all over you!

Finding a quiet spot to read by candlelight is easy, for the officers dine in the captain's cabin while the men sing and dance upon the deck. You find space, but not quiet. Still, perhaps that's good officers' training in its own right? Learning to think while distracted? Not often will the distraction come in the form of gaiety, laughter, and celebration, but the point stands.

For now, your only company is a chapter defining rhumb lines.

The next few days are a flurry of activity. The morning starts off with funeral rites for the fallen in battle, then goes straight into resupply. Once the ship gets fresh water, provisions, and timbers, the *Hornblower* heads out towards Caribbean seas and an urgent mission to the West Indies.

Weeks go by in this way, the ocean gradually changing from indigo to turquoise as shallower seas, reefs, and sandbars threaten the ship's path. The sun hangs longer in the sky, giving warmer, near-equatorial heat, and rain becomes a welcome relief for an English sailor.

It's a particularly hot day when you're to make for port. You're sailing along a series of islands, and the men are practically frothing at the bit for some shore leave. A change of pace would certainly be welcomed.

"Sails, ho!" Lieutenant Dalton shouts.

"What colors? Spanish? English?" you ask.

"No… she's flying the black," Dalton answers.

Could it really be? A pirate vessel?! Best quickly alert the Master and Commander of the ship.

Reporting in as you've been trained, you relay the sighting of the black flag with only minimal excited stammering. Captain Longwick gives the briefest hint of a nod, then rushes out to the quarterdeck. Examining the situation through a looking glass, the captain practically growls, "The *Cooper's Pride*."

Something in your memory clicks. You've heard that name before….

"A merchant ship, under the command of Arthur Bullock, or at least she was last. A draconian captain by all accounts, but still an Englishman." Then, lowering the spyglass, adds, "Well, then, if the *Pride* has been taken by pirates, I suppose it's only proper we take her back."

"Sir, my cousin last served on that ship," you say. "I'd like to lead the attack on the pirates, with my cousin in the boarding party."

Captain Longwick shakes his head. "Too personal. Your cousin's the gunner's mate, is he not? Find out what you can from him, but he stays here. You will lead the attack, sure enough, Ward. Pray to the Almighty your cousin can tell you something useful."

He's waiting for you to acknowledge the order. Say:

- "Understood, sir. His emotional connection might cloud his judgement. I shall learn what I can from Cousin James and use against these pirates. Would you prefer their leader be taken dead or alive?" Go to page 192
- "Sir, all due respect, the first task you assigned me was to question the veracity of your orders. Cousin James will serve better by my side on the front lines of battle than he would in the back of my mind." Go to page 295

Separation Anxiety

"**A** good plan," James says, not without a twinge of disappointment. "You find the carriage home, and I'll find the liquid courage t'head home with ya, and face me mum…"

He trails off, looking away, lost in thought. Seeing your curiosity, he continues, "Never did have her blessing, d'ya know that? 'A boy-o'-sixteen playing at a man' she called me when I told her my intentions. Said no son-o'-hers would ever have salt on his boots. So I signed up as none other than Jimmy Saltboots, and sent a letter to her by post using that very name. That bit make the family gossip?"

"No…" you admit, slowly. "Though it does explain her insistence that I bring you home straightaway."

"Aye, you've always been one of the good ones, coz. Honorable to a fault, as they say. Go find your cabbie, then look for me in there."

He points down the muddy promenade to a far tavern, where you can just barely make out the sign. SPENCER'S FREE HOUSE. Offering a curt nod of understanding, you part ways, seeing your cousin painted in a different light. No wonder he's so keen on a drink. Those high spirits are simply an act. He may look like a man of the world now, but at the heart of it, he's still a boy nervous about disappointing his mother.

"You ain't no Londoner, nor a sailor," a harsh voice croaks out.

Turning, you see a haggard-looking man. The boils on his flesh make James's scars look angelic by comparison. Hunched in such a way as to hide his great height, perhaps even from a long ago mis-healed wound. Presently, he grins at you through a maw of chipped and missing teeth.

"Matter-o'-fact, I'd say what you is, is lost. Plain obvious—more outta place than tits on a fish!" he crows, laughing uproariously at his own joke.

"My business at the port is nearly concluded, thank you," you say, trying to hide your nervousness around the man. "Once I find a carriage, I'll be on my way."

"Taxi service? Well, why didn't you say so? Me mate runs the only honest cabbie in port. Richard, they call me. Spotted Dick to me friends. Come, follow your new friend. Dick'll make sure you get in safe. Can't trust the ruffians 'round here."

➤ What good fortune! Take him up on his offer and say, "Much obliged, so long as your friend doesn't mind a longer route. My cousin and I are headed back to Buckinghamshire this evening." Go to page 324

➤ Turn your nose up at the man. Say, "Indeed, not. Why don't you and that foul stench leave me be and return to whatever hovel you crawled out from?" Go to page 286

➤ Turn him down politely. Go find a carriage in the cobbled streets after you say, "My business is *nearly* concluded. And so, sadly, I must make haste. Ta-ta!" Go to page 253

Setting a Bad Precedent

⚓

You take the tool and hand it back to the carpenter's mate. The Master-of-Arms laughs to himself in disbelief. "Are ye daft? Was sort of in the middle-o'-somethin' here, in case ye couldn't tell!"

"I'm aware," you answer, coolly. "I've listened to you berate this man long enough."

It has the intended effect. The Master-of-Arms chokes on his laughter and sputters out, "I—I'm in charge-o'-bloody shipboard discipline, damn you!"

"As you'll holler at anyone unfortunate enough to be within earshot, yes, I know. I waited patiently just over there for you to finish, but this mockery went on beyond what good sense would tolerate."

"You... you *little*... wait—ya didn't just happen by—you were *spying* on me!"

"I was doing no such thing! I was performing my rounds, as ordered."

"Like hell. You're intents be easier t'see than that of a shark drawn to the sounds-o'-battle!"

The shouts have attracted Lieutenant Dalton and Mr. Magnus, and they now intercede.

"What's all this, Geoff?" Dalton asks. "What exactly is going on here, Ward?"

➢ Perhaps there's another way out here. If you challenge him to a duel, he'll have to back down! Say, "This man is calling me a liar! I demand satisfaction!"
  Go to page 309

➢ Tell these men you think you got off on the wrong foot and want to start over. Say, "Gentlemen, please. This is all just a misunderstanding!" Go to page 305

Setting Sail

"The sirens call for this family in particular, it seems, and so I must answer…"

You pen the most eloquent, vociferous letter you can muster, though you know that won't be enough for the family left behind in Buckinghamshire. Still, they managed to forgive Jimmy—Cousin James—once he hopped ship and left without permission, so perhaps they will do the same for you in two years' time.

"…like Odysseus, though I may voyage to the ends of the earth, I shall never forget those back home."

The next morning, once you've sent your letters and settled your affairs, Billy the mate meets you on the waterfront. The merchant district is a sprawling metropolis in its own right. The docks creak in a chorus of cranes, which load and unload ships. A blue man, like an explorer from Neptune, walks before you, colored this way from his labors in the indigo trade. Warehouses store mountains of the dyestuffs, more valuable than ingots of gold.

There appears to be enough treasure in this port to make every family in England wealthy. Passing this quay, the air becomes fragrant with tobacco. The next, with the vapors of rum. The spice of peppercorn and the acres of cork, copper, and timbers. Goats bleat out and sows squeal.

Passing unfathomable treasures, Billy brings you aboard the *Cooper's Pride*. She's a sleek and clean ship, loaded with fresh supplies ready for the colonies. The figurehead on the front is an enormous carved octopus, or more likely, in this case, the legendary Kraken. With a fearsome glower the beast stares ahead, ready to ride forward atop the waves, a pair of swords held out in its multitudinous arms.

When you climb aboard, the first thing you see is a group of four seamen bound upon the main deck. You look to Billy; a guilty countenance washes across him.

"We're happy to have ya volunteer, but sadly, we had t'recruit in other, less scrupulous ways," he confesses.

"Were these men… pressed into service?" you ask.

"That'd be the Navy. We use crimps in the merchant service, but 'tis more-o'-less the same," Billy replies. "Bein' pressed'd be far worse, trust ole Billy on that account! This here's a payin' job with little chance-o'-bein' fired upon by the dagoes."

There's a rhythmic tapping sound and you turn, along with Billy, to see a man walking on deck with a cane. The cane is the source of the tapping, yet he doesn't move with any appearance of a limp. He's dressed in finery like your father might wear when entertaining guests at the country estate, but a broad tri-corn hat hides this man's features under a mysterious shadow.

"Cut 'em loose, Robin!" Billy cries, then turns to you and adds, "Cap'n Bullock requires a vow-o'-service from those who'd serve aboard his ship. Yourself included, I'm afraid."

➢ "I thought you said Captain Bullock is fair and just? An oath spoken under duress is no oath at all." Go to page 89

➢ "I already signed papers with you, Billy. I shall give my spoken word of honor to the captain as well." Go to page 186

Shameless

The men nod, faces cold and stoic, not belying any emotion. These seamen are no strangers to death, but if they find you coldhearted, they do themselves credit not to show it.

"Send his body back over, and make sure his crew knows. They're at our mercy, so they'd better be on their best behavior."

Both men nod at your orders, then step to. You stay inside the cabin, mind running wildly. *If Bullock was poisoned....*

At length, Rediker reports in. "Christ Almighty. It's true. Look at that poor sod. Looked at ya cross, eh? Just as well. Crew says he were a cruel master, serves him right, I say. Bloodbeard's legend grows."

"And the prize?" you say.

"Massive haul, Cap'n. Sugar, indigo, cacao, tobacco, leather, silks, silver, gold, and jewels. Once we divide the shares, hell, I'd say each man just earned himself three years' pay! Not bad for a first-timer."

"Refit the ship first. Take their carriage guns, plus any weapons. Once the *Deleon's Revenge* is made stronger, the rest is profit."

"Aye, Cap'n. It'll take a few hours t'move all the cargo, but we should be full up. Afterwards, shall we plot a course for New Providence to unload our ill-gotten gains?"

"Do it!" you say.

➤ "I'm going to go through the Porto captain's cabin to see what I can find. He was right, I need a manner of dress befitting the name of Captain Bloodbeard."
Go to page 70

➤ "'Twas a grand first catch, Rediker. Once we make sail, open the rum stores for the men. I'd like to make another toast... to the first of many! And the start of a prosperous partnership." Go to page 137

Shanty Town

These funds were meant for a hot meal and a carriage ride home, but caught up in the moment, you use it to buy the bar a round. Billy takes his second drink and his muttonchops part as he belts out, "Oooohhhhh, we'd be all right, if the wind was in our sails!"

Then the whole tavern echoes, *"We'd be all right, if the wind was in our sails!"* and you join in for the third, *"We'd be all right, if the wind was in our sails!"* and the whole chorus sings, *"And we'll all hang on behind!"*

The womenfolk, Spence included, give a harmonizing *"Ohhhh!!!!"* while the seamen sing in concert, *"And we'll roll the old chariot along, we'll roll the old chariot along, we'll roll the old chariot along, and we'll all hang on behind!"*

Billy continues to lead, "Oh, we'd be all right, if we make it round the horn!"

To a chorus of, *"We'd be all right, if we make it round the horn! We'd be all right, if we make it round the horn! And we'll all hang on behind! And we'll roll the old chariot along, we'll roll the old chariot along, we'll roll the old chariot along, and we'll all hang on behind!"*

Billy belts out, "Oh, a long night ashore wouldn't do us any harm!"

Now you join in with the rest of them, noting the cadence of the tune and its echoes.

Finishing your drinks as a group, Billy now offers, "Oh, another round from Jimmy wouldn't do us any harm!"

James takes it good-naturedly and offers up more coin. In response, the tavern sings, *"Another round from Jimmy wouldn't do us any harm!"* bringing the new verse into the chorus.

Now James lifts up his courtesan into his arms and shout-sings, "Oh, a roll in the clovers wouldn't do us any harm!" before retreating into a back room.

His exit is marked by enthusiastic singing of the line. So the night goes, drink after drink, song after song, in the revelry of the seamen, until coin purses are empty and you black out from too much gin. Not much choice here:

Wake up the next morning and face the consequences of your actions. Go to page 93

Shipmates

Billy shakes his head with disappointment. "I seen me fair share-o'-dreamers and scoundrels, and I'm afraid you're lookin' t'be both. Can't beat the Crown, Saltboots, and, as they say—if ya can't beat 'em, join 'em. Only way I know to earn riches is through hard work, one guinea at a time."

"I truly appreciate your concern, Billy, but I'd rather take fate into mine own hands—danger and all. Why toil to earn another man his treasure?"

"Spoken like a true buccaneer. I s'pose 'tis goodbye then, Saltboots. I'll say a prayer for your health. Just one last thing. I know ye let me live, so I'll pay off the debt here and now: take a look-o'-this building upon which your old mate now enters. If ye would be a pirate still, do so with haste."

With that, he turns and heads inside the nearest building. Taking a step back to get a better look, you see what he meant—clear as the printed sign at the main entrance: The building next to you, as it turns out, is the Admiralty Court building. That must've been Billy's destination all along, and soon the Royal Navy will know of the pirates here in port!

Fear surges through you and a new burst of adrenaline sends you running back for the ship. The Admiralty here in Boston likely won't be any kinder to pirates than those you saw hanging in iron gibbets on the River Thames. You haven't a moment to lose!

Billy took so many twists and turns through the alleyways that you find yourself lost—navigating only by the sounds of seabirds at the port and the distant smell of salt in the air.

Finally, you make it back to the wharf and the *Cooper's Pride*. Joe the bosun is here, supervising the final unloading of the goods, shaving with a razor as the lad often does to calm his nerves.

"Bosun!" you cry between heaving breaths. "Has Rediker returned?"

Joe simply points up to the ship. You make to hurriedly board, but the hulking gunner Robin emerges, blocking your path. It's a fair guess he'd like to know of Billy's fate.

"He—I'm sorry, Robin. Billy left you and the ship. But there's a place here, should you want it."

"Cap'n!" comes Rediker's cry from aboard the ship. "Goods sold as ordered, and I even gotcha a new crew. How's that for a day's work?"

He waves forward those standing behind him. A dozen new faces appear at the prow. Several Africans look down at you, bloodied and feral, fresh from a brawl, as well as a handful of ne'er-do-wells—likely out-of-work sailors. They gleam with golden-hooped piercings and leer with lusty grins, swaying under the influence of alcohol.

➢ "Fine! But we must make sail, and with haste. Up anchor! Shove off! Loose all canvas for the wind!" Go to page 128

➢ "I think not! Get those men off my ship. I'll choose my own crew, thank you very much!" Go to page 126

Shoreline

Stepping forth from the jungle, the pirates recoil in a mixture of surprise and fear. Cutlasses fly forth into ready hands, pistols drawn and cocked for action.

"Saltboots?" Rediker says. "By God, 'tis you!"

"Welcome to my island, Rediker," you reply, coolly.

Rediker grins. "That'd be Cap'n Rediker now, elected master-o'-this here ship, rechristened the *Deleon's Revenge*."

You look around to many familiar faces: Barlow, Chips, Marlowe, Butch, and Joe. But many more unfamiliar faces, hardened pirates ready for action.

"Revenge against the likes of Bullock and Billy, I take."

"Neither-o'-whom sail with us," Rediker says with a shrug. "Robin, neither. All these men here are loyal t'me now. Each his own man, sailing by choice, as brothers. I'd ask ye t'join our merry crew, but I can see it in your eyes. Desire t'see me swing in the gallows, wouldn't ya? Must've been tough, marooned out here for a crime ye were innocent of.

"Sure, I knew ye didn't kill Bullock, mate. Never had it in ya. But what's done is done, eh? Could just leave ya here now, but other ships're bound t'stop in, and you'll talk, won't ye?"

"You came back... to silence me?" you say, somewhat dumbstruck by the idea.

"Don't flatter yourself. There be a Spanish warship about, and I knew-o'-one island sheltered from prying eyes. Now that we found ye, alive, well... I want t'be merciful, I do, but try as I may, I can't think-o'-why I should. So how about you, Saltboots? Give me one reason we shouldn't just kill ya now and be done with it."

➢ "You can try, but you die first." Go to page 35

➢ "Because I know who truly killed Captain Bullock." Go to page 3

Shove Aboard

⚓

Captain Longwick gives a curt nod, which you take for tacit approval to join him in the longboat to go see the flagship. A dozen questions flutter in your mind as the men row towards the enormous first-rate ship of the line, the supersized HMS *Rochambeau*. While the Spanish warship *Don Pedro Sangre* dwarfed the HMS *Hornblower*, the flagship is as impressive as they get. The pride of England—even if she is a prize from the last war fought against the French.

The longboat crewmen hail out to the sailors aboard the *Rochambeau* and a rope ladder is thrown down. As you board, the seamen offer salutes to Captain Longwick, and he's greeted by an officer who introduces himself as Lieutenant Aubrey. The lieutenant leads you to the quarterdeck, where several Spanish officers stand captive.

"And where is Vice-Admiral Maturin?" Captain Longwick asks.

"Ah, his lordship will be joining us shortly, Captain."

Longwick studies the Spanish officers, then says, "These men still have their swords. Has no one accepted their surrender?"

"No, sir. The Lord Admiral will see to that personally as soon as he's able."

"How long does it take to put on a bloody wig?" Longwick snaps. Then a gay sort of laughter rings out from across the deck, followed by the sing-song of friendly banter. Your captain looks towards the voices sharply.

"Please, sir," Lieutenant Aubrey says. "The Admiral will be—"

Captain Longwick moves past the underling and rushes towards the sounds. You follow, and soon see the source of the gaiety. Several of the ship's officers play at shovelboard, a game where they knock at metal weights with sticks, trying to hit them into marked sections of the deck.

"My Lord Vice-Admiral!" Aubrey starts by way of warning.

The eldest of the players, an imposingly broad man with auburn hair tied into a long ponytail, raises a hand to silence the lieutenant. He keeps his back towards you, attention on his game. Surely this must be Vice-Admiral Maturin, but why is he so focused on a trivial game?

"My Lord, there is a war to be fought," Longwick interjects, sharply.

"The war can wait," Vice-Admiral Maturin replies, still not turning around.

Captain Longwick fumes, but holds his silence. The admiral aims his stick, which you recognize as a capstan bar borrowed from the ship for purpose of the game. He lines up, deliberately taking his time, and makes the shot. Then he stands proudly erect and says, "Match point scored! That's game, gentlemen."

Vice-Admiral Maturin then takes his nearby wig, dons it, and tops that with an enormous hat befitting a man of his rank and stature. He allows his steward to help him into his admiral's coat before finally turning back to face Longwick.

"Charles," he says without any hint of emotion. "I see my patronage has paid off. I knew putting you on the *Hornblower* would be the right fit. Come now, let's go see the Dons who gave you so much damnable trouble, shall we? Oh, who's this with you, then?"

For this last part, the admiral looks your way.

Captain Longwick says, "That's Ward. Or my ward, rather. Midshipman."

"Midshipman Ward. Come aboard the *Rochambeau* to see the 'great and powerful' Vice-Admiral Maturin, have you?"

"I, well, aye, sir, your lordship," you say, stumbling over the answer.

The admiral smiles to himself, then continues, "This was a French ship, did you know? Why do you think I keep her as my flagship, eh? And why might I have the Spanish brought aboard to surrender here rather than allowing them to be taken aboard their own ship?"

"I'm sure the Midshipman wouldn't care to guess at the lord admiral's motivations," Captain Longwick says, eyeing the shovelboard court.

The admiral ignores the jibe, continuing, "This ship was a prize, the capture of which ended our last war at sea with the French. I sail her to remind our enemies of the outcome they can expect when sailing against us."

"And bringing the Spanish aboard her?" Longwick asks.

"To ensure the message isn't lost, of course. Subtlety is the purview of the English, Charles. Come now, let's go collect their sabers."

Perhaps that explains the shovelboard as well, you think.

The Spanish surrender occurs via translator, with the officers being afforded every possible courtesy—until they can be transferred to an English prison. This transit is an honor Captain Longwick clearly fears will be bestowed upon himself, for at the first possible opportunity he asks the admiral his orders for the *Hornblower*.

"Repairs, of course. I understand the *Don Pedro Sangre* gave quite a bite to your hind flanks as she gave chase. No wonder you were so keen to see the captain's surrender!" Admiral Maturin says with a brow raised. "Then you'll resupply and depart the fleet with haste."

You can see the disappointment on Captain Longwick's face as he says, "Bristol?"

"What? No, don't be absurd. I'll have some schooner or other sally forth to the prison. The *Hornblower* made fantastic time finding the Spanish vanguard. We intercepted some dispatches from the enemy, and I need you to make sail for the West Indies to deliver word of their plans in the Caribbean. Have you ever been to Barbados?"

"Lord Vice-Admiral, if I may be so bold, the seat of action is here—against mainland Spain."

Maturin throws his head back in hearty laughter. "You won't miss the war, Charles! I'm not taking you out of the fight, but entrusting you with a pivotal mission, man. Once you've brought word to the Governor and given his reply to London, you'll rejoin us off Cape Passaro."

"Aye, sir. Very good. If you'll excuse me, then, my lord, I should be getting back to my ship."

"Oh? I had hoped you'd join me for dinner, Captain."

"If it's all the same to the Vice-Admiral, I'd like to celebrate with my men."

The admiral gives you a glance, then turns back to Captain Longwick. "It's all the same, then. Go on. Celebrate your success. We'll speak again before you depart for colonial waters. Dismissed."

After salutes are exchanged, you return to the longboat and the small crew rows back towards the *Hornblower*. After a few minutes' contemplation, Captain

Longwick turns to you and says, "Right, then. What are your thoughts, Ward?"
You take a moment to choose your words wisely, then say:

➤ "The men will be pleased to toast to your success, sir. I take it the rum stores can afford to be run out before we're resupplied?" Go to page 207

➤ "I should think these dispatches important. There are Spanish ships in the West Indies, so perhaps we won't be completely out of the action sailing in the Caribbean?" Go to page 103

➤ "The Vice-Admiral is rather eccentric, isn't he? Have you known one another very long?" Go to page 213

Showered in His Glory

There's an enormous thunderclap, such that would rival cannon fire, but no accompanying jolt of electricity. Instead, the lightning hits against the dead tree once more, sending flaming splinters into the air. Your prayers have been answered! Perhaps this truly was divine intervention, perhaps also you were spared because this position of supplication is very similar to what modern experts call "the lightning crouch."

Either way, the heavens do not strike you down. You are, however, caught out in the open for another rainstorm, soaking you through. After the threat of the lightning blasts have passed, you take shelter beneath the trees.

The squall over, the clouds part and warm tropical sunshine pours down in its stead. Back out to the clearing, you find a spot with a view of the coastline that's semi-dry, due to a natural protection from a rocking outcropping. Plenty of time to set up camp here, start a fire, fortify a more permanent shelter, and even cook dinner. The rest of the day is looking up!

As a two birds/one stone sort of effort, you clear the area surrounding your camp of underbrush. This vegetation can be used on a new shelter or for kindling your fire (especially the driest bits), but its removal will also help minimize insects, rats, and snakes around your camp.

Once you've cleared out this growth and built a sleeping area for the night, you set out your clothes, journal, and pistol shot to dry. The pistol is a flintlock, which you can use to start a fire.

The flintlock mechanism works by literally striking a piece of flint, which creates a massive spark. So all you have to do is hold the pistol near the kindling, cock the hammer, and pull the trigger. Flash! The sparks leap into the kindling.

After coaxing the spark into a flame, you carefully reload the pistol and store it back into your waistband. Best not to use that trick too many times, or you'll wear out the mechanism before you have a chance to use the weapon.

Sitting back, you enjoy the warmth of the fire as the sun sets. This was a fine day. Though it very well could be the crackling of the firewood echoing off your rocky outcropping, you could swear you can hear something or someone wandering around out there, watching you. Keeping close to the fire, you try to shrug off the feeling.

Maybe you should take your mind off things. Think back to the time on the ship and Captain Bullock's true killer. If Rediker and his ilk were the likeliest of suspects, then Joe, Chips, and Robin were the trio with the most opportunity. After all, these three were the first to arrive, so that means they were close to the captain's cabin.

What do you really know about these men?

> Reminisce on your time spent with Chips, the crusty old carpenter. Go to page 42

> Think back to your experiences with Joe, the young olive-skinned bosun.
  Go to page 73

> Reflect on your knowledge of Robin, the tattooed hulk of a gunner.
  Go to page 279

> Keep your mind off of the *Cooper's Pride*, and simply enjoy the fire's warmth.
  Go to page 320

The Siren's Call

Though it was a costly victory, 'twas victory nonetheless. The *HMS Hornblower* completes her mission in the West Indies, and you depart Caribbean seas to head for English shores. The rest of the journey is relatively uneventful. There are a few storms to contend with, but nothing quite as exciting as Spanish enemies or battles with pirates. So it is that you return to London, collect your pay, and depart the *Hornblower* for the last time.

Cousin James falls to the muddy banks of the Thames and scoops up the muck, kissing it like a long-separated love finally reunited.

"God, 'tis good t'be home!" he exclaims. He stands, wipes his hands on his breeches, turns to you and adds, "Never again, aye, coz?"

"Never again," you agree.

"Let's get us a carriage back to Bucks."

You nod, somewhat reluctant be leaving this world of naval brass and brine. Despite all the trials and travails, the *Hornblower* came to feel like home. And, by the end, you'd earned your title of Jack Tar. No more a Landsman, but an able-bodied Seaman through and through.

"Cabbies up ahead," James says, bringing you back from your reveries. "Ready?"

"Well… maybe just one drink first?"

A broad grin stretches across James's face. "Yeah, why not? What could one drink hurt?"

That's it! You've survived and thrived in the world of an enlisted seaman. But there's plenty more to explore. *MAROONED* has three unique storylines (look for anchors, skull and crossbones, and the palm tree symbols) and over fifty possible endings. Maybe things would have worked out differently against the pirates if you had been an officer aiding in the attack? Or, what if you were a pirate yourself?

Or, if you're finished, please consider leaving a review to help others find this book. It's an incredibly helpful and easy way to support the author (who thanks you in advance, and in third-person, no less!).

When you're done, don't forget to check out the other exciting titles in the Click Your Poison multiverse! You can also sign up for the new release mailing list, or check out James Schannep's blog for updates.

http://eepurl.com/bdWUBb
http://jamesschannep.com

Sodden Mess

You crawl beneath the driftwood, pulling in whatever broad pieces and leaves you can, in an effort to shield yourself from the rain and storm. It's a miserable way to spend a night, and you can't help but think your time might have been better spent erecting a dwelling before the storm hit. Still, it's better than being out in the open, and the token amount of insulation offered by the detritus helps warm your body enough so that eventually you stop shivering.

You could swear you can hear someone or *something* walking around out there, so you keep as silent as death. Maybe it's just the sounds of the storm and your imagination conspiring against you?

The pistol digs against your side as you try to sleep, but you keep it close lest the storm spoil the gunpowder. The idea of revenge, of justice, is the one thing keeping you going right now. But who could have killed Bullock? He was slain by his own knife, in his cabin, so the killer couldn't have gotten far. Moreover, who might have had a motive to kill the captain? There was a page missing from the ship's log–that cannot be a coincidence.

Then it occurs to you: you kept your own log all this time. Since your journal faithfully recalls a month spent with these seamen, you might actually know them well enough to ascertain their motives. Perhaps if you think hard enough, the answer is already there, waiting in the recesses of your memory! At the very worst, it should help keep your mind off the storm and whatever's "out there."

You start with the most obvious suspects. Three men in particular, thick as thieves, come to mind:

- Barlow, the mustachioed man always at Rediker's side. Go to page 181
- Rediker, the ringleader of the crimped men. Go to page 166
- Marlowe, the oldest sailor on the ship. Go to page 281
- Actually, no. Best way to keep my mind off things will be just to get some rest. Go to page 86

So Fresh and So Clean

⚓

Most of the water casks are unceremoniously dumped into the sea and scoured of rot and algae in preparation for refilling them. Which means you can't set sail until you find more fresh water. No pressure.

You're assigned to teams and rowboats and told that the first to find a goodly stream and to signal the others will be rewarded. More rum? Or choice beef, now that the larders should be resupplied as well?

This coast is most likely French, should geography serve you correctly, and seeing as how they're an ally of your Spanish enemies, the men have hopes of looting a farmhouse while you're out and about. They will ultimately be disappointed, for this section of coastal forest seems devoid of Frogs.

You too are disappointed when a single *crack* of gunfire signals another team finding water first. Still, that means less time spent searching.

When you arrive at the stream, you find the men first filling their gullets with the fresh water, and second, stripping bare for a wash. The sailors' faces and hands are tanned like leather, but their backsides practically blind you with their paleness.

It's to be a fleeting clean, as you afterwards sweat out the previous night's booze with the backbreaking work of pumping the water into the casks and reloading them onto the ship. With fresh supplies exchanged with the larger ships of the fleet, however, you're greeted with one of the better meals you've had in weeks once you're back onboard.

"We're to set sail tomorrow," Cousin James says when you're in your hammock. "Cap'n oughta be giving orders for our new course, if you're curious. Rumor has it we're not returning to Spanish waters."

➢ "Where else might we go? Okay, you've got me wondering now. Let's go see!"
  Go to page 40

➢ "I sail at the pleasure of His Majesty. I'll not leave this hammock to trouble myself with whereto." Go to page 311

Son of a Gun

While Captain Bullock's godlike authority inspired great terror, the man with the most frightening presence in the crew might have been the tattooed, shaved-bald, musclebound gunner, Robin. Though Robin was usually a man of few words, you got to know him as a soft-spoken, gentle giant while the weeks at sea flowed by.

There was plenty of time at sea to explore the ship, whether officially on errands, or during your down time when you might've either had trouble sleeping or felt too restless to sit and journal. On one such occasion, you were exploring the belly of the *Cooper's Pride*, noting her eccentricities and peculiarities, when you stumbled across a bit of vandalism. The name "Martin Underhill" was scrawled upon an interior passage, carved right into the wood.

But there was no Underhill in this crew, nor any man who might've known him. Many said there never was a Martin Underhill; that carving the name was some inside joke amongst sailors, so old as to be lost to time. Others said Mr. Underhill sailed every ship launched from London, inscribing his name upon each to add them to his collection.

You were running your fingers over the inscribed name, pondering your own pet theories, when you heard voices coming up from the ship's magazine. The magazine is the gunner's home, where all the ship's ammunition is held secured, but it was Captain Bullock's voice that rose to your ears.

Curiosity getting the better of you, you had crept down for a closer listen.

"How did it happen?" Robin said.

"A weak heart," Bullock had replied. "Painless, in her sleep. I understand that's where your wages had been sent. I can see to a stop order, if you wish."

"Aye, Cap'n. Many thanks."

"It… well, the letter mentioned something else, Robin. She doesn't simply leave a grieving son on my crew, but also… a widower. Her will contained a special request, you see. That her son, Robin, might finally reveal the truth to his father… William Greaves. Is this true? Is Billy really your father?"

"Aye. God's honest truth, Cap'n. But Billy himself don't know, and I don't want him to, neither."

Robin is Billy's son? You could hardly believe your ears.

"Come now, Robin. A man's got a right to know who his son is, surely. 'Twas your mum's dying wishes. I'm afraid I'm honorbound to tell the man, if you won't."

"Got me own rights as a man, don't I? Billy don't know 'cause I'm a true son-o'-a gun, such as the sayin' goes. Like to think he respects me as a man, Cap'n. Might be he'd look at me different, would that he knew I were his bastard."

"I see. Hard to earn your father's respect, I know that as well as most. Very well. Swear you'll tell him one day, when you've finished sailing together, and I'll consider my own duty fulfilled."

"I… I swear it, Cap'n. One day."

But that day hasn't come, has it? So far as you know, you're the only other person to know Robin's secret. And with Bullock dead, the gunner very well may believe that the secret died with the captain. Could that have been what was written in Bullock's journal? The page found torn and taken from the captain's cabin?

Would Robin have killed to protect his anonymity?

It seems unlikely, especially as how Captain Bullock agreed to keep the secret safe, but it's certainly a motive to bear in mind. Who else might have a motive of their own?

➤ What about Joe? Was there any secret the bosun might kill to protect?
  Go to page 73
➤ What about Chips? Did the carpenter hold any ill will towards the captain?
  Go to page 42
➤ That's enough for tonight. Best to take your mind off things and enjoy the warmth of the fire. Go to page 320

Spinning Yarn

Marlowe was—is—the oldest sailor in the crew, and those on the *Cooper's Pride* respected his expertise. In the storms that ravaged the ship (likely the same storm that has now caught up to your island), it was Marlowe the men would turn to and ask "How bad?," for his was the encyclopedia of experiences with which to compare the present.

What possible motive could he have against Captain Bullock? One particular incident comes to mind. Only a few days ago, you were picking oakum with Marlowe and Butch, the surgeon. These old ropes were meticulously untwined and spread apart so that they might be braided anew and made useful once more.

It's a tedious task for the hands, one that certainly built up the callouses on your fingertips and the muscles in your forearms. But it wasn't a particularly demanding task in the mental sense, which led to telling stories and shooting the breeze.

Butch told of how he came into the service of the *Pride*, putting this succinctly, "Always was destined to be a butcher. My father had the shop 'fore me, and his father passed it t'him, who got it from his father's father and so on *ad infinitum*, all the way back t'when God invented the cow, pig, and sheep. Only taxes kept goin' up while the cost-o'-mutton stayed constant. I lost me shop, and on the very same night, lost me wife. Died-o'-a broken heart, she did."

"Consider yourself lucky," Marlowe said with a wry grin.

"And how, pray tell, might a man do that?"

"A sailor's wife be the worst kind! There's only one reason t'marry a sailor, and that'd be to take what's his when he's at sea. Mind ye, they either know this when they sign up in the first place, if they'd be the cunning sort, or they figure it out soon after. A wife never spent a man's wages like one whose devoted husband is an ocean away! Mark me words, Saltboots. Never trust that what wears a petticoat."

This last bit he directed towards you, but Butch had a good laugh all the same.

"I guess when ye'd put it that way!" the surgeon had said, chuckling.

Then Marlowe let out a sharp cry, like a man in pain. He dropped the rope, cradling one hand in the other. His fingers curled into a claw and he sucked in air through his teeth from the pressure. Arthritis, most likely, though the ship's surgeon sitting next to him lacked the education to diagnose the ailment.

That's when Captain Bullock had descended upon your group. The man must have been watching, perhaps even listening to the idle chat, but at Marlowe's injury, the master of the ship rushed down from his perch on the quarterdeck.

"It's nothing, Cap'n," Marlowe had tried to pre-emptively defend.

"It's your bloody age, man. I knew you were getting too old for work as a deckhand, and now look at you—a disgrace to your profession."

"Every man gets cramps now and again," Marlowe said.

"Don't lie to me! You lied when you said this work wasn't too much for a man of your age, that much is clear! Lucky I don't flog you for it. Would too, if I didn't know the beating might kill a man of your age. I swear to God I will have my satisfaction yet! The Admiralty Courts in Boston will see to it that I garnish your wages for this deception. Why, if I get my way, you'll get no wages at all and I'll leave you to beg on the streets, like I should have done in London!"

To this tirade, Marlowe offered no response.

"I suggest you prove your worth before that happens," Bullock said at length. "I am not an unreasonable man. If I see you outwork the younger men, well, I might leave you with your wages intact. But know that this is the last time we sail together, *Methuselah!*"

And then the captain had stormed off. To make a note in his journal perhaps? A note that Marlowe was to receive no wages and not to be hired on by another captain? Something like that—the prospect of losing one's livelihood—might make a man desperate, perhaps desperate enough to kill for. Certainly, at the time there was a darkness that came flooding into Marlowe's eyes, a detail that wasn't lost on you. Only then, you didn't have the foresight to see a murder on the horizon.

Where was Marlowe at the time of the killing? Hadn't he been on watch, with you? That's right! The old man of the sea was one of the three figures you'd seen conspiring in the moonlight, of that you're certain. He had left his post and went down into the hold with the other two.

Yet… if he went below decks, his couldn't have been the hand that put the knife to Bullock's throat. Indeed, if he lacked a steady hand, he might have conspired with someone else to do the dastardly deed. But who?

➤ It could certainly have been Barlow. What motive might the mustachioed sailor have held? <u>Go to page 181</u>

➤ Rediker himself, obviously. Think back to what you know… could his have been the hand on the knife? <u>Go to page 166</u>

➤ That's enough for one night. Time to get some sleep. You'll need your energy for tomorrow. <u>Go to page 86</u>

Spooked

Barlow unfurls the flag; a sea of black upon which rests the iconic skull and crossbones—but with one change: There is a beard of blood sewn onto the death's head, formed by a dozen or more crimson droplets, which, when combined, give the appearance of a beard. *A Bloodbeard.*

A glint on the deck betrays their use of a spyglass, and the way they make full sail to run betrays that they've seen your flag. Might've shown your true colors a bit too early.

"Make all sail! We've got to catch her. Gunner, ready a warning shot!" you cry.

"Aye, Cap'n," come the replies from the crew.

You're gaining quickly on the *Dos Santos*, which is a good sign. Most likely, it means that while your ship is nearly empty and glides easily across the sea, she's laden with treasures, dragging heavy with a belly full of loot to be plundered.

Robin lets them have a warning shot, but your former merchant vessel has no more guns than they do, and they're not cowed into submission. Rather, they give as good as they get until you're right alongside them.

It's odd, being so close to another ship that you can hear each other in conversation. Sizing one another up, it's the Portuguese captain who speaks first. He does so in English, clearly wishing you to understand when he says, "Fear not, men! Look at these ragged sailors in their torn breeches. These are desperate *desperados*, not the pirates you fear them to be!"

Glowering, you raise a hand to signal the attack. "Show them who you are!"

Here, the boarding party throws grappling hooks, drawing the prey in ever closer until they can leap aboard. The Portuguese crew does their best to cut the ropes binding the two ships together, but they only slow the progress, not stop it. Once your first men leap onto the prize ship, the enemy crew scatters, heading below decks.

Your pirate crew holds a motley medley of armaments. Wielding boarding axes, wooden and iron beams; whatever makeshift weapons they could find. Weapons aren't generally found aboard merchant vessels, so you'll want to upgrade your armaments as soon as possible. For now, it looks as though the crew has raided the carpenter's toolset.

"What d'we do now, Cap'n?" Barlow asks.

"Could smoke 'em out?" Marlowe suggests.

"No. We don't want t'start a fire on a wooden ship," Chips says.

"How about we rig up some *grenadoes*? Can ye do it, Robin?" Rediker asks.

The hulking gunner nods. "Might blow a hole in the ship, though, if the magazine's open."

"I say we hack our way in. Break down the door and make 'em pay for resistin'!" Butch offers.

As captain, the say is yours.

➢ Break down the door! A few axe strokes and you'll be inside. Go to page 135

➢ Have Robin rig up some *grenadoes* and blow your way in. Go to page 96

Spotted

You point past the guards, back towards London. "What's that?! A fire?!"

They turn, and you dart off back towards the port. Into the nearest alley, running as fast as your legs will carry you. Or rather, as far as a belly full of steak-'n'-ale pie will allow your legs to carry you. When you can run no further, you clasp your hands around your knees and take deep gasps of air.

"There, there," a familiar voice croaks. "Town Guard can't getcha now. You're safe with your ole friend, Dick."

When you look up, you see the same crooked man who spoke to you outside Spencer's Free House.

"If it's money... you want... I'm afraid... I don't have... much," you say between heaving breaths.

"Ya know, normally I'd try to come up with some clever ruse, but I'm tired, same as you. I've been followin' ya 'round all night, see? So, I'll just cut to the quick."

He produces a black, leather-bound object, the lanyard looped around his wrist on one end, and a heavy ball wrapped in sailor's line on the other. You realize, just as he starts to swing it, that this is a blackjack club, or cosh.

"Wait!" you cry, to no avail.

One of the blows glances your head at the temple, sending you down to the muck underfoot. He must've been a seaman once, because despite his crooked spine, Dick is able to deliver terrible attacks when provoked—a lesson you learn a bit too late. The savage beating is enough to make you lose consciousness, though not enough to kill you. Time will tell if that would've been a mercy.

Wake up and face the consequences of Dick's involuntary conscription on your behalf.
<u>Go to page 93</u>

Stern Expression

⚓

You turn away towards the rear of the ship and hurry off. The Master-of-Arms approaches and growls, "Where'd ya think you're going?"

"I have urgent business with the Captain," you say, hoping to use this as authority to take leave of the man.

"Ain't ye on watch? Ring the bloody bell if there's an emergency!"

"I shan't be a minute!" you cry out before running off.

If Lieutenant Dalton and Mr. Magnus heard you nearby, you haven't much time to lose. And from the looks of it, the Master-of-Arms is headed to further collude with them anyhow.

Best to make haste!

Captain Longwick glowers as you explain what you've just overheard. He shakes his head with disappointment. But not for the reasons you might've hoped.

"Ward, your admission into the officer ranks was sold upon the understanding that you would better serve in this capacity. Yet, here you are, proving to be a burden."

"But—but, sir! These were direct threats!" you stammer.

"Made to you personally?" he asks.

"Well... not exactly...."

The flesh about his neck reddens, but rather than showing his temper, his voice goes quiet as a whisper. "Do not mistake my earlier kindness as showing favor. Prove yourself, navigate the murky waters of shipboard politics, and earn your place amongst us. Until that day, until you earn the rank of Midshipman, I will not be entertaining another personal audience. Am I perfectly clear?"

"Aye, sir," you answer. What else can you say?

"By God, I should have you flogged for abandoning watch to bring me this trifle. Out of my sight!"

With tail sufficiently tucked between your legs, you head back out to the decks. By now the storm is in full force, and the men rush to brace the ship to weather against it. Mr. Magnus glares at you, then marches over.

"Up the foremast with ya!" he commands with an evil smirk.

You know it's incredibly dangerous, especially for someone so green, but you've just been given a direct order. What'll it be?

> That's on the opposite end of the ship. In a gale like this, he'll never know if you go or not. Agree, but hide until the storm has passed. Go to page 204

> Do your duty with gusto! He must be underestimating you. Maybe you can earn the trust of these men though hard work? Go to page 223

Sticks and Stones

Your words cut to the quick, and Dick's eyes go dark with rage. He produces a black, leather-bound object, the lanyard looped around his wrist on one end, and a heavy ball wrapped in sailor's line on the other. You realize, just as he starts to swing it, that this is a blackjack club, or cosh.

The first blow hits your wrists as your hands come up to protect your face.

"Better get used to these! Your bosun or ship's mate'll deliver worse for a vile tongue like that!" he cries, just before striking you again. "Been mollycoddled in the country too long, friend. But Dick'll break ya-o'-that!"

One of the blows glances your head at the temple, sending you down to the muck underfoot. He must've been a seaman once, because despite his crooked spine, Dick is able to deliver terrible attacks when provoked—a lesson you learn a bit too late. The savage beating is enough to make you lose consciousness, though not enough to kill you. Time will tell if that would've been a mercy.

Wake up and face the consequences of Dick's involuntary conscription on your behalf.
<u>Go to page 93</u>

Superiority Complex

A low growl comes from the predator as you step forward. Its ears fold back against its head, fur bristles on its neck as it cowers. Maybe you really are intimidating? You stare harder into the creature's eyes. The jaguar suddenly springs off its back legs, lunging out, with claws extended to their fullest and most lethal.

What should you do?

- Fight back! Aim for the head with punches and kicks while protecting my jugular as best I can. Go to page 261
- Play "dead." The jaguar is asserting dominance and will lose interest if I don't fight back. Go to page 48

Suppressed

⚓

You stay quiet, walking in line with the rest of the sailors. You're marched back out to port with an escort of redcoat soldiers—Lobsters, as the sailors call them—past the docks that house the merchant vessels and off to a section where the ships-of-the-line reside. Huge command vessels, waiting to be filled full of military fighting men. There are smaller sloops and gunships too, looking fast and fearsome. England is readying herself for war against Spain, and these wooden ships and iron men are the tip of the spear.

And then there's the HMS *Hornblower*. She's not the biggest in the fleet, but much larger than some. Her timbers are newly scrubbed, pitched, and held tightly together; sleek yet powerful. She leans forward, ready to speed off as soon as her sails are unfurled. A colossal, carved figure from Norse mythology looms proudly at the bow.

The figurehead is a musclebound, bearded warrior, who holds an enormous ox horn as a trumpet that he's set to blow into eternally. It's so large in fact, that he needs both hands to hold the horn; biceps bulging from the effort just to hold the instrument in place. From your studies, you recognize the figurehead as Heimdall and the Gjallarhorn he'll use to signal the coming of Ragnarok—the end of the world.

"A frigate," one of the other recruits murmurs, letting you know which class of ship looms over you now. You know practically nothing about ships and seafaring, so this designation doesn't tell you much. To your eyes, it's an impressive vessel, with too many cannons for you to count before you're marched forward yet again.

The ramp is extended and dozens of seamen bring supplies onboard. Your motley gang of recruits pales in comparison to the mighty beast of war. How many men does a frigate hold? 100? 200? Far more than the sparsely-manned merchant vessels down the docks, that's for sure.

You're greeted by the Master-of-Arms, a fastidiously groomed sailor who doesn't bother with introductions further than his title. As each man passes, he gives them a position and a location to report. "Convicted pickpocket? S'pose a man with nimble fingers can wrangle the rigging. Bosun's mate. And you? Fear not, we'll work that love-o'-gin outta ya. Seaman. You, any skills? Woodworking, eh? Carpenter's mate."

James makes it to the front of the line where he reports, "Two years' experience aboard the *Cooper's Pride*, merchant vessel."

The Master-of-Arms looks him over and says, "How many fingers ya got?" James shows off all ten and the man concludes, "Gunner's mate."

And then it's your turn. "Any skills?" the Master-of-Arms asks.

"I can read," you offer.

"And what can ya do with your hands?"

"Umm, write?"

He glowers in response. At length he roars, "Landsman it is, then!"

"Landsman? That's a funny name for a sailor."

Now he laughs and says, "Well, then! Keep your nose clean and, provided ya live long 'nuff, we'll make a seaman outta ya in no time."

You gulp. "To whom do I report, sir?"

"Anyone and everyone. Landsman is as low as ya can get on the totem pole! Now help us get these crates loaded up!"

- Wait! I come from a good family! Surely there is a berth more befitting my breeding? Go to page 224
- Get to work. Idleness will only make things worse. Go to page 133
- I've made a terrible mistake. I don't belong here! Sneak off the ship in the commotion of loading up. Go to page 204

Sweet Relief

The berries are sweet, plump and ripe, with a nice, tangy aftertaste. It leaves a pleasant tingling sensation in your jaw muscles as the tart mixes with the sugary, releasing a flood of saliva. Most of a seaman's diet is composed of salted meat or flavorless coarse biscuits, so a bushel full of berries feels like Christmas morning.

Once you've had your fill, to the point of where you really could eat no more, you fill your pockets with extra berries for a snack later. The entire experience is intoxicating; leaves you feeling lightheaded, with a pleasant numbness in your mouth.

A bit of a stomach-ache sets in, but that's not all that surprising due to the rich and unfamiliar nature of the snack. It is a bit surprising, however, when the stomach-ache sets into a full-blown cramp, and you double over in pain.

Your abdominal muscles seize up, sending you into a fetal position on the sand, clutching your gut. It's an excruciating pain, and your hands form themselves into claws as you try to dig in to stop the cramping.

Then the paralysis sets in.

Even though we humans eat plenty of red fruits, in the natural world, red means dead. This bright coloration is actually a warning. "Don't eat me, or you'll regret it." Despite those on the menu and in our markets, about 90% of wild-growing red berries are toxic.

As are the sort growing near the shores of your island.

THE END

Taking Flight

You sprint away from the quarterdeck, frantically scanning the ship for signs of Billy. Joe and Chips run after you, frantically crying "Murderer!" as they give chase. While Joe is nimble-footed, and Chips would have an iron-grip if he could catch you, neither man can. Too great is the fear that propels you onwards.

But where can you really hope to run on a ship out in the open ocean? All you really need is to find Billy. Your heart soars when you see the doors to the fo'c'sle open, but falls back into despair again when you see Rediker emerge.

"You!" you cry, unable to help yourself. "You did this!"

Rediker grabs hold of you, and Barlow helps when he emerges from behind his companion.

"What's this now?" Rediker says.

"Hold there! Saltboots killed the Cap'n!" Chips cries from across the ship.

Rediker's eyes grow wide and he turns to his co-conspirator. "Quickly! Help me get Saltboots overboard, we've been made out!"

The two of them pick you up and throw you into the sea. The shock of the cold and wet causes a reflexive gasp for breath, bringing a salty drink to gurgle as you struggle to stay afloat.

"Saltboots jumped for it!" Barlow cries.

You try to scream out, but your sodden clothes pull at you from below.

"Too good an end for a murderer!" Chips says, arriving at the side.

You finally manage cries of innocence, but they fall on deaf ears and the men ultimately turn their backs and walk away. The *Cooper's Pride* sails on without her captain, and without you too.

THE END

Tarnation

This group of "Jack Tars" (as seamen are commonly called) certainly fit the name, with their wide, baggy breeches tarred for weatherproofing. Their loose-hanging linen shirts and jackets look to have been sewn and resewn over and over again at sea. The whole kit has clearly survived age and beatings; both by weather and shipboard labor—perhaps even by an unruly master.

The nearest sailor catches you eyeing the odd-shaped buttons on his coat and offers them up for closer inspection. "Shark vertebra. Can make ye a set, if ya like, exchange for your daily rum tot."

"Cheers. I'll keep that in mind," you say.

The leader of the group steps forward. "Call me Chips, ship's carpenter and lead-o'-this-here starboard watch." He has this moniker roughly tattooed on each forearm.

"So you won't forget," you say good-naturedly, pointing to the tattoos.

"So *ye* won't, lest I lose one or the other… or me head," is his humorless reply.

"Can carve your initials for ya, then rub in the gunpowder so it keeps. For another tot," the nearby sailor offers.

"Jack of all trades, master of rum," you mutter.

"Ye be Saltboots, Jimmy's cousin, eh? And you there, hear tale ye were a privateer," Chips continues.

"Scuttlebutt wastes no time. Call me Rediker, or Red, if it suits."

"Just you stow such liberal thinkin' aboard the *Pride*, hear me? Privateer's more freebooter than he is common Tar, and we don't need no such trouble."

"Don't fret," Rediker replies with mock sincerity. "Won't forget me rightful place."

"See that ye don't! A troublemaker in the crew damns us all to a harsh voyage, seen it meself time and again."

➤ Say, "Excuse my ignorance, but I understood a privateer to be a perfectly legal position, no?" Go to page 174

➤ Say, "So… Starboard watch? What, pray tell, does that duty entail?"
Go to page 177

A Three-Hour Tour

This group is formed by Robin, the heavily tattooed gunner, Butch the surgeon, and two more common seamen. The others introduce themselves, and you do as well, but Robin wastes no time with small talk.

"Call me Robin. I be the gunner, and this here's the second starboard watch. Saltboots, stay with me. The rest-o'-you lot, we form up in four hours; eight bells."

Your three compatriots depart, headed back down into the fo'c'sle to rest. Waiting to see what Robin has in mind, you take a moment to measure the man.

He's shirtless, which shows off his musclebound frame as well as his ink. There are the traditional cannon and anchor tattoos, common among many sailors, a Jerusalem cross, and, most peculiarly, a treasure map. A dashed-and-dotted line runs along his leathered skin, ending in an "X-marks the spot" atop his heart. He keeps his head and body shaved clean, perhaps to show off this art.

"The *Cooper's Pride*, she's a sloop," he says. "Near fifty-feet at the keel. Her mainsail there, ya can see the short-gaff type with long boom. Square topsail flying on the topmast, see? Topmast stay has a flying jib, too, but she's furled—rough seas ahead. Foot ropes on her standing yard, mind those. Up there be staysail and jib."

Following Robin, it comes to you with sudden realization: he's giving you a tour! For someone who appears so gruff and brusque, menacing even, he proves to be genuinely interested in helping you learn your place.

He continues, "Four carriage guns, two swivel. Show ya how t'use both 'fore the week's up."

Robin points out the different parts of the ship, from the helm to the hold, and everything in-between. You learn where you'll have your meals, and where you'll go to relieve yourself once they've passed. You learn where the animals are kept, where their feed is stored, and where the muck-raking gets shoveled once they've passed their own meals in turn.

It's a three-hour tour all told, taking up nearly your entire "off time" before the watch. Robin goes to get the report from the leader of the current starboard watch, so that they might change over positions seamlessly. Soon, eight bells are rung and your watch officially begins.

You look idly about, awaiting orders.

"What a bunch-o'-soddin' rubbish," Butch says, arriving on deck. "Ever heard-o'-a surgeon on the watch? Should be learnin' me trade. So many books and potions down there, without a clue on what t'do with 'em. God help the first man t'get sick, his surgeon's stuck on watch!"

➢ Listen to the man vent. Ask, "Why do they have you on watch, then?"
  Go to page 20

➢ Nod sympathetically, then excuse yourself to find Robin and see what duties you should perform. Go to page 18

Thy Cup Runneth Over

A bottle of wine is opened, but only those deemed in charge—that is, yourself and Rediker—are offered a glass. Hierarchy and propriety must always be honored, it seems, even when punishing a pirate crew. As the Captain, you're allowed to go first.

"Health to His Excellency the Governor, and prosperity to the colonies," you begin. "Wine is a fitting tribute offered from a wayward seafarer, for it is Homer's wine-dark seas that so dominate our destinies. Like Odysseus, I too was blown off course, and I pray the magistrate sees a repentant soul who might be worth pardoning. The Greeks say they invented wine, seafaring, democracy, and even civilization. Perhaps seeing this wine now will remind us of our civility and the chance to show that the greatest gift of a democracy is the power to raise up the people and give us voice.

"Homeric wine was described in several different ways. Often it would be *melas*, or dark, used lyrically to compare wine to blood, death, and the depths of unforgiving seas. But it could also be called *aithops*, or bright, to compare to the play of sunlight shimmering upon the waves at dawn. Will this wine I hold in my hand be a portent of death and darkness? Or will His Excellency show the world and the rest of Britannia that Boston is to be a shining light of civility?

"Health to His Excellency the Governor, and prosperity to the colonies," you say again, ending the toast and drinking from the wine.

Rediker steps forward and raises his own glass. "I say damnation to the Governor, and confusion to the colonies! Looks like a fine day t'die, so do your worst, ye devils!"

Gasps ripple through the gathered crowds, and the magistrate's face flushes red. The reverend clasps a hand to his mouth in disbelief. Rediker smiles, then gulps down the wine, finishing off both the libation and any chance of liberation.

"Hangman, dispose of these knaves!" the magistrate cries.

With that, a rope is strung about your neck, prayers uttered, and the platform falls out beneath your feet to leave you swaying in the breeze.

THE END

Together, As One

⚓

"Very well. You'd know your cousin best; I trust your judgment. Bring me that pirate captain, Ward. Alive, if possible."

"Aye, sir," you say, before saluting.

Rushing below decks, you find your cousin in the ship's magazine, as expected. Word of the impending pirate battle has already flooded through the ship, and the *Hornblower*'s crew surges forth to action stations.

"And I'd like you by my side, cousin, if you think you can face those who likely murdered your old shipmates," you say, finishing the tale.

James pauses, considering your words. "These were good men. If you're leading the attack, coz—count me in!"

"What about your duties here, lad? Call came for action stations!" Monks interjects.

"I shall send a replacement down from the boarding party. Come, we haven't a moment to lose!"

The drums beat for war as the *Hornblower* sails towards the pirate ship. The plan, insofar as you've been made aware of it, is to pin the *Cooper's Pride* up against the coast, without letting them slip through an inlet and escape into the shallows. Once they realize the only way to flee is over the open seas, you'll cut off the smaller ship, board her, and take the pirates with flintlocks and steel.

The cannons boom, making what could be considered a warning shot—but more likely is meant to shape the fleeing ship's course. It works, and the *Cooper's Pride* alters its course to flee further along the coast.

The *Hornblower* follows the pirate ship along the convex bend of the coast, until another ship is revealed from around the curve. A Spanish Man-o'-War, not too different from the last you've seen. She's moored in this hidden inlet, and the pirate ship dares not sail into her. This is an unexpected tactical wildcard—neither ship is allied with the Dons.

Captain Longwick continues with the present course, and you have the boarding crews ready themselves. Sharing a knowing look and a nod with Cousin James, you steel yourself for battle. Then the order comes to attack at will.

"FIRE!!!" you order, and the muskets discharge in unison. Not waiting for a reload, you draw your saber and shout, "Charge!"

The boarding party drops muskets and instead launches grappling hooks and walkways across the open sea, bridging the two ships. It's a ferocious and bloody battle from the start. The pirates are brutal fighters, but numbers are on your side. The sailors rush against the gilded barbarians, taking the others by sheer overwhelming force.

James sticks by your side, fighting like a man out for revenge. With a shout of, "For Billy! For the Pride!" he goes after the brutes. You watch his back and he watches yours. Together, fighting as one, you cut through the lines of pirates, making your way towards the center of the ship in hopes of capturing the pirate captain.

That's when you spot him. He has a red skullcap, a pierced eyebrow, and fire in his eyes. He's not distinguishable from the rest of the crew, but you recognize a fellow leader of men when you see one. They fight in a circle radiating out from this man, keeping their trust in his leadership, ready for whatever orders he may give.

"Cap'n Rediker, look out!" a mustachioed man shouts as you approach.

"He's gonna blow the whole bloody ship!" James cries, noting the setup near Rediker.

The pirate captain, rather than turning to cross swords with you, dashes back and lights a fuse—the long tendril of which ignites and runs down below decks. Without another thought, you dash over, leap and slam your cutlass down upon the fuse; cutting the head off this fiery serpent just before it would retreat below decks.

Rolling to your side, you see James fighting the mustachioed pirate who warned his captain. The pirate called Rediker joins the melee, but, together with your cousin, you're able to best the pair of them in outright combat. At nearly the same moment, you each raise a blade to the throats of your foes.

"Surrender!" you growl, sword pointed with menace.

Rediker looks to the blade at his throat, then to that of the man at his side who shares in his predicament.

"Surrender!" you call again.

"I yield!" the pirate says.

<u>Go to page 27</u>

Too Easy

It takes a few stabs with the spear to get the hang of it, as the refraction of light shifts where you perceive the fish to be versus where they actually are, but eventually, you're able to catch a meal of red, yellow, green, and purple fish.

Making a great feast from your bounty, you eat like you truly are the monarch of this small island. It all goes down swimmingly. Huzzah! Lots of fish, no issues. Unlike plants, brightly-colored does not necessarily mean toxic in the fish world. Indeed, their rainbow scales might make them more camouflaged against the brightly colored reef, or perhaps they simply need to recognize one another amongst so much visual noise. Either way, you get a wonderful source of protein and fish oils.

It appears as if your luck has only just begun, for the very next day you're out hiking when you startle a feral pig on the island. Most likely a sow that was released by passing ships in hopes of growing a native population, she now frightens when you step near her, astounded that she didn't hear your presence. Unwittingly, the pig dashes off a rocky outcropping, falling to her death once she's been dashed on the rocks below. All you've got to do is gather her up and have a real feast.

How do you prepare a wild pig?

- Remove all the organs to remove risk of tainting the meat with fluids, such as from the musk gland. Go to page 15
- Tie the pig to shore; soak it in your local pond overnight. This will cure the meat and remove parasites. Go to page 202
- Eat only the head and/or organs. The pig likely has parasites that it will pass on to you through its flesh. Go to page 321

To the Trees!

The best way to avoid lightning is to make oneself as dissimilar to a lightning rod as possible. Becoming just another part of the undergrowth in the forest is a great way to do just that. Indeed, this was probably your best choice, because when the rainstorm starts in earnest, you don't get soaked through or have to sit for a long time in an awkward position.

After a short time spent cowering from the fury of Mother Nature, the storm has passed. With any luck, that means you can now set up camp and not have to worry about sleeping through the deluge for a second night.

The squall over, the clouds part and warm tropical sunshine pours down in its stead. Back out to the clearing, you find a spot with a view of the coastline that's semi-dry, due to a natural protection from a rocking outcropping. Plenty of time to set up camp here, start a fire, fortify a more permanent shelter, and even cook dinner. The rest of the day is looking up!

As a two birds/one stone sort of effort, you clear the area surrounding your camp of underbrush. This vegetation can be used on a new shelter or for kindling your fire (especially the driest bits), but its removal will also help minimize insects, rats, and snakes around your camp.

Once you've cleared out this growth and built a sleeping area for the night, you set out your clothes, journal, and pistol shot to dry. The pistol is a flintlock, which you can use to start a fire.

The flintlock mechanism works by literally striking a piece of flint, which creates a massive spark. So all you have to do is hold the pistol near the kindling, cock the hammer, and pull the trigger. Flash! The sparks leap into the kindling.

After coaxing the spark into a flame, you carefully reload the pistol and store it back into your waistband. Best not to use that trick too many times, or you'll wear out the mechanism before you have a chance to use the weapon.

Sitting back, you enjoy the warmth of the fire as the sun sets. This was a fine day. Though it very well could be the crackling of the firewood echoing off your rocky outcropping, you could swear you can hear something or someone wandering around out there, watching you. Keeping close to the fire, you try to shrug off the feeling.

Maybe you should take your mind off things. Think back to the time on the ship and Captain Bullock's true killer. If Rediker and his ilk were the likeliest of suspects, then Joe, Chips, and Robin were the trio with the most opportunity. After all, these three were the first to arrive on scene, so that means they were close to the captain's cabin.

What do you really know about these men?

- Reflect on your knowledge of Robin, the tattooed hulk of a gunner. Go to page 279
- Think back to your experiences with Joe, the young olive-skinned bosun. Go to page 73
- Reminisce on your time spent with Chips, the crusty old carpenter. Go to page 42
- Keep your mind off of the *Cooper's Pride,* and simply enjoy the fire's warmth. Go to page 320

Town Rats

Your hands ball up into fists, and you send a right hook into the man with the wounded nose, aimed right at that same bull's-eye. An unpracticed boxer, you're signaling your attack and could probably be easily dodged, but the drunken man's reflexes are too slow and you ring his bell with more strength than you knew you had in you.

A terrible *crack* sounds out and you're not sure if it was your knuckles or the last bits of his cartilage. Either way, a new fountain flows from his face and he curses you as he backs away.

Stunned that you even knew how to throw a punch, you look at the other man is if he knows what should happen next. As it turns out, he does. He waylays you with a haymaker of his own, sending you reeling back across the muddy boardwalks. You trip over a loose board, and hit the soft ground.

The kick that hits you in the ribs is a ferocious one, and the attacker seems to realize it. He takes a minute to help his friend while you catch your breath.

"I'm fine! Finish the bastard off," a newly nasal voice cries out.

Vision turning red, you grab hold of the loose board, find your footing, and spin around just in time to connect wood to skull with your would-be assailant. It's such a brutal strike, full of such unbridled rage and pent-up aggression that the man falls with just the one blow.

"Good God Almighty," says a man behind you.

You turn to see two town guards looking at you with mouths agape.

"You better hope this fella wakes up in the morning," the other says.

"Just in case, you'll be sleeping in a cell tonight."

Not much choice here:

Go directly to jail, do not pass go, do not assault officers of the peace and make matters worse.
<u>Go to page 188</u>

Trapper

The pirates give chase through the jungle, hot on your heels, slashing their cutlasses as they go. None fire their pistols, for it would be a waste of the flintlock's single shot to discharge the weapon without a clear line of sight.

Lithe and swift, you manage to pull slightly ahead of the men. In this way, you're able to leap onto the perfect precipice before the men come tumbling down after you. A ravine you've explored serves to decimate their ranks as they fall into the crevasse with bone-crunching finality.

The remaining pirates give chase more warily, but the natural well you had found is hidden by ferns, and Marlowe and his men fall perfectly into the trap. From here, they struggle to free themselves, collapsing the earthen walls of the hole and burying themselves alive. Those who were pursuing you are now gone, buried like so many distant memories, but more pirates still remain nearer the shore. You've come too far not to end this…

Claiming a pistol off the fallen pirates, you now stalk the rest of the men, armed to the teeth. They respond in kind, setting fire to the underbrush of your island. Soon, only Barlow and Rediker remain—and you've got a pistol for each man.

The flintlock you've been carrying all these weeks is the one you save for Captain Rediker. Stepping from the underbrush, they turn to face you, faces full of surprise. Out here, on the very beach you were abandoned upon, only the three of you stand living.

➢ Fire at Barlow first—savor the victory. Go to page 315

➢ Fire at Rediker first—he's the bigger threat. Go to page 189

Treachery Afoot

Rediker nods quickly at your orders. "I got this, Cap'n. Go!"

Then you find your feet and take great strides out of the cabin, across the quarterdeck, and towards the larboard side, where the ship is moored in port. From here you see Billy running down the wooden planks of the wharf and into Boston. He's an older seaman, not used to sprinting, and his hefty frame waddles with the extra weight.

Not wanting to waste a moment, you grab hold of a rope hanging slack from the yardarm and swing off the ship like a marauding corsair. The rope brings you over the crates being offloaded and down onto the wharf with a bit too much speed. Boots hit first, then you tumble and roll forward, before finally finding your footing. Even so, that move helped you get on Billy's trail much quicker than simply climbing down the gangway and darting between the mazes of crates would have.

This tumbling clatter upon the wharf causes Billy to look back, and, upon finding himself pursued, he renews the frenzied pace of his attempted escape. He shoves bystanders out of his way; one of them splashes into the harbor, and the commotion brings all eyes towards the pair of you.

"Deserter!" you shout, thinking quickly. "Stop that man!"

The bystanders move aside, laughing now at the familiar scene.

Billy changes tactics, tries to lose you in the alleyways of the port town. He's clearly been to Boston before and navigates the narrow streets as easily as if he were leisurely consulting a chart. You look about desperately from intersection to intersection, only to catch a fleeting glimpse before he disappears again.

But you're faster than the husky old sailor and gaining on him with every turn. Finally, he slips up, and you corner him in one of the alleyways. He tries to double-back, but now you're blocking his path—heaving for breath, sweating, panting, and looking for all the world like a cornered and wounded beast ready to lash out and defend himself.

The old mate pulls a dirk from his waistline and you do the same with the dueling pistol, pulling the hammer back for emphasis. His eyes go wide with the move. At length, Billy tosses the knife aside, catching his breath and shaking his head.

"Saltboots, ya might be a lot-o'-things, but a murderer ye are not. I dunno who killed Bullock, but I don't believe ye killed the man, nor do I believe that ye will murder me now. Lemme go. The *Cooper's Pride* was good t'your family and I been kindly t'ye, have I not? Look at me. I be but an old man without a taste for the pirate's life," Billy pleads.

➢ Take pity on the man. Agree to let him live out his days here in the colonies, and return to the ship. Go to page 178

➢ Fire the pistol, and set him free of this life. Dead men tell no tales. Go to page 56

Treeline

From the jungle, you watch the men as they arrive on the beach. They've already transferred the carriage guns to the shore, erecting a makeshift fort in case any ships were to follow them to this cove while the *Pride* was careened and vulnerable.

They now fly the Jolly Roger—a black pirate flag, of custom design. Crossed cutlasses serve as the outline to an hourglass, with a death's head in the upper chamber and a drop of blood pouring out as the sand in the lower chamber. The message is simple, clear. Surrender while you still can.

The crew ravages the beach, felling trees, digging up turtle nests for eggs, dozens of pairs of boots tromping everything in sight. Their ranks have swelled since last you met the crew, and indeed, at least half of their number are now African pirates or perhaps former slaves.

Each man is more fearsome a sailor than you've ever seen, armed with cutlasses and pistols. They're dressed flamboyantly in leather and silk, with golden hoop earrings and jewelry about their necks and fingers.

"Orders, Cap'n?" one of the sailors says. Then you recognize the man, it's Marlowe. And the seaman he addresses is none other than Rediker, now made captain.

"Have Chips lead the careening on the *Deleon's Revenge*," he says, indicating a new name for the *Cooper's Pride*. "Take a few others inland in search-o'-fresh water. Remember, Saltboots might be here somewhere, if only as a skeleton."

"And if we should stumble across a living, breathing Saltboots?"

"Bring our former shipmate t'me. If Saltboots be alive, no doubt we could learn-o'-freshwater and food caches all the more quickly. Hell, if t'were me, I'd offer t'be our guide in exchange for a block-o'-cheese after a few weeks out here sucking on coconuts and turtle's eggs."

They both have a good chuckle at that.

➤ Seems Rediker might find your knowledge valuable. Step out of the jungle and return from the dead. Go to page 271

➤ Haunt the men from a distance. These are pirates, after all. Go to page 94

True Colors

As ordered, the men abandon the top decks of the ship and rush into the hold. The African pirates are already here, waiting.

"Barricade the door," Rediker starts. "When they break in—"

"No. Leave the doors open. Spread out; let them come," you say. All eyes go to you. "We kill every last one, no prisoners. Just try not to get too much blood on the uniforms."

The bloodthirsty pirates grin, ready for revenge against the crown.

"Lamps out," Marlowe says, getting it.

Boots clatter from above, announcing the arrival of the Royal Navy aboard your ship. Soon they rush below decks, scouring the ship for any sign of you. Waiting until the last possible moment, you cry, "NOW!!!" and the bloodbath begins.

The naval soldiers were expecting a barricade, like Rediker had in mind—not an ambush from an inferior force. It's a brutal battle in the confinements of the ship, but this is your home, and the crew of the *Deleon's Revenge* have a decided advantage in the dark depths of the ship's hold.

"We must move quickly, once the fighting is over," you say to Rediker. "The half of the crew who played at plague victims, get them into these naval uniforms. The other half—into irons. Find me an officer's uniform. Are you ready for your debut as Captain Bloodbeard?"

Rediker blinks, confused. Then a smile slowly creeps across his face.

Back out on deck, you move in the Lieutenant's uniform, large hat pulled low on your brow. Marlowe, also dressed as a military man, lowers the pirate flag, raising the English colors in its place.

"The ship is ours!" you cry out to the man-o'-war.

The pirates in irons are lined up on the deck, put on their knees and held at bay by the remaining Royal Navy seamen. Or, at least that's how it appears. At length, the commander of the *Hornblower* comes across to the *Deleon's Revenge* to accept Captain Bloodbeard's surrender.

"So this is the rogue giving the colonies so much trouble, eh? Well done, Lieutenant!" the captain shouts, turning to you.

Then his smile drops. At this, you raise a pistol to aim at the man and the pirates all stand up, tossing the unclasped irons away. Those pirates pretending to be Royal Navy seamen also follow on your signal, taking captive the naval captain's entourage.

"Actually, *this* is the rogue giving you so much trouble, Captain. Your sword, if you please."

Go to page 7

Two Bits

You climb out to the ship's waist—the main deck for green hands that sits recessed between the rear quarterdeck and the fo'c'sle upper deck. The yardarm swings cargo down into the hold, and you nearly bump into the fleshy pink snout of an enormous sow. She squeals in your face, triggering further squeals of laughter from above.

When you look up, you see a boy of about seventeen, thin as a whip, with hair of obsidian and tawny skin. He's fair-looking and exotic, and gives a tilt of his head in response to your prolonged stare.

"I'm sorry, it's just—you're not…" you stammer, trying to find the words.

"British? But of course I am! You'll be this tanned too, in a month or so," he says.

Your face must be priceless, for he erupts in a new gale of laughter.

"I'm Yousefah," he says, his accent becoming plain. "From British India. Though most just call me 'Joe.' I'm the Bosun here on the *Pride*, so when I pipe me whistle, you come."

You nod and Joe produces a straight razor, then begins to dry-shave right there on deck. Captain Bullock haunts the quarterdeck, notes Joe, and shouts to Billy, "Mr. Greaves! Send the new surgeon to my cabin with his cutting shears. I'm in need of a haircut."

"Aye, Cap'n!" Billy cries in response.

"The surgeon gives haircuts?" you say, thinking aloud.

But Joe hears and answers, "Perhaps you think the captain is flaunting his own importance?"

"Apologies. I—I didn't mean anything by it."

"Don't be too quick to judge Captain Bullock," Joe continues. "While it might look like a frivolous request, might be something more. He said *new* surgeon, did he not? Could he be ensuring the man better have a steady hand?"

Before you have a chance to respond, Billy arrives at the bosun's side. "Ho, there, Saltboots! Cap'n Bullock wants a word. Where's the rest of 'em?"

"Still below, I should think."

"Christ Almighty, we still got cargo t'be loaded before we can set sail! C'mon now!"

Not much choice here:

Best not keep Captain Bullock waiting… Go to page 105

Under Pressure

⚓

You go back to the watch, saved somewhat ironically, by a deadly storm surge. The sea swells, sending your stomach into a worse state than it's ever been. If the carriage ride into London had left it unsettled, this storm now swoops in to leave your stomach downright conquered. You find a bucket meant for swabbing the deck and use the vessel to store your day's vomited rations. Lieutenant Dalton raises the alarm. "Up! Every soul, and nimbly, for God's sake, or we perish!"

"Up into the maintop! Take in the topsail!" Mr. Magnus adds.

Rain comes down upon the deck in sheets. Gale-force winds pick up anything not battened down (nearly yourself included!) and lightning fractures an otherwise black sky. The crew—those who were on rest included—rush from below decks to help prepare the *Hornblower* to weather the storm.

Some sailors notice you clutching your bucket, but few bother to give you a disappointed shake of the head. You're no use here, not yet, and it's speed that saves lives, so they're content enough just to have you out of the way—for now.

That night was certainly the worst the storm had to offer, though a weather system does follow the ship for the next few days. The more superstitious of the sailors (that is to say, nearly all of them), start looking for something or *someone* to blame.

And that night was just the start of the difficulties for you personally. Because of your position of Ward, you're constantly asked questions you couldn't possibly know the answer to, then berated for not knowing anyhow. Lieutenant Dalton gives you extra volumes to read and study during your "free time," but Mr. Magnus and the Master-of-Arms make sure you have none to spare by adding additional duties. Swabbing the deck, scouring the hull, and pitching new lines are added on top of your requests from Dalton, with both sets of supervisors demanding timely obedience.

And sleep? A distant memory. The few times you're afforded to lie down, either someone suddenly shouts or drops cannonballs or other equipment right over your head. And you could swear those same two conniving men are always smirking nearby when that happens. Either that, or Lieutenant Dalton has you woken and brought up to the top deck during your sleep shift to witness this or that procedure.

As a result, you're starting to fall asleep elsewhere. Once, while using the privy. Worse, while on watch. You've already had two warnings, each time with a bucket of cold seawater over your head, and you've been told there won't be a third.

They've done nothing wrong, according to the letter of the law, so you can't go to the Captain. And your immediate supervisor, Lieutenant Dalton, is either in on it, or simply willing to turn a blind eye against their cruelty. What other ally do you have, save for a cousin who's a common Tar.

"Good God, coz. Ya look in an awful state!" James says.

➤ "…it's nothing. Just taking a while to 'learn the ropes' as they say. I'll be fine."
   Go to page 217

➤ "…it's the other officers. It's like they want me to fail! I'm at my wit's end."
   Go to page 151

An Understanding

Though the Jaguar does not understand your words, the calm, soothing tones cross the barrier from human language into the animal kingdom. Your body language, more than anything, is saying, "I am not your prey, nor you mine, we are two hunters who can live together in mutual respect."

The jaguar holds its ground and allows you to retreat.

Granted, that could just be today. You're still best to keep a roaring fire at night and look over your shoulder as you hike through the jungle. And watch your footing—nothing screams, "I'm prey!" like falling and flailing. Just ask that little piggy.

Although this final lesson you'll have to learn the hard way.

You're hiking through the jungle, looking for signs of a larger pork population, when the underbrush goes out from under you. Falling into darkness, you lash out for a handhold, but just too late. You slam down at the base of a natural well. It's not a manmade trap, for there are no spines at the bottom. Still, the fall was incredibly painful and it's pitch-black down here.

Anything broken? You don't think so. Regardless, it's best to take a moment to catch your breath before finding your way back out. What's the best way out of a natural hole?

- Leaning forward. Feet planted on at the rear wall and hands on the front, you can back slowly up. Go to page 172
- Try to dig your way out. By pulling down the earthen walls, you can make a ramp and climb to safety. Go to page 64
- Leaning back. With your shoulders and hands pressed on the wall and feet out in front, walking. Go to page 108
- Like a starfish. With your arms and legs spread on opposite walls, you can totter your way up. Go to page 92

Universal Gravitation

You must be coco-nuts to use a tree out in the open as shelter! Though this is the tropics, hypothermia is still a real danger and leaning against a tree offers negligible protection from the rain, while adding absolutely zero protection from the wind. You tuck your knees into your chest and shiver while the storm rages on.

WHAM! A coconut blasts against the beach, sending wet sand into the air like a mortar strike. *WHAM!* Another coconut hits just off your foot, bouncing against your thigh with enormous force. These fruit pods are falling from fifty feet up, carried down by the storm with devastating speed.

Then the final (as far as you're concerned) coconut hits squarely upon your own melon, striking you dead with an instantaneous demise. You've now joined the exclusive, but very real, list of people unfortunate enough to experience Death by Coconut.

THE END

Unlucky

Admittedly, there's more to the game than a simple toss of the coin, but in only a few minutes, the outcome is the same as if you'd done just that. The dice clatter to the table, showing a loss for you. All that coin, gone!

Wycombe takes a deep hit from his opium pipe and Monks divides your ante amongst the winners, while Argyle keeps tally on a scorecard.

"You look as though you have an albatross about your neck," Wycombe says. "Fret not, 'tis only money."

"Aye, wages come and go," Argyle agrees.

"But we ain't scavengers," Monks adds. "Double or nothin', and ya could winnit all back."

They're giving you a second chance, but at a double-or-nothing rate, you'd owe more than you have in your coin purse if you were to suffer another loss. Still, they don't know that, do they? And if you win, they'd never be the wiser that you bluffed your way into winning your money back....

If you want to say no, enough excitement for one night:

➤ Cut your losses and return to the bar to wait for Cousin James. Go to page 233

To try double or nothing, go again! The winning choice has been randomized, and the outcome of these choices may or not be the same. Play the dice/coin game again, or simply pick your luck of the draw:

➤ Heads on the coin toss, or a one, two, or three shown on the die. Go to page 183

➤ Tails on the coin toss, or a four, five, or six shown on the die. Go to page 230

Unprecedented

⚓

"**W**ard, use caution. There's much weight behind such words," Lieutenant Dalton warns.

"Indeed, words have weight, sir. Though I was simply on my rounds, as ordered, I'll ask him again, directly: as the Master-of-Arms, are you actually accusing me of lying? Of spying, no less?"

"I'll not back down," the man replies.

"Geoff, please, this is not the—" Dalton tries, but the Master-of-Arms cuts him off.

"If the Ward would challenge me to a duel, I accept!"

Mr. Magnus says nothing, but smiles at such a prospect. Clearly he does not think your chances against the Master-of-Arms to be very great.

"So be it," the Lieutenant says with a resigned sigh. "I shall inform Captain Longwick of your intentions immediately."

The raging storm postpones any thoughts of duels or satisfaction, but the Captain promises to address the issue first thing the next morning. That leaves you all night to think about just what you've gotten yourself into. The way the ship rollicks violently would forbid sleep anyhow.

Did you think the Master-of-Arms would hope to avoid the conflict? Or were you just feeling cornered, with no other way out? It's an awful storm that buffets the ship, but nothing compared to the tempest of dread within your soul.

Cousin James tries to convince you to forego the duel, or at least forestall it, but you turn him down. "I'm sorry, Cousin. But I don't think I can. Events are already in motion… if I were to relent now, these scoundrels would treat me all the worse for it—and now, with good reason."

James simply nods, knowing the truth of your words. An officer's greatest asset is their word of honor, and so the same is true of an officer candidate.

"I don't know much about duels," James confesses. "A common Tar cannot challenge a peer, much less an officer, so 'tis a privilege reserved to your own rank and file. Still—I can tell ya this: if ya rush the shot, you'll miss. But so will the Master-of-Arms. Maybe try to get him to rush and shoot first, then ya can take your time and aim true."

The noontime sun shines brightly in the sky over the main deck. *A fine day to die,* an inner voice says darkly. The officer cadre has gathered to bear witness, with Captain Longwick in full dress uniform yet again.

"The Commander's Ward is not typically in a position to challenge an officer to a duel. Indeed, this is a highly unusual request. Yet as a Ward is not directly under the Master-of-Arms in the chain of command, it must technically be considered within regulation. If the aggrieved parties truly want to continue, I am in no position to deter this course," Captain Longwick says, as much to you as to the gathered crowd. "Will neither party relent?"

"My honor has been besmirched," you say, the words leaden in your mouth.

The Master-of-Arms clears his throat and offers, "Sir, your Ward ain't nothin' but a spy; I tell it true."

"Very well. Without resolution, there is little choice but to settle this in a gentlemanly fashion—by means of duel! We should traditionally attempt landfall, but I will not turn the ship back into the storm we've just weathered. Ten paces, one shot, then if both parties miss, to be decided with cutlass. First to draw blood will be declared the victor. Select your weapons."

Twin pistols—the Captain's very own—sit inlaid in a velvet-lined case. They are ornately designed, but as will soon be proved, as deadly as they are beautiful. Once you each take a pistol, you march out your ten paces, heart thumping and stomach more sour than ever.

When you turn, the world becomes calm and clear with the certainty of mortality lingering over you. The sun is brighter than you ever remember seeing it, the gulls seem to flap their wings one feather at a time, and the swell of the sea undulates as regularly as a metronome. That wave of calm washes over you as well, and your hand steadies on the pistol, despite the rolling of the ship beneath your feet.

The Master-of-Arms raises his own weapon, as you do the same.

➢ Wait him out—force him to shoot first. Go to page 185

➢ Aim for the body. All you need to do is draw blood to be declared victor. Go to page 154

➢ Aim for the head. If you don't kill the man, you'll never be rid of him. Go to page 225

Up She Rises

⚓

You're awoken the next morning by a shouted, "Weigh anchor!" from one of the midshipmen. The *Hornblower* is fully resupplied and ready to depart the safety of the fleet once more. You head towards the capstan, helping fit the capstan-bars, ready to do your part to turn the wheel and raise the cable attached to the anchor. And you'll start, just as soon as the sea shanty does.

"*Ooooob!!!*" belts out one of the older seamen. "What shall we do with a drunken sailor? What shall we do with a drunken sailor? What shall we do with a drunken sailor? Ear-lie in the mornin'!"

That's when you start to push with the other seamen, while you shout in chorus with them, "Weigh-hey, and up she rises! Weigh-hey, and up she rises! Weigh-hey, and up she rises! Ear-lie in the mornin'!"

Another of the men takes the next verse. "Put'm in the long boat 'til he's sober! Put'm in the long boat 'til he's sober! Put'm in the long boat 'til he's sober! Ear-lie in the mornin'!"

"Weigh-hey, and up she rises! Weigh-hey, and up she rises! Weigh-hey, and up she rises! Ear-lie in the mornin'!" you all shout in refrain.

"Give'm a taste of the Cap'n's daughter!" another sailor starts in. "Give'm a taste of the Cap'n's daughter! Give'm a taste of the Cap'n's daughter! Ear-lie in the mornin'!"

Finishing out the sea shanty, you bring up the anchor and set sail for foreign seas. Oh, and a taste of the captain's daughter, in this sense, is to be on the receiving end of a flogging. Fortunately, Captain Longwick has not shown much interest in corporal punishment. Yet.

Days go by, each with the same duties performed in myriad ways. Sundays are usually easier; when the men tend to sew garments, cast lines into the sea in hopes of fresh provisions, or a few even read books or write letters home.

Weeks go by in this way, the ocean gradually changing from indigo to turquoise as shallower seas, reefs, and sandbars threaten the ship's path. The sun hangs longer in the sky, giving warmer, near-equatorial heat, and rain becomes a welcome relief for an English sailor.

Events of note during this month-long voyage: Monks, the gunner, manages to catch a sea-turtle when fishing, and there's a frenzy of bidding to get a taste of something other than salt beef. The carpenter's mate breaks an ankle, and is reassigned as the cook's mate. The carpenter is promised his old mate will be offloaded and traded out at the first Caribbean port upon which you make landfall. The scurvy has set in, with four sailors starting to show signs. One has already lost three teeth.

It's a particularly hot day when you're to make for port. You're sailing along a series of islands, and the men are practically frothing at the bit for some shore leave. A change of pace would certainly be welcomed.

"Sails, ho!" Lieutenant Dalton shouts.

"Looks like one'a ours. What flag's she flying? England?" Midshipman Magnus asks.

"No... she's flying the black," Dalton answers.

Could it really be? A pirate vessel?!

"Landsman, rouse the cap'n!" Magnus shouts, pointing your way.

You rush up to the quarterdeck and to the captain's cabin, remembering only at the last second not to barge in on the Master and Commander of the ship. Reporting in as you've been trained, you relay the sighting of the black flag with only minimal excited stammering.

Captain Longwick gives the briefest hint of a nod, then rushes past to discuss the situation with his officers.

"Sir, it appears we've happened upon a band of brigands," Lieutenant Dalton says.

Examining the situation through a looking glass, the captain practically growls, "The *Cooper's Pride*."

"You know her, sir?" Midshipman Magnus asks.

"A merchant ship, under the command of Arthur Bullock, or at least she was last. A draconian captain by all accounts, but still an Englishman." Then, lowering the spyglass, adds, "Well, gentlemen, if the *Pride* has been taken by pirates, I suppose it's only proper we take her back."

"Shall I set a course to intercept?" Dalton asks.

"We don't want to spook them just yet. If there's a hidden way through these islands, you can bet your hat these pirates will know it. Best not force them into the shallows, where we can't follow."

"Those scoundrels ain't no match for the *Hornblower*, sir!"

"Magnus, why must you speak when you have nothing to say?" Longwick replies. "Dalton, bring the relevant maps and charts to my cabin. We will use the terrain to our advantage, not the other way around. As for the men—action stations!"

"*Action stations!!!*" Midshipman Magnus bellows in response.

The order means you should muster with your gun crew, but likely you could also form up with the boarding parties. How often will you get a chance to fight pirates face-to-face?!

➢ Gun crew. We'll rake her with the broadsides. This time, we're the bigger ship! Go to page 5

➢ Boarding party! These pirate dogs will need to be captured and tried for their crimes against the crown! Go to page 61

Useful

"Into the pump room with ya!" Billy cries, then, turning back to the other sailors, continues, "You there! Grab the second axe and go aloft! Waste not another minute!"

You head down inside, battered about by the rolling of the ship as you go, into the pump room as ordered. She's a tight ship, but not immune to water cresting over her sides, and all that excess is weighing her down. The muscle-bound and tattooed Robin is here with a pair of other seamen, manually working the pumps to free the *Cooper's Pride* of bilge water. At your arrival, Robin simply nods, and you take a turn at the pumps. It's backbreaking work, but it serves as a much-needed outlet for your panic and adrenaline.

In this way, you help keep the ship afloat, and survive the storm. Sadly, as you'll later learn, three of your crewmates did not. It's only the end of the first day, but with the man crushed by crates and the three casualties, this ship of twenty-one souls is already reduced to seventeen. The workload increases proportionally, though, much to the grumbling of the men, the rations and pay do not rise to meet the intensified demands.

There's barely time to mourn the fallen, for their deaths are overshadowed by the need to re-mast the ship from that lost in the storm. Extra timbers are stored for exactly such a case, with nearly all of Sherwood Forest cut down sent across the seas. It's a Herculean effort, but the ship's carpenter—Chips—is an expert in his field. Still, short-handed and exhausted, raising a new mainmast in the face of continuing tempests feels like a somewhat Sisyphean endeavor.

Sevennight passes, each evening with wicked weather. Your digestive tract gradually empties itself of countryside finery (butter and milk and cheese), and is resupplied with hardtack and "Irish Horse" (coarse sea biscuits and salt-beef), which helps harden your constitution.

Then a fortnight goes by, finally without any seasickness, and with skies clearing up. In this time you "learn the ropes"—what to call them, what they do, how to tie, knot, and splice them, crawl upon them, with muscles and skin hardened from their handling.

Yet your education is not a solely physical one. The deep-sea ship is the height of technology in this era, with its own language for operations. You familiarize yourself with the *Cooper's Pride* forwards and backwards, bow to stern, larboard and starboard. In addition to the names of ship quarters and knots, there are whole vocabularies for sails, masts, and rigging. You learn the lexicon of winds, currents, basic navigation, stars and constellations, maneuvers at sea, other manner of ships seen on the horizon, as well as that of your crewmembers and their swears.

Despite a youth spent in scholarly pursuits, the low-threat environment of Latin and the classics was nothing compared to this new education and to what Rediker cynically calls "The Seven Liberal Sciences" one learns from a life at sea: Cursing, Drinking, Thieving, Whoring, Killing, Deceiving, and Backstabbing. Thankfully, you've only been exposed to the first two, so far as you know.

A month passes as you gradually become a useful member of the ship's company. There are no other major injuries or fatalities in this time, save for a pig that appears to have been strangled. An odd occurrence that Butch says could "possibly" be due to disease, which thankfully fails to spread. Captain Bullock orders the sow thrown overboard just to be safe, and the men watch on hungrily as the sharks feast on gammon. Indeed, a constant grumbling these weeks has been the worsening of the ship's stores and a lack of fresh provisions, with the occasional speculation as to the fineries feasted upon by the captain and his mate.

"Those chickens' eggs got t'be goin' somewhere, and it ain't our bellies," is a common refrain.

You're presently idling between watch duties, journaling about this month past, when you're given a sobering reminder of the need to learn one's duties properly. All hands are called to witness a flogging.

When you reach the top deck, you find most of the crew already assembled, gathered around a shirtless young sailor whose hands are tied to the larboard gangway. Joe, the bosun, holds a green broadcloth bag, from which Captain Bullock removes the infamous cat-o'-nine-tails.

"What'd the poor soul do?" an older sailor, Marlowe, asks in a low whisper.

"Used the wrong sheet in sew'n a sail. Ruined the whole bolt-o'-cloth and wasted two days' work, so I heard," Barlow replies, stroking his mustache.

"Oh, Christ be merciful," Chips swears. "'Twas me ordered the lad t'the task. Shoulda kept an eye on him…"

"Too late for that now, cat's out-o'-the bag," Rediker says.

All eyes go to the captain as he calls out, "Mr. Greaves! As I call out a full dozen!"

Captain Bullock passes the whip to his mate, who accepts the burden with a simple nod. Then Billy raises the cat and lashes the young man across his back. The snap reverberates over the silent deck, each man on the crew flinching in empathetic pain. Nine red lines appear, marking where each of the tails ripped across skin.

"One!" Bullock cries and Billy pulls back for another swing.

Abused, cross-hatched flesh seeps blood down the youth's back, staining his trousers crimson. On and on it goes, painfully slow, until the twelfth and final lash.

"Take him down," Captain Bullock orders as Billy passes the cat to the bosun. He gives no other reprimand, letting the whipping speak for itself. "Bosun, strict orders to the surgeon: nothing for the pain. Once he has dressed this man's wounds, have Butch report to my cabin."

"Aye, cap'n."

"Market day's over!" Billy cries. "Back to your watches!"

Murmured prayers are offered, and the men disperse, with heads hanging low.

➤ That's awful. I'm going to take my next tot of rum down to the man.
Go to page 76

➤ That's a lesson this sailor won't soon forget, nor I. Best keep my head down and steer clear. Go to page 30

Vengeful

Crack! You fire the pistol and Barlow falls to the beach, dead.

Rediker goes for his own pistols, and you bring out the other flintlock; the one you've saved for revenge. But his hand shakes, unsteadily, and just before you fire he lowers his weapon. Rediker looks to Barlow on the sand, swallows hard, and turns to face you.

"Go on then, finish it, ya devil," Rediker spits out, hatred in his eyes.

"You brought this on yourself, Rediker. The day you decided to be a mutinous pirate, judgment started following you like a shadow. Only now, it's finally caught up."

At this, he laughs. "Ye've murdered more men than I, by a long shot. The mutiny were never about Bullock or the *Pride*. Living life as a free man, as a privateer—that ain't a life a man can turn his back on. Never did spill blood that ain't deserved it, but you? Look! Gunned down an innocent in cold blood. How can that be justice?"

A splash pulls your attention to the shore, where Dudderidge the cook and a few others launch the jolly boats out for escape. They must have seen the island aflame and decided to flee.

Crack! Rediker's shot echoes out on the beach. You clutch your gut from the wound, drop the pistol, then stagger and fall.

"I make me own justice. Thank ye kindly for the reminder, Saltboots." Rediker stands over you, watching you slowly die. But with his crew dead or fleeing, this is the end for him too. He can't sail the ship by himself, so in essence, he's the marooned one now. He claims the pistol you dropped for himself, examining the weapon. "Kept this the whole time?"

"One shot, to end it," you say, then with your last ounce of strength, pull out the fifth and lay it out at his feet. "And… for the courage… to do so."

All goes dark as consciousness fades away.

THE END

The Volley of War

⚓

Learning to be a sailor these last few weeks has been essential to your survival, but unlike a merchant vessel, on the HMS *Hornblower* you've also been training for battle. This is the Royal Navy in wartime, and war against the Spanish is the whole reason they're impressing sailors, so in addition to seamanship you've been also been drilling on how to fire the cannons.

Yours is a crucial position: you swab the bore before the cartridge and shot is loaded, thus preventing accidental ignition (and the accompanying fatal explosions). You've got your bucket of seawater and your swab at the ready. Soon, you'll get to put all this training to practice. Soon, you'll fire upon the enemy!

Only you're stationed on the wrong side of the ship.

The enemy warship approaches from the starboard side, yet you've been set up on a gun team under Lieutenant Saffron on the larboard side; the complete opposite from the action! Still… that might be a good thing. You peek out across through one of the starboard gun ports at the approaching ship, and swallow a throat dry with fear. The Spanish warship is identified as the *Don Pedro Sangre*, a first-rate ship of 74 guns. By comparison, the *Hornblower* has only 36, of which only eight point in the right direction here on the lower gun deck. A daunting prospect, to say the least.

"Lieutenant, would you please keep your men out of my gun ports," the starboard broadside commander says to you, despite his words directed at your superior.

"Back to stations," Lieutenant Saffron orders. Then mutters to himself, "We'd do better to put oars out these gun ports."

The report of musket fire from above decks brings back the threat of action, and the men ready themselves at battle stations. The gun deck feels like a tinderbox—ready to blow. Finally, the time for battle comes.

"Rear battery, fire!" the Captain issues loudly, which is relayed down to your command. "FIRE!!!" the starboard broadside is ordered, signaling the last two guns.

The resultant explosion is unlike anything you've ever heard. As the cannons boom, your ears ring out, and the guns themselves slam backwards against their breech ropes. Seeing the several-ton weapons hurled violently backwards is a shock to the system, more so even than briefly going deaf from the cannon shot itself.

Then all hell breaks loose, as the Spanish return fire. The gun deck as cannon shot from the *Don Pedro Sangre* bombards your ship. Several men take splintering—though you yourself are spared, with the men on the starboard side acting as unwitting human shields. One of the men is blown apart by a direct hit to the ribcage. The pressure from the blast sprays viscera across the gun deck. It's complete carnage, with all the seamen dumbly looking to the ranking lieutenant for an order. You don't even remember falling, but you find your footing and look to Saffron. The man is shell-shocked, and every minute counts.

➤ See to the wounded. Several who need to be shuttled down to surgery are clearly unable to do so of their own accord; yet they can still be saved! Go to page 242

➤ Rush over and replace one of the wounded men on the active gun teams. You've got to keep those rear batteries firing! If you don't return cannon fire, the *Hornblower* will be blasted to pieces. Go to page 90

Volunteer as Tribute!

⚓

Pushing your way through the crowd, you shout, "Take me! Place me on the same ship as my cousin, this man here, and I volunteer to serve in His Majesty's Navy!"

The gathered crowd is shocked into silence, with all eyes on you. James's are the widest and he shakes his head, either in a mix of disbelief and terror, or perhaps trying to silence you.

Too late for that now.

"I don't suppose you have any naval experience?" the magistrate asks at length.

"Admittedly, no. But I'm a fast learner and a hard worker."

"Silence, cousin!" James hisses.

"Very well. We need more honorable sorts sailing our seas," the magistrate says, before continuing to address the confined men. "I hope the rest of you lot can learn from this. Defending the realm is a matter of duty! And so, by the authority of a wartime hot press, I hereby order your sentences commuted to the HMS *Hornblower*, under direct supervision of Captain Charles Longwick."

The crowd cheers and your head swims, unable to accept this new reality. You've just been pressed into the service of the Royal Navy! Finally, the ceremony is over and you're led away from the court. Where are they taking you? Will you head directly to the ship?

➢ Stay silent, stay in line. Go to page 288

➢ Find your way to James. He'll know what's going on. Go to page 59

Waiting Game

The three seamen sit on three sides of a square card table, leaving the fourth side conveniently open for a new player. Introducing yourself, you inquire as to the nature of the game. The ancient mariner across from you seems to be the leader of the bunch, a clean-shaven bastion of civilization amongst these brutish men. He introduces himself simply as Wycombe, surgeon assigned to the HMS *Hornblower*. Clearly prone to vice, at least while on shore, he cradles an opium pipe with an ornately carved tiger on its head.

The gruff man on your left says, "Everyone calls me 'Monks,' on account's me name's too hard t'say, and also I hail from the little parish of Monks Risborough." He has several facial scars and two tattoos: a cannon along one forearm, and a cutlass on the other. "I'd be the gunner on the same ship."

"We're all on the same bloody ship, we got pressed into her service," the third man says in a crisp Scottish accent. He'd look just as gruff as Monks if it weren't for the spectacles he wears. "And I suppose ya want to know my role? Call me Argyle. Able-bodied seaman, according to the logs, which I happen to keep. I got the best penmanship in the Royal Navy, and the Commander has no taste for bookkeeping, so 'tis a win-win."

"Gentlemen, may we get on with it?" Wycombe asks.

The sailors offer you a seat at their table and explain the rules of their game. Though they have several fun names for it—*Set the Rigging*, *Seaman's Bastard*, *Dog Watch Downs*, and most hilariously, *Fleeting Booty*—seems as if it's essentially just a 50/50 win-or-lose scenario. And despite the extreme odds, they bet heavily.

So, Dear Reader, grab a six-sided die or a nearby coin. Give it a roll and/or a flip, as appropriate. Or, just pick one of the two choices if you have no taste for the theatrical. But know this: to keep the process honest, I've randomized the outcome, and I'm not telling you which is the win or the loss. Good luck!

➤ Heads on the coin toss, or a one, two, or three shown on the die. Go to page 308

➤ Tails on the coin toss, or a four, five, or six shown on the die. Go to page 183

Walk on the Wildside

You set off into the jungle, the plants tugging on your seaman's clothes. What was meant to be light and airy on a ship is now easily tangled on thorns and brambles. If only you had a cutlass to hack through the undergrowth!

It's slow going through the thick vegetation. Unlike the public footpath trails that crisscross the English countryside near your Buckinghamshire home, mankind has left no route for you to follow here. Indeed, you might be the very first human to set foot on this island. There's something exciting about such thoughts, even if they are terrifying.

Then you hear it—the telltale roar of water.

Rushing forward, you find a clearing with a great pond, fed by a waterfall. The source must come from somewhere up the mountain, and though it's no gushing river, it is more than a trickling brook. This water will sustain you!

Drinking straight from the waterfall itself, you taste the purest water you've had since becoming a sailor. Possibly even the best water of your life. Untainted by civilization, purified by the rocks and the motion of the waterfall, this is pure mountain stream water.

But this sense of elation is to be short-lived.

After you finish congratulating yourself, you realize the sun has set, with you still in the interior of the jungle. You generally know which way you came from, but could you hope to retrace your steps in the dark? Could you sleep somewhere near the pond?

And that's when you see the shape moving through the jungle. You fumble for the pistol at your waist, but before you can find it, the jaguar leaps out.

Turns out, tromping through the jungle at night might not have been the best idea.

THE END

Warming Up

The fire keeps you warm that night, and it's a much better night's sleep without any rain, though you do have nightmares of marauding pirates lurking in the shadows of your encampment. Even now, the next morning, you have an unshakeable feeling that you're being watched on this island. It's hard to say how much of that is in your imagination.

The embers in your fire still pulse with heat, and you're able to stoke these coals to get a morning fire going. If you keep the coals alive and insulate the burn pit while still allowing airflow, you won't have to keep using your flintlock to start a fire every night. You can also use the coals to make a bowl.

By finding a piece of wood of roughly the desired size and shape, you can put the embers on the center and scrape out the charred pieces with a rock. By repeating this process, you will eventually find yourself with a wooden bowl.

Then you'll just need something to fill it with. Your stomach growls at the thought of food. From the views afforded at your camp, you see one section of coastline dotted with rocks. If you stand on them, you can try to spear any fish that might swim by.

After forming a few wooden spears, you hike down to try your luck. As it turns out, many different types of fish cluster near these rocks as reefs, where they might find protection from larger fish. Yet, they won't be so easily shielded from your spearing once you've perfected your technique.

What sort of fish might be the best to eat?

- The brightly-colored reef fish. Easy to spot, probably easy to catch and eat. Go to page 297
- Fish that look like rocks. Muted colors keep them safe, but you can see them when they move. Go to page 229
- The biggest fish I can find. As an apex predator, best to set your sights high. Go to page 323

Wasting

Yes, you can eat many of the organs. Kidney, liver, heart. And there is some meat on the head, so you won't go hungry, but the truth is that you wasted the best parts of this hog. If it had parasites, they'd either be killed off by the fire (largely why we humans cook our food), or you'd end up with the same parasites anyway, just by living on the island. Porcine anatomy isn't that different from person anatomy.

If you make it off this island alive, people will likely give you strange looks when hearing this part of the tale recounted. Still, there are worse mistakes to make, and more serious situations to consider. Like the one that will occur tomorrow morning.

The next day, you're off from camp, hiking down to the pond for fresh water, when you come face to face with a jaguar.

Its golden fur glows tawny in the early light; black splotches break up the outline of the animal, even as it stares at you out in the open. Is this who's been following you these last few days? Likely so. What was once curiosity to size you up now very well may put you on the menu. What do you do?

- Stand tall, but slowly back away. Speak calmly. Say, "It's okay, I don't mean you any harm." Go to page 306
- Almost as if in slow motion, remove your pistol and shoot the beast. Can't get revenge if you're dead. Go to page 326
- Shout, "Look, over there!" and then run in the opposite direction as fast as you can. Go to page 226
- Scream loudly to frighten the animal and climb up into the nearest tree for safety. Go to page 69
- Confidently walk towards the jaguar. Lock eyes to show dominance. Say, "This is my island now!" Go to page 287

Waylaid

You put up your fists, prepared to defend yourself. The two seamen smile at another chance to fight. Deep down, you fear that even one of them might prove too much for you, if it were to be a fair fight. Yet it's to be anything but.

Dick sidles behind you and the sound of wood sliding on wood makes you turn around, just in time to see Dick claim a loose beam from the boardwalk.

The pair of sailors grab you by the arms and Dick clouts you on the head with the board. It's enough to make you lose consciousness, though not enough to kill you. Time will tell if that would've been a mercy.

Not much choice here:

Wake up and face the consequences of Dick's involuntary conscription on your behalf.
<u>Go to page 93</u>

Whaling

Though the larger fish such as groupers, sturgeon, or tuna may be appealing, to a single castaway, they're a bit much. Not only more than you need for a meal, but more than you can haul in, as well. Despite how easily these fish glide through the water, once you bring them above the surface, you feel their true weight.

After hours of hit-or-miss fishing, you manage to spear a few of the leviathans, but each time they snap your lances. One by thrashing, the other when you tried to pull it from the water once the weight sat in.

Still, you filled the sea with blood and thrashing fish, which attracted sharks. Now, not only were you left without a meal, but you had to sit atop your rock for several hours before it became safe enough to swim back to shore once again.

Looks like you're going to bed hungry.

But it appears as if your luck may have changed, for the very next day you're out hiking when you startle a feral pig on the island. Most likely a sow that was released by passing ships in hopes of growing a native population, she now frightens when you step near her, astounded that she didn't hear your presence. Unwittingly, the pig dashes off a rocky outcropping, falling to her death once she's been dashed on the rocks below. All you've got to do is gather her up and have a real feast.

How do you prepare a wild pig?

- Eat only the head or organs. The pig likely has parasites that it will pass on to you. Go to page 321
- Remove all the organs to remove risk of tainting the meat with fluids, such as that from the musk gland. Go to page 15
- Tie the pig to shore; soak it in your local pond overnight. This will cure the meat and remove parasites. Go to page 202

What a Dick

Spotted Dick produces a parchment, ink and quill, and instructs, "I just need full name, home address, next-o'-kin up top, then make your mark at the bottom, past all the legalese."

"A contract, for carriage service?" you ask.

"We don't often drive to Blenheim, is all. Just insurance and liability, ye understand."

"Buckingham, not Blenheim—*Buckinghamshire*."

"Right, right, of course. Write your address legibly, m'friend!"

Once you've signed, he walks with you down the port as if you're a dignified guest of honor. "Right this way, please," he'll say, ushering you along. "After you, of course!"

He eventually escorts you to a dilapidated carriage, the body splintered and hastily resealed, the upholstery moth-eaten and likely ridden with bedbugs. Dick holds the door open for you, then, noticing your hesitation, adds, "She may not look like much, but old Spotted Dick passes the savings on t'you!"

Pushing you inside, he closes and locks the carriage.

"You said your friend owns this carriage?" you ask, nervously.

"What? Oh, right. That, uhh, he's lent it out t'me. Or rather, I'm a driver for him, on occasion. Don't worry, you'll be home, soon enough."

"But, my cousin!"

"Shh, shh… settle down, your cousin will join you, trust Dick on that account."

Yet, rather than heading out into the countryside, the carriage goes into the city streets of London, only to park in front of a rather impressive-looking government building.

"Is cousin James in here?" you ask.

"He will be, you'll see. You just shut up now."

A redcoat soldier comes out and greets Dick with, "Mr. Martin, I'd thought ya left the press gang and turned crimp?"

"Well, 'tis a hot press, innit?" Dick replies. "Sides, I got one in here that's already signed the papers. You pay more for those, if memory serves."

"You truly are a bloody fear merchant," the soldier laughs. "And what charge should I give the magistrate?"

"Idleness? This one's a bit soft in the head, so do as you please."

"Sounds like a perfect candidate for His Majesty's Royal Navy."

They both have a good laugh, then the soldier motions for another pair to come claim you from the carriage. Not much choice here:

After a night in a holding cell, await your fate before the courts in the morning. Go to page 188

The Whipping Boy

Hustling so as not to lose the men in the labyrinthine belly of the ship, you follow the third figure down into the hold. It's pitch-black down here, but the first man must wield a candle or lantern, for the others follow by his light. Being the furthest one back, there's only the ghost of lamplight to illuminate your path, but having wandered these corridors daily for the past month, you could navigate the hold with your eyes closed.

Finally, they stop and gather where they think none will overhear. They hatch their plans, as it were, tucked down amongst the chicken coop. Rediker is the leader of the bunch and—as you might have suspected—Barlow stands at his side. The third man is the older seaman, Marlowe.

"Gotta be tonight," Rediker says.

Barlow simply nods.

"Do we have the support we need?" Marlowe asks.

"After what the Cap'n and Mate did t'that poor lad, I'd say so. Each day under this tyrant is a bloody nightmare, but today's cruelty 'twas the last straw. If we lose any more men, we won't be able t'steer the damned ship! Billy and Joe know this, so they won't resist."

This is more than idle chat; they're plotting mutiny!

➤ Oh, it's mutiny all right. And you want in! Step forward and offer to help. Go to page 195

➤ Remember the gallows at Gravesend? You know how mutineers fare. Billy will know what to do! Go to page 10

Wild West Indies

The *BOOM* of the pistol is frightening, even to the most experienced shooter. So, to the jaguar, it's terrifying. Had you wasted your shot by discharging the flintlock into the air, you might have frightened off the predator by the sound. As it is, you wasted your shot by discharging the pistol into the jungle cat itself, and now the beast is angry.

Nothing quite like small-caliber arms fire to piss off a wild animal.

The jaguar now comes at you with great ferocity. The animal might not survive this wound and might starve in a couple of weeks, but you won't survive the next few minutes.

THE END

The Wooden World

⚓

Given an axe and pointed towards the nearest forest, you join the contingent headed out to resupply the ship with timber. The Carpenter and his mate are nominally in charge here, for it's their expertise that will instruct you just which trees to fell.

This coast is most likely French, should geography serve you correctly, and seeing as how they're an ally of your Spanish enemies, the men have hopes of looting a farmhouse while you're out and about. They will ultimately be disappointed, for this section of coastal forest seems devoid of Frogs.

You sweat out the night's boozing by cracking down tree after tree, loading them onto the longboats, and performing a full day's backbreaking work. With fresh supplies exchanged with the larger ships of the fleet, however, you're greeted with one of the better meals you've had in weeks once you're back onboard.

"We're to set sail tomorrow," Cousin James says when you're in your hammock. "Cap'n oughta be giving orders for our new course, if you're curious. Rumor has it we're not returning to Spanish waters."

➢ "I sail at the pleasure of His Majesty. I'll not leave this hammock to trouble myself with whereto." Go to page 311

➢ "Where else might we go? Okay, you've got me wondering now. Let's go see!" Go to page 40

Worry about Your Own Neck

"The old aphorism goes, 'Three men can keep a secret… if two are dead.' I already took care of Bullock; now you're up, quartermaster. Rediker, have your men give Billy a send-off via the yardarm," you say.

Rediker smiles, signals Barlow towards Billy, then looks back to you. The smile disappears and his face goes slack before something akin to panic washes over him.

"Saltboots, look out!" he cries.

You turn just in time to see Robin, the hulking tattooed gunner, reach out with his two burly arms, wrapping his hands around your neck. A *crack!* echoes inside your skull as he breaks your neck like a twig.

THE END

The Book Club Reader's Guide

If you want a Monet Experience (no spoilers), avoid these questions until after you've read through MAROONED to your heart's content. OR.... Take 1-2 weeks, progress through as many story iterations as you can, while keeping the following questions in mind. Then, meet with your reader's group and discuss:

1) In an interactive book, the main character is often a blank slate, requiring the supporting cast to take on a bigger role. Was this the case in MAROONED? What did you think of the other characters in the book? Was there a specific character whose story you found particularly compelling?
2) How did the book end for you the first time? Share your experiences with the group. What would you say was the "best ending" you found?
3) There are certain expected norms in historical/naval fiction. To what extent did MAROONED uphold these traditions? Has Schannep added anything new to the genre, or simply sailed upon well-established routes?
4) Many choices that might feel like the "right thing to do" lead to death. Did you feel like you were unfairly punished for altruistic choices? Or did it make the story seem more grounded in reality? Did you find the move away from larger-than-life swashbuckling cliché refreshing or frustrating?
5) There are several vignettes off the beaten path. What was your favorite "hidden gem"? Did you find any Easter Eggs or references to other CYP books?
6) The three unique storylines are identified through palm trees (deserted island survival), skull and cross bones (piracy), and the anchor (Royal Navy). Did this encourage further exploration of the story world? Did you enjoy any path more than the others? How did knowledge of one affect the experiencing of another?
7) How did you feel about being "in control" of the story? Did you feel more or less involved than you do with traditional books?
8) Compare and contrast being "Crimped" (sold into service to a merchant ship) vs "Pressed" (conscripted into the Royal Navy during wartime). Are these functionally the same practice? Is one more justified than the other? Why or why not? Compare with the military drafts of the last century.
9) Though it is possible to be stranded on a deserted island in the book, the reader can also find themselves "marooned" in many other situations. For example, the books open with the fish out of water experience at the Port of London. In what other ways did you feel stranded or at the mercy of the elements in the book?
10) The author uses several historically-inspired toasts and "sea-shanties" (sailor's songs) throughout the course of the book, though these have been edited to fit the situations your character finds themselves in. Did any of these stick out to you? Did you perhaps have a favorite?

BONUS: If there's anything else you'd like to ask the author, feel to send your questions to author@jamesschannep.com

Printed in Great Britain
by Amazon